T0128143

DRAGONS & DINOSAURS

The New World

Timothy Martin

Order this book online at www.trafford.com
or email orders@trafford.com

Most Trafford titles are also available at major online book retailers.

Print information available on the last page.

ISBN: 978-1-4907-9779-3 (sc)
ISBN: 978-1-4907-9781-6 (hc)
ISBN: 978-1-4907-9780-9 (e)

Library of Congress Control Number: 2019916453

Trafford rev. 10/18/2019

 www.trafford.com
North America & international
toll-free: 1 888 232 4444 (USA & Canada)
fax: 812 355 4082

CONTENTS

Prologue: Diary of a Madman?..ix

Chapter 1   Springtime in the North...1
Chapter 2   Transition..9
Chapter 3   I Don't Think I Am Home Anymore 15
Chapter 4   Ogres, Etcetera..21
Chapter 5   Travelling Man 28
Chapter 6   Captivated..37
Chapter 7   Gizmo Saves the Day! 45
Chapter 8   To Wiz or Not to Wiz (I mean wizard—not pee!)......51
Chapter 9   North To —? 61
Chapter 10 The Voice 77
Chapter 11 Love Comes to Town..91
Chapter 12 Into the Dark 100
Chapter 13 New Home 107
Chapter 14 Trouble in Paradise 115
Chapter 15 Into the Great Forest...124
Chapter 16 The Wings of Mercury 134
Chapter 17 Enemy at the Gate...139
Chapter 18 Air Time 144
Chapter 19 The Dragon's Dark Secret 147
Chapter 20 Quest for the Answers...151
Chapter 21 Road Trip..154
Chapter 22 Chavez's Story...160
Chapter 23 Holiday Time..164
Chapter 24 Secret Rebellion..175
Chapter 25 Godfrey...182

Chapter 26 Godfrey's Story..186
Chapter 27 Don't Wake the Dreamer...189
Chapter 28 Of Seashells and Submarines....................................192
Chapter 29 Portals 197
Chapter 30 New Companions...204
Chapter 31 Wrongful Accusation..210
Chapter 32 Betrayers?...216
Chapter 33 Spy or Assassin? 228
Chapter 34 Bandit Hunting...237
Chapter 35 Emancipation 249
Chapter 36 Gaol Break...258
Chapter 37 An Unexpected Event..266
Chapter 38 Surgery..273

Character Index..277
Items of Magic 283
About the Author...285

Message from the Author

This book would not be possible without the loving support of my wife Gayle. We have been together for 30 years of ups and downs.

I suffer from Post-Traumatic Stress Disorder, after working 25 years with the Royal Canadian Mounted Police. Without Gayle's loving care, I would not have been able to be an author or even be here in this world.

A portion of the money received from the sale of this book will be dedicated to a non-profit organization that trains and provides service dogs at no charge to veterans and first responders suffering from Post-Traumatic Stress Disorder.

~ PROLOGUE ~

Diary of a Madman?

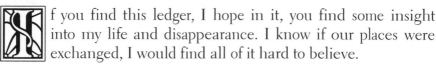f you find this ledger, I hope in it, you find some insight into my life and disappearance. I know if our places were exchanged, I would find all of it hard to believe.

I am not much of an illustrator, so my sketches are at times a little rough, depending on how soon I get an opportunity to sit down and have some time to draw and make some notes.

To give some validation to my story, you will find that, if you wish to have it examined, the material that the ledger is wrapped in to protect it from the weather is, in actual fact—dinosaur hide.

Dragons & Dinosaurs

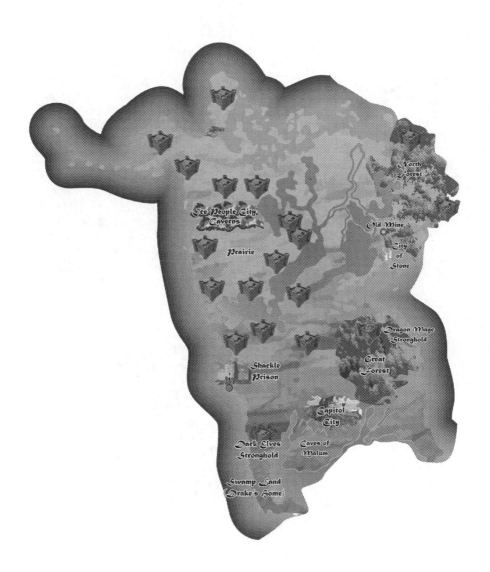

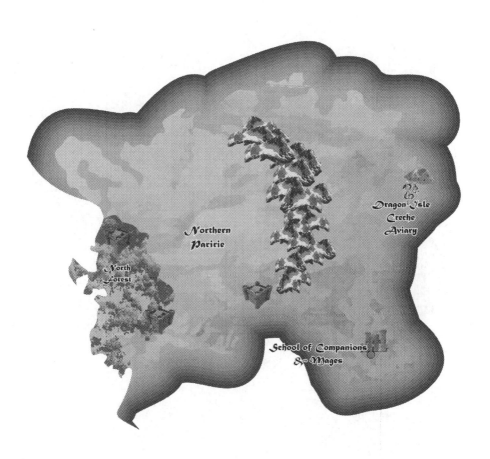

Dragon Isle
Creche
Aviary

Northern
Pariric

North
Forest

School of Companions
& Mages

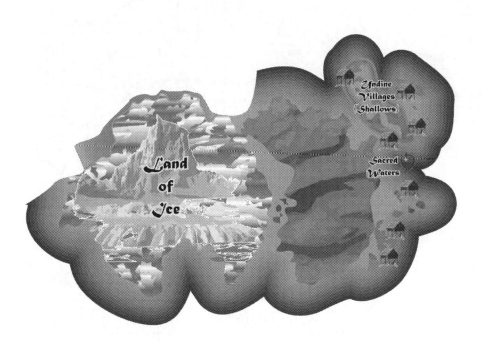

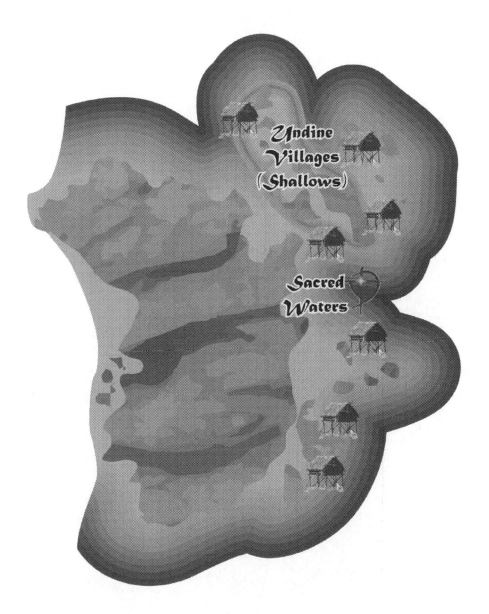

~ One ~

Springtime in the North

I pulled into the parking lot at the sheriff's office around seven o'clock in the morning. The office staff and dayshift officers had yet to arrive, which suited me just fine, since I enjoyed the peace and solitude of working alone.

The office stood out in the little town of North Fork, Washington. It was built on an empty lot that was to be developed at a later date; unfortunately, the mine that was to be built in the area had pulled out, so the building was sitting all by itself at the north end of town.

The building was showing its age, and was long overdue for a paint job. I could see the paint peeling down in patches, in the areas where the sun shone most on the office. I liked it. The building had been built to resemble something much older, it was encased with wood siding to give it the appearance of something from the eighteen hundreds with an overhang out front and a boardwalk. When the sun hit the building it gave off that warm cedar smell that made me want to pull up a chair and just enjoy the atmosphere. The rest of the lot had a forested area around it, which helped keep the place cool in the summer heat.

The town was just waking up; I could hear the distant sounds of vehicles headed for the local diner for morning coffee. There was no heavy industry in the area so the air was fresh and clear and further improved by the occasional hint of wood smoke and pine trees.

The main street led from the elementary school at the south

end, and headed up to the Sheriff's office at the north end. It looked like something out of the old mail order catalogs in the early nineteen hundreds. When the snow fell in winter, the main street was decorated with wreaths and lights.

I soon learned who the troublemakers in the area were, and could spot them or their vehicles from a distance. I found the major part of my job was just keeping tabs on these potential juvenile delinquents. The more I kept an eye on them, the less trouble they caused. Since the town was only a tidy six blocks square, I could resolve any problems rapidly.

Once I got over sweating the small issues and started concentrating on the real crimes, I quickly found a reliable source of information from the teenagers in town. Information would flow freely about who was doing what. Everyone in town knew my name, and I was always greeted with a smile or a nod.

The great thing was that if the teens wanted to party or cause trouble, they would leave town and go to the city, which was located about one hour south. It was not uncommon for someone from the day shift to have to drive there to pick up one of our wayward teens.

As I walked into the foyer of the building, I was reminded of an old bus station. There were some comfortable benches with padding along the walls, and a few rows of them in front of the huge counter. This area made up almost one third of the office space. I could smell the coffee brewing in the large urn; it didn't smell or sound like it was ready yet.

In a few hours the old timers would come in and sit in the back, drinking coffee, exchanging gossip, and listening for anything new that might be reported. This was the highlight of their day that they could share around town later.

I saw the night shift dispatcher nodding off in his chair by the radio transmitter. George was his name and he cleaned the office as well as answered the phones; all the while acting as dispatch for both the local fire department and the police. There was a small room just behind the desk with a cot for George to catnap during the long, usually quiet, night shift.

"Morning George; anything happen in the hours we weren't

speaking?" I said with a grin, knowing that he was probably sleeping part of the night.

"No, other than the sheriff wants to talk to you about a file before you go home," George said softly.

"Thanks George," I said, knowing that he was not someone to make angry; I could end up with a lot of files that could wait for the dayshift.

I was lucky enough to work mostly night shifts. It gave me time to think and learn a lot about the community before I had to switch to day shifts. I was pretty much a loner, keeping to myself and only dealing with people when I had to. I knew that the sheriff would only let me work so many nights, before expecting me to finally work day shifts. Fortunately there was no great rush from the other officers for volunteers to work at night.

I took my time getting out of my uniform, sitting on the bench in the locker room; wondering if I had made a mistake on an investigation and was being called to task. I shook my head and smiled, knowing there was nothing that could be done on the few files I had picked up in the short time I was working in this department.

Sheriff Malone had his door open, waiting for me to call on him. He had held down the job for over twenty-five years, and his office was as antiquated as he was. It was filled with reference books and overstuffed chairs, just like a reading room in an old library.

I had only been working in this police detachment for six months, having spent the majority of my career working in the bigger centers. This was quite a culture change for me.

My full name is Jonathon Isaac Martin, but most people who know me just call me Jim. I stand about six feet tall and weigh a respectable one hundred and ninety pounds; a little flabby, but in decent physical condition. Not bad for forty-five years of age.

Single—again—because my wife did not like the long hours and I was away from home all the time. She couldn't deal with the stress of me being out in the line of fire, so she found someone who would be home all the time, and moved on with her life.

I found a small rural area that would get me away from the big city, with the opportunity for plenty of work and overtime to keep me busy. I was really starting to enjoy it, getting to know the residents of the area, and sometimes driving miles between farmsteads. This was the biggest town in the area and boasted a small movie theatre and a population of about four hundred people.

I rubbed the sleep from my eyes, grabbed a fresh cup of coffee, and headed into the office to find out if I was in trouble, or if there was some other issue that Sheriff Malone wanted to talk to me about.

"Come in and have a seat—I'll be with you in a second," Malone said, not looking up. As usual, he was going over reports from the day before.

I let out a silent sigh of relief; if I had screwed up, the sheriff would not have allowed me to sit down. It was his habit if you were in trouble to make you stand there and sweat until he was ready to speak.

"I wanted to talk to you about the mutilation of livestock that has been happening for the last month in the northern district. I've been studying old articles dating back almost one hundred years. It seems that every so often when the moon is right, strange things happen. It only goes on for about a month or two and then—nothing for another ten or twenty years," Malone said, with a concerned look on his face.

I had heard about it, and had seen some of the pictures of the severely mutilated carcasses. The dry weather and hard-packed soil had left no tracks in the area of the kills.

"We got a little break. The last animal mutilated had been in a field where the irrigation was turned on, and we found a footprint, along with some blood from the victim animal," Malone said, and then waited for a response from me.

Malone pulled out some photographs from a file, laying them out on his desk in front of me. Examining the photos, I noted the prints were like nothing I had ever seen.

"Does the game warden have any idea what it might be"? I asked gently.

"He hasn't got a clue. He sent a copy to the state university and they could not identify it from any living species of animal. At this point it's anyone's guess as to what is mutilating that livestock,"

4

Malone stated, as he paused to rub his temples in consternation. "It may even be someone trying to pull some pranks on us, like crop circles and such."

"The killings seem about a week apart, and it's almost been that long now. I want you to patrol the north area, and if there's anything suspicious, check it out and find out what you can," Malone stated with authority, not expecting nor even wanting an answer from me.

I got up from my seat, gave the chief a nod as I left his office, then walked out the front door of the building down two blocks to the apartment I was renting. It was in an older, two-story house, painted green. The yard, as well as the entire area around the house, were immaculate. The owner was retired, and by renting his room to one of the police officers in town, he had no worries. With time on his hands, he took extreme care of the old house, and would sit on the porch in the mornings with a cup of coffee and some pastry for me. That way he could get an idea of what was occurring in town, ahead of all the gossip hounds. Since he did not share any confidential information with anyone, he was a great sounding board for anything I might be stumped on. Since he knew the area so well, he quite often pointed me in the right direction if not telling me outright who the perpetrator might be.

After our usual morning conversation, I went inside and crawled into bed, to try to get some sleep before having to search for this "imaginary" beast that was killing livestock and leaving the mutilated bodies behind.

I awoke to the sounds of a typical springtime afternoon and the smell of fresh mown grass. I made myself a simple meal and prepared my lunch for the night. I then sat and read the documents that Malone had found in relation to unusual events over the years.

As I was perusing the papers, I found a reference to a John Martin who had disappeared in this area over one hundred years ago. I wondered if he was any relation; my parents once told me of a great grandfather, who had been a Texas Ranger. He had left home and never came back.

The sun was starting to get low on the horizon as I headed back to the office for another quiet night patrolling the countryside. I strolled into the locker room to change, then went out front to the reception area where the day shift officers hung out at the end of the day. I spent ten minutes chatting with the younger guys, listening to the local gossip of what was happening in and around town.

After I finished getting organized, I fueled the police vehicle and made sure everything that I might need was ready and available in the vehicle. As I pulled out of the parking lot, the sun was just going down behind the hills, and the air was starting to cool.

The next five hours were spent peacefully, as usual, the silence broken only by the sound of crickets and the occasional owl. I felt the night envelop me, with the only light coming from the twinkling of stars shining down on me.

I rolled down the windows of the vehicle, letting the cool air and natural sounds of the countryside enclose me in their loving embrace. It was shaping up to be another uneventful evening, with the occasional barking dog complaint from town, and not much else. This was the reason I had moved here.

I was patrolling the quiet back roads, enjoying the cool of the evening, when a call came in to visit one of the farms in the middle of nowhere; something about someone stealing pigs. I thought it was probably a bobcat or cougar, which was common in this area. But at that point, I was unprepared for what the evening was going to bring.

It was about as far as I could go and still be in the district. This was the last homestead before the woods headed up into the hills and out of sight. Although this was a serious complaint, I was greeted with the usual offer of coffee and cake. I turned down the kindness, as much as I would have loved to have taken the time away from work to chew the fat.

"There are no tracks in the ground around the pens," the farmer said, as he handed me a cup of fresh coffee, ignoring my rejection of his offer.

I walked out with the farmer and examined the area where the pigs were penned. The smell of the sty was almost overpowering, and my eyes were on the verge of watering. I found myself wondering how a predator could smell livestock over the stench.

There was next to no evidence around the pens, but I noted a faint trail of blood leading off the property toward one of the old logging roads that led off the farm.

"Whatever or whoever did this, they headed up that way," I said as I looked toward the forest that encroached upon the farmer's field. I handed the farmer the now empty cup of coffee, and prepared to do some searching.

Walking out to the police cruiser, I was glad that it was a four wheel drive, which could handle the sometimes very rough logging roads; especially since most of the roads in this area had not been used for many years. I felt this was going to be a long and probably uneventful night. The odds of finding the culprit or animal were slim to none, but I had to try and locate whoever, or whatever, had taken down the pig.

As I started driving down the dusty and disused trails, I spent the time pondering my life and how it had brought me to where I was now.

Until my nineteenth birthday, I had been a bit of a "geek." Studying was the most important thing in my life. Girls never paid much attention to me, and I was a prime target for bullies. I set my eyes on becoming a police officer so that I could protect the victims and underdogs.

Then—of course—I got drafted right after my nineteenth birthday and ended up in the Marines, which gave me a whole new perspective on life and death. They taught me how to survive, how to kill, and how to perform emergency first aid. All of these skills came in extremely handy after I finished my tour and throughout my career as a police officer.

I came into my height and physical shape during the years with the Marines. The exercise regime and training turned me from a wimp into a warrior.

I pulled out the forestry map showing all the logging roads in the direct area, checking to see where they ended up. I stopped the car every so often, and looked to see if there was still blood on the old road leading away from the farm.

I didn't bother to buckle my seatbelt, since I was in and out of the cruiser almost every other moment, checking the road. On a smooth stretch, I was not paying enough attention to notice that I had the cruiser speed up to almost fifty miles per hour.

The sky suddenly went from black with the twinkling of stars to bright daylight with the sun shining in my face. I struck something on the road and was thrown forward into the windshield of the cruiser, losing consciousness almost instantly.

~ Two ~

Transition

hen I came to, I was suffering from a throbbing headache. Dried blood was caked on my face and hair. I stepped out of the vehicle, noting that I must have lost control after hitting whatever was on the road because the front end of the cruiser was wrapped around a tree. All I could think of at that moment was the mountain of paperwork this would involve when I got back to the office.

Standing beside the vehicle, looking around, I could not see an opening to the clearing or the road anymore. It looked as if I had been suddenly transported to northern California; giant redwood trees dotted the forest, visible from the clearing. The air was warm and muggy, heavy with the scents of the forest; different from what they were the night before.

I was a little dazed and having trouble focusing on precisely where I was and what was happening. Still, my head was starting to clear, and the longer I was awake, the sharper images were coming into focus.

It was broad daylight. The vehicle battery had died sometime while I was unconscious. Looking at the crumpled front end, still wrapped around the tree, I didn't think the car or any electronics in it would work. I tried my portable radio, and it wasn't working either. This puzzled me because I had put a new battery in the radio before heading out on shift. I didn't think I would be able to transmit with the portable enough for anyone to hear me this far into the bush. But, at least it should have worked.

The road was gone. My vehicle was at the edge of a clearing, but there didn't appear to be any openings wide enough for the cruiser to have been driven through. I saw my tire tracks leading back from the cruiser; that was when I saw the "thing" lying in the middle of the clearing.

Realization slowly came over me that it was—honestly—a giant lizard.

Sheriff Malone and I had discussed the situation, and we knew there was nothing alive that could have made those marks. From my avid reading as a single guy with lots of time on my hands, I recognized the marks as being from a moderate-sized dinosaur called a Velociraptor. It was supposed to be extinct, but there one was, lying in the clearing. What was this beast doing here and now in these woods? Mind you, what was I doing here? Nothing looked recognizable, from my point of view.

I closely examined the raptor, glad that it was dead. If the creature had gotten close to me, I might not have stood a chance. No wonder the livestock had been mutilated. Looking at the teeth and claws on this thing, I knew it would leave a hell of a mess. I was very close to losing it at this point and I tried to suppress a shudder that swept over my entire body, thinking of what the raptor was capable of doing.

It looked to be about twelve feet long from the tip of its tail to the very sharp teeth in its mouth. What really surprised me was that it had feathers covering most of its body. Chuckling in spite of myself, I pictured a killer ostrich.

Grabbing my canteen and some paper towelling from the wrecked cruiser, I used a little bit of water to clean up and assess my injuries. The cut on my forehead was minor, and other than being stiff and sore from being tossed around, I counted myself lucky to be alive. I still had some water in my canteen, and had packed a lunch for the shift that now was going to be a lot longer than I had intended.

With the sun shining high in the sky, it was time to put my Marine survival training to use. I climbed the biggest tree I could, to get the lay of the land. The tree was some sort of redwood, like the giants that can only be found in some national parks where logging is not allowed. When I got as high as I dared, I could see over the top of most of the forest. I saw no roads near the clearing, which begged the question: how did I get here, and—where was *here?*

The tree I had climbed was very high, but it was still dwarfed by some of the giant ones spread out in this forest. The forest swept down a valley and led to a prairie, which opened up to the south. There seemed to be a road of some sort on the prairie that ran straight toward the opening.

The air was fresh, without the distinct smell of wood smoke; the air was warmer than it should have been for this time of year. When I climbed down, I pulled out the camera to take pictures of the damage to the cruiser and the dead raptor.

"If the Sergeant doesn't see any evidence, he will not believe this friggin' fairy tale," I said, as I could imagine the argument with Malone about the damage done to the vehicle.

But of course, the camera would not work; that seemed to be the way my day was going.

Pulling my emergency survival gear out of the cruiser, I used the buck knife to cut out a couple of teeth and a foot claw from the raptor's remains. If scavengers got to the carcass, there would be nothing left. I was going to make sure I had something to show for the written-off cruiser—when and if I ever made it home again.

It was still early in the day, so I set off toward the south, where I had seen signs of a riverbed. I left a note in the cruiser indicating my path of travel, just in case anyone came looking for me.

It was unseasonably warm, so I put on my Stetson, and walked into the cool shade of the forest and down the gentle slope toward the riverbed. Without water I would not last very long, so I trudged through the brush, walking back to civilization (I hoped). The water in my canteen would last only so long, and I was reluctant to walk away from a source of water until it was absolutely necessary.

It was going to be a long day, and the headache I had awakened with was not easing. I kept my ears cocked, listening for a search and rescue plane. Since I didn't know how long I had been unconscious, someone could be looking for me already.

As I hiked through the trees, I soon found a game trail and decided to follow it, knowing that eventually it would lead me to water. It took me a couple of hours to reach the gully where I had seen the stream bed.

The sun was almost directly overhead, and despite the shade of the trees, it was very warm. I heard the welcoming gurgle of the stream before I reached it, and it was all I could think of. I took my boots off and soaked my feet for a few minutes, relaxing for the first time today. The water was clear and cool, fish could be seen swimming in pools nearby.

I looked around for berries or something edible to supplement my limited supply of food, but I couldn't find anything I recognized as safe to eat. The plants and trees down by the river looked odd, but I could not place initially what that difference was.

As I sat enjoying the cool water, I had a very disturbing thought. What if that raptor I ran over last night had buddies? I quickly looked around to make sure I was alone by the stream, and decided that I had better get a shelter set up, with a fire, well before dark, in case of unwelcome visitors.

Locating a small overhang where the stream had dug away the embankment during the spring runoff, and working with the hatchet in my survival kit, I made a shelter that was protected on three sides. The shelter was at least five feet from the water's edge, giving me a nice dry location. Unless the weather changed to rain there was no danger that the stream would overrun the banks and flood my campsite. Gathering wood, I set up a healthy supply that should last me the night.

I ate part of my lunch sparingly, having difficulty stopping as the food tasted better when seasoned by hunger; saving the rest for later, I settled down to watch the stream and see what sort of game was in this area. It was impossible to tell from the marks near the river's edge, which looked as though it had been trampled down by a lot of animals. I realized it might become necessary to set up a snare or try to shoot something with my handgun if I got a chance, as my supplies at hand would only last another day maybe two if I ate it very sparingly.

My little shelter should be adequate, I thought. The weather looked clear. It was going to be a long night, in a strange place, in an uncomfortable bed. Sleep would be hard to come by. If recollection served me, there would be no moon tonight, but the sky was clear.

Of course, the matches in the survival kit didn't work. The emergency rations looked intact, even though they were a few years old. The emergency blanket made a good backdrop in the shelter to reflect the heat from the campfire.

I coaxed the fire to life using my knife, the flint from the kit, and a few choice words that I would not repeat in front of children. The flashlight, guaranteed by the manufacturer never to fail, failed to work. I threw it out across the gulley as hard as I could, and heard it land somewhere on the streamside rocks.

"What next? I feel like I'm in an old episode of *The Twilight Zone*; any minute now some alien is going to come out of the woods and abduct me," I said as I chuckled out loud.

Only the gentle babbling of the stream answered me, as the late afternoon sun began to set. I could feel the air cooling rapidly as the sun left the sky.

Lying there, relaxing in front of the colourful flames, feeling warm and comfortable in their glow, I slowly drifted off to sleep. I awoke with a start to a group of pale eyes staring at me over the dying embers of the campfire.

Without thinking, I grabbed and quickly threw a few logs on the fire, and I fired a few shots in the direction of what my mind told me were the hungry eyes. I thought I heard a cry of pain, followed by a lot of scrambling and squealing in the dark.

Looking up, I was shocked to notice two moons in the sky, giving a fair bit of light to the area around the camp. I was too overwhelmed by the encounter to stir from my position of safety. Besides, because of the brightness of the fire, I wouldn't have any night vision initially, even with the moons.

I was having problems focusing, and my head was pounding. I thought maybe I had a concussion from the crash, which would explain a lot in regards to seeing the double moons. Plus, with the fire roaring again, I couldn't see if there was anything else out there by the stream in the darkness.

Despite my confusion and the rush of adrenaline, once the threat had passed I felt sleep overcoming me again. This time, I slept soundly until the morning sun woke me. I lay there listening for the sounds of the morning birds, but there were different noises, ones that I could not place as belonging in the forest. The fire had died down to just warm embers again.

After remembering the previous night's incident, I checked the ammunition clip in my gun,. Finding no rounds missing, I wondered if I had dreamed the whole thing. I felt certain that I had fired shots, but there was no brass on the ground or rounds missing from my sidearm. Taking it apart, I saw that it was as spotless and oiled as it had been two days before when I cleaned it thoroughly. Had the whole incident, including the two moons up in the sky, been a nightmare or hallucination of some kind?

I surveyed the campsite carefully before stepping out of my shelter, looking for any critters that may have been left from the night before. As I headed toward the creek and the area where I had seen the eyes, I saw blood on the ground, with bits and pieces of meat scattered near the edge of the water.

The mystery was going to bother me for a while. If I had shot some of the beasts, where were the missing rounds? At that point, I was wondering if maybe I was in a coma on a bed in the hospital and all of this fantasy was because they were pumping me up with all sorts of drugs. When I woke up to the real world, there was going to be hell to pay for the damage to the cruiser.

Always a realist though, I figured that would be too easy an explanation. The pain in my head was increasing that morning, and the aches in my body from lying on the ground were enough to tell me everything felt all too real.

I debated about either staying at the campsite and waiting for help to arrive, or heading toward the valley with open fields that I could see down below, where there would be a clear view for me to wave down a rescue helicopter or plane for pickup. The more time I spent out in this wilderness however, the more I was getting the feeling that rescue was unlikely.

For anything to happen, I would have to be responsible for the results. I could not rely on anyone saving my butt; that would be unrealistic.

~ THREE ~

I Don't Think I Am Home Anymore

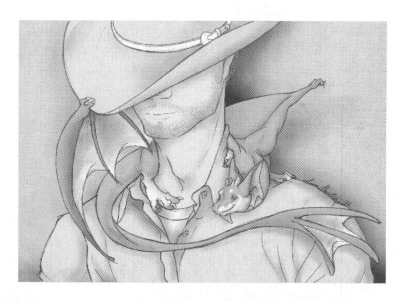

started to walk slowly down the gentle hillside toward the open prairie, which inspired my every step. As I neared the edge of the forest, I heard a noise that sounded like a puppy in pain.

As I approached the noise, I noticed something trapped in what appeared to be a bramble bush, being harassed by a couple of very large wolves. They were snapping and snarling, getting more worked up, and were getting thorns embedded in their faces from trying to push into the brush to get at the animal inside.

Normally I would not have intervened in this cycle of nature, but the creature caught up in the bushes did not look like anything I had ever seen in my life. As our eyes met, I felt that I had to help the creature. I could do nothing else.

Without hesitating, I drew my sidearm out and fired a couple of head shots into the wolves, dropping my targets with one shot each. After ensuring the wolves were no longer a threat, I holstered my weapon.

As I walked up to the bush, I saw that the creature appeared to be something out of a fantasy book. I got as close as I safely could. It was the size of a Chihuahua, black and tan in colour, with a three-foot wing span. Tiny claws shone at the tips like ivory, reminiscent of an iguana I once had when I was a child. The belly was a light cream color, with the outlines of fine ribs showing through.

Determination of the creature's sex proved difficult, with no sex organs visible, plus I had never seen a course on how to determine the sex of a dragon. I'll have to call it a dragon. I may be crazy, but who's to say otherwise?

I spoke softly to the little dragon, telling it that I was just going to help it. The little dragon cocked its head sideways listening to my every word, almost as if it understood me. I kept talking softly and reached through the bush, extricating the shaking little bundle.

The creature had a reptilian face, but had light, down-like fur on its skin. It weighed at the most eight pounds, and was about 18 inches long, snout to tail and its wingspan was three feet across. All in all, it reminded me of a stuffed toy one would find at a carnival or toy store.

"I'm going to call you Gizmo," I said softly to the little dragon, as I handled it gently.

I whispered softly to the dragon, as I noticed a tear in its leathery wing. The damage was superficial, but enough of a tear to make it impossible for Gizmo to fly with it. I looked into my medical kit and duffle bag. The only thing I could find that might do the job was duct tape.

Now a thousand and *two* uses, I thought, but even if I got back to the real world, no one was going to believe me. Once I was done, I set the dragon down on the ground and it climbed on top of my pack and curled up, just lying there, patiently eyeing me.

"Well, which way should we head out now"? I spoke out loud, even though I did not think the little dragon understood me.

Gizmo cocked its head, looking around it completely, and then stared down one of the game trails. I looked at my new little traveling companion.

"South it is, my friend," I said to the little dragon, as it seemed to react to my voice.

I gently lifted my backpack, with the creature comfortably settled upon it. The next thing I noticed was that Gizmo had wound its way around my neck with its back resting against the backpack. It was so comfortable that I soon forgot the little one was there.

I traveled as far as I could, following the stream as it trickled down the gentle hillside toward the valley ahead. I noticed as I walked down near the stream that the type of tree changed slightly, they appeared to be something that you would see in a tropical jungle. The difference though was that these trees were at least ten times bigger than any I had seen on any tropical holiday. I was surprised by how domesticated my dragon friend was, as I offered it what was left of my lunch to share. Gizmo took it, after examining it closely, gently grabbing the bits of food without snapping at my fingers.

I occasionally heard movement in the bushes around me, which made me a little anxious, but nothing ever showed itself as a potential threat. As the day progressed into late afternoon, I started to look around for a place to make camp for the night. If the previous night was any example, it could be another interesting experience.

Finding a small cave near the stream, I decided it was an ideal location for the night. It did not smell of any prior occupant, so I moved right in. It was only a matter of some short work to gather soft boughs for my bed, and enough dead branches to make a decent fire for the night.

Gizmo remained quietly curled up on my pack, watching all of my preparations.

"Well Gizmo, looks like I have to go look for something to eat, since I don't have any food left to share with you," I said. Gizmo cocked its head to one side as if listening to everything I was saying, and gazed into my eyes intently.

After searching the surrounding area for half an hour, I was able to find some berries that looked familiar: enough for me to risk trying one, and more later if they did not make me sick. Returning to the camp, I was stunned to find two decent-sized fish sitting on a rock, with Gizmo standing guard over them, looking very proud.

The fish looked like a type of sturgeon, but I did not recall anyone ever seeing a sturgeon in the rivers or lakes of this area. At least, there was nothing ever reported and that kind of word spreads fast in a small community.

I knew enough not to interfere with Gizmo's dinner, but it pushed both fish toward me with its beak. This was an obvious open invitation for me to share its catch. I laid out the berries that I found and watched Gizmo, fascinated by the fact that it examined each of the different types of berries, sweeping one type on the ground, then sat there patiently watching me.

"Well, obviously I made one bad choice with the berries, but otherwise didn't do too badly with my harvest. We shall have a fine feast tonight with the fish," I said as I bent over the wood shavings in the fire pit. With my flint and knife, I tried to get a flame going to cook dinner and after trying unsuccessfully for several minutes, I leaned back to take a breath.

Gizmo jumped down to the ground and walked over to the base of the kindling where I had been failing to start the fire. It looked intently at the wood and out of its mouth shot a small flame, which rapidly caught the kindling, and the fire was soon going strongly.

I sat there with my mouth wide open, not believing my eyes. Gizmo strolled back to the rock and hopped up near the fish, looking pleased with itself.

"Holy crap! You are full of surprises, my little friend," I said in wonderment, as the fire started to blaze.

I cleaned and cooked the fish, sharing everything equally with my new little friend who seemed to have a healthy appetite. Banking the fire, I settled back for what I hoped would be a quiet night.

Gizmo hopped into the shelter and quietly settled itself in my arms. I dozed lightly and every time I woke, I made sure to stoke the fire.

I was awakened partway through the night by a sharp pain in my ear. Thinking it was an insect, I tried to brush it away. I awoke with a start to realize that Gizmo had grabbed my ear to get my attention. The fire was still burning well, but there were some eyes staring out of the darkness at us.

I drew my pistol out of the holster, but did not fire. I kept my pistol handy just in case, stoked the blaze, and threw a flaming brand out toward the eyes, hearing a yelp of pain. Then it looked like we were alone again. I quickly drifted off to sleep, confident now that Gizmo would alert me to any trouble. The rest of the night passed without any interruptions from uninvited visitors.

The morning dawned, warm and clear. We quickly shared what was left of last night's fish before heading out on the trail again and Gizmo settled in behind my neck as we headed out. The trees started to thin as we came to the edge of the forest. I thought this was a good place to take a break in the shade of the trees, before starting out into the open prairie ahead.

I can't explain it, but I felt strangely uncomfortable looking at the tall grass in the fields ahead. The wind was blowing one way, but the grass at times seemed to be moving in different directions. Gizmo seemed more alert than I had ever noticed before, and was watching the prairie closely. The grass was a height of five feet consistently as far as the eye could see. It gave the impression of a yellow ocean with what appeared to be waves as the wind hit it.

"We're going to skirt the edge of the wood, so that we have firewood for tonight and a measure of safety from predators—that is, until I can figure out why I feel so darn uncomfortable going out into it," I said speaking aloud, partly because I liked sounding out my problems to help myself think, and partly because I liked the idea of getting Gizmo used to my voice.

Gizmo must have been someone's pet; it was too well trained. Bringing fish for the dinner plate, and starting fires—someone must have spent a lot of time training this animal. This creature was better than having a well-trained dog with me.

The next question was, where the hell was I? I decided by this point that it was all too real and painful at times to be a dream or a drug-induced coma at the hospital. The next thing to worry about was if there was any way to get home, or if I was stuck there in the wilderness with wild animals and trained dragons.

Only time would tell if I could solve each of these mysteries. Gizmo seemed less stressed as I started to skirt the edge of the wood, without walking out into the prairie. That made me feel better. I felt that Gizmo's hearing and sight was probably better than mine. As well, Gizmo was a creature of this new world which I found myself in.

~ FOUR ~

Ogres, Etcetera

I found a roadway in the late afternoon that seemed to stretch back as far as the eye could see along the valley. The road led across the prairie about ten feet wide, and then narrowed down to a width of four feet as it came into the forest.

The roadway appeared to be paved with stone, but nothing was growing between the paving stones. This must be the path that I had viewed from the treetops. It was either well maintained or something had been done to keep the weeds and grass down.

Stopping and examining the roadway as it stretched to the east and west, I crouched on the edge of it and closely examined the road. I tried to pry up one of the paving stones and experienced a strong shock, as though the road was electrified. Well, that would explain why no plants could grow between the stones, and why there did not appear to be any animal droppings on the road. The stones, upon closer examination, appeared to be bricks made out of clay or mud, but that did not explain how they would last so long... with weight applied on them you would expect them to crumble in no time.

I felt a mild shock as I stepped onto the road. Almost like an invisible electric fence, this would explain why animals would try to avoid this experience if possible.

I thought I heard something coming down the road toward me—almost a scraping and shuffling sound. Gizmo seemed very agitated, and that should have been my first clue of trouble. My curiosity got the best of me, however, and I just stood there as a man came into view, walking along the roadway toward me.

The man, (I use that term loosely) was hard to describe, and looked like an escapee from an old horror film. He was about seven feet tall, all muscle, carrying a very large club and dragging one foot. When I looked closely, I could see why. There was a large set of shackles on his left leg, with a length of chain trailing behind. The major attention-grabber was that he was dark green from head to foot!

For lack of a better description, he looked like an ogre out of some fairy tale that my grandmother used to tell me when I was a child. I felt a shiver down my spine as the ogre noticed me and stopped, staring at me intently. The ogre was having a hard time deciding what to do next, or even what I was.

He shambled toward me and spoke in a deep, guttural voice, "Pass?"

"I am a traveler; I don't understand what you mean," I said to him, standing with my right hand near my pistol. Since he did not appear to be very bright, I reached into my pocket and tore a piece of paper out of my notebook and handed it to him. He looked at the paper for a couple of minutes and then stuffed it in his mouth, chewed a couple of times and swallowed.

The ogre stood there for almost two minutes, thinking of what I had said, then spoke again, "Show pass."

"I do not know what you are talking about—I don't have any kind of pass," I said angrily to this ogre, who appeared as dumb as a post.

The creature immediately lifted its club, and with a cry, lunged toward me. At that moment, Gizmo flew off my shoulder, distracting the creature and giving me time to draw my pistol and fire, dropping the creature onto the roadway.

Grabbing a stick on the side of the road, I poked the creature to ensure that it was indeed dead. Once I was sure, I walked over to it and closely examined the body. Big, mangled teeth, green, all muscle, small head—yes, it definitely fit the description of an ogre.

I checked his scraps of clothing, finding nothing of interest. I saw a small brand on the ogre's left shoulder. It appeared that this creature was someone's property. I tried to lift the ogre's club; it was a huge hunk of wood weighing about eighty pounds. Anyone or anything hit by even a glancing blow would suffer major damage.

As I crouched there over the body, I looked out along the road, which made a gentle curve in the distance. I chuckled to myself, expecting any minute to see Dorothy, the Tin Man, the Scarecrow, and the Cowardly Lion coming down the road.

As I finished my examination, I found nothing else which identified the ogre or where it came from. Then, I thought I heard something else coming down the road and Gizmo was getting agitated again. Instead of ignoring the little dragon this time, I thought it best to find someplace safer to watch the road and see what other wonder came down it.

I ran to the forest edge and climbed up the nearest tree, giving myself a clear view of the ogre's body and the area where it lay. I climbed into a position where the branches of the tree protected me from view by anyone or anything that came down the road. I did not have to wait long. Racing down the road came three creatures.

The only way I could describe them is that they were raptors. They resembled the creature I had run over; however, they were much smaller than the one I had killed. These creatures were around six feet long, very skinny, maybe fifty pounds. All three had collars of some kind on their necks – stiff leather and ruddy metals. They ran up to the ogre's body and sniffed it before they started to dine. Obviously they were allowed by their owners to help themselves to anything found dead on the ground, or maybe anything they killed.

I sat quietly, not moving a muscle or making any noise, deciding to try to wait out the raptors rather than disturb them and face their ire. My backside was getting a little sore sitting in the tree watching the creatures below, and I was wondering how long I would have to wait for their owners to show up. The sun was climbing into late afternoon by my estimate, and I was feeling drowsy.

A shrill whistling in the distance caused the raptors to raise their heads and then run off toward the source of the sound. As they raced off, I thought alone I might handle one, but as a pack, they were incredibly fast and frightening.

I climbed down the tree and headed into the forest, away from the road. I wanted to find someplace I could sit out the night and not have to worry about those large reptilian predators I saw on the road, or their owners.

Fortunately it did not take me long to find the perfect location for a base camp. It was a large cave in a butte, with a dry, sandy floor and a small underground stream running through it. The entrance was easily blocked off and defendable. There was even a large hole at the top of the butte, climbable from inside, giving a view of the road and the prairie down below.

The walls were covered in jewel-like crystals, left behind by the stream's flow. It would have been a miner's dream; I was more interested in survival and hiding from the unknown.

The walls were polished by the running of water over the centuries. With the crystals in the ceiling, it looked like a starry night when I lay on the floor looking up. The nice thing with the sandy bottom was that it kept the cave dryer than one would normally expect.

I spent the rest of the afternoon gathering wood and rocks to prepare my temporary home. Then Gizmo and I went out to do some fishing and gather berries. I picked as much as I could into the late afternoon, getting enough to last a couple of days. I cut some brush and covered up the entrance so it would not be visible unless a close search was done. I carried some clay from the river and sealed the entrance to block out any light from the fire.

I set up a small fire which Gizmo lit for me, then set up a line to slowly smoke the fish, and put the berries (wrapped in leaves) on a ledge. After that, I climbed to the top of the butte, and found a nice comfortable spot where I could look out and see all around me with the binoculars from my survival kit. I had forgotten that they were in my kit until I had decided to climb to the top of the butte to check out my surroundings. I could not see any sign of the raptors, but could just barely make out the ogre's corpse.

As I watched the road, the raptors returned, running back to where the ogre lay. They were followed by a group of figures I could not make out. I wondered why they had taken so long to return to the body, as I has spent a good part of the day doing other things. It was possible that they had been there before and had returned to their superiors to report this unusual event. It would have been very confusing as when I examined the ogre's body there was an entry wound for the bullet but I could not see an exit wound. So just a little circle in the ogres head would surprise them as well. As the raptors started to tear into the ogre again, the figures pulled the raptors away. A couple of the figures closely examined the corpse, stopped suddenly and looked up and around.

Some of the figures ran back the way they had come. The rest headed up the road in the direction I had taken, with the raptors held in some type of harness, like bloodhounds, leading the way.

In the growing twilight, a cold sweat trickled down my back as I lost sight of the creatures and their handlers. I lay there listening to the noise of movement in the bushes. It grew closer, and then slowly moved away.

I stayed where I was until the moons came up. All was quiet so I climbed down. Curling up next to the fire with Gizmo, I was soon fast asleep. Nothing disturbed us and I woke up with the sun shining down through the hole in the butte, warming up the spot where we lay.

I carefully climbed to the top of the butte, and stretched myself out to watch the road my new acquaintances had come down. The ogre was gone. Either very efficient scavengers had gotten him, or whomever he belonged to had retrieved him.

I could see wisps of smoke rising from where the strangers may have set up their camp the previous night, but it was too far away to discern much else, even with the binoculars.

As I watched, I heard wings flapping and looked up to see Gizmo fluttering up to the top of the butte to join me.

"Well, it looks as if someone is feeling much better. You'll probably be headed back to where you came from soon?" I asked Gizmo gently, knowing I would miss my little companion.

Gizmo gave a very human gesture, seeming to shake its head no, and proceeded to curl up closely to me. I ran my hands gently over Gizmo's body as I said softly, "It's almost as if you understand me, my little friend."

The sun was almost completely overhead before I saw any movement coming along the road. The first living things to appear were a pair of riders headed toward my location along the road, astride the same type of raptor as the one I had hit with the police cruiser.

As they got closer, I started to make out details with my binoculars. The riders' skin colour was obsidian. They had elongated faces, sharp teeth, and pointed ears which flopped down: all of which gave them a very canine appearance.

The armour the riders were wearing looked ill-fitting and in poor repair. I could make out what looked like rust or old blood stains that were never cleaned off. I could see arrows carried in a quiver, and one of the riders pulled out his bow to shoot at an unseen animal of some sort in the tall grass. Even from a distance, I could make out cruelly-barbed tips on the arrow. The riders also carried large, serrated swords on their hips and each had a long lance or spear with a wicked-looking tip on it.

I could envision them riding someone down in open country atop their raptors. These steeds could quickly outrun anyone, and leave them easy prey to finish off at the riders' leisure.

A chill overcame me; the riders had stopped at the trail that I had taken to the butte! One held the reins, while the other climbed off and appeared to be sniffing the air and ground near the trail head. Then the one on the ground was peering right where I was for a good minute before turning back, climbing onto his mount and continuing up the road.

I continued to watch the riders until they were out of sight. A larger party then showed up, slowly traveling along the road into visible range. The first thing I saw was more ogres, followed by the three smaller raptors in harnesses, with their handlers. Then there was a large group of riders similar to the scouts I had seen earlier.

Following this was what looked like two giant iguanas. One had a large, flat frame attached to its back with a tarp roof, and a number of archers lounged on it. The other one had supplies on the frame and was towing a large wooden cage on two wheels. I gasped in surprise when I saw there were humans in the cage!

I could not make out much in the way of detail, as all of the cage occupants were huddled together. Some of the soldiers were poking the occupants with long sticks, or throwing rocks and laughing at them. This caused a continual shifting of the occupants to try to stay out of the reach of their captors' torments.

I stayed where I was for a long period of time, well after the caravan was out of sight, to make sure it was safe. I climbed down and prepared to venture out to see if they had left anything at their camp which might help me unravel this new mystery. I made up a small pack of food and headed out with Gizmo, wondering what else I would encounter out on the prairie.

After a half-hour of steady walking, I finally arrived at the camp of the obsidian people. The first things to draw my attention were two heads mounted on pikes at the edge of the roadway.

"Well, they must have pissed somebody off, big time, to deserve that!" I said as I looked closely at the heads, which were of members of the obsidian people, impaled on the poles.

As I walked into the camp area where the group had spent the night, I found the two headless bodies. They had been stripped before being left to rot and there were a large number of some sort of small scavenger dinosaurs working on the corpses. The body of the ogre from my encounter was nearby as well, it definitely was not fresh and was starting to smell foul so I quickly bypassed it to examine the headless bodies.

As I approached one of the corpses, the little dinosaurs scattered, only to rush back the minute I walked away. The area was littered with garbage and debris, including a small wagon with a broken wheel, and a couple of tents.

Gizmo suddenly took to the air and flew toward the centre of the encampment, with me following as fast as I could. My little friend landed near a human body that had been staked to the ground, and was attacking any of the scavengers that came near. When I got close enough to scare away the scavengers, Gizmo took up its place on my shoulder again.

As I looked closely at the elderly man on the ground, I saw him take a shallow breath. I immediately grabbed my knife and quickly cut the leather straps that held the man down. The man briefly opened his eyes, saw me with Gizmo on my shoulder, and gasped out,

"Mage," before lapsing into unconsciousness. Obviously, I could have replied to his comment, but he would not have been able to hear me.

~ Five ~

Travelling Man

I carried the elderly man into the shade of the broken wagon, cleared the ground, and used parts of the wagon to shelter him from the wind and sun. I treated the man's wounds as well as I could, but I wasn't sure how he would fare, due to his advanced age. The man was very emaciated; looking like a stiff wind would blow him over.

I didn't feel safe out here in the open, but wanted to ensure my patient was stable enough before trying to move him. I took the opportunity to check the man over and examine him closely. He was about five feet tall, maybe seventy pounds—nothing but skin and bones. He was wearing tattered clothing, and had welts and bruises all over his body. He had not been treated kindly by his captors.

Later when he woke up, I was able to get a little food and water into him. In his weakened state, he was only able to tell me that his name was Samuel, and impress upon me that I should get out of there before more 'orcs' showed up, as this was an area that they frequented. I weighed the risks of transporting Samuel, or staying in a possibly dangerous area. Moving, I decided, was definitely the safer alternative.

I slung Samuel over my shoulders and headed back to my camp. The sun was setting, so I set as fast a pace as I could to get back to the safety of my camp. Gizmo was not adding its weight, instead flying in wide circles overhead.

At one point, almost halfway back to my camp, I saw movement in the tall grass, headed toward me. I gently placed Samuel down to the ground between my legs, as the adrenaline started pumping madly through my body, readying for the possible fight to come.

When a massive head broke through the tall grass and hesitated before crossing the road, I sighed in relief. It was a Triceratops, not known for violence unless cornered or provoked; an herbivore, I thought. (I hoped the books I read were right).

The triceratops stopped on the roadway and watched me intently, while seven others in the herd crossed the road and headed back into the tall, waving grass, toward the setting sun. I remained absolutely still, not wanting to upset this giant. It must have been over thirty feet long, weighed about eighteen tons, and had three sharp horns for defence.

I thought my bullets would just make it angry enough to crush me to a pulp, unless I was lucky enough to hit a weak spot. And since the part of the dinosaur facing me was mostly bone, I didn't know where I would shoot him anyway, without becoming some kind of goo you scrape off your boot when you come into the house.

Once the herd had passed into the tall grass again, the leader gently turned and followed. It obviously felt that I did not pose much of a threat to it or the herd, and I agreed.

We reached the cave, and with a little help from Samuel, I was able to get us both inside and settled down for the night. I set up a warm blaze and wrapped the old man up in my emergency blanket on a bed of moss, with some food and water in reach. I settled down to a couple of hours of restless sleep, after which I piled more wood on the fire, and then climbed up the butte to check out the countryside.

Both moons were up when I settled in to view my little area of this world, giving enough light to make out shapes in the prairie below. I mused that if there were not so many animals that scared the crap out of me outside, this would be a nice place to live. I climbed down and made myself as comfortable as possible, falling into a deep slumber.

I awakened to the loud crack of thunder and the sound of water pouring down from the opening above. Samuel was lying across the fire from me with his eyes open, watching me intently. I stoked the fire and proceeded to heat some water and make some hot chocolate from my survival kit.

I handed Samuel the cup of hot chocolate and some dried fish and berries, and his eyes widened in surprise. He seemed confused that I was offering him food before I ate. When Samuel was done, I ate my meal, sharing it with Gizmo as usual.

As Samuel relaxed, he slowly overcame his fear of me and he decided to tell me a bit about himself. Surprisingly, Samuel spoke English! When I asked, Samuel explained to me that this was the common trade tongue and that his people spoke a different language amongst themselves. He spoke a few words of his native tongue, which sounded a lot like Spanish, to demonstrate.

Learning more about Samuel, I found that the 'People,' as they called themselves, were mostly rural farmers. They were forced into labour for other races, a practice that had decreased in the last few years, as the People learned to defend themselves.

Samuel then shared information about where he was from, and daily life when he was at home. He explained how the creatures called orcs were law enforcement for the government in certain parts. Whenever people were needed for the mines, the orcs would go out and take an entire village. This included women and children to work in the mines, and once there, no one ever left alive.

The leader of the government was a powerful wizard named Chavez, who had come to power several hundred years ago. (I wondered if this was a hereditary name passed down for the leader from generation to generation. Otherwise, how could someone be over 200 years old and still hold power, or for that matter, stand up).

Chavez, I concluded, ran a typical dictatorship; if anyone voiced discontent they quickly and quietly disappeared, never to be seen again. Any information that went out to the People was strictly censored and controlled.

Samuel, it turned out, was a village elder, and had received some education from the Elves. Elven education, he explained, was free and uncensored, and the elves rarely followed the government rules.

They were unofficially at war with the orcs, but kept their

fights low-key enough that the government ignored them. "Elves now," I contemplated. I was kept in a state of continual surprise by everything I was coming across in this world.

Samuel further explained that since this was such a violent world, it was not uncommon for an entire troop of soldiers to be taken out by a Tyrannosaurus Rex or some other type of large predator. I was glad that I had not run across one of those monsters yet.

In this world, the land masses had never separated so it was one large continent. There were several large island chains scattered around, but they were mostly inhabited by dragons. The dragons enjoyed the solitude of the islands, but spent the rest of their time in the mountainous regions with the Dwarves (Again, a familiar name from the story books. I wondered if the dwarves looked anything like they did in the stories).

Around the islands, the seas were, for the most part, poorly explored. There were no vessels large enough to contend with the giant sea monsters and rough seas.

Elves were apparently very close in height to me, and I was the tallest person that Samuel had ever seen. Samuel had heard that elves were very tall and slender, but had never met one in person. The training he had received was from another of his race, who had been trained as a teacher.

The People were no taller than Samuel's height of five feet, with the average being four and one-half feet. Dwarves were around four and one-half feet but stockier and broad shouldered. Orcs were between the two races in height, being between four and one-half to five feet. They rarely walked without being hunched over or hobbling, so their actual height was hard to tell. It appeared as though it hurt them to walk straight. It was thought that orcs originally came from living in caves in the mountains, which would explain why they walked hunched over (maybe a hereditary thing).

The road had been there as far back as anyone could remember; no one knew its origins. Cities and towns had been built with the road running through them, or at the intersection of roads. This allowed for easier travel for all, including trade caravans that didn't have to blaze trails through woods or prairie. Most animals steered clear of the roads, and crossed them only when necessary.

When a new town or village was built, they would request a wizard (what didn't they have in this storybook world?) to come from one of the bigger cities or towns to put a spell on the perimeter of the town to keep the predators away from the set boundaries around the town. The boundaries were then usually marked out in colourful stakes or a wall was built just inside of the perimeter so that the People knew where it was safe to go without worry.

The rain finally let up after a couple of days, so I ventured out, after Samuel assured me that he would not leave the cave. I went back to the camp where the orcs had been, salvaging enough material to fashion a small cart to carry my supplies and Samuel to the nearest village of the People.

Even in his weakened state, Samuel did not want to ride in the cart while I pulled it along the roadway. He finally agreed to it after I explained that he could watch over the supplies and watch for dangers coming up the road behind me. Gizmo thought it was a new and novel way to ride instead of on my shoulders, deciding to sit on the low rail of the cart, and seeming to be enjoying it.

Our arrangement paid off in the early afternoon of the second day traveling through the prairie. Samuel yelled, "There is something coming down the road!"

I stopped the cart and ran to the back. Three raptors bolted into sight. We would not have stood a chance without the warning! The firing stopped with the last raptor falling to the ground by my feet. A shiver ran through me. Either I was going to get used to this, or a nervous breakdown was on its way.

These raptors had collars on them. I quickly dragged the dead animals off the road into the tall grass, out of sight and I cut their collars off, hoping that it would slow down their handlers with another mystery to solve before trying to chase us down. I was hoping their handlers were not too close; if they were, we may not have enough time to get away. I grabbed the cart and put on speed, to put as many miles as possible between the area of the altercation and my little group.

The rest of the journey, thankfully, was uneventful. We arrived at the nearest town late in the morning of the third day. The town was surrounded by a wall of brick and straw, but the gates were made of dinosaur bones. When we got closer, I was met by a welcoming party consisting of eight to ten young males and a couple of older men.

All the young men were armed with spears and hide shields. When I got within hailing distance, I stopped and presented both my hands palm-up, indicating that I was unarmed. Two of the young men approached me warily.

"I come in peace, and I have an Elder who needs his injuries treated," I said, pointing to Samuel. Seeing Samuel, the men began talking in the other language that sounded like Spanish.

Four young men immediately took the cart away, hustling it down the road into the town and quickly disappearing out of sight. I was left standing there for a couple of minutes while the two elders talked to each other. The guards were sent away, which made me feel better, as one of the elders approached.

"I am Joseph. Come, you must be hungry and tired. I will show you a place where you can rest and refresh yourself. We can talk later," Joseph said, with a broad smile on his face.

I was escorted to a small house near the center of town, where I was able to clean up and lie down for a little bit on a bed. I was so tired that I immediately fell asleep; not waking until someone gently touched my shoulder. The sun was just setting; lamps had been set to illuminate the house.

Sitting on the edge of the bed, I noticed that my pack, with all of my belongings (nothing was missing), had been brought into the house while I slept. Someone had been busy, because I found that a clean pair of loose-fitting pants and a shirt in my size had been laid out.

My "alarm clock", who was a pretty young girl of the People, appeared to be around eighteen, and was trying to undress me. She seemed very disappointed when I thanked her and sent her out of the house. She watched me with disappointed and hungry eyes as

I shooed her out of the hut. I said to her glum face, "I am quite capable of doing for myself. Thank you, though."

A basin of warm water sat on the table, inviting me to clean up and refresh. The clothing was rough-spun, but extremely comfortable. I put my gun belt back on over top of the new clothes, and stepped outside into the cool of the twilight. My hand-crafted cart was parked outside the house, with a few children playing on it. I observed that there were no guards posted outside my door, indicating that the villagers either trusted me or were so scared they did not want to interfere with anything I wanted to do.

Joseph was sitting on a bench across the road, so I walked over and sat down beside him as the lamps were being lit around us to hold back the darkness. We sat in silence, watching people moving around us, working on their own personal business for about ten minutes. I asked him, "How is Samuel doing?"

"You took great care of him. Without your help, he would not have lasted the night. He told me how you saved him and brought him back to us. There are very few wizards who would stoop to helping a servant, or someone of lesser rank," Joseph said kindly.

"I consider Samuel a friend, not a servant, and I am not a wizard," I replied.

Joseph ignored the comment and escorted me to the biggest building in the town. It appeared to be a communal eating hall, as well as a main meeting place. Joseph showed me around, advising that this was also a strategic building. If the town were overrun by enemies, it could be closed up and defended easily. There was a deep well in the building, as well as enough food stored there to last up to a month.

Samuel was relaxing in a reclining chair at the head table. Gizmo had its very own little perch, right by the seat I was escorted to. The flagon they gave me contained a very strong and flavourful beer. There was a party atmosphere in the hall, obviously a celebration of Samuel's safe return. Instead of the simple fare I expected, the table was covered with all sorts of meat, cheeses, and fruit.

When everyone was settled in their seats, one of the elders told the story of how Samuel's village was destroyed, leading up to how

I had saved him and brought him to this village. When the speaker was done, the people present banged on the tables, yelling and raising their flagons to me in toast for my actions.

Then it was my turn to speak. I explained as much as I could that I was a traveller from a faraway land, and roughly explained how things were there. I went on about my adventures since coming to this land, leading up to the point where I brought Samuel to the town. After that, things settled down to an evening of eating, drinking and singing.

Joseph advised me that he knew I had questions, and that they would answer them in the morning as best as they were able. That was a good thing, because by the end of the evening a couple of young men had to help me get home and tuck me into bed for the night because I was very inebriated.

I had a nasty hangover the next morning, fortunately, the People had a cure for that – more beer! But after the breakfast that most heavy drinkers prefer (a couple of smaller glasses of beer), I actually felt almost normal again. A couple of strong young men in their early twenties approached me and introduced themselves as James and Joshua. They showed me around the town, although they could not or would not answer most of my questions. The buildings were made up mostly of packed clay, or grass and clay mix. The streets were simple packed dirt, beaten down over the years by hundreds of footsteps. I saw torch brackets which were obviously made for the night time illumination of the town. The walls of the town were a combination of grasses and mud, with wooden rods to strengthen the walls to make it able to stand up to most dinosaurs. It would also slow down the largest predators so that warriors could gather to defend the town.

Shortly after the tour, I was taken to the hall to meet with the elders, which included Samuel. Joseph shooed off my escort, and when it was just the elders, said, "I think you left out a few things when you were telling your story to the townspeople. I need you to be honest with us, so that we can help you if possible."

I described the world I had come from, and how I had ended up here, in more detail. I could see that all of the elders were paying close attention to my every word, and when I was finished, they asked me to step outside for a few minutes while they discussed in private.

Sitting on a bench outside the hall, I watched children chase a couple of dinosaurs that looked remotely like chickens (not knowing what else to call them). They were obviously small dinosaurs with feathers on them, although I had no idea if they laid eggs. I had not observed any at the banquet table last night, although that did not mean anything.

After a thirty-minute wait, I was called back in to the hall again. Samuel was sitting up in his recliner chair and talking to someone else. Everyone stopped talking when I entered. It was never a good sign when I could get a room to stop talking the minute I walked into it.

"Jim, I am too weak to travel with you and show you the way to someone who can help you understand everything about this world of ours, and the powers that you are starting to manifest. There is nothing more dangerous than an untrained wizard and whether you believe it or not, you are a wizard. Joshua and James will travel with you to show you the way, and act as your servants. You will attract much less attention in the bigger towns and cities with servants, and it is this village's repayment for saving my life," Samuel said quietly as he lay on his reclining chair.

Now was not the time to start an argument with Samuel and Joseph about the two young men traveling with me. I did not know where they were sending me, and having someone who was familiar with this world would be of great benefit.

Samuel gestured for me to step closer to him, and whispered, "Is Jim your birth name?"

Before I could answer, Samuel stopped me and said, "In this magic world, knowing someone's birth name gives you possible control over them and their powers. Remember that always!"

I nodded my head yes, not saying anything else.

~ SIX ~

Captivated

arly the next morning, James, Joshua, and I (with Gizmo, of course) were seen off by the whole town. James and Joshua were a little taller than the average amongst the People, standing at five feet. Both were very muscular and toned, looking like they could hold their own in a fight. We headed north toward what I was told was an inland sea, in the direction of a small mountain range with cave dwellings scattered along them.

The wizard Godfrey had a modest dwelling in these mountains, where he kept mostly to himself. However, Godfrey also liked to put on a good show for anyone who wanted to watch, and so spent part of his time teaching anyone who exhibited the least amount of magical talent.

The only thing that Joshua and James would let me carry was a small pack, with a little bit of food and water. Meanwhile, they were loaded down with the rest of the supplies, including a tent, cooking pots, utensils, and foodstuffs. The first couple of days were uneventful. The group would halt partway through the highest heat of the day, and then resume traveling after a couple of hours. When the sun started to set, we would look for an appropriate site to set up camp.

After a few days of travel, I thought I could get used to having servants. The two young men were very keen to fulfill my every need—from preparing meals and cleaning up, to setting up and taking down our camp in short order. When I expressed an interest in learning their history and how things were run in this world, both

Joshua and James took turns keeping up a running commentary while we traveled down the road.

We passed a few caravans of travelers or merchants, but no words were exchanged, and each time the other parties passed in sullen silence. When children tried to strike up a conversation, they were shushed or cuffed into quiet again by their parents. We were checked about twice a day by patrols of orcs, but fortunately they could find nothing wrong with the paperwork the village prepared for me. Later James explained that, knowing I was a wizard, the orcs were hesitant to cause any trouble in case I got angry.

As we approached the tree line again, I saw what looked like a large structure with a gate stretched across the roadway. I felt we were far enough away to make camp and approach the structure in the daylight, at which point we would have the time to figure out what it was. We set up camp and turned in for the night as soon as it got dark; banking the fire so that it did not give off light that would draw unwanted attention. The prairie gave way to the tree line, which would explain the heavy wooden fort that the orcs had built blocking the road before you could travel further in the forest and eventually the mountainous regions.

The moons were high up in the sky, but were waning, so there was not as much light, when Joshua grabbed my boots and hissed that a large group was moving down the road toward us. Most of the group walked right by the camp, but a squad of eight orcs, led by one mounted leader, came directly toward the tent.

They surrounded the camp, and the orc officer started screaming at me and my companions, demanding to know why we did not go to the checkpoint. He was obviously an officer by the cleaner uniform and rank markings on the epaulettes of his jacket. I knew how to deal with people like him; just like with any other bully. I screamed back at him, asking, "By what right do you disturb my sleep? I wonder if you might look good as a toad!"

That stopped the captain dead in his tracks. He stepped off his steed and walked over to me with a torch. By the fact that I was still dressed in my slowly deteriorating uniform, and by my height, he could tell I was definitely not one of the People.

"I am very sorry that I may have insulted you, master wizard.

All must report to the checkout," The captain said hesitantly, now a little unsure of his standing in this argument.

From that point on, the orcs were no longer pushy, but waited patiently while my travelling companions took their time taking down the camp. They gave us plenty of room, fearing the wizard's wrath if they pushed too much.

The area of the checkpoint was well lit by lamps and torches, and smelled like a pigpen. I observed two different enclosures: a very large one for the People (which was quite full), and a smaller one, which held six or seven small, stocky, bearded men (these must be dwarves).

The dwarves were just being released, and were very loud and indignant about their incarceration. I did not initially get a good look at them, as I was being steered toward the pen full of the People. The language the dwarves were using, swearing at the orcs, would make a pirate blush, but it brought a smile to my face, and I momentarily forgot about the pushing around I was receiving.

The dwarves stopped in their tracks, stared at me for a minute, and then spoke among themselves. They spent a few minutes staring at Gizmo and talking to it like it was intelligent. Gizmo flew over to the lead dwarf and sat on his arm for several minutes. The leader walked up to me and handed Gizmo over to me.

"You two are made for each other; I can sense the bond growing. Take care of each other and be safe, great mage," the dwarf leader said, before going back to his group and speaking to his men, who handed him something. Then he walked back to me.

"Bow your head, please. I place this amulet around your neck to show that you fall under the protection of the dragon clans. Mage, we will stand by until you are done with the offal here," The dwarf leader said, with unveiled anger.

"Do not question his word. He would step in and fight to the death any orc that might threaten you. A dwarf's word is like the gold they cherish; it is unquestionable once given." Joshua said as he stood beside me.

"Thank you for your offer, kind sir. It will certainly cause these others to think twice before dealing unfairly with me," I said, while looking at the orc guards and leader.

The dwarf leader nodded his head, and went off to stand with his group of men, waiting to see the outcome of my dealings with the orcs. The dwarves were exactly as described in fairy tales: five feet tall, with long, braided hair. They wore heavy leather armour enhanced with metal chainmail, and each carried a bow and arrow, as well as either a heavy war hammer or a hatchet for fighting.

I decided that, since this was a Mickey-mouse government operation, it was time to bluff and bully my way out of there as soon as possible. I immediately stopped outside of the pen and refused to enter.

"You will take me to see whoever is in charge of this pigsty, as I have important business to attend to and do not have the time nor the patience to have to wait to be processed," I told the leader, with as much anger as I could muster in my voice.

He was not sure who I was to begin with, but with the dwarves standing there glaring at him, the leader was quick to escort me to a well-lit building. He went inside, and I could hear the yelling start the minute he entered the office.

The orc leader and whomever he was addressing were initially yelling at each other but then the conversation dropped below hearing level. Although I could not hear what was being said, their voices could be heard for at least ten minutes before they obviously came to a decision.

When the door opened, I walked right in to confront the boss while my companions waited outside with the luggage. The commander quickly looked over his paperwork and smiled. This was the first time I had seen an orc smile, and it was almost more frightening than the scowl they usually had on their faces. He was a fat, slovenly male, his uniform covered in food and wine stains. He had to weigh at least three hundred pounds.

"I am so sorry for the way that you have been treated, Great One. Is there anything we can do for you?" the commander asked, still grinning.

"I appreciate your expediting my processing. It will be noted so that you will receive your just reward," I said with confidence.

The commander personally escorted me through the camp to the other end of the checkpoint.

"Is there anything I can do for you; provide you with accommodation for the rest of the evening, or provide you with an armed escort to ensure your protection and speed you on your way?" The commander asked, with that scary smile still on his face.

"Thank you very much, but I am able to take care of myself and my servants. I will continue on, now that the sun is starting to come up in the sky," I said, with sarcasm in my voice.

As I stepped through the gate, I could hear the captain and the officer congratulating themselves on managing to avoid future trouble from what to them appeared to be a very important person traveling incognito on government business (or so they thought).

We took short breaks throughout the day, to get as much distance as possible between the orcs and our party. We even took the extra precaution of finding a place where we could hide away from the road for the night, in case the orcs realized that they had been tricked.

When there had been no indication of pursuit in the last two days, I was feeling pretty safe trekking along the road toward my destination. I was really looking forward to sleeping on something softer than the hard ground, and we would reach the wizard Godfrey's home sometime tomorrow.

Gizmo perked up on my shoulder and was getting agitated. I noticed that the normal noises were suddenly absent. Abruptly, from the trees all around us stepped thirty or more orc soldiers. Gizmo shot up out of its resting place on my shoulders and took to the air. One of the orc archers strung his bow and took aim. I rushed the orc soldier, throwing his aim off, and the fight was on!

I pulled out my pistol, getting ready to defend my party, when one of the orcs threw a spear straight at my chest. It would have killed me if it had connected, but Joshua leapt in the way and took the spear straight through his back. My recollection from that point is blurred. All I saw was red since one of my new friends had just been killed.

I spread my wrath upon the orc soldiers. I kept firing, dropping soldiers left and right. I was told later that I had killed twenty orcs before I was knocked unconscious.

When I finally came to, it was very dark. I grunted and groaned as I tried to sit up. I felt like I had been hit by a semi-truck, or maybe one of those ogre clubs.

"Master. It is I, James. I have some water for you and I am right beside you. Just reach out and take the container," James said. I reached out and felt around, finding the container that James handed me. I drank half, and handed it back to James.

"What happened, and how long have I been out?" I said groggily.

"When Joshua took that spear for you and died, you went berserk, killing many orcs before one was able to get behind you and knock you out. They immediately grabbed me and held me down but master, you were able to dispatch twenty of them before they stopped you! Once you were down, they laid a severe beating on you, even though you were unconscious. You have been out for two days. They grabbed your magic fire stick and tried to use it on you, but nothing happened," James said with awe.

James explained further that I had been placed in a small cage and transported back to the checkpoint, then thrown in a little underground cell with him. He had been taken out and beaten a few times to elicit more information about who I was and what I was doing, but since his knowledge was limited, he was unable to help them. They had sent for a wizard who was very skillful in interrogation, but he had not arrived yet.

"Now that you are awake, they may take you out again to question you," James said.

"Is it dark in here, or have I been blinded by my injuries?" I asked.

"No, it is dark as a moonless night, without the stars," James replied quietly, as he reached over to touch my arm and try to calm me.

Apparently there were some torches in the room, but they had been extinguished when the guards had left.

I felt the overwhelming need for light and heat, as it was

suddenly very cold in the dark cell. I closed my eyes and remembered the heat and the brightness of the summer sun back home. I suddenly felt warmer, and could see light from behind my closed eyelids.

When I opened my eyes, I saw a small orb of yellow light floating in the air just in front of me. James was sitting there with his mouth wide open in awe. He just stared silently as I located the torches. One by one, the orb drifted over, touched them and lit them ablaze.

"Master, you truly have the gift of magic inside you!" James said in awe.

James gave me some food, advising that he had been putting parts of his meal aside for when I woke up. Feeling better after getting some food inside me and a little warmer with the torches lit, I drifted off to sleep again.

I woke to the sounds of the guards cursing at each other for leaving the torches lit in the cell. There were ten of them (I felt complimented that they thought me that much a threat even without my weapon). Two watched James, and the rest half carried, half dragged me down the hallway, up a ramp and into the sunlight.

They placed me in a wooden chair, tied my hands and feet so that I could not move, and a gag was put in my mouth. As I listened to the officers talking to the commander, I found out the compound commander had been away when I came in. He came in the next day, and did not get word of anything strange happening until two days after I had passed through. He was immediately suspicious and sent a large group of soldiers to bring back the supposed wizard for questioning.

When the orc in charge of the soldiers who had taken me captive explained his story, the commander got very angry and called him a liar. The captain brought out my gun belt and pistol, explaining that no one else was able to make the fire stick work. The commander examined the pistol for a few minutes and suggested an experiment. A group of ten of the People were brought out and put into a line in front of me.

The pistol was placed in my hand and I was ordered to kill all ten of the People or I would be killed. I shook my head no. The captain grabbed my hand and pulled the trigger for me; fortunately nothing happened. I let out a sigh, and closed my eyes in relief. The last thing I wanted was to be made to kill innocent people. Before they thought to pull the gun out of my hands, I managed to fire one shot, killing the commander's bodyguard.

Angrily, the commander advised me that a wizard was coming from the capital, and that he would find a way to get information out of me. The squad leader asked the commander a question that I did not hear; who grinned evilly and answered, "Of course."

Several of the larger orc soldiers were ordered to beat me severely, while the other soldiers looked on laughing and making suggestions. By the end, I knew several ribs were broken because when they threw me back in the cell I was having hard time breathing. They even removed all the torches, so I could not relight them even if I wanted to. I found that I could generate the light at will, but in my weakened state I could not maintain it for long.

James gave me the good news that Gizmo had managed to escape during the initial fight with the orcs. I hoped my dragon companion was happy and free somewhere away from the enemy. I really had grown quite fond, and would hate for anything to happen to it.

I did not like what appeared to be coming for my immediate future, I felt that once they got the information they wanted I would no longer be of any use to them; and my life would be forfeit. I lay there in the dungeon drifting in and out of consciousness thinking that I would die in a strange new world with my comrades back home not knowing where I was or what happened to me.

~ Seven ~

Gizmo Saves the Day!

was awakened by James shaking me vigorously.

"Master, wake up! Something is happening outside—it sounds like a big fight! I can smell smoke, and it sounds like weapons clashing," James said excitedly.

"I am so weak right now, I could not fight a kitten," I replied feebly.

For the next little while, I lapsed in and out of consciousness. Suddenly, I heard the cell door bang open. I didn't have much energy left, but I was going to try to struggle. Then I was grabbed by someone.

"It is all right, master—they are friends!" James said to calm me.

I vaguely remember being put on a blanket to be carried out of the cell. When I came out into the sunlight, I thought I saw a huge dragon, surrounded by a lot of heavily armed dwarves. Then I felt something alight on my chest; when I looked, it was Gizmo! I was so overwrought that I burst into tears when Gizmo cuddled against me.

"Welcome back little friend, and thanks for bringing help," I said to Gizmo.

"You're welcome," an unknown voice said in my head.

The next time I woke up, I was in a very soft and comfortable bed, being attended to by a young maiden. I surmised that she must be a dwarf, as she was only four and a half feet tall, with a stocky build, but very beautiful. She had long, dark brown hair fashioned in a single braid, falling down almost to her ankles. She had dark brown eyes, which seemed to swallow me up when I gazed too long into them.

The maiden was giving me a sponge bath, and since I am a typical male, I started to get aroused. When she noticed that, she looked into my eyes and giggled. "You are still too weak for things like that, but thank you for the compliment," she said, smiling.

Humming merrily to herself, she dried me off, and then pulled the covers back over top of me. She then strolled out of the room with a broad smile on her face.

"She is right, you know. You are still too weak to even think about that, and her father—the war chief—would not be impressed either," that unfamiliar voice in my head said again.

I looked around, but there was no one else in the room except for Gizmo and me.

I mumbled to myself, "I must be dreaming again," before drifting back to sleep.

I was up and partially mobile within a couple of days, and starting to feel a little claustrophobic in my room, even though James and the pretty little nurse came in to check on me often.

I felt like I was getting the royal treatment. I had a lavish bedroom and a bathroom close by, and they had some way of running the water in the toilet all the time so that it was continually flushing. The water must have been warm, because the stone seat was not cold at all.

I really itched to get outside into the fresh air and sunlight, to start regaining my strength. When I talked to James about it, he said he knew the perfect place, and promised to take me there late the next morning, when the sun was shining brightly.

When the morning came, it took a good fifteen minutes of hobbling, with my body complaining every step of the trip, but when I reached the large balcony area, looking down on the valley and the inland sea below me was well worth the effort. It was just so amazing, with different types of herbivorous dinosaurs visible, eating around the small sea. I could even see people in the distance harvesting some crops fenced off to keep the dinosaurs out.

As I was reclining there in the sun, I saw a far-off bird winging its way toward where I was relaxing. As I watched the bird get bigger, it finally dawned on me that it was huge, probably twice as large as any of the dinosaurs that I had seen on this world so far. It was a dragon, headed right for me! I began to panic, but saw that no one else on the balcony seemed concerned and they were also watching the approaching dragon.

"Good morning, Wizard Jim, how are you feeling today? You had us worried for a while that you were not going to make it," said the dragon loudly, once it had landed on the balcony.

I sat there with my mouth open for a moment, and then remembered my manners and how many strange things I had seen so far. I replied to the large dragon, "I am feeling much better; just a little tired still."

"I am Adoronac, Guardian of the North and provider of counsel to the dwarves in this region," Adoronac said in a voice that carried across the balcony quite clearly, "...and of course you remember your traveling companion, Gizmo?"

James handed me a flagon at that point, and Adoronac said, "You must drink this. It will help you heal faster, as well as other things."

It smelled horrible and tasted even worse. It burned going down and I wondered if it was going to burn equally if it came back up. I managed to keep it down, while thinking to myself that it was quite disgusting, and wondering what was in it.

"It is full of slimy things mixed with dragon's blood. Potions are not supposed to taste good; otherwise, men would be taking them all the time to see what they would do." Again, I was hearing that mysterious voice in my head.

"Who said that?" I questioned aloud.

"It is I, the one you named Gizmo. Now that you have tasted of my blood, we can communicate with each other 'til we are but dust in the pages of history. Magic is only amazing to those who have not lived with it. Only those without it in their lives do not realize the limitless boundaries it has. And for the record, I am over two hundred years old, which is young for a dragon, and I am not someone's pet," Gizmo said, with a little bit of irritation in its voice.

"What happed after I lost consciousness again at the checkpoint?" I asked, wondering what had happed with the orcs.

Gizmo proceeded to explain the series of events leading up to my arrival at the dwarf stronghold. Apparently I had only been a captive for a short period of time before Gizmo found a small party of dwarves hauling a load of silver to one of the larger cities in the area. When Gizmo communicated our need for help (I did not know this, but dwarves and dragons can talk to each other naturally), the dwarves immediately sent half of their warriors to watch the checkpoint.

Gizmo then flew on to the dwarf stronghold and told Adoronac of our needs. A large contingent of dwarf warriors was dispatched immediately to the checkpoint. The dwarves were strong and could cover a great distance in a short amount of time, only taking a day and a half to reach the checkpoint. Once they were in place, Adoronac received notice, came, burned down the front gate with his flame, and demanded that the wizard be released.

Orcs do not take well to threats so they prepared to shoot down the dragon, which became a little difficult as the dwarf warriors had had time to enter the checkpoint by then. At that point, the orcs fought for their lives.

Dwarves made short work of the orcs, killing thirty out of the sixty in about ten minutes (half the garrison) and hauling up the commander in front of Adoronac for questioning. He denied any knowledge of trying to kill the little dragon, and stated that those responsible for the attempt had been themselves killed by the dwarves.

When asked about the wizard, the orc commander kept trying to change the subject, saying that the wizard was not protected by the law, unlike the dragons. (Apparently dragons are a protected species—who knew?)

"Did you look to see if he was marked as one of the dragon companions?" Adoronac asked, in his loudest booming voice. The commander admitted that the thought never crossed his mind, but it could be checked then and there.

"Have one of your underlings show my men where he is and bring all of his belongings to me," Adoronac said angrily.

The orcs hustled to gather my belongings in a stack in front of the dragon. Apparently, after they had placed me on a stretcher, with James close at hand, a couple of orcs died. They had tried to stop James from being with his master, at which point Gizmo attacked them and the dwarves finished them off. There, on top of the pack, was the medallion that one of the imprisoned dwarves had given to me.

Gizmo settled gently on my chest, checking for heartbeat and breathing, then looked up at Adoronac, and nodded its head. Adoronac picked up the stretcher, with me in it, and flew away to the stronghold.

The dwarf chief stepped in and informed James that Adoronac had taken me for much-needed healing. James was to travel with them to meet up with me. The commander apparently put up a big fuss about James going with the dwarves.

"By violating the right of the protection of dragons, you violated all your rights. You are lucky that we are going to let you live to explain this to your leader when he gets here. Not only did your men attack the small dragon, but as you can see on the pack a protection amulet for the dragon clans; and they also mistreated a wizard under our safeguard," The dwarf chief said.

The commander visibly paled. With that, the dwarf chief walked over to the pen where the rest of the People were being kept and broke the locks, letting them all free. The commander started to protest the release of the People, but when the chief glared at him, he thought better of it.

The dwarves escorted all of the orcs into the pens that had been used to hold others and locked them there. Then, the dwarves and the People who had been held disappeared into the country, leaving the orc commander to ponder how he was going to explain this one to the leader. Maybe he should have let the dwarves kill him; it certainly might have been quicker and less painful.

The trip back to the stronghold had been uneventful for James and the others. I, on the other hand, was there within minutes. Since they knew I was coming, there were stretcher bearers and healers present at this very balcony to take me into immediate care and treat me. I did not wake up until James had been by my side for a week. Potions were given me to sleep and heal quickly.

Apparently the potion that I had been given to drink was a mixture of some of my own and some of Gizmo's blood. This, combined with some serious dragon magic, bonded the two of us together. Gizmo had hesitated initially, but after getting to know me during the past few weeks, she saw how good and strong my personality was. Yes—SHE! I found out that Gizmo was female, but my ignorance was not my fault. There had been no biology class in school on how to tell the sex of a dragon.

Gizmo finished bringing me up to speed on the last few days I had missed.

"You have been chosen to become a dragon mage, something that has not been seen for over ten thousand years. It is a great honour, and holds great responsibility for the bearer of the title. You will learn magic that few have ever known existed," Gizmo said, sounding like she was reading something from a history book she had memorized.

"It's nice to know that I have a decision in this matter," I replied a little sarcastically.

~ EIGHT ~

To Wiz or Not to Wiz
(I mean wizard—not pee!)

he next day, a large contingent of orcs showed up at the dwarf stronghold, carrying a white flag of truce. Adoronac went to meet the leader of the group with a large number of dwarves manning the battlements, in case of trouble.

Not being allowed to attend the meeting due to my weakened state, I had to wait for someone to come back and tell me what had transpired. Watching through a telescope that the wall commander had given me, I saw the orcs approach and lay down on the ground, humbling themselves in front of Adoronac. The orc leader, after a long, ranting appeal, brought forward a large sack. He then emptied the sack, which contained several orc heads, before the dragon.

The orcs also left two large chests, which appeared to be very heavy, and walked away. The party from the stronghold waited until the orcs were well out of sight, then workers came from the stronghold. They made a large bonfire, burned the heads, and inspected the chests before packing them back behind the walls.

Gizmo explained what had happened later to me in my room; how the government apologized for the incident at the checkpoint. The leader of the orc delegation explained that the offending parties had been beheaded for their flagrant disregard of important laws. When the orc leader had enquired into my health, Adoronac had explained that I was very weak and my likelihood of surviving was very slim.

The orc leader could not hide his happiness at this comment, but stated that the chests of gold were in compensation for any difficulty and for the dwarves that had died in battle. The orc leader was not thrilled when Adoronac explained that there had been no loss of life from the dwarves' contingent.

The orcs left two spies behind to monitor the stronghold, but both had unfortunate accidents within a short period of time. The dwarves graciously assisted in the process of their untimely end.

The chests were examined closely to ensure there was no poison or negatively-magicked items that could cause harm. The chests and contents were then turned over to me, to do with as I pleased. After learning that the dragon's treasure troves were mine for the asking, I had the contents of the chests distributed among the rescue party.

Eating in my spacious rooms by myself was beginning to grow monotonous. I was resigned to the prospect of another typical night ahead, until I was perked up by Gizmo joining me for the meal.

"They are having a wake in your honour tomorrow evening, since you are believed to be dead. We have time to make some arrangements and start your training before they get wise and possibly try to hurt you," Gizmo said with a laugh.

"Why would they try to hurt me?" I asked.

"Because if they find out that you are being trained as a dragon mage, they won't take it well because that makes you an unknown entity and a potential threat to the ruling wizard of this country. Even now, just the hint of your existence is giving many of the People hope, and stirring up the embers of a revolution," Gizmo said.

"And what happens if I decline this prestigious honour you have given me?" I asked Gizmo when my mouth was empty of food.

"It is not a choice that was taken lightly. The eldest of the dragons, Elijah, foretold your coming. He had a vision and predicted three places where you might appear, and a little dragon was dispatched to each location to watch for your arrival. It was fortuitous for me that you showed up where I was watching, or I would be wolf excrement by now," Gizmo said laughingly.

"So do I need training, or do these powers just show up?" I asked, staring at Gizmo.

"Even before you were chosen, you were demonstrating powers. The fire stick you carry never stops or runs out of spears, as I can see in your mind would normally be the thing that happens. James told me how you lit the torches in the cell, bringing light to darkness. These were manifestations of just a fraction of the power that you have in you," Gizmo said.

Gizmo could read my mind thoroughly, but I was only able at this point to see and understand whatever Gizmo wanted me to. I wondered what she might be holding back from telling me. I was still unsure of my role in this world that I had found myself in, and not sure if I was a pawn or a king in a cosmic game of chess.

The next morning I was alone again with James, who seemed in an excellent mood.

"I am to show you around the fortress and help you pick out new clothing and a holder for your magical weapon," James said cheerily. We walked out of the keep down to the street of vendors, which was located within the walls of the stronghold.

The first thing we located was a tailor who measured me from head to toe, not asking what I wanted, just shooing us away when he was done his measurements.

Our next stop was at a leather crafter. I showed him my holster and explained that I wanted a shoulder holster, and roughly how to construct it. The leather crafter nodded his head just like the tailor, and shooed us away again. The cobbler was next, and again I got the same treatment.

"They are not asking what I want. How come?" I asked James.

"They have been given instructions already on appearance; they just needed your size," James replied. "I think that you will be impressed by the end result, but it is to be a surprise as per Adoronac's instructions."

Walking around the stronghold for several hours, I realized that with a dragon for backup, there was no way someone could break the fortifications. I walked with James to my rooms, realizing how much this stronghold resembled the old castles in my world, but of course better maintained and newer. After James left, I lay down for a long nap, I was awakened just as the sun was starting to set, and brought over to a hot bath that had been prepared for me. Afterwards, I felt clean for the first time in weeks, and walked into the bedroom to find a new outfit laid out for me.

I didn't know what they used for underwear in this world, but they had duplicated mine pretty closely. Shirts were similar to my tattered clothing, with pockets in the chest and some sort of crest that resembled a dragon above the right hand breast pocket. Pants again resembled my older worn out clothing, but in a tan colour.

The boots were a supple leather that fit perfectly; I felt very comfortable walking around in them. The shoulder harness and holster were exactly how I requested them to be (they must have borrowed my holster to make such an exact duplicate).

When I walked out into the main room, I found James dressed in a very similar uniform, with crests on both shoulders. Gizmo showed up and curled into her usual place, and we headed for the main hall. On the way I asked Gizmo about the crests on the uniforms.

Gizmo replied "the crest marks you as a dragon companion. You are marked as a leader, and James as a regular companion."

The hall was huge. Large doors folded away so Adoronac could sit comfortably on the large balcony and look into the hall. He could interact with everyone present, but not be in the way due to his immense size. I was first introduced to clan leaders and their wives. When they came to my lovely nurse, I found out her name was Susie.

When we were introduced, she giggled and leaned into toward me whispering, "Maybe we can take care of that problem you had the other morning."

I turned beet red, while Susie's father, the war chief, looked on with a scowl on his face.

After the feasting and toasting, I was feeling light-headed. The alcoholic beverages I drank were definitely a lot stronger than what I was used to. I headed off to my room, with James giving me support along the way, so I did not bounce off walls or guards.

Early the next morning, I woke up with a hangover. As I lay there thinking, a soft arm reached across me and a warm body smelling of lilacs snuggled up to me. I thought to myself; *Please don't let it be Susie.* If her dad catches us, I will never make it to my next birthday, never mind wizard training. I rolled over, and OH CRAP, it was Susie.

"Good morning! Everything seemed to be working fine last night. My father does not approve of the companions, so last night will have to tide you over 'til you find another girl friend," Susie said, before she jumped out of bed. She dressed swiftly and gave me a quick kiss on the lips before flitting out of the room, giggling.

"Tsk, tsk, I warned you to stay away from her," Gizmo said, scolding me.

"Well, I was alone when I went to bed, and I don't remember inviting her in. Speaking of which, is there a spell or something that I can have to stop or reduce the effects of alcohol? The stuff you people brew here is just too darn potent!" I said to Gizmo.

"Of course there is, but most wizards like to get drunk once in a while to forget their problems," Gizmo said, laughing.

"Just give me a spell that will reduce the effects, so at least I can remember when I have a good time," I replied, as my head was pounding with a nasty hangover.

Gizmo was still laughing at me when James came in to announce that breakfast was ready in the main room. I noticed that there was a small bed and a perch being brought into my room by servants.

"What is this?" I enquired.

"I am moving in with you, so that you can start being a companion, and start your magic training," Gizmo said.

"What does the companion job entail, by the way?" I asked Gizmo.

"Why—to protect me, of course; something you have seemed very capable of doing since we met," Gizmo replied.

"With all these companions around, you shouldn't need protection," I said to Gizmo.

"It is a title that helps keep you out of trouble. There are few people willing to get on the bad side of dragons and their companions," Gizmo replied to me.

Apparently, there had been a war several centuries ago, and the dragons had laid waste to a large area of land. Their enemies had been trying to eradicate the entire species, although it was never clear as to why.

There was another banquet a week later, to discuss the trip to the North and to get counsel from the oldest and wisest of dragons who was so ancient that he could no longer take to the air. There was a table set up near the leaders, with a variety of items stacked on it.

"These are from the other clan leaders to welcome you as a dragon companion, to help in your future endeavours, and to become the dragon mage," Gizmo said with respect, adding that givers achieved status by giving the best gift to the possible dragon mage.

"This is the one of the most important gifts. It is a mithril shirt, to be worn under your clothing," Gizmo said, explaining that mithril was a magical metal that dwarves worked with their earth magic to make weapons and armour. The shirt could not be punctured. Gizmo then pointed out what looked like a set of mithril vambraces (forearm protectors) saying, "These are from the dragon lord Adoronac, to help focus your magic as you learn to control it."

"Is there anything from the war chief?" I asked.

"No, he said that Susie had given you a very precious gift, and there need not be any others from his family," Gizmo said with a laugh.

I could almost hear the chuckle from the voice in my head. I noticed as I looked around that there were more young maidens than at the first banquet. It was a good night not to get inebriated, so I could make proper decisions later in the evening.

Samuel, the elder of the People, was talking to some of the clan chiefs. I approached him and offered my condolences and gratitude for Joshua saving my life. I promised that if there ever was anything I could do to repay the debt, all Samuel had to do was ask. Samuel reassured me that the dragon companions had been very generous to Joshua's family.

"And this is the gift from the People, to the new dragon companion and future dragon mage," Samuel said, pulling aside a curtain to a side room. There stood ten identically-dressed men in uniforms like James had worn, and leather armour with swords and bows. They were to be my bodyguard, and were an elite corps of men trained in all forms of combat.

After being introduced, both Gizmo and I felt very tired and headed off to our room. I could not understand why both of us were feeling so tired, I would expect one of us but not both of us at the same time. There was nothing left to do but plan the trip and our opinion was not needed for that.

When I awoke, I had twice as much of a shock. I woke up wedged between two maidens, both beautiful, one with jet black hair and the other yellow like the sun. I looked at Gizmo, who was just waking up on her perch.

Both maidens dressed and with smiles on their faces, they each gave me a kiss and sauntered out the door.

"This is not possible," I said to Gizmo, as I watched the maidens leave. "I only drank water and juice—no alcohol at all."

"There is something fishy about this, as your people would say. Let me get to the bottom of it. I will find out and let you know," Gizmo said, leaving. She returned to me later in the afternoon and said, "After having delved into this, I learned that the maidens purchased a sleeping draught that will not affect your performance. In the vernacular of your world, you have twice been the victim of a date rape drug."

Apparently, the girls wanted a baby by me, so that my bloodline could be merged with their clan's. All three were from the same clan, which would make the clan very powerful if and when children were born.

Not liking the idea of being used as a stud, I did not hesitate to very loudly and angrily share my anger with Gizmo. Gizmo explained it would be dealt with, and as soon as a punishment was determined, I would be advised.

"Not to mention the fact that they drugged me as well, going against everything that our law allows for. If these were warriors, they would be placed in prison for a long period of time," Gizmo said. "I will seek out Adoronac immediately and consult with him as to what should be done."

With that, Gizmo flew out the open window. After quickly dressing, I headed out into the main room where I found James sitting and scratching his head.

"Should I prepare for three guests for tomorrow morning, master?" James asked, with a broad smile on his face.

"There will be no further breakfast guests, unless I advise you the night before. I will explain later. Let's go down to the courtyard and see how the troops are preparing for departure," I growled at James, who realizing that I was angry lost the smile and became very business-like.

We found one of the members of the troop standing guard over several packages, including tents and foodstuffs.

"Good morning, master," the soldier said, and bowed deeply to me.

"That has to change, James. Tell the men that they will not call me master, nor bow to me in the future. They may call me commander and slightly nod their heads; that way it does not indicate me as an officer to some archer hiding in the bush, and it does not take their vision off the surrounding area to watch out for enemy units," I said, still angry from my morning encounter while I examined the cart that was to bear the equipment for us.

"Were you present when your superior purchased this cart for supplies?" I asked the soldier, who replied simply, "No."

"Then you go fetch him and bring him back here to talk to me right away," I said to the soldier.

"But I was told to remain here with the supplies," the soldier stated.

"And who outranks him?" I said, raising my voice so that a few heads turned from the crowded vendors stalls to see what was happening.

"You do, sir…right away, sir!" the soldier stammered in reply to me, then hastened away to find his supervisor.

A scruffy-looking individual tried to steal a package of supplies while I sat there on the pile.

"Unless you want to lose some fingers, you had better put it back," I said, not being in any mood to accept any problems from anyone.

The individual put his hand on his knife and started to say

something, then took one look at the emblem on my shirt and my gun in its holster.

"Thank you," he spoke softly, as he turned pale as a ghost. He quickly put the package down, and ran as fast as he could in the other direction.

Two soldiers returned, with the more senior one ranting and not letting the younger one speak for himself.

"Who was this boob trying to countermand my orders?" the senior soldier loudly demanded. The junior soldier replied, "That one," pointing at me. They walked up to me, and after taking a good look, were completely silent.

"I have had a bad morning," I said gruffly to the senior soldier. "You obviously have, too. Let's start things over with a fresh start, and the previous conversation will be forgotten. I will not let it affect our working together."

He replied "Thank you, sir," turning a little pale.

"I have noticed some problems with the cart, which you must have been too busy to notice, or the shopkeeper who sold it to you might have pulled the wool over your eyes. Get the shopkeeper, and I will deal with him directly about the missing or broken parts on the cart. That way, you can get on with other important matters that need to be attended to," I said to the senior soldier, to which he replied, "Yes, sir!" having moved on from his earlier brash attitude.

The soldier returned with the shopkeeper in tow within moments, and then wisely disappeared to get other tasks done. I looked at the shopkeeper, noting that he was not the typical-looking dwarf. He was heavy and balding, and sweating profusely (either from nerves or from the short run to the cart). I introduced myself to the shopkeeper, who went a little pale.

"You sold these soldiers a defective cart, but since you are an honest and upstanding citizen, I am sure you want to correct this as soon as possible," I said to the shopkeeper, giving him a ready-made excuse and a way out of trouble.

The shopkeeper apologized profusely, stating that the workers in his shop had brought out the wrong wagon. A brand new one would be brought out immediately, and this piece of junk scrapped. He left, and within ten minutes, a couple of young men from the wagon shop brought a brand new one to me, and took the old cart away.

By the time James came back, all the soldiers were gathered. He had them load the supplies onto the cart, and located a driver and team to haul the supplies to the compound. The senior soldier noticed the new cart, and started to ask me about it.

"On another day, when I have time, I will explain it to you," I told him.

By the time I got back to my rooms, I was feeling a little better after bested the shopkeeper and the thief. Gizmo was sitting on her perch.

"Things have been sorted out and whenever you are ready, Adoronac has an appropriate punishment arranged for the maidens. Their fathers have not been spoken to yet, and are in the dark about what is to happen," Gizmo advised.

I told Gizmo what had happened at the market. Still feeling groggy, I was going to sleep for a couple of hours. James was told to call me with lunch and I crawled into bed, after dead-bolting the room door. Gizmo, noticing my actions, said, "Good choice."

I curled under the covers, and Gizmo quickly cuddled in beside me like when we were traveling. I was sound asleep in moments, and did not rouse until James pounded on the door.

While I was eating a hearty late lunch, I suddenly realized how I could use this situation to my advantage. I asked Gizmo if I might be able to have a private meeting with Adoronac prior to his passing sentence on the maidens. Gizmo lifted her head, tilting it sideways, and then responded, "It is arranged. As soon as you and I leave these rooms, we will go directly to talk to Adoronac."

Leaving the rooms, we took an alternate path to where Adoronac was waiting. Gizmo spoke to Adoronac mind-to-mind, so that the dragon's loud voice did not boom out. I explained my concerns and needs through Gizmo, and Adoronac was in complete agreement. The meeting was done incredibly fast. It is amazing how quick a conversation can go when you don't have to speak.

~ NINE ~

North To —?

izmo and I walked back, arriving in the hall at the same time as the three maidens and their fathers. There at a table were all of the clan chiefs and Adoronac, waiting to pass judgement in relation to this incident.

Gizmo and I were given a comfortable spot to sit, off to the side of the table. The fathers were placed in front, as supporting counsel for their daughters. The three maidens were ushered down the centre of the hall to stand in front of the great table of the clans.

"You are charged with drugging one of the little dragons—those beings that you have sworn to protect against all harm. You are also charged with taking, without his consent, the seed of the dragon companion and mage, Jim, and also drugging him. How do you plead in relation to these charges?" Adoronac said to the maidens and their fathers.

"Guilty," Susie said, and the other two maidens replied similarly, staring at the floor, ashamed of themselves. They knew that they could not lie, as I found out that the little dragons were masters of reading the minds of anyone and would detect the truth immediately.

"The little dragon known as Gizmo has agreed that since no harm was done, she is willing to have you work in the lords' kitchens for a period of three years. This is very lenient, as the usual penalty for this offence varies from ten years to life, depending on the level of injury done to the dragon," Adoronac stated, and then carried on with the sentencing, stating: "The charges against the dragon mage are more serious, because they deal with the balance of power in the clan, which could throw the whole order into chaos with the possibility of dragon-born mages that are also dwarves. If the dragon mage had chosen to drink spirits, this infraction would have been missed. I ask the fathers to stand with their daughters for judgment."

"The penalty is for the maidens to be made barren for the rest of their days," Adoronac said loudly.

All three fathers were on their feet, protesting the unfairness of the ruling.

"I do not make the law," Adoronac said in reply.

"Maybe I can offer a less drastic solution to this situation," I said, as the maidens and their fathers eyed me hopefully. I addressed Adoronac, as the penalty had been decided between us. "I would accept that no prodigy comes from these unions, and that each of the clan chiefs whose daughters have taken advantage of me, provide me with their best warrior as part of my personal guard."

Adoronac said to the chiefs, "You have one day to ponder this option, which is acceptable to me. The maidens, in the meantime, will remain with the clan chief wives, sequestered so they do not try to escape from the stronghold. This meeting is dismissed until tomorrow at this time, if not sooner."

I sat enjoying a drink in front of the blazing hearth in the main room, when, one by one, each of the clan chiefs showed up with a warrior in tow. Each one was extremely grateful that I had given them an honourable way out of this incident. I arranged for a large room across from mine to be set up for the three warriors, and since they were all of the same clan, there were no hard feelings amongst them.

The warriors were named "Blaze," "Blade," and "Fire-Tongue." After consulting with the other companions, Gizmo was able to determine that Blade was the most gifted.

I had a quiet dinner with him and James, to talk about organizing my people into a core group that I was forming, with me as commander, James as my personal assistant and bodyguard, Blade as captain, Blaze and Fire-Tongue as sergeants, and John and Frank as corporals, followed by Bill, Joe, Fred, Samson, Kevin, Karl, Larry, and Lionel.

The organization allowed for the men to be broken down to smaller groups, or to operate on their own if I needed the dwarves in a protective situation for Gizmo.

During our meal, I learned that we were leaving in two weeks, to head north to the stronghold of the dragon they called Elijah, who was the oldest known dragon in the world. Elijah was old and he preferred to remain in the warmth of his volcano home, surrounded by his guardian companions.

But, it was Elijah who would make the final judgment on whether I was a dragon mage or not, so the trip had to be made to see him. The decision always fell to the eldest dragon, and then my training could begin.

I learned that over two hundred from another clan (Gold) were traveling to a northern stronghold below the snow line so that was why it was going to take longer for them to prepare the provisions and dinosaurs for the trip. The dwarves used Ankylosaurus that they put platforms on, or to tow large trailers. Also, a number of merchants wanted to travel in the safety of the large contingent traveling north.

Delays… when I was hoping to just sneak out and get to our destination without a lot of pomp and ceremony. Also, the clan sending men north was not on friendly terms with my companion warriors, so it could be a very interesting trip. The dwarves were now dragon companions, and that should have separated them from clan rivalries, but accidents could happen.

The Gold clan had six or more of their most beautiful maidens riding in the group. (Tell me someone had not planned this and was trying to coerce me into freely donating my seed to another clan.) I gave very clear orders to my companions that they were to run interference between the maidens and me.

I also told Gizmo that I would appreciate her company, telling her to feel free to bite anything soft and pretty-smelling that crawled into my bed without my express permission.

Word obviously got back to Blade's clan (Diamond) about the maidens, and my attempts at avoiding them during the trip. Within a couple of days the contingent was bolstered by fifty warriors, two healers and kitchen staff. If they could not have me as part of the clan, then they were going to make darn sure the others would not convince me to give it up unwillingly.

As it was, it took two whole days to pack and load all the provisions for the week-long journey. The destination was a stronghold that dug into the side of a chain of mountains that ran from east to west, forming a natural barrier to the north. The mountain chain was rich in rare metals such as gold and platinum, which bore a high price for jewellery.

Now, with my contingent of dragon companions strengthened to fifty, plus my own small elite group, I spent much of my time planning. A large part of this was making sure officers understood the chain of command under my direct orders, or those of my three dwarven warrior commanders. Being under the command of my three dwarves presented no problem, as each of them held a rank of general in their own clan.

I slept soundly each night and after the lesson of Adoronac's punishment, I felt very secure in the stronghold that the women would leave me alone. However, I was awakened one night by the equivalent of someone mentally biting on my ear. Gizmo spoke clearly to me in my mind.

"There is something soft and pretty-smelling just entering the room. I can detect no malice in her thoughts; it is obvious what she wants," Gizmo said to my mind.

"Let her climb into the bed, and then give her something to remember you by," I replied, thinking the answer so that the interloper did not hear me.

I continued to pretend to be asleep. I listened to the rustling of clothing, and then felt a naked female crawl into the bed beside me. Gizmo lunged out, and I heard a loud squeal of pain. I then heard the female streaking out of the room. I got up, locked the door, got back in bed and drifted off to sleep again, after thanking Gizmo for a job well done. After she finished laughing, both Gizmo and I drifted off to sleep again.

As I was finalizing the arrangements for provisions, I noticed a maiden buying ointment and salves from a healer. When she became aware of me, she turned her head and strode off so I was unable to make out her features. I asked the healer what she had purchased. He hesitated initially, but was forthcoming after he noticed my uniform, advising that she had purchased salves for pain and to heal an animal bite that she had received from her lover's pet. I chuckled all the way back to my rooms and told Gizmo.

"I am not your pet!" Gizmo said angrily.

The night before the caravan was to set out, I wandered around inspecting the dinosaurs used by the dwarves, and the solidly-built platforms. A small cabin in the center of the platform, to protect from weather and attack, was very visible. The trailers were large, two-wheeled affairs that could be disconnected by a simple lever on the platform, which would allow for the ankylosaurs' tail to be free for combat. The dinosaur's tail was a formidable club that could take out quite a few enemies.

I was with Gizmo, which opened all parts of the caravan to me. Otherwise, clan honour might have prevented me from looking, as there was always a level of distrust and animosity between the clans.

I spotted defects on the trailers and harness which could have delayed us on the road, and after I showed these issues to caravan leaders, they came for other pointers in the trip preparations.

I was trying to foster trust between the clans, in the hope that more things could be accomplished in the future.

"Good luck. We dragons have been trying for centuries. Since you are closer in appearance, they may be more likely to listen to you," Gizmo told me.

Crawling back into bed, I made sure the door was locked, leaving instructions to wake me at sunrise. The morning dawn was just lightening the sky when the sound of knocking and the smell of breakfast awoke Gizmo and me.

Blade, Blaze, and Fire-Tongue joined us and advised that everything was prepared for departure. With one Ankylosaurus and trailer, they packed lightly. They also had two small trailers, with two Gallimimus towing for speed. Gallimimus are like raptors, six feet in length, but herbivores, gentler and easier to handle.

Moving ahead as quickly as possible, with the entire kitchen and heavy equipment left with the Ankylosaurus, we were able to scout ahead and find a campsite and also to avoid spending time with the maidens. Those girls' biological clocks ticked extremely fast and you could almost hear them, when they were around me.

The trip, which would normally take one week, would take two, due to the fact that they had so many more animals and equipment in the caravan. The Gold clan was ready to leave by the time I arrived at the front gates, so we immediately set out. The day was cloudy and cool—a good day for travel. We scouted ahead to find a campsite area by early afternoon; the rest of the caravan catching up and setting up camp for the night.

The area between the two strongholds was well known, and there was a high volume of traffic between the two. When we reached where we would normally set up camp for the night, we found a way station (which was a small stone keep), completely gutted by fire; the lake polluted by a carcass.

This was not a normal bandit attack. A dead animal had been deliberately dragged into the lake to poison it. I immediately sent word back advising the caravan so that the keep could be repaired and the lake cleaned out by a crew from the stronghold.

I, with Gizmo's permission, also ordered that all the maidens and merchants be sent back to the stronghold until the path was cleared and safe. I had all the men clear the area for hostiles. As soon as the first Ankylosaurus arrived, the warriors began the process of pulling the carcass out of the water to allow the lake to clean itself from the streams feeding through it.

When the caravan arrived, I was glad to see that they had taken my orders seriously, sending the maidens and merchants back to the stronghold with an armed escort. If it was just bandits, I doubted they would attack a well-armed contingent of fighting men but the guard was doubled regardless and everyone spent a restless night waiting to see if anything would happen.

Since there were no civilians to slow us down, the striking of the camp went quickly and was well organized. I was able to get the whole caravan to leave at the same time. Gizmo and I traveled ahead with the scouts, watching for signs of trouble.

As we travelled, I kept thinking back to the way station. I asked Gizmo as we walked, "Do bandits take prisoners, or leave valuables behind?"

"No, they do not take prisoners. All things of value would have been taken, and victims left where they were struck down. There were no bodies found, and there were a lot of valuables left behind, so they could have been in a rush, or maybe they were slavers. But dwarf warriors would have fought to the death rather than be enslaved," Gizmo stated, looking back toward the way station.

"I think it is time to take a detour back to the stronghold, to see what we are missing," I replied loudly, so that my companions heard me as well. I could not overcome the strong feelings that something was wrong and I needed to see what I had not noted before. Gizmo said, "You feel it too—there is something wrong about the whole thing."

I gave a shrill whistle, which was passed up and down the line, stopping the caravan and recalling the scouts to our location.

"Is this sixth sense normal for dragon companions?" I asked Gizmo, and he replied, "No, but it is normal for mages to be able to sense deceit and find missing items or people that are essential for the mage's needs."

The feeling about the missing bodies was so strong, I should have noticed right away, so I had the entire regiment of men rushing back to the way station. The men searched, looking for anything out of the norm and it was not long before shallow graves were found, a half-mile from the way station.

The keeper and all of his staff, including men, women, and one child, were buried together. They also found their weapons with the bodies, as well as many broken orc arrows and blades.

I found out later that the dwarves favoured cremation rather than burial, followed by internment of the ashes. Bandit groups would never bother burying the dead, as it would cut into their looting time.

Why would someone bury them that far from the way station? We found tracks in the softer soil of large machinery and footprints of the large Iguanodons and orcs headed in the direction toward the stronghold. By the quantity of prints in the soil, it appeared to be a large contingent of orcs.

"Gizmo: call Adoronac if you can, and tell him to call for help from other dragons. The stronghold is about to be attacked very soon by a large number of orcs. If reinforcements cannot be there shortly after nightfall, it will be too late to do any good. We are on our way back as quickly as possible, with ground forces to come in from the rear of the attackers," I stated to Gizmo, as all the troops followed me back toward the stronghold.

I left the Ankylosaurus behind with all of the heavy equipment and just enough men for protection. We began a forced march as fast as possible, with what we could carry for weapons. I kept a lookout for more tracks in the soil headed toward the stronghold.

It was not long before we found more marks on the ground. I estimated that there was at least five hundred orcs, and twenty to thirty heavy siege engines of some sort: catapults, siege towers, or battering rams. This was a war party; they were planning to take out Adoronac's stronghold.

We surprised orc perimeter patrols an hour before sunset. My troops were very diligent in dispatching them quickly and quietly. The enemy camp was hidden in the woods northeast of the stronghold. We silently approached as close as we could. After receiving reports from our scouting parties, it turned out that my estimate was seriously wrong. There were near one thousand orcs hidden near the stronghold...

"Are you in communication with Adoronac?" I asked Gizmo quietly with my mind.

"Yes," Gizmo said, and she also advised me that five dragons were nearby, ready to attack the orcs.

"Tell him in fifteen minutes, I need a very large diversion so I can see about destroying at least the ten catapults, which could cause the most damage to the stronghold," I said to Gizmo.

"It will be done," Gizmo replied.

I called in my men and laid out my plan to attack the catapults; the men would pull back and attack the orcs in smaller parties, drawing them away from the main party as they looked for the dwarves in the woods.

There was a contingent of fifty orcs protecting the catapults, battering rams, and siege towers, which were all clustered together in a group. The orcs were not expecting any trouble from behind; they were lying around playing dice or sleeping. A group of dwarves stepped into sight and led a good number of the orcs on a merry chase before stopping to deal with them, aided by a larger group waiting in ambush in the forest.

While the attention of the remaining orcs was glued to the chase, my group stepped out of the woods and attacked.

The five dragons appeared and laid down fire, destroying the front line troops, fifty to one hundred in a breath. I realized there was not much time before the catapults would be used, but when I tried to set the catapults on fire with torches, I was unsuccessful. Nothing I did started the fire.

"They are enchanted—only dragon fire will destroy them. I can generate enough to destroy only one or two. I need you to help do all of them," Gizmo stated.

"Leave us, and try to distract them with an attack on the other flank!" I said to the dwarves that were still with me. "If the flames get too close or you have to withdraw, good luck be with you!"

I watched the warriors. They withdrew, but only to the forest line, where they set up their archers to shoot down anyone who attempted to stop the barbeque party. I held Gizmo in my arms so she could see the catapults.

"Now close your eyes." Gizmo directed me. "Focus on your inner power—feel it coming up through you to me. Let it channel to me, and let your rage fuel it to destroy the catapults."

I could feel the power envelope me, like that springtime rush when your sweetheart realizes you love her, and she kisses you passionately, when it becomes more intense and full of heat. Gizmo's body grew red hot, burning in my hands, but I did not let go.

"Now!" Gizmo said, and I opened my eyes to see the flame erupt from Gizmo's mouth and envelope all of the siege equipment, causing it to erupt in a fireball that seared my face and eyes. That was the last thing I remember seeing until I woke up several days later.

When I opened my eyes, I was in my room at the stronghold. Well, at least that was a good sign. I was alive, and if I was a captive, experience told me that I would not be treated as well. The person treating my wounds was an older male dwarf healer named Thomas, who did not seem to smile, and was all business when he was dealing with me. This beat the heck out of young maidens who were only interested in my body.

Gizmo, sensing I was awake, showed up to visit with me shortly and let me know what had happened during the battle. Gizmo said, "I am in deep trouble, my friend. You have so much power in you that once we started burning things we could not stop until you exhausted yourself. Fortunately for us, the only real damage was to one half an acre of forest, five hundred or more orcs, all of the siege equipment, and their camp. The problem is that I almost killed you, by letting your powers manifest themselves without more control."

Gizmo was to speak to Adoronac and the four dragons that came to the aid of the stronghold, to see what they suggested to help me control my enormous potential.

Gizmo came back and woke me up from a nap. She had been chastised for letting this happen. The only saving grace was that she was young and impetuous (Only two hundred years old!), so she had a tendency to act without thinking.

When I was ready to travel, we would be headed to see Elijah. This time, only a small group would be going; my squad and accompanying dwarves were to cover their uniform markings and were to travel with a caravan, disguised as mercenaries.

Two days later, we left the stronghold and headed north again. Gizmo and I sat inside the cabin on the back of one of the Ankylosaurus, comfortable but bored to tears. Contact was only with our own men, who served us food, sharing the accommodation when they were not on duty. James remained near the door to the cabin at all times, preventing the caravan crew from looking inside. They had not been informed as to the nature of the valuable cargo.

Gizmo started me on the basics of magic training. Since I was attuned to her, I could not only see and hear through her eyes and ears, but I could also see in the dark, and my sense of hearing was greatly enhanced.

As my training progressed, I was able to sense what was going on outside the cabin. This extended from hearing tiny bugs to the "sensing" of the platforms and trailers, right up to one mile around the caravan. Twice during our trip to the next stronghold, this came in handy, once by advising James that a wheel needed fixing the next time they stopped, and also giving them enough warning to avoid an orc patrol that might have asked too many questions.

The dragon lord was aware of our coming so no need to send notice of our impending arrival. Most of our supplies were ready to head out as soon as we were ready. Two more days, and our personal equipment was ready for the cold weather travel, especially since they had to farm out my requests to several stores, so as not to raise suspicions around the town.

We ended up with what appeared to be a hairy relative of a rhinoceros towing a cart, which had a set of skis that could be attached when the snow got too deep for wheels. I devised a sling to carry Gizmo close to my chest under my outer clothes, where she could stay warm and still see.

We were still two days away from Elijah's home when we came across the massacre. A large contingent of orcs had been killed along the road, left for the scavengers to finish. I did not feel comfortable in the open, and so we moved to a more defensible location among the trees and boulders.

Though it was early in the day, it was getting darker by the minute. A powerful winter blizzard arrived within an hour of getting the camp organized. Visibility was limited to only a few feet.

Kevin, who was one of the trained People warriors, came into my tent looking pale. He handed me a letter he found in his coat pocket after coming back to the camp from perimeter guard.

The note read: "Had you been orcs, your entire party would be dead by now. We wish to speak to the dragon mage, and we will send someone to your perimeter, so that he may enter and speak to him."

I looked at Gizmo with a questioning glance, and she said, "Yeti."

So Big Foot's northern cousin could be found in the north of this world. The abominable snowmen were part of this new world I was slowly learning about, and they were intelligent. That is not to say that the ones in my world were not; but no one had had the opportunity to talk to one. I walked out to the camp perimeter in the cold and blowing snow.

"I am here, so if your desire is to kill me, then get it over and done with, or come and talk with me!" I yelled out to the blowing snow and limited visibility.

Out of the snow stepped a being of pure muscle and white fur. I could not detect any fat on the Yeti. It wore a small belt with pouches, and a spear slung on its back. I stepped into sight, with my hands wide open, showing no weapons.

"I take it that you are the mage Jim," the Yeti said.

"Yes I am. Please, come out of this wind so that we may talk," I said, and the Yeti followed me into my tent. While I took off my outside clothing, the Yeti sat in the back corner and accepted a cup of tea, sipping quietly for a few minutes.

Gizmo climbed out of her carrier and onto a perch near the fire, where she could be warm and focus on our new acquaintance.

"I have heard of the Yeti from dragon teachers, but have never met one in person." Gizmo said. "Yours is a very reclusive race that seldom deals with others. A few are selected from amongst your tribes to trade with certain merchants. It may take years or several generations before a merchant family can gain your trust. Once that trust is in place, the merchant can become very wealthy, if they deal fairly with the snow people, and can become very rich off the rare furs and jewels you collect."

"This is true," the Yeti replied, and I was amazed again, because like the dwarfs, the Yeti could hear a dragon's mind talk when it was directed at them.

"How is it that I am honoured by a visit by the snow people? Especially since the great people of the north seldom grace others with trade or conversation," I asked, choosing my words carefully so as to avoid any slight to this amazing being.

"We have heard of your skills, dragon mage, and how you have helped others that would normally be trampled or passed by without a moment's hesitation. My name is Ice Wind, and I have been chosen to be your voice to the snow people, that we may help each other. The orcs are waiting up the road, trying not to freeze to death, hoping for the opportunity to dispatch you, should you get this close to the great dragon of the north, Elijah," Ice Wind said, looking back and forth between Gizmo and me.

Ice Wind looked curiously at me and around the tent, while I tried not to stare at him. The Yeti was of average height for a human back home, being around five foot eight inches. He was all muscle without a trace of fat, weighing around one hundred and eighty pounds. Other than a loincloth, he wore a white belt to hold weapons consisting of a few throwing knives, a sword, and a short spear. Later I learned that the Yeti preferred to use their claws and sharp teeth to take an enemy down, because it was more honorable than using other weapons.

The orcs had set up a large camp, with lookouts posted watching for any party heading north. They had set up in a narrow valley, so it was impossible to sneak around them without being caught by the contingent of one thousand. Several merchants had tried, and were lucky if they were allowed to leave again with the clothes on their backs and enough supplies to reach the northern stronghold.

The next passes to the east and the west were at least a week's travel to get to, and we did not have enough supplies for that.

"There is a way that goes underground and passes under the camp. These have been dwellings of the snow people for centuries. No outsider has been allowed past the secret entrance in over one thousand years. But now our caves are growing dark.

Some of the foods we grow need the lights, which are dying. Without your help, the snow people will starve," Ice Wind stated in a matter of fact tone, and then he continued, saying, "You must break camp now, and follow me. The orcs will have scouts looking for you as soon as the storm dies down, which will be four hours from now."

Ice wind further explained that the massacre we had found was another expedition of orcs looking for game to fill their larder. Because of the limited visibility, the snow people had been able to slip in and out, killing the orcs swiftly and silently.

Camp was broken down quickly and quietly, with Ice Wind leading. Without the snow people, we would have been hopelessly lost within moments. We walked into a box canyon out of the blowing snow. As the snow stopped blowing in our faces, I noticed that there were forty of the snow people around my men. Coming to the end of the canyon, Ice Wind made a signal, and a section of the cliff parted, showing darkness ahead.

"The animal cannot come any farther, and will be taken by another route, with your supplies waiting for you on the other side of the pass. This is sacred to the snow people and animals are not allowed," Ice Wind stated.

Once the opening was closed again, I noticed that it was quite warm in the caves. I pulled out a magical staff given to me at the stronghold of Adoronac. I concentrated and created a ball of light on top of the staff. It took no extra energy to keep it lit because of the magical properties of the staff.

"You will sleep here for a few hours, and then we will move to the City of Lights, as it is known to our people," said Ice wind.

We settled in to try to sleep. Gizmo and I sat together, discussing what spell would be able to get the globes on the ceiling relit. We decided on the appropriate spell, and I provided the power to help Gizmo light most of the thousands of globes, as only a few still glowed, giving just a little bit of light.

I did not sleep well at all during the rest period, because I was afraid of losing control again, as had happened in the past. I was hoping that in this case, where everything was calm and there was no threat present, I would be able to hold it together.

When it was time, I explained what was happening and gave strict instructions to James to knock me unconscious if necessary, to stop things from getting too crazy. Gizmo flew to the ceiling, and I felt the bond between us strengthen again. This was different; there was no anger, just a feeling of power flowing like a cool mountain stream. When Gizmo reached the spot, I concentrated on the spell, letting the power trickle out of me and into Gizmo.

It did not seem to be working initially, but eventually the globes that were very dim brightened up, and the globes that had been out were glowing dimly, but getting brighter by the second. The globes reached a certain level and stopped, but were still spreading across the ceiling of the huge cave. The natural jewels embedded in the ceiling and walls of the cave enhanced the light, turning it into something so beautiful that mere words could not describe it.

"It may take a few days, but every intact sphere of light will be burning, renewing the splendour that once was. If you have a loose light sphere, I will enchant it to regenerate any of the other ones that may be in other caves or dwellings," I said.

"The snow people thank you. Anything in our power to give will be yours without fail," Ice Wind said. You could hear the tremor in Ice Wind's voice as he was trying to control his emotions.

"As a sign of trust, other than personal weapons, everything is to be put in the cart, along with the winter clothing while we are here. We have been entrusted with a very important secret that could jeopardize the snow people if it got out. These gems are so wondrous that many unscrupulous men would not hesitate to take lives and plunder this great hall. I hold you now to your strongest oath that no one is to hear of this other than the dragon lords themselves," I said to my companions.

"I was hesitant when the elders said to contact you without careful study, which is what we do with all our normal contacts, but your comments show me the strength and the steps you are willing to take to keep this place a safe haven for ages to come." Ice Wind stated with pride. "Your names will be recorded, and if ever you need shelter in the north, you have but to announce yourself and the snow people will aid you in any way possible,"

I looked up and the lights on the cavern ceiling had reached the city. It appeared as a giant jewel in the centre of the cavern. Standing up to walk toward the city, I suddenly felt light headed and weak in the knees. James came up to me to give me balance and support, and we slowly walked toward the city.

Most of the snow people left us behind, but Ice Wind, with eight others, escorted the group, carrying our packs so the companions were unencumbered as we walked. Within thirty minutes, I was feeling much better, and was able to walk on my own. I thanked James.

"You treat me like a man, not a servant. I would have been poorly treated if I was an indentured servant. The other companions of the People and I would lay down our lives in a heartbeat, to die free men instead of like some animal," James said, looking at me. I could hear the pride in his voice.

"We are almost there, Gizmo. How about climbing back on my shoulder so they can see a little dragon and you can get a closer look at Yetis of all ages and genders. Or are you sound asleep in there?" I asked Gizmo.

"No, I am wide awake, my friend, but I think I will take you up on that kind offer," Gizmo said, as she climbed up onto my shoulder and around my neck, her normal resting place.

The streets were not lined with cheering snow people, neither were they empty. The Yetis were going about their daily chores as if nothing had changed. No one seemed to realize how much brighter it was with the overhead globes brilliantly shining, although they stopped and stared at our group as we passed.

The snow people came in all sizes. There were the six-foot tall warriors, and females that were slightly smaller, covered up in the appropriate places. Small ones could be seen running around and playing until they saw the strangers, and then they just stood and stared until we had passed.

There were elders stooped over, walking with canes to aid them. One elderly male approached Ice Wind and challenged him, asking why the prisoners were not in chains. Ice Wind pulled him aside and had a short, whispered discussion with him, pointing at the lightening day from above. The elderly male bowed at Gizmo and I after realizing the mistake he had made.

"Please forgive an old fool's ramblings, lady dragon, dragon mage. I spoke before thinking. Friends, of course, would not be shackled," the elder stated.

Then he wandered away, doing something other than putting his paw in his mouth.

Ice Wind brought us to the travelers' lodge. We were taken to a suite of rooms with a large common room in the center, surrounded by six bedrooms. The common room had a small pool with hot water flowing into it. We were shown how to darken the rooms since with the light globes repaired, it was like daylight outside all the time.

The city of light was built out of a white stone, possibly marble, which reflected the light coming down from the roof of the cavern. The streets were immaculate, without a trace of any rubbish or food products. In the center of the city was a large tower which stretched up to the ceiling of the cavern, it was some sort of polished black stone standing as a lone sentinel guarding the city below.

~ TEN ~

The Voice

he rooms consisted of multiple stone platforms, covered in well-tanned animal pelts and some exquisite handmade quilts. Blade insisted that we have one companion awake (just in case) at all times. I bathed in the hot pool, using pumice stones and soap after which both Gizmo and I were very tired and went right to sleep.

James woke us to inform us that a large breakfast had been delivered. Gizmo and I joined the men, sitting around a low table on pillows, eating our fill and listening to the general chatter. Most of the meal consisted of stewed vegetables of some sort, with very little meat present. No wonder, the lights were needed to grow the crops they lived off. I did not recognize the flavour of the meat, but it was well cooked and very savory; I was learning not to ask as I did not want to lose my appetite.

Ice Wind came in about thirty minutes after we had finished breakfast. He walked up to me looking very excited and said, "The Voice of the snow people wishes to talk to the lady dragon and the dragon mage. It is a great honour, as he has never spoken to anyone other than the snow people for as far back as I can recollect. He only wishes to talk to the two of you. Your men can remain here and relax."

"I protest! We have sworn to protect the lady Gizmo and the dragon mage with our lives," Blade said loudly.

"We are in their city and they outnumber us one thousand to

one. If they really wanted to hurt us, they would have done so by now," I said to Blade, to calm him down.

Blade grudgingly accepted, advising that the men would be ready to go on a moment's notice should I call for help. I thanked him and headed off with Ice Wind toward the great hall in the centre of the city.

At the hall, we were stopped by The Voice's bodyguards outside his chamber. Ice Wind and the head guard were having a heated argument over the pistol and dagger on my belt. We heard a voice yell from within the chamber.

"Damn it, just let them in! I don't care about their personal weapons. If he wanted to kill you or me, he could do it with or without his weapons," The Voice yelled from the other side of the door.

The guards sheepishly opened the door, and then closed it behind us as we entered The Voice's chambers. The blinds were drawn part way so there was a kind of twilight in the room. There was a large sitting area near a roaring fire on one side.

"Come in and make yourself comfortable," The Voice stated as I approached, and found an ancient Yeti sitting in a very large overstuffed chair, with a blanket covering his legs.

"I would get up and greet you, but I am not as mobile as I would like to be in my advanced years. Let's see: it was Eighteen-Twelve when I found the portal from our world to here. What year was it when you crossed over?" The Voice asked quietly.

"T—Two thousand fifteen," I replied, as I stuttered the answer out. I hesitated for a moment with my mouth open before answering. The Voice was from my world and had crossed through a portal into this world over two hundred years before.

"Yes, some bloody jerks from a British museum were out looking for a specimen that they could stuff and mount. I lost them and their Sherpa guides in a blinding snow storm when I fell down a ravine. I awoke here, and managed to survive for a couple of weeks before the snow people of this world found me and brought me into their caverns," The Voice said, and then continued on. "They thought I was a seer sent to guide them. They were a little too peaceful, and were being massacred for sport by the orcs. The monks in the Himalayas had taught me many things, including weaponless fighting. I was able to teach them to defend themselves against their enemies. I have been trying to guide them ever since. I suggested trying to enlist your aid when I heard you were going to see Elijah. Tell me a little about yourself. I already know how you met the fine Lady Gizmo. That is public knowledge in the strongholds. What is not known is your history from the home world. A little bit of knowledge of you to start, then what you can remember from the history books."

Telling The Voice about my life took me over two hours, leading up to my transition to this world. Then I had to sit and think, dredging up what tidbits of information I remembered from high school history lessons. That took some doing, as history was never my strong suit. When I was ready to leave, The Voice gave me a golden ring, with intricate inscriptions in what looked like Latin.

"This will boost your physical strength by at least ten times. You never know when it will come in handy," The Voice said.

The Voice thanked me and said that Ice Wind was my servant for as long as I wanted him. Before I could object, he advised me that it was by Ice Wind's request.

"It is quite the motley crew we are building up for our companions. What next, eh?" I said to Gizmo.

Gizmo just nodded her agreement and we were on our way back to the comfortable rooms that had been prepared for us.

Expecting a peaceful night's sleep, I was surprised to be awakened by Ice Wind, advising that there was another blizzard outside. He stated that the snow people would escort me and my companions to Elijah's stronghold, to avoid the orc patrols. We were quickly escorted to the northern gate of the cavern, where our rhino patiently waited for us. When I went to grab my outside gear, it was gone, having been replaced by finer, better-fitting white furs. This would allow my companions and me to blend into the snow.

Ice Wind advised that there would be a regiment of the snow people with us. One warrior would be attached to each of the companions to ensure he kept on the right path and to protect us from any dangers. The rest of the warriors were there to hunt orc.

Tucking Gizmo into my carrier, I closed up my new winter coat as tightly as I could. We headed out into the snow toward Elijah's stronghold. Things went slowly, but smoothly, for most of the day.

Late in the afternoon, I could hear the occasional scream and the clash of metal on metal. I asked Ice Wind what was going on, and he replied. "Orc patrol; we are tearing them apart, but our main concern is to get you to the safety of the stronghold."

We went from wandering in the blinding snow to standing at the front gates of the stronghold, beating on the gate to get someone to answer.

No one appeared for a while but someone inside must have finally heard us, because the gate at last opened, just wide enough for us to enter the stronghold. The other snow people disappeared into the storm but Ice Wind entered the stronghold with us.

Once we were inside, I did a quick headcount to ensure everyone was there. I looked for Ice Wind, only to find that the guard had him pinned to the ground and dwarves were trying to get shackles on him! I yelled at them and pushed a couple of dwarves out of the way. The spears started to point toward me. The companions swung into action, and in no time the guards were on the ground—immobilized.

Before the rest of the stronghold guards could come to the aid their fellows, Gizmo popped her head out of my coat and got everything under control. The gate guardian apologized profusely, saying the snow people never came into the stronghold unless it was pre-arranged, and they always had an escort for security and safety reasons.

I apologized to Ice Wind for the poor behaviour he had just experienced at the hands of the dwarves. Ice Wind replied, "They are afraid, and when a warrior is afraid, he acts on instinct first. After the dust settles, then he starts to think and deal with things more appropriately."

We were escorted to the keep in the middle of the fortress where we took over the first two floors. I sat down by the blazing fire in the main room on the ground floor, while James scouted the building, finding appropriate rooms for the companions.

Once everyone was settled, I called the senior members of the companions together. I asked Blade if he knew the Bronze clan, which kept this stronghold secure.

Blade said to me, "There has been little communication with other clans. It is believed that this group has taken back the old beliefs of Asgard and the northern gods such as Odin. It is possible that they might feel threatened by the dragons. The old gods and the dragons clash on certain fundamental issues. Why do you ask, commander?"

"Because there is definitely something going on. The guards at the gate had a difficult time looking me in the eye, like they were ashamed of something. Then they escorted us to this keep, which is in the dead centre of the stronghold, and impossible to sneak in or out of. This is not the typical hospitality of the dwarf people. I have seen them treat others far better," I said angrily.

"Yes, normally they would have taken us into the guard room and offered us some hot spiced mead to warm us up while someone would have arranged for the watch commander, at least, to formally greet us," Blade said.

"Keep alert, and be ready for anything, but try not to look like you are expecting trouble," I said, as there was a pounding on the door. When we opened it several servants came in, bearing large plates of steaming food and pitchers of mead. The head servant said that his master would be here in a couple of hours, as he was in an important meeting.

They bowed and left immediately. Several of the warriors sat down, digging into the food like they were starving. James yelled out loudly, "Stop! Don't eat the food; it is drugged!" James was reading from a note that had been slipped to him. "You are in great danger if you stay here."

"It is time to spring the trap on our hosts, to see if we can get to the bottom of this intrigue." I said in a commanding tone. "Obviously, they do not want us dead, or they would have poisoned the food. There is not much time.

I sense there is underground access hidden in this building, leading to the tunnels and dungeons. We need to find it quickly. Also, we need to move that large beam, so we can drop it in place and barricade the door,"

The companions were amazed when I picked up the two hundred-pound beam, holding it until the others could get ropes in place to secure the door.

Gizmo helped locate the tunnel entrance quickly, and opened the access to the underground tunnels. We packed all of our travelling gear in the tunnels and dumped most of the food and mead down the cesspit. We set up the warriors in various states of apparent slumber around the room. After we had been in the keep for thirty minutes, there was a pounding on the door; a servant entered to clean up after the meal. When he saw the companions sprawled around the room, he ran to the guard, to tell them what he had observed.

The guard quickly checked for himself and then ran to get a war chief of the clan, who came in to look at the sleepers. There were ten warriors with the chief. When they entered the keep, Ice Wind slammed the door shut. I cut the ropes holding the wooden block above the door, sealing them into the keep with us. Having a spell handy, I quickly uttered a few words, causing the clan chief and his associates to fall immediately into a deep slumber.

"Okay, boys, time to go to work again—nap time is over. Blade, grab the war chief and two of the top warriors. Tie them up and pack them down in the passageway. Tie up the others and we will leave them here, for their friends to find. Gizmo, we need to disable the control for the passageway from the inside to delay anyone following us," I said, issuing orders.

I was the last one in the entrance. Gizmo explained a simple way of locking the access to the tunnel.

"Can you get a hold of Elijah and find out if he knows what's going on?" I asked, with concern in my voice. Gizmo said, "He is very weak, and I can sense an evil presence with him, but I can locate him in the tunnels."

"Wake up our guests and see what kind of information you can get out of them, Blade," I said.

Blade nodded grimly, and set off to question the other dwarfs. I asked, "Lady Gizmo, can you go with him and ensure that the information they give is both accurate and truthful?"

Gizmo dipped her head in the affirmative. I sat down on the rocky floor, and asked Ice Wind to patrol the tunnels to check for intruders. His night vision was as good as mine, and I watched down a fork at the other end, listening for footsteps. When Gizmo and Blade returned, they had the war chief untied, as well as his two officers.

"They were under a spell that put them under the magician Torlak's control. I was able to break the spell, and they are loyal once again. Torlak will be unable to take over control again, as I have conditioned them against tampering," Gizmo said.

"Good. Welcome to the companions, for the time being. I'm sure you are up to saving Elijah and disposing of Torlak. The important question is: how many warriors does Torlak have under his control?" I asked the war chief.

The war chief answered that there were only a handful who dealt with Elijah, so that all had to obey or put Elijah's life in danger. He offered his officers to help me find the chamber that Elijah was kept in, and to get more reinforcements.

After what seemed like an endless series of twist and turns, we reached Elijah's chamber. Elijah was lying there, not moving. I was concerned that maybe we were too late to help.

"Not so. He still breathes, but he is very weak," Gizmo said.

I searched around the surrounding chambers and found some cattle. I quickly slaughtered two of them, bringing them into the chamber in front of Elijah.

"You are a fool for coming here even when you know it is a trap. Your strength may not be enough to vanquish Torlak, and Gizmo cannot join you, because Torlak has sealed access to the chambers," Elijah said, with concern in his voice.

"I was expecting a little more common sense, especially when you know that you do not stand a chance of defeating my warriors," Torlak's voice echoed through the chamber, but I could not see him. He suddenly appeared alongside a dozen very large orc soldiers, as he let his cloaking spell drop.

"I will help as I can, dragon mage," Elijah said weakly, as he wolfed down the two cows. Not waiting for the orc soldiers to start the attack, I pulled out my pistol and fired until all twelve were dead.

I looked closely at Torlak. Other than his height, Torlak did not look any different than other orcs I had seen in my travels. He was very slight, almost looking like he was starving. He carried a staff and wore the typical mage attire — a long robe with a hood.

Slipping the gun back into my holster, I stood waiting for Torlak to make the next move. I did not have to wait long; the air around me was rapidly getting very cold. My anger boiled up inside of me, heating up and dissipating the cold instantly.

Torlak then used a cloaking spell, and started to shoot lightning bolts at me, hitting me several times and burning my skin. I fired off a few shots at random, and by Torlak's laughter I could tell that I wasn't even close. Then I remembered a lesson Gizmo had taught me early in my training: *When all else fails, go back to the basics.*

I closed my eyes and concentrated on listening for the noise of movement on the rocky floor. I let loose a fireball, which squarely struck my enemy. Listening intently, I closed my eyes again. I drew my dagger, sidestepped, and drove the dagger back with all my strength. I heard a gasp of pain, and Torlak reappeared with the dagger embedded in his chest, blood bubbling out of his mouth.

When Torlak dropped at my feet, a rushing wind blew past me. Gizmo flew over and landed on Torlak's shoulder, gazing down at the dead orc.

"Just talented enough to take control of things… my guess is that he was expendable, or they would have sent someone with more power. He probably knew in the long run he was going to be defeated. They wanted to test your strength. I can sense several magical talismans on his body that may be of use to you," Gizmo said.

"Are you all right, Great One?" I asked Elijah.

He answered, "I will be, with time, and if you bring me a couple more of those delectable cows, Great Wizard Jim."

The group of companions slaughtered another couple of cows, bringing them to Elijah to feast on.

We heard banging on the door to Elijah's chamber, and then booming from a battering ram hitting the wood and iron door. Elijah looked intently for a minute.

"Let them in before they hurt themselves, or break my nice

door. I can sense that they are free from the power of our enemy," Elijah said.

I signalled Blaze and Blade to unbar and open the great door. When the door was open, in flowed almost a hundred dwarf guardians, looking for a fight and focussing on the first dwarves by the door. Blaze and Blade had to withdraw quickly to Elijah. Before the new arrivals could get to my men, Elijah's voice boomed out, "Cease this nonsense right now! These companions are with the Lady Gizmo and the dragon mage, having saved my life and yours by breaking the wizard Torlak's spell!"

The dwarfs put their weapons away and approached me with respect, meekly asking my name. I said, "I am the great Mage Jim, and I had an appointment with the eldest of dragons, Elijah. But right now my men and I need a hot meal and a suitable place to sleep. I hope to be presentable to continue my discussion with the Eldest Dragon. With your permission, Lord Dragon, I will take my leave until tomorrow, when you have had an opportunity to rest as well."

Elijah nodded his head yes and after bowing deeply, my companions and I walked out of the chamber and up the tunnels to the courtyard of the stronghold.

On his way up, Blade addressed one of the soldiers headed down into the dragon chambers, telling him that the dragon mage wanted the bodies searched and that everything, including clothing, was to be brought up for inspection. The bodies were to be disposed of as quietly as possible, to avoid word getting to the enemy.

As I climbed into a hot bath, I sighed deeply, knowing that this was just another day in my new life as a dragon mage. I had been in this world for a couple of months, but I was ready for a holiday. I knew though that a holiday was not in the foreseeable future. No wonder mages liked to get drunk to relax; we didn't have time for anything else.

After a long soak, I felt so relaxed that I lay down in the wonderful soft bed, cuddled up with Gizmo, instantly falling asleep.

When James arrived to tell me that all of Torlak's belongings were here for inspection, I felt revitalized, and went to examine them. Someone had the foresight to gather even the belongings from his rooms in the stronghold.

Gizmo came with me to examine all of the talismans and jewellery that Torlak had on his body. There was a cap of silver that could be worn below a helmet or by itself. Gizmo was able to divine that it could be used as a device to control the people under the wizard's power.

There was a staff (which explained the lightning bolts), and a ring. There were a few ledgers on dark magic. Not much else was in the cases and chests but clothing, silver, gold, and whatever booty Torlak was taking with him.

"See that the clan chiefs of Elijah's stronghold get this valuable stuff for their dispersal and use. Destroy the cap. I will take the ring, and the chiefs must secure the staff of lightning somewhere safe," I said, and then walked out of the room.

Toying with the ring for a while, I discovered its magical power and how to control it. The ring generated a field of invisibility around the wearer; this field could be adjusted to cover a ten foot radius. It allowed for me to carry weapons, Gizmo, and a few companions as well, if they stayed reasonably close around me.

Elijah's companions brought a message, asking if I would not mind waiting another couple of days before the meeting. I agreed, stating that Elijah's health was more important than our meeting. This new plan gave me time to focus on my daily lessons with Gizmo and relax and revitalize for a couple of days.

I was glad my small group had made it to the stronghold safely because the last two days had brought several feet of snow and blinding winds. Staying indoors, resting in a large overstuffed chair, letting the heat from the blazing fireplace soak into me, I felt at peace.

Gizmo already knew my life history from my mind, since she was much better at reading my mind than I was at reading hers. I was, however, getting better at grasping little tidbits that Gizmo may have tried to hold back from me. I sat there with my eyes closed, listening to Gizmo narrate her story and show me scenes from her memory, as viewed through her eyes.

I learned that there were two types of intelligent dragons. They both had extremely long lives, with the only difference being size. Both species were vastly intelligent (but if you live long enough, I guess you would be smarter than others with a shorter life span). Gizmo was hesitant to provide much information on the caves that had been her original home, and how she had been raised.

Ice Wind was in his element, running around the stronghold in the blowing snow, helping the dwarves with his hearing and sight in this weather. Normally, everything would be done through the tunnel system that ran under the stronghold, but a lot of supplies were still above ground as the winter storms had come early this season.

Ice Wind came to ask my permission to leave the stronghold for two days. He said he wanted to consult with The Voice about a certain matter and it could not be discussed until afterwards. I gave him permission, and he slipped out into the snowstorm and quickly out of sight.

When he returned, there were five snow people with him. This surprised not only me, but the dwarf leaders, who had never seen more than one or two together in the past. Ice Wind asked if he could come with another of the snow people to the meeting with Elijah. It was agreed that he would stay outside the chamber while I dealt with Elijah, then Ice Wind and his companion, Ice Storm, could be brought in.

Gizmo had arranged for a tailor to make me a formal wizard's robe, with dragon images emblazoned on it. It reached slightly above the floor, and was of the darkest blue colour, with all the markings done in a blood red. She had also located a long staff that stood half an inch above my head. It, too, was intricately fashioned, with symbols carved on it. Gizmo said that the meeting was but a formality; Elijah was ready to proclaim me a dragon mage. Having participated in the fight to save Elijah's life, I had earned the right to become the first in over ten thousand years.

When they entered the dragon lord's chamber, Elijah boomed out in his great voice, with a touch of humour in his tone, "A little presumptuous of you to have Jim outfitted already, little one!"

All the clan leaders were present in the room, as well as all of the magically-trained dwarves, wizards, fire starters, and others. Ice

Wind and Ice Storm had been brought in with the rest of the snow people to witness this.

"In front of those in attendance of this historic event, I introduce you to the dragon mage. There has not been anyone suitable in over ten thousand years. He will be a very formidable foe to the enemies of the dragons who will make themselves known in these troubling times that are approaching us," Elijah said.

The warriors slammed axes and swords on their shields, and the wizards clapped and came forward to pay their respects and congratulate me. When all had settled down, Ice Wind approached Elijah.

"Illustrious master of the skies, The Voice has heard of your wishes, and another of the snow people is here to speak to the clan chiefs to make arrangements for mutual aid and trade," Ice Wind said proudly.

I noted that the clan chiefs were surprised, but smiling. It turned out to be a most unusual day since this type of event had never happened in the history of the either the snow people or any stronghold dwarves.

"Let The Voice of the snow people know that I will miss our conversations. I am leaving with the dragon mage to warmer climates, so that I may guide him to the full potential of his powers," Elijah said.

The clan leaders began to loudly protest these last comments from the Great Dragon. Elijah interrupted, loudly exclaiming: "Silence! Are you like little children, that you must be suckled and cared for every minute of the day? The Bronze clan is to have the prestigious honour of having a bonded Lord and Lady Dragon pair to guide and protect you."

Gizmo explained to me that lady dragons very rarely left the Island chains, where they lived for their entire lives. If they held council at all in a stronghold, it was in secure areas, where there was little chance of having to fight. If there was any danger at all, there were several other strongholds nearby for male dragons to assist in time of need. Dragons, for beings who were so intelligent, were also very much male chauvinists, keeping the females safe and cloistered as much as possible.

"There is more we need to discuss, but it is only for the dragon mage, war chiefs, clan leader, and the snow people. The rest of you will leave us, please. The dragon mage's companions may stay behind in case of problems, though none are expected," Elijah said.

Elijah got up from his resting place and slowly walked down the great hallway. This was important for Elijah; he was having difficulty walking but still making the effort. Although he had to stop three times, he persevered slowly down the hallway to a bend. Around the bend, he came to a huge, vault-like door. The head engineer stood waiting patiently by the door. Several dwarf warriors in light coloured armour and leathers were stationed there to protect this portal.

Elijah nodded at the engineer, who walked over to the door, unsealing and opening it. The door opened, and there stood a very wise looking old Yeti. It was The Voice of the snow people! Stretched out behind him were light spheres leading back to another open vault door, guarded by a small group of Yeti warriors.

"The snow people will be doing their trading at the stronghold. This will be an extra measure of safety, as no one can be traced back to their homes. Since the snow people grow their own food, allowing them to trade with our people makes it impossible to starve us through an extended siege. We have come to an agreement, to help each other. One thousand warriors can traverse this highway quickly, and non-combatants can be moved either way," Elijah said, explaining the tunnel system to those present.

"The four warriors with Ice Wind are yours, from the snow people, to be part of your companions. As a dragon mage, you are entitled to your own companions, and the Lady Gizmo will have more companions dedicated to her. We will traverse with the Great Dragon through the mountain tunnels to a safer place before traveling south," The Voice said to me.

One of the Elijah's companion protectors came running up. He approached the Dragon Lord to tell him of two dragons just arriving at the ramparts to see him. The elderly dragon lord slowly headed back to his chambers to greet the new arrivals.

I sensed that I was dismissed, and gave the signal to my party that we could head back to our rooms to rest. Elijah said as I walked away, "We will have a council around dinner time, dragon mage. It would be appreciated if you would join us. By the way, Gizmo, your husband is here as well."

I was a little surprised, but should not have been, as Gizmo was in her prime as far as dragon years went. She said, laughingly, "Sorry, there was never a good time to tell you there was another man in my life. His name is whatever you choose, so that you may be more comfortable with him."

"Thank you for this honour; I think we should call him Isaac, as it is a strong name that has roots in the Bible. It means, 'to laugh'," I said, and Gizmo replied, "I will tell him. Knowing him as I do, I am sure he will be very pleased with the name. I must go and meet him! I will see you later, Dragon Mage."

~ Eleven ~

Love Comes to Town

Going up to my suite of rooms, I decided to lie down so that I could be fresh and alert for the dinner meeting; I was still run down from my struggle with Torlak. James was given instructions about a bath and light meal, and I was to be awakened in no more than four hours. I knew that I had lots to think over for the trip south with the Dragon Lord Elijah.

The door to the room opened. I asked James what he wanted, but when I looked up, I saw a beautiful dwarf woman. She was no more than thirty years of age, of average height, with shiny, silky blond hair that stretched to the floor in a single, long braid. She flung the drapes open, standing there before me, I was overwhelmed by her deep blue eyes. I tore my eyes away from hers, as my manhood began to react to her presence.

"I thought this was thoroughly discussed with your clan chief, that I was not interested in company," I said, trying to ignore my body's urges.

Her name was Sylvia, and her husband had died in a skirmish with the orcs two year previously. Sylvia had started as a seamstress for the upper class, being aware of the height of fashion and had to find a way to support herself. This world had a long way to go in the support of families left behind by a death of a loved one. She was independent and very strong willed, able to put up with her former friends who now looked down on her because she was no longer married to a great warrior.

91

"My husband was killed while battling orcs. I am barren and cannot have children, and the Dragon Lord Isaac has requested that I be your companion for the rest of your stay at the stronghold," Sylvia said. With that, she slowly undressed, showing me all of her attributes. She then closed the drapes and crawled in beside me.

"I will do nothing if you do not wish, dragon mage. Sleep, my lord, and I will warm your bed if you want nothing else. I will be your dinner companion and entertain you,' till you leave. I will be by your side when needed. There will be no jealousy from the other women, as they know I cannot bear a child," Lady Sylvia said.

"Thank you," I said to Sylvia.

I allowed her to snuggle up to my back, warming it with her body, and I slowly drifted off to sleep. When I awoke, she was there. She helped me into the bath and then crawled in with me, thoroughly scrubbing my body. She was doing such a good job, one thing led to another.

"Wow. That was fantastic. Thank you," I said.

"Thank *you*, lord. It is my pleasure to be able to please a man after so long a time," Sylvia said, with a kind of sad smile on her face.

"How long has it been since you lost your husband in battle?" I asked.

She was silent for several minutes and I thought that maybe I had overstepped by asking the wrong question "Over two years, my lord," Sylvia replied finally.

"I am very sorry, I did not mean to bring up painful memories. If I cross the line anytime, do not hesitate to call me on it I may be the so called dragon mage, but I am still a man and men make lots of mistakes. Do not call me my lord. Lord Jim, maybe—but just Jim would be nice. If you are to be my companion, formal names are not required," I said.

Sylvia replied, with a smirk on her face, "Yes, Lord Jim, I will definitely enjoy putting you in your place!"

I just smiled, hugging her, and then jumped out of the tub. Sylvia assisted me with drying off, helping me put on my formal wizard's outfit for the dinner. She then left and went to prepare herself.

When she came back to the suite, Sylvia was dressed in the finest of her apparel, which was worn, and did not do her beauty justice. When I asked her why, she told me that, since she was a widow, she couldn't afford quality clothing. I knew she was hurting inside, but she was a very strong woman and was not going to give anyone the satisfaction of seeing her cry.

I excused myself for a few minutes, and asked Gizmo to get the Bronze clan advisor right away. When the advisor showed up, he looked annoyed about having been disturbed while he was busy preparing everything for the formal dinner.

"You know who I am, and I am very upset that you did not ensure my companion had something nice to wear for this formal occasion. This is what I want: a handmaiden to assist the Lady Sylvia, and appropriate clothing up here in the next fifteen minutes. I also want you to arrange for a room near mine. If this is not done, I will not be going to the dinner, and you can explain that to the clan!" I said angrily.

I did not like pushing my status around, but was always willing to do so for someone else's benefit. The advisor turned pale and left, storming down the hall and yelling out orders left and right. In less than ten minutes, workmen were in the old storage room across from my suite of rooms, cleaning it out and bringing in furniture. Three young maidens showed up with clothing for Sylvia to try on, and from the look on her face, it was like Christmas back home.

Going to Torlak's chest, which had been left in the room, I found some very nice earrings, a necklace, and a small tiara for Sylvia to wear to the formal dinner.

"These are for you Sylvia. You should not be looked down upon because your husband died in battle. You should be proud that he died protecting what he believed in," I said to Sylvia. "I do not expect these back; they are yours for the keeping. Maybe they will be suitable for your daughter's dowry."

Sylvia had a confused look on her face and started to say something when I kissed her passionately, and she stopped and returned my kiss. She was overwhelmed, and she dropped to her knees, holding on to me and crying. She then gathered her composure and said, "I do not understand, Lord Jim."

"I still have a surprise or two up my sleeve, my dear Sylvia. When it is time to leave, I have a greater present than these fine jewels to give you."

As Sylvia and I entered the hall for dinner, she was glowing on my arm—the arm of the Dragon Mage. I left her briefly, and found Gizmo and Isaac sitting on a large perch, side by side, enjoying each other's company.

"I am grateful for the name, and I am grateful to you for saving my wife on several occasions. I see you are enjoying my gift to you. You have brought life back into her household to strengthen her and her family for generations to come," Isaac said in my mind.

"You knew that I could do nothing else. She needed a reason to show how strong she can be and a little one to care for and nurture is what she needs," I said.

Isaac nodded his head. I rejoined Sylvia and moved further into the crowd. Sylvia received some strange looks as she walked past some of the ladies of the clan. Little did they know that I had gifted this barren widow with a daughter who would grow up under her care. Her strengths and stubbornness would make her an excellent teacher, leading by example making the daughter a strong independent soul. One that would not be afraid of the standards that were set in this backward world where women were second class citizens, only fit for breeding. I knew instinctively that she would be capable of doing whatever she wanted to do.

When the nobles found out, they would bend over backward to curry favour in her eyes and hopefully that of the dragon mage as well.

One of the wives made a loud comment about finding a more suitable concubine to service the dragon mage. Sylvia heard the comment, but showed her inner strength by acting as if she had not heard the remark. But I felt that I could not ignore the insult, so I stopped and stepped back to where she was on the greeting line, looking down at her as if she was an insect hardly worth my attention.

"The Lady Sylvia is my guest, and should I hear any more snide comments, I will take them as personal insults to me as well," I said gruffly.

The woman went pale and stepped back from the receiving line. I was confident the woman would be spoken to about how to address the Lady Sylvia in the future. "Thank you," Sylvia whispered, squeezing my arm gently.

After walking through the receiving line, I walked directly up to the clan chief and said "the lady Sylvia should be treated as a proper lady, not some lady of the evening." The chief just looked blankly at me, asking "Why do you care? She is simply there as a distraction for your pleasure and when you leave she will return to her duties, as required of any unwed spinster."

"She has imparted strength to me and I feel she is part of my family, to be treated as a proper lady of the household, in the care of clan Bronze. If she is not treated with respect and honour, I will take it as a personal insult and deal with it appropriately."

Tears formed in the clan chief's eyes and he thanked me profusely. He gave a promise that on his life, no one would mistreat the Lady Sylvia ever again. I was welcome to come and visit and check on her whenever I wanted, or ask for any information and it would be provided immediately.

"Because of my bond with Gizmo, my mate, I am able to communicate with you and hear your thoughts." Isaac said quietly from his thoughts to my mind. "But I think this is a good thing that you do. From my understanding she has been treated no better than a servant; she has managed to stand up for herself to a point as the rules of this world will allow, and now she will be treated as a proper lady. Plus, the gift you have given her is more than was ever expected, which is important. It is not that she asked for a child, but it was given freely, knowing her need."

I was aware that word was spreading and the Lady Sylvia was being treated with proper respect. She was radiant as she looked back at me, as yet another dwarf warrior or chief asked her to dance with him.

"She will find a more than suitable mate, once you are gone. With your seed planted inside her, she will be the most sought after female in this clan. Anyone that can capture her heart will be a lucky man," Isaac said.

"I will have to talk to the dragons to ensure that she is matched with an appropriate mate, and not just someone who wants the position," I said. Isaac replied, "Don't worry. I have already spoken to them, and they will watch. As a matter of fact, she is to be the first female companion guardian in this keep to attend to the female dragon. She will be placed in charge of a group of companion warriors, whose sole duties are to protect the lady dragon."

"Thank you," I said to Isaac.

As I made the final preparations to leave the stronghold, I pulled Sylvia aside to speak with her in private. "If you need anything, talk to the dragons. You need to know about the special gift I am giving you. This comes from my heart. I wanted to give you something to show you how much you mean to me. You are to have a daughter, and she will have magic. This will show the clan that women can be powerful; not just for cooking and cleaning. If the dragons cannot provide what you need, they will contact me and I will come to take care of both of you."

"You have provided so much, and the whole clan has accepted me, and are treating me as an equal. I do not think there should be any problems," Sylvia said.

We were interrupted by a loud BOOM coming from the area of the gates. I looked at Sylvia, who was startled, but kept her cool. I said, "Run to the keep and tell them there are enemies at the gate!"

Sylvia nodded her head and ran off. I grabbed a nearby warrior: "Run to my quarters and get my wizard's robe and cloak, so I may greet our guests. Then tell Elijah's companions to start move him into the tunnels at once, for his safety," I said. The warrior nodded and ran toward the main keep to give orders. I walked up to the gate and asked the gate keeper what was going on.

"The—the orcs are at the gate making demands to enter! I—I have been stalling, waiting for word from the keep," Stuttered the gatekeeper, as he realized to whom he was addressing.

"Stall just a few minutes longer, and once I am in my wizard garb, I shall speak to the orc leader. They can wait outside a moment or two longer. Let them know that you are waiting for someone in charge, as you are not allowed to open the gate otherwise."

James showed up with the wizard gown, which I quickly

donned, while asking if Elijah was secure. I was advised that he was on the move, and the two remaining dragons were ready to take flight and assist in any way that I might need.

"Tell the companions to enter the tunnel with Elijah. Ice Wind and the snow people are to be here, with me when I meet the orcs. And of course James, you can stay with me, otherwise I would have to tie you up just to keep you out of the way." I said this last bit with a chuckle in my voice.

When walking out near the main gate, the Yetis spread out in a defensive arc behind me, and James took up a position covering my back. I could see around a thousand orcs, with their siege equipment set up to engage the stronghold. I walked up to the leader of the group, demanding to know what they wanted at this holy site of the eldest dragon.

The orc did not bat an eye, simply looking at me as if I were a simpleton, and said, "I am here to inspect the buildings for safety."

"Fine, what do you want to see? We have nothing to hide from you," I said to the orc leader.

He stepped through the entranceway heading into the stronghold, but, other than his personal guard of ten, others following were blocked by the dwarf warriors. The orc commander noticed this but continued on. As he made his way through the keep, he was given access to all public places; the only place he was forbidden was the dragon quarters. Some of the orc soldiers got anxious waiting outside the walls, and fired one of the catapults. The stone lofted toward the stronghold hit the outside wall, but did little damage.

I looked out the corner of my eyes, as I saw movement. I observed Sylvia in armour and standing with her warrior companions ready to engage the enemy if needed.

Word was sent to the lord and lady dragon, suggesting they destroy only the orc siege equipment. The dwarf archers were ready to provide covering fire, if the orcs should start anything else. The orc leader saw the dragons in the sky. His eyes went wide, and he drew his weapons, rushing toward me. Wanting to question him, I quickly side stepped, tripped and then pinned him to the ground.

Without even looking up, I knew from the sounds that the snow people had taken care of the orc escort.

As I stood there with my boot on the orc's chest, Isaac flew up and landed on my shoulder. Sylvia and her fellow companions stepped in and surrounded the surviving orc officer with grim looks on their faces and weapons drawn, pointing at the orc.

"The dragons have destroyed all the siege equipment. Once the enemy realized that the equipment was the only target, the orcs backed off and let them burn them down," Isaac said.

"Isaac, can you listen in to my conversation with this cockroach squirming on the ground under my boot, and determine if he is telling the truth?" I asked loudly.

"Yes, of course," Isaac said.

"What is your name?" I directed the question to the orc, and he answered back, "Morlack."

"Tell me the truth, Morlack. One does not send one thousand soldiers for a safety inspection," I said, grinding my foot down on his throat.

"We are seeking a wizard named Torlak, who was last seen entering the stronghold to speak with the eldest dragon," Morlack raspingly replied.

"I don't believe you need that many men to look for someone. You have seen enough, and Torlak is no longer here," I said.

I let him stand up and Sylvia and her men escorted him to the front main gate of the stronghold, where the bodies of the orc escort were deposited, just outside the gate. I said to Morlack, "Take your men with you, and dispose of them as you wish."

The gate was secured, and watch was kept until the orcs were out of sight. I looked at the sky, noting that it was starting to snow and visibility was dropping fast.

"Please run ahead and tell The Voice that there are prime pickings moving through the forest, and I would appreciate it if only part of the group made it back to their camp."

The young Yeti I was talking to smiled which was a frightening thing, as his fangs showed and then he ran off toward the tunnel entrances.

"We must move out," I said, as I headed for the tunnel entrance.

Lady Sylvia was standing near the entrance. With tears in her eyes, having a little trouble holding it together, she hugged me saying, "I will never forget you; be safe dragon mage. I know James will watch your back in my absence."

Isaac said, "By the way, I am going with you so that my mate and I can spend some time together. The Lord and Lady are aware of how special the Lady Sylvia is to you, and will let the clan chief know when the time comes and she starts to show that she is with child."

Changing back into my travelling clothes, I looked back to where I could see the Lady Sylvia waving until I was out of sight. I hesitated for a second, as a pang of guilt swept through me about leaving Sylvia behind, then I set off at a fast pace to catch up and made my way with Elijah through the land of the snow people.

"I forgot to ask, Isaac, were you able to determine why the orcs were really there at the stronghold?" I asked, and Isaac replied, "Morlack was an open book. With his orders in the forefront of his mind, he was there to ensure that both the eldest and you were still there. Their orders were to either take the stronghold by force with the aid of Torlak, or at least ensure that you were still there. That way, they could keep tabs on you. Their great leader Chavez was very interested in finding out as much as possible about you."

~ TWELVE ~

Into the Dark

ue to his extreme age (no one was brave enough to ask), the eldest Elijah could no longer fly nor could he walk very far without resting. Elijah had fully expected to spend the end of his days here in the Bronze stronghold, having delayed the trip to the warm south too long.

The dwarf engineers had spent many hours in hard labour, designing and building a special carrier for Elijah. It was comprised of an extremely large platform, with walls that could be taken up or down to allow air in, or to protect Elijah from cold or inclement weather. It was too large to pull with one dinosaur, so two huge Ankylosaurus were hooked up in tandem to the platform.

Running down the tunnel, I quickly caught up with the platform. I climbed up onto the deck, leaving my companions to walk along the road. I walked into the shelter where Elijah, The Voice, Isaac and Gizmo were all in attendance.

"Good. Now that you are here, you can bring us up to date on what happened in the stronghold, and why you felt it necessary to rush everyone into moving out so soon," Elijah said.

I explained what had happened above ground and that because of the host of orcs, I was concerned for Elijah's safety.

"Very well; a wise precaution. My companions, who are not used to moving fast any more, need the practice of making snap decisions. I did not want to give this to you until we had started the trip—it is your dragon staff. Carved from a femur bone of one of the first-born dragons, legend has it that it took ten years to craft and enchant before it was ready to be used by the first dragon mage," Elijah said. "It cannot be given. You must take it out of the chest. If it allows you to take it, then it is yours 'til the end of your days. Should any other wizard try to use it, they will be destroyed by the backlash of power from the staff. It, like many things of great power, has a name. It is called Draco."

I walked over to the ornate chest sitting in the corner of the room, and saw that it was carved with intricate designs of dragons fighting with men and other mythical creatures. Opening the chest, I saw that the staff was lying in a bed of black fur and silk. The staff was white, like ivory, and was carved in great detail to resemble a dragon without wings. In the open mouth of the dragon's face was a clear crystal ball; the only colour were the eyes of the dragon, which were flawless rubies.

When I tried to lift it out of the chest, the weight felt to be at least one hundred pounds. A spark jumped from the staff to me and I dropped it back into the chest. I braced myself to try to lift it again, and suddenly it was so light that I was afraid it would float away in a breeze.

"Good. Draco has accepted you as the dragon mage. This was the final test. If Draco had not accepted you, we could not teach you certain dragon spells. You will find that with it, you need less energy for spells, and also, the crystal will light your way as long as you need. Now go and play with your new toy! The Lady Gizmo will teach you the basics before I teach you the complex spells," Elijah said.

I bowed and walked away, as Elijah settled himself for a nap. I felt energized with Draco in my hand. Not feeling tired, I walked the perimeter of the caravan, checking everything personally. Ice Wind trailed behind me, with the snow people companions spread out in front and after me. Ice Wind advised me that the other companions were resting; they would not be needed today, being in the safest area of the caverns.

I thought about asking a question, but let it lie for the moment ("safest" area of the caverns)? That seemed to imply there were less safe areas, or perhaps even downright dangerous areas. I had enough on my mind that day so it was a question I would broach at meal time or in the morning. Of course, the question was never asked, as it slipped into the back of my mind.

With the slow pace, it was not until late in the second day that we reached the City of Lights. The Voice had prepared a large banquet for Elijah, as a dragon had never visited any of the underground cities. A dozen of the snow people elders from the other cities were there, to see the great dragon elder Elijah.

"Elijah likes his food fresh, but with his advancing years, having a cooked meal or two will not hurt him. Sit back, enjoy your meal, and relax. We are well protected among our friends and no enemies could enter the caverns without the snow people knowing," Isaac said.

Relaxing, eating and talking with my men, getting to know them as individuals, I felt that I was bonding with them. I excused myself early and headed to my room. Sitting on the little balcony looking up at the fake sky twinkling with jewels and light globes was one of the few times I was able to fully unwind in a long time.

I spent the rest of the time on the balcony planning for the rest of the trip ahead. There was little to do until we came out of the tunnels. I spent time looking at the lights on the ceiling of the cavern and thinking of Sylvia, who had captured my heart and whom I was going to miss dearly.

The next few days were uneventful, and I had lots of time to practice with the dragon staff. I learned how to adjust the light in Draco's mouth, from blinding to light which just barely illuminated. I was taught a few simple spells under Gizmo and Isaac's guidance, finding that less energy was needed than when I had done it previously. Gizmo told me that I was becoming used to it so my body was less fatigued. I thought that it was just like being a long distance runner; the more I trained, the less toll it took on my body.

Elijah summoned me on the fourth day. When I entered the chamber, I found him in deep conference with The Voice.

"I sense danger ahead, and my dear friend here (indicating The Voice), advises that this area has been unexplored for many years. There was no need, prior to our trip, to use this particular area of tunnels. You will scout ahead with your companions to ensure we have safe passage. Isaac and Gizmo will accompany you for support," Elijah said.

The Voice said, "There is a species of giant spider, as well as some Trolls, that inhabit the deeper caves. There is also the possibility of encountering a demon from the underworld. With the noise from the workmen in the area, there are many that could come out of the dark to grab hapless victims before fleeing down deeper again."

Great, I thought. I always had a bit of fear when it came to spiders, the thought of giant ones made me shudder a bit. Ice Wind explained that this area had not been excavated properly yet. There was had been no need to use this section until now but dwarves and snow people were working frantically to make it passable for Elijah and his caravan as soon as possible.

As we started to enter the undeveloped tunnel areas, I noted that tunnel lights had not been strung yet. Ice Wind brought light spheres with him and as we went along, I lit spheres and rolled them down the incline to see if there was anything ahead. I also generated a bright light with my mage staff, illuminating the way for a long distance.

Ice Wind explained that we would only have to use this passage as a temporary path. A better tunnel was being built higher up, which could be patrolled and protected. Everything was going well, with the exception of some large rats (about the size of a Rottweiler back home). There was very little movement in the tunnels. The rats did not like the light, and scurried away as our party approached.

After passing a bend in the tunnel, we reached a low point in the path. I heard a cry in my mind from Isaac.

"I am trapped in what appears to be a giant web near the next tunnel mouth, and I can feel a lot of movement around me!" Isaac yelled in my mind.

"Move! The Lord Isaac is in danger—we must save him!" I screamed to the companions.

I had Ice Wind throw up a light sphere and I was able to use my magic to guide it up to the area where Isaac was stuck. I caught a new web strand before it reached him but what I saw gave me a dry throat, and my heart began beating rapidly. There had to be at least one hundred of the giant spiders, ranging in size from large wolf to grizzly bear.

Immediately burning the web strands around Isaac and catching him as he fell to the ground as his wings were pinned together, I instructed Gizmo to stay on the ground, out of the line of fire. I laid a circle of flames around all the warriors and dragons to prevent a ground attack and then concentrated my dragon magic fire overhead to ensure there were no surprise visitors from above.

Then I let loose a storm engulfing everything around us in flames and watched the huge spiders perish as they were quickly overcome. I relaxed for a second, and then I realized that there were more streaming in from the side tunnels! There must have been a huge nest somewhere back through the old tunnels. I had to act quickly or we would be overcome by the sheer number of the creatures.

I took Draco and focused on each of the ten side tunnels one by one, sending forth a bolt of energy that caused them each to collapse, sealing them off. I would leave the magical sealing of the tunnels to the lesser mages, as it was not needed at that moment. I saw that the companions had dealt with most of the remaining spiders and were just dispatching the last ones left in this corridor.

Suddenly, one of the monster spiders jumped over the companions and grabbed Isaac as if to devour him. I did not want to blast it with magic, as I might hurt Isaac accidentally, so I quickly wedged Draco between the spider and Isaac and pried the spider loose. Once it was free, I blasted it with a bolt of fire. Isaac was not moving, and was barely breathing.

"The venom is lethal—we must get him to a healer before it is too late," Ice Wind said with concern.

"He is so small. The poison is already coursing through his body." I said, laying my hands on Isaac, feeling the heartbeat growing weaker and weaker. We would not get him to help in time. I had to try to save him, or at least buy him some more time. "Go quickly and get help, while I do what I must," I instructed them. I was exhausted from the battle, but I could not let Isaac die without at least trying to save him.

I stretched my mind into Isaac, keeping the heart beating, drawing the poison out of him. I worked on him for ten minutes before he opened his eyes. "Thank you my friend. I am forever in your debt," Isaac said weakly.

That was the last thing I remembered for a while, as I felt blackness overcome me. When I awoke, Ice Wind was forcing liquid down my throat. I was being carried on some type of litter, moving at a very fast pace.

"You must run as fast as you can to get him back to the great dragon Elijah, so he can be healed completely before the venom kills him," I heard Ice Wind say loudly to the litter carriers before I faded out again.

When I awoke, I was lying on the litter in Elijah's shelter. I looked up and saw Elijah looking down at me.

Elijah said, "You are coming into your full powers, I see. That venom should have killed you by now but with your magic and the dragon blood in your system, you are stronger than any man or little dragon combined. I did not have to cure you. Most of the venom was cleaned out of your body by the time you arrived here. Nevertheless, it was dangerous and stupid of you to take that risk. I want your word that you will not do it again."

"I cannot give my word that I may not again try to save a friend or companion from death," I replied calmly.

"The impetuousness of the young and their foolish ideals. I guess, then, that we must ensure you have as much training as possible to ensure that you and your patients survive," Elijah said, laughing loud and long, his booming voice carrying across the caverns. "We will stay here another day to recuperate and to let the lesser mages seal up those tunnels, to ensure that we do not have any surprise visits from our eight-legged acquaintances."

I got up and slowly wandered back to my tent and bed, falling into a deep and dreamless sleep for the next twelve hours. Waking up, I found James sleeping in a nearby chair. I walked out to relieve myself and then covered James with a blanket, letting him rest as long as possible. In the main room, I found only Isaac and Gizmo.

"Good morning. We were not sure if we were going to have to

haul you up to Elijah's transport to let you sleep for a while longer. How are you feeling this morning?" Isaac said.

"Like I have been in a stampede of ankylosaurs, beaten up, and then tossed aside," I said.

"That is actually better than others who have survived the bite of this spider have felt, and usually, it lasts for a longer time so consider yourself well on the mend," Isaac said.

"Where are the companions?" I asked them.

"They are finishing the preparations to leave; we are headed out again within the hour," Gizmo replied.

One of the snow people came into the room and saw that I was awake. Within minutes, a plate of hot food and drink were brought for me. I thanked him and then roused James out of his slumber to join me.

He came out with a smile on his face when he saw me and plowed into his food as if he had not eaten since my illness (which, I felt, is what probably happened).

The caravan started, and things fell into a routine. The camp was torn down in the morning; the equipment was moved in faster, smaller wagons, meals were prepared, and tents were up by the time Elijah's transport arrived each evening. It was monotonous, but it allowed the dragon companions to rest as the snow people scouted, ensuring nothing happened to Elijah in the underground kingdom.

Three weeks later, we reached the tunnel entrance to the outside world. We waited inside the caverns for two more days until the dwarf warriors arrived to escort the great Dragon Lord Elijah. Another month of travel before the stronghold of the Diamond clan came into sight, and Elijah was settled into his new abode. He declared that he would rest from all this travel before we started my training in the magical arts.

~ THIRTEEN ~

New Home

The Diamond stronghold was built on the edge of a great lake that was teeming with life. I often sat for hours in the sun, watching dinosaurs of all sizes come to the lake for water and to consume the large abundance of plant life. The herbivores, in turn, attracted a variety of carnivores. Patrols around the stronghold, dangerous as they were, had to consist of at least ten men for safety, and even then, sometimes they did not all return.

The temperature during the day usually reached around eighty-six to ninety degrees Fahrenheit, but dropped down to a cool sixty-six to sixty-eight degrees at night. There was a nice, steady breeze normally coming across the water, which kept the air comfortable. In the room, it was either bake in the heat at night with the windows closed, or suffer from the bugs.

After a few sleepless nights, I was able get a craftsman to construct a fine light metal mesh to place on all of my windows to allow the air to flow and keep the pests out.

The introduction of the mosquito screen to this world was an instant hit, and within a week all the sleeping quarters had been fitted with similar screens. I learned that within the month, all of the strongholds had them on the residential rooms, and some had even begun to show up in the great city.

The lesser mages were also taught by the dragons a variation of the light globes the snow people used in their caverns. They could enchant specially sealed glass containers of various sizes and shapes.

The enchantment caused the container to glow with a strong white light, and they could be covered by a thick cloth to block out the light when not needed.

The Diamond clan was told that they must share this information with other clans but this obligation did not prevent them from trading for something else to increase their coffers. There was an increase in caravans coming and going from the stronghold, as word of these new inventions reached others.

One day, a familiar face showed up wandering in the market, making a few purchases. I immediately recognized him; casually, I walked up behind Morlack and said, "I see they let you take a break from the cold climate."

The orc started to be polite, as normal— that is, for orcs: swearing a blue streak, demanding what business it was of mine, wondering why a peon was addressing an officer of the government in such a friendly manner—!

When he turned around in mid-sentence, his eyes bugged out and his jaw dropped as low as it would go. He dropped his purchases and ran for the gate. I had one of the Yeti run ahead before the orc. They delayed him and questioned him at length as much as they could before giving him back his purchases and letting him proceed out of the stronghold.

It turned out that, although I had been joking, the orc leader was in fact traveling to his new position in this region of the country. It was a promotion at the nearest orc encampment. He probably would get a pat on the back for finding the dragon mage (whom they thought was still safely ensconced in the north). I was sure I would be seeing him again in the very near future.

I knew Morlack would not try anything in public, as there were four other strongholds close by, with dragons and dwarf warriors for backup. Elijah and the clan chieftain were advised of my run-in but they did not think there was anything to be concerned about at this time.

The next couple of months were spent honing my skills at healing, and at "attack magic". The healers requested my assistance when they could not recognize or were unable to heal a disease or major injury. I was able to save most patients, and ensure that the passing of those I could not save was both peaceful and painless.

Sylvia was not being mistreated by the Bronze clan, but was the subject of much rivalry between warriors, including a few deaths. I requested an audience with Elijah, which was immediately granted and I explained what was bothering me, and what I had heard.

"I am aware of the issues in the north with your concubine. It has been dealt with, and you need not worry," Elijah said.

Trusting Elijah completely, I sat in a large, comfortable chair next to him. I closed my eyes, relaxing, and when I opened them, I saw a mage companion of Elijah's approaching, with a flagon.

"Place some of your blood in the flagon so that we can share our minds, for there is much I would teach you and it will be better if I do not have to talk. At my age, my voice gets hoarse and there is nothing worse than a fire-breather with a cough," Elijah said laughingly.

I did not hesitate to take a knife from my belt, slice my hand, and drip blood into the flagon. When the flagon was stirred, I drank deeply of the fiery brew, and passed it back to the companion, who poured the rest into Elijah's mouth.

Elijah closed his eyes, as if deep in thought. While waiting, I idly looked down at the cut on my hand, which had healed rapidly. I could feel a tickling in my head, and then Elijah's voice spoke inside my brain.

"Now that we are of one mind, leave me for a time so I can absorb the knowledge of your complex world," Elijah said.

Bowing deeply, I went back to the surface, feeling energized and alive. As I scanned the sky, I could see a speck approaching rapidly. I went over to the guard captain, asking if they were expecting a dragon to arrive. The captain replied that they were and asked me why. I advised that I had seen something approaching.

The captain, obviously skeptic, looked out over the ramparts. If it had not been for my rank, he would have called me a liar. One of the guards called out that a dragon was seen approaching the stronghold. The captain looked questioningly at me, and then bowed, going back to his business.

The dragon had a large bundle in its claws, which it gently

placed on the ground of the courtyard, in front of me. "Dragon Mage, I have a very special package for you alone, courtesy of the Eldest," said the dragon.

Stepping back and bowing, it immediately lifted off and flew off into the distance. I gently opened the bundle and there was the Lady Sylvia! She appeared to be sound asleep and was just starting to show her maternity bump.

"She is merely under a spell, so that she would not be frightened during the flight. You have but to kiss her to awaken her," Elijah said in my mind. I obliged, bending down and giving the lovely lady a long and lingering kiss. She opened her eyes, and hit me with a strong right hook across the face so hard that I was seeing stars for a second.

"Lord Jim, I am so sorry, I did not realize at first that it was you! Please forgive me," Sylvia said apologetically.

I laughed at her, saying, "No apology necessary, Lady, but it is obvious that you do not need help to fend off the advances of some unwanted suitor."

As she turned beet red with her blush, I took her in my arms again and gave her another long kiss.

I told a companion to arrange for a suite of rooms for the Lady Sylvia, and also to ask the clan chieftain for a meeting at his earliest convenience. I asked Sylvia how she felt, and she told me that she was well rested and full of energy, especially now that she was once again with me.

I escorted her to the main building and the clan chieftain came out to meet me. I explained to the chieftain who Sylvia was and that I expected her be treated with all honours, as she was bearing my child.

The chieftain replied, "I have handpicked four young maidens to attend her, and she will be treated with the upmost respect and hospitality while she is under our roof."

Sylvia was escorted up to the same floor as I, and her suite of rooms was right across the hall from mine.

The chieftain had the ladies show Sylvia her rooms, and then they went shopping with her as she had only the clothes on her back. The chieftain advised that there would be a banquet tonight to greet the Lady Sylvia. I kissed her on the cheek, to the tittering laugh of the young ladies, and Sylvia's face turned red.

"I will be up in my room should you wish to talk," I said to her. Before entering my rooms, I reminded my guards and companions that Sylvia had complete access to me at all times.

Awakening briefly from my slumber, I felt the gentle presence of Sylvia as she crawled into the bed beside me. With her beside me, I felt eased, and fell back into a deeper sleep than I had experienced in months.

When I woke in the early afternoon, Sylvia was gone. For a brief moment I wondered if I had dreamt the whole thing. But then I caught a strong waft of her perfume on the pillow beside me, and knew that she had indeed been there. I felt conflicted about our future together, knowing that anything could happen in the upcoming struggle. I knew that mine was a dangerous path to travel and that I would have to straighten things out soon with Sylvia. It was not my intention to enter into a marriage when I might not live long enough to care for my family.

After dressing quickly, I walked into the main room where Sylvia had made lunch for the leaders. After having an excellent lunch with my men, I asked Isaac and Gizmo to step into my room for a private meeting. I instructed James that I was not to be disturbed by anyone. As soon as we were alone, Isaac spoke.

"I know what is on your mind Jim, and you need not concern yourself. I have looked deeply into the mind of the Lady Sylvia, and she understands the situation more than you give her credit for. Although you have given her a gift beyond what she could ever hope for, she just wants to be a part of your life, as much or as little as she can." Isaac said.

"Thank you Isaac. I will go off in search of Sylvia, to speak with her," I said, relaxing as another possible issue was taken off my hands.

I found her standing on a large balcony area, looking to the south and the huge lake. She was watching a herd of brontosauruses grazing at the water's edge. I coughed politely so as not to startle her. She turned toward me and her smile broadened. The handmaidens retreated, as I obviously wanted a private word with the lady Sylvia.

"Yes, my lord, how may I be of service?" Sylvia asked smiling.

"I just wanted to clarify some things about our relationship. You hold a special place in my heart. But I…" I stammered. Sylvia stepped close to me and put her fingers on my lips.

"Shhh. I understand that I may not be your number one in the household, but I am content to be a part of your life regardless," Sylvia said.

"You are more understanding than anyone I have ever met in this world or where I came from. Should you find another, more appropriate person, you have my permission to step away from my clan and join another," I said warmly.

"That would never happen, as our daughter has a right to know her father and feel the honour of being the firstborn of the dragon mage. Without you, I could not feel the joy of childbirth, and even more, your love is unconditional. If I married someone else, I would never know if he wanted me for status or actual love," Sylvia replied, almost in tears.

I thanked her for being so understanding, and gave her a very passionate kiss. I could hear the young maidens' tinkling laughter in the background. "I would be greatly honoured if you would grant me the pleasure of your company this evening after the banquet," I said.

"Yes," Sylvia whispered, turning red and snuggling closer into my arms.

Later I had a chance to speak with the Diamond clan leader. "I have a special request, leader of the Diamond clan."

"Anything that is in my power to give you, just ask and you will receive it," The clan leader said.

"I would like you to care for the Lady Sylvia in your household as if she were one of your own, should something happen to me. I know that she would be cared for and loved," I said to him. "I am still learning traditions and proper etiquette amongst your people. If I have overstepped my bounds, I apologize and will no longer bother you," I added as the clan leader appeared to be overwhelmed by my request. He finally said, "No, you misunderstand my reaction. It would be the highest honour to accept part of your family under my protection. It brings me great joy that you trust me with something as valuable as the life of your unborn child."

"I have yet to speak to the Lady Sylvia on this matter, so I would greatly appreciate your discretion until it is resolved," I said.

"Of course, I await your decision on this, dragon mage," The clan leader replied.

Walking out of the hall with a smile on my face, I found Isaac perched in an alcove, looking like he was waiting for something. Isaac said, "That was a wise decision, as the Diamond clan is the oldest and strongest of the dwarf clans. I suspect the Lady Sylvia will defer to your judgment, but one never knows with the female of any species."

Sylvia was not happy at the prospect of joining the Diamond clan, but agreed that she would do it only if something happened to me. She agreed that this was probably the best clan to protect her. I wrote a note to the clan leader, suggesting that he could make the announcement at the banquet tonight and had one of the companions deliver it to him personally.

When the announcement was made at the banquet, the ladies in waiting swarmed around Sylvia. They insisted that she must meet the important people in their clan, to show her that she could feel safe under their roof. That was the last I saw of her for the rest of the evening. When I took my leave of the banquet, no one noticed I left; the party was in full blast, with a lot of drunken warriors.

I made sure that my guards were aware that the Lady Sylvia was not to be hampered in any way, as she had free run of my quarters. I felt her crawl under the covers and snuggle beside me in the large bed, a few hours later.

Waking up in the morning, I felt alert and full of energy. Sylvia was gone. I started to get out of bed when a rapping came at the door. When the door opened, it was Sylvia, with a broad grin, carrying a platter heaped with food.

"Lord Jim, being this far south is paradise. More fruits and fresh vegetables than I have ever seen in my life. And the kitchen help were practically stepping on each other to give me the very best of what they had to offer for the morning meal. I feel like I have been welcomed completely into this clan, unlike the way I was treated by my own clan. To them, I was only a piece of meat to be taken by the strongest, as a way of climbing the ladder. My joy has no limits! With you here and my new friends, it is like a fairy tale come true," Sylvia said beaming happily.

Chatting quietly, we shared our breakfast and enjoyed each other's company. James came to the door and announced that my presence was requested by Elijah when it was convenient. I told James that I would be along in about a half an hour. James brought a wash basin with hot water and I started to clean up but Sylvia stepped in and quickly helped me finish.

I knew that my hair was growing long when Sylvia washed and tied a pony tail at the back of my head. It stretched almost to the middle of my back. *Wow,* I thought, *have I been here that long?*

~ FOURTEEN ~

Trouble in Paradise

ressing in my everyday clothes, I stepped out into the common room and sent a thought down to Elijah, advising him that I would be along momentarily.

"Take your time, young one; sometimes we have to spend time with those we love as much as we can, for who knows how long it will be before we are together again. Do not rush. Take your time for a leisurely stroll through the stronghold before you come to me. I want the guards used to you checking things out at different hours, so that I may see through your eyes how things are run in the defense of this clan. And by all means take the Lady Sylvia for a nice stroll; I hear it is a beautiful day," Elijah said, and I could feel the chuckle in Elijah's mind. When I extended the invitation to Sylvia, she simply glowed. She ran to her rooms to prepare, and was back in a short time. Isaac and Gizmo came into the common room before Sylvia and I were headed out for our walk, and I extended the invitation for them to join us.

"Are you sure the Eldest would appreciate the delay to his summons?" Isaac said.

"I have already cleared it with Elijah; he suggested the stroll himself," I said.

"Always one to consider the younger generations." Isaac said. "Elijah was an excellent parent—thinking of others first."

When Sylvia came, ready for the stroll, I looked for her

handmaidens. She said, "It is too early for them to be organized, other than to help me get ready."

We laughed and chatted with each other as we strolled out into the stronghold. I tried translating for the little dragons, but Sylvia, being dwarven, could understand and feel a part of the conversation and needed no translation.

I started getting an uncomfortable feeling as I walked toward the market. Blade had taught me some signals for battle when talk was not appropriate, so I signalled him to be on the alert. The dragon companions and dwarf warriors understood the signal; instantly, every one of the companions was on edge, scanning the market.

"Is there a problem Jim?" Isaac asked, as he saw the warriors and companions come to be alert and to take defensive positioning.

"I don't know, but it feels wrong, like something is about to happen very soon," I said. Isaac instantly took to the air to scan the market from above. Two arrows flew out of a dark corner of the market toward Isaac! Without even thinking of my actions, I raised my staff and the arrows burst into flame before they could reach him. The companions raced to where the arrows came from.

"Take them alive if possible!" I yelled as the companions reached the dark corner.

Moments later, they came back carrying two bodies between them and they saw the look of concern on my face.

Ice Wind said, to quell my concerns, "It is all right, my lord, they were just knocked unconscious, and we removed the poisoned teeth they had in their mouths before they had a chance to use them."

I noticed that the would-be assassins were not orcs, but were of the People. Both Isaac and I examined them closely.

"Wherever there is money, there are people prepared to do anything to earn it. Mercenaries and assassins are an evil that cannot be avoided," Isaac said. The stronghold guards ran up in a group, once things were well under control. When they saw that the problem had been dealt with, they focused on crowd control.

"Show the snow people where to take these two where no one can talk to them, or interrupt me when I have time to talk to them." I directed the guards and companions. "Ice Wind, please make sure that extreme measures are taken to ensure that they cannot harm themselves. Comb their hair to look for hidden wires and place them in separate cells, tied down to their cots. I want you to have one of the companions watching each of these criminals at all times. Do not speak to them; just be there to stop them from escaping or ending their own lives before we talk to them."

"It will be as you command, dragon mage," Ice Wind replied.

"Our meeting, given the circumstances of the last two minutes, can wait." Elijah said to me. "Deal with the assassins as soon as they awake. That way, they do not have time to make up stories to try and cover their tracks."

As I started to head back to the keep, a male in the cloak of a traveling merchant stepped out of the laneway between stalls, and thrust a knife at my heart. If not for my mithril undershirt, I would have been immediately killed. As it was, the blade only left a bruise on my skin. I pushed him back with the added power of my strength and magic, sending him flying, into a stone wall ten feet behind him. He was dead the instant he hit the wall, his head twisted in such a way that it was obvious his neck was broken.

"Guards, seal the stronghold. No one enters or leaves until it is cleared by me or the dragon lord Elijah! I want the caravan leader brought to me unharmed, and I want all property that belonged to these three men seized for us to examine," I said loudly.

The guards rushed to do my bidding, and hauled the body to the keep, stripping it in a search for any clues as to where the man came from. The attackers had only a minimum level of skill, but even if they had been well-trained, they should have known this was a suicide mission, whether or not they succeeded in killing anyone.

"Fire Tongue, I want you to take four companions with you, and escort the Lady Sylvia back to her quarters. You will remain with her and take her orders without question. Ensure that we and the clan leaders are all safe, so that we can concentrate on the mystery at hand," I said quietly.

"I will treat their safety as if they were my own family," Fire Tongue replied.

"I ask your leave on behalf of the companions to allow us to step down, to be replaced by someone better trained, like those of the companion guardians who had been trained from a young age to protect the dragon lords," Blade said contritely.

"Is this the wish of all of my companions?" I asked with anger in my voice.

"With the exception of the snow people, who were not present during the last attack, yes." Blade said.

I replied, "I will consider the request and we will have a meeting after we deal with these men who tried to kill us."

Blade bowed and the companions fell back into order. Walking back to the keep, I met the chief of the Diamond clan, who wrung his hands and tried to apologize profusely for what had happened inside his stronghold.

"The guards responsible will be severely punished, as they have been getting slack about checking visitors to the stronghold during this time of peace between the nations," the Diamond Chief stated apologetically.

"I will leave the punishment to you, but these men were well-enough trained in concealment that I missed one who was able to give my mithril shirt a test with his knife. I have a request," I said.

"Whatever you want, if it is in my power to give you, it is yours." Diamond Chief said.

"I wish for the Lady Sylvia to have a group of guards assigned to her protection and under her direction. Maybe the guards who were working the gate? They will ensure that no harm comes to her, and they will strive to show how worthy of trust they are," I said angrily.

"It will be as you requested before the day is out!" the Diamond Chief said with enthusiasm.

The caravan leader, a dwarf well into his years named Argentum, was escorted into the keep and shown the body. Argentum said, "Yes, I know him. He joined our caravan in Capital City, he and his two brothers. He had fine jewels from the sea, pearls and beautiful rare scales of sea creatures that are difficult to find. He also had some of the finest animal pelts that I have ever seen—all to be sold to some of the larger strongholds, where jewellery could be made by craftsmen. The three kept mostly to themselves, only dealing with others in the caravan when they needed to."

"These men were assassins. I am sending a group of guards to seize all of their belongings to be examined, but you will be given a healthy finder's fee if you make certain that we have all of their possessions," I said.

Argentum bowed and directed one of his men to go with them to make sure nothing was missed.

"You will be held up here for a few days while we speak to all of your people to determine if they noticed anything, or if they have more information we can obtain about these three men," I said to Argentum.

He started to sputter and complain about loss of revenue, and about still having to pay his people without any income from trading, etcetera.

"You will receive one thousand gold coins in compensation for any loss of trading time until we are finished," I finally said, a little exasperated.

"I agree that would be a fair price, and my men will be at your disposal for at least two weeks for that level of compensation," Argentum finally said.

As it turns out, the assassins, when they joined the caravan, had provided their own transport. It was an Ankylosaurus with a large platform—more elaborate than any of the ones I had seen so far. Argentum's assistant made sure that all belongings owned by the group, and their equipment, were on the beast of burden.

We went to look over the platform, with the aid of Isaac and Gizmo, to ensure that there was not another assassin or trap lurking inside. Once it received a clean bill, it was searched closely, top to bottom, by the companion mages.

All the material and chests were examined; anything with the taint of magic or the least bit suspicious was separated and brought into the keep.

Several of the chests contained false bottoms containing documents, including maps of all the strongholds in the area. They also contained detailed descriptions of me, and a note that any little dragon with me was to be killed as well. The chests contained the genuine article when it came to jewels and fine furs ('a king's ransom,' as the saying goes, or the price for killing a dragon mage).

The two surviving assassins were still unconscious, so I had a healer come in and give them something to make sure they slept through the night. This would give me time to reflect about the attempt and have the documents examined. I told my staff that I would be in my quarters, and if they found any new information, they could bring it to me there.

The little dragons and I went back to my common room where perches and bedding were provided for the dragons. I cleared out most of the companions, with the exception of the commanders, as there was just not enough room to move around—let alone think—with everyone in the room. Of course, James was there as well, sitting in the background trying to blend in and not be noticed while he watched over me. I noticed him, but knowing how disappointed he would be if I sent him out of the room; I chose to not worry about his being in the room with all the commanders.

The clan historian came to help with the document examination, and muttered to himself for hours on end, periodically sending scribes to the library to get reference documents, and at one point to search for the stronghold map as he suspected the map found in the assassin's possessions was that document. It turned out that someone had stolen the original map of the stronghold, but since it was not examined very often, no one had noticed that it was gone.

The dragons' perches were moved into the bedroom, and we went to grab a few hours' sleep. I was so on edge that out of surprise, I jumped and almost struck Sylvia when she crawled into bed beside me. But with her warm body comforting me, I managed to get a few hours' sleep before being called by James. The historian had finished with the documents. I quickly dressed and headed to the common room. "Isaac, let the ladies sleep," I said on my way out.

Stepping into the common room to talk to the historian, we saw that the documents had been laid out on the main table. The historian was able to decipher the written documents, which showed that the assassins in the market were just delivery boys. They were novices in the assassins' guild, and were to deliver jewels, furs, and important documents to someone else, who would give them a pass phrase to accept delivery.

That meant that we still did not know who the assassin might be, but with that much treasure on my head, it was obvious someone really wanted the dragon mage taken care of.

These three had tried to take the opportunity of killing Isaac and me when they had the chance. They did not think it through, and wouldn't have stood a chance of escaping alive from the stronghold, even if they had accomplished the task.

It appeared from the documents that they were to meet the person they were looking for at the caravan's next stop. I instructed my people to finish interviewing the caravan employees, to see if they had any more information, and then send them on their way as soon as possible.

We then contacted Elijah so I could request that he send some of his trusted people with the caravan in the morning. That way they could see who came looking for the three apprentice assassins disguised as traders.

The next morning, when the caravan left, six observers shadowed it. They were not to challenge anyone, just to watch and report back on what they observed. A single trained assassin or a small group of them might be too much for the observers to tackle.

The members of the caravan had been spoken to. Without mentioning their mission, those that had been captured or killed had been very talkative about where they were from, before being hired by their new 'merchant" employer. They had come from a larger community, near the sea, on the other side of the great forest to the east.

The historian had given us the first map I had seen of this world. I already knew that it was one land mass; the continents had not separated but this map showed different areas marked out. Some of them were controlled by the elves, some by the dwarfs, but most were controlled by the government. The government, of course, was under the control of the great wizard Chavez.

There were also large patches that were either unexplored or not worthy of anyone's interest, with little in the way of resources to gain.

When asked about the large village near the sea, James knew little about it, although he had heard of it. We asked Elijah about getting a letter of introduction to the village chief, so that they could get more information about the assassins. Elijah advised that it would be done up shortly.

When I went to interview the two surviving attackers, I was not surprised when they turned out not to be the brightest of individuals. A couple of fisherman's sons, leaving home and hoping to make it rich with the money they were going to make, they would come back home with money and fame. They were named John, Luke and Mark. Mark had been the knife-wielder who died in the market.

They had made it to Capital City without being kidnapped by orcs for the mines or some other nasty venture. Whatever money they had been quickly stolen, and they were at the mercy of whoever approached them first with a job.

In Capital City, they had finally come across a merchant named Mortimer. He had had a dwarf for a father, no one knew who or what his mother was, and no one had had the guts to ask. Mortimer was a front for the assassins' guild in Capital City and as such had had a big contract come across his desk, but he had needed the money delivered for completion.

He had promised the boys a membership in the guild if they could deliver the jewels and furs for the assassination. The contact had known they were idiots, but had not figured they would find the target first and try to fulfill the contract by themselves.

They were very cooperative with their information, stating that their contact would be a dwarf (name unknown) who would give them the pass code. Then they could arrange transport back to Capital City to be paid (more than likely to be killed). John offered to show all the neat features such as trap doors and secret compartments in the platform, but the dragon companion engineers were good, and had found all the ones that these boys knew of, as well as a couple they did not.

When all the information was gathered, which was not much, I untied the captives and left them in a cell together, eating a hearty meal. I had had the healer put a sleeping potion in their meal so that they would sleep.

Finally, after two days, I went down into the underground to speak with the eldest dragon, about how things had transpired. It only took a moment for Elijah to get caught up, as he had been watching quite often through my eyes and ears.

Elijah said, explaining the situation, "I understand your compassion for all of mankind, but they must pay the penalty for the attempted murders. However, I see what is in your mind and I give you permission to poison them in their sleep, so that they may go peacefully, rather than have to face a public execution with the headsman. This way, there will be nothing public that may get back to the assassins' guild.

"The other matter I wanted to speak to you about was that I wish for you to learn proper combat with sword and shield, in case you do not have your magical weapons, since you are headed that way anyway. The Elvin warriors are the best. Since you are of the same stature as most elves, it makes the most sense for you to train under them.

"You can leave shortly after the letter of introduction comes from Samuel. I will be keeping tabs on you. As I can speak over long distances, I will still instruct you mentally on some more magic training."

Since the orcs knew where I was, it was decided that a diversion would have to be created to distract their attention from this stronghold. Elijah arranged for some battle exercises from a nearby stronghold a day's travel to the west. The snow people also went out for a hunt, during which they located and eliminated six orc scouts watching the stronghold.

Once the command was issued for the battle exercise to begin, five hundred dwarf soldiers and siege equipment set out toward the orc base. I gave them half a day to allow for the orcs to run around, send for help and get ready for battle, then we double checked the area around the stronghold. When everything was clear, we set out. Once we had set up camp for the night, the battle exercise ended and the dwarf soldiers headed back to their stronghold, leaving the orcs very confused for the moment.

~ Fifteen ~

Into the Great Forest

here was little traffic on the main road; we only ran into a couple of bored orc patrols. Once a little bit of gold exchanged, they did not even bother to examine the caravan any closer.

As we approached the great forest, we could see a large fort in our path. We stopped, as it was the end of the day, to discuss what we wanted to do. It was likely the orcs in the fort knew we were there. We decided that we would tell the truth about being on dragon business, and see what transpired.

The Yetis were kept under cover on the platform so the orcs would not get worked up immediately. When we got within one hundred yards of the gate to the fort, they ordered us to stop. The gate opened just enough for a captain and twenty of his men to exit, and approach the caravan.

I stepped down to meet the captain as he approached. He asked, "Where is your pass and paperwork for this caravan?"

"This is a dragon caravan, with little dragons aboard. We do not require passes, as per treaty stipulations. We are on dragon counsel business; we must not be delayed beyond the time required to confirm our credentials," I replied haughtily.

"Who are you to spout off, telling me the rules?" The Captain asked angrily.

"I am the Dragon Mage, Lord Jim. I would appreciate it if you would expedite our passage through your lovely fortress," I said with a smirk at the captain in my most annoying way.

"I will get the commander of the fort to talk with you, dragon mage, if you truly are who you say you are," the Captain responded and turned around, returning to the fort in record time. It was a good fifteen minutes before the commander showed up. It was easy to tell he was in charge. He was a grotesque mass of fat, with grease and wine stains all over his uniform. Seemed normal, from the stories that I had been told of orc hierarchy, and what I had witnessed before when I had been a captive of the orcs.

"I must see further proof that you are who you say, and that you are companions to dragons," The commander demanded.

"Please step into the platform structure, where you may speak with the small dragons we are personally escorting, I said respectfully.

"I will not come in. If you have a small dragon with you, it will have to come out and speak to me in the open," The commander demanded.

Relaying this information over my mind, Isaac agreed that he would come out to show himself to the commander.

Raising my voice, I had all of the companions out around the platform draw their weapons, and all the archers scan the walls of the fort. I said to the commander, "If an arrow even comes close to Lord Isaac, you will die and then we will destroy your precious fort, stick by stick."

"Are you threatening me?" The commander yelled.

"No, just stating facts. We are not keen on exposing the dragon lord to possible hostile fire. If something happens, it will be your responsibility as commander of this fort. And as such, punishment for you will be swift and merciless," I said to him, as Lord Isaac exited the structure, landing on my shoulder. The commander bowed deeply.

"Open the gates immediately for the Lord Dragon and his companions," The commander yelled at the fort.

I listened to Lord Isaac for a moment, and then stated very loudly and angrily at the commander, "THE LORD DRAGON IS UPSET AT THIS AFFRONT. A FORMAL COMPLAINT

WILL BE LODGED AGAINST YOUR COMMAND AT THE EARLIEST POSSIBLE TIME!"

The caravan made its way quickly through the fort, making as much speed as possible eastward into the Great Forest. Isaac warned me to expect trouble, sensing the orc commander wanted to do something about the caravan, but had not decided before we had passed through the fort.

We allowed both of the ankylosaurus to graze in a field until nightfall, and then they were secured so they wouldn't run away. I settled down for what was obviously going to be a sleepless night. When the orcs finally showed up, both moons were high in the sky, giving the camp as much illumination as twilight.

They must have cleaned out as many warriors as they could spare from the fort, because there were about two hundred of them screaming down on the companions.

As the horde reached a distance of one hundred yards, they started dropping mysteriously, and I could hear the sound of arrows whistling through the air. Only one out of five managed to get close to the companions. They would not last long, as the companions were sure to strike them down with relative ease. Pulling my pistol out, I started picking them off the orcs at around one hundred yards, after they got by the volley of arrows. Afterwards, I learned that the companions had suffered injuries to only ten men, and just three were serious enough for the healers to be involved.

Now that we had dealt with the orc soldiers, I spotted platforms in the trees. This must have been where the mystery archers had been shooting from. Soon, I saw ropes drop down to the ground and several warriors climbing down. I signalled to Blade to stand down, and to attack only if the fight was brought to us.

One of the warriors came into the torchlight, and I recognized an elf from the descriptions I had been given. He was six feet tall, with a slim build, was all muscle with long blonde hair, wearing camouflaged clothing that would blend in with the forest. His weapons were a bow and quiver of arrows on his back, and a sword and shield but had no other armour of any kind. He started speaking in a tongue that almost sounded like Latin to me. I just stood there, and Isaac flew out of the platform, landing on my shoulder.

"My apologies, dragon mage. I thought you were one of my people, since the similarity is very close. We had heard you were coming and I am glad we could be of assistance with the enemy," said the elf.

"Yes, thank you. Without your assistance, I could have lost several men," I replied.

"My name is Gladius. I am the leader of the nearest Elf complex in this area. Come, we must move before the scavengers infest this area, with the huge number of dead bodies. My warriors will quickly search the officers to see if there is any intelligence. They will catch up with us later," Gladius said, and the camp was taken down quickly.

We were once again headed to the east, away from the carnage in the clearing. Isaac chose to stay with me, as we walked down the road beside Gladius, listening intently to whatever he had to say.

This was the first time that the orcs had been audacious enough to set up a fort on the edge of the Great Forest. The commander was going to have a hard time explaining that the fort now needed a complete new garrison as he had just lost two hundred men overnight.

As we walked, Gladius explained the workings of the elf world. He clarified that he was just a guiding force on the Council which consisted of Elders who made all the important decisions in the running of each community. In an emergency, Gladius was mandated with the authority to make decisions promptly.

The sky was lightening when the elves guided the caravan to a side path off the main road, and headed north. After a couple more hours of travel, we finally came to a clearing that had a stream running through it. Several large buildings on the ground included stables and barracks. As I looked skyward, buildings of all sizes, interconnected by bridges in the trees, were visible.

Gladius explained that the buildings on the ground were for visitors. The elves were uncomfortable with strangers being in the trees with them. Until the visitors were well known and trusted, the trees were off limits.

Isaac and Gizmo were sitting on the edge of the platform for time, absorbing all that they could see. They both took wing suddenly, flying around the clearing, working their way up to the buildings nestled in the trees, high in the sky. I started to protest, but was interrupted by Gladius, who said, "Do not fear. They are safe; there are no large predatory flying animals in this area. Guards are posted day and night and anything dangerous will be shot down. They are familiar with the dragons, large and small, and no harm will come to them."

Knowing that the dwarves had no love for heights, I ensured that my men were set up properly and were comfortable then asked Ice Wind and James to accompany me. We climbed onto a large platform with short sides, and were lifted skyward into the treetops. I looked down at the clearing and tried to ignore the size of the scant platform I was on.

"Have you ever considered putting walls up around the clearing, to protect the property on the ground and make it more defendable?" I asked.

"It had been considered, but resources were always needed elsewhere. Dwarves, who are great builders, are not always on speaking terms with the elves. At least we have a common enemy, which is bringing us together as the atrocities spread to all species," Gladius replied, deep in thought.

Arriving at the main hall, I saw that a banquet had been laid out. Lord Isaac and Lady Gizmo were in places of honour, waiting for me to arrive. Once everyone was seated, the speeches began, welcoming us to this community. Lord Isaac replied for the party, through an elf interpreter who dragon speech. I gave a very short but well-received speech about the beauty and majesty of the community in the sky.

Things settled down and a great meal was laid out. During the evening, Gladius and I were able to have a quiet conversation. I said to Gladius, "One of the reasons that I am here is that the great dragon Elijah thinks it would be best if I received training in sword and shield combat. He explained that Elves are the best warriors, so here I am."

"Our best warrior lives in this community. This one is away at the moment, but will be back within a couple of days. I am sure that this person would be happy to teach you," Gladius said cheerfully.

After the incidents at the Diamond stronghold, I abstained from alcohol. I wanted to be in complete control of my faculties. Besides, I had only been in this community for one day and didn't want to develop a bad reputation. I slept fitfully in the room the elves gave me; it moved too much with the wind. The next day I returned to the ground to wake Blade up (who had been drinking fairly heavily the night before). Blade had a hard time getting himself out of bed, but did not complain. I called a meeting with all of the companions and the little dragons.

I laid out my plan about putting up walls in the clearing to make it more defensible, and about building a series of tunnels, including a dragon lair underneath the stables. It could be hidden from view, serving as a safe site for dragons. I also explained this to Elijah through our link and he was elated about the idea, as long as we could get the elves to cooperate.

Gladius and the Council discussed the idea for a short two days before they agreed ecstatically. I suggested that it could be done in all of the elf communities, to create safe havens for dragons and their offspring. Gladius stated that he would approach the head council, and that they would make a ruling on it shortly.

"The animosity between dwarf and elf has prevented anything like this from even being considered 'til now. If it were not for the fact that you are an outsider, and that you are not of either species, it would not have even been considered," Gladius said.

"Elijah, the resolution has been agreed upon for this community and is being considered for all of the others," I communicated.

Elijah replied, "Excellent. A regiment of engineers is on its way to Gladius' community, to begin work right away."

While waiting for the elf champion, Ice Wind spent time teaching me the art of hand to hand fighting (no weapons).

"This only just begins to pay our debt to you for saving our people by regenerating the light spheres. I am eager to teach you all that I know on this subject, although it probably will be a very rare occasion that you have no weapons and do not want to use magic," Ice Wind stated.

I was extremely stiff and sore for the next few days, as I used muscle groups that I never knew existed on my body. I found that that my muscles adapted quickly, however, and I remembered all the lessons, so by the end of the week of rigorous training, I was able to surprise Ice Wind with a couple of moves. I was even able to teach him a few tricks, and I now could fight him to a draw several times during a session.

Then, the elf trainer showed up, and was not at all what I expected. He was not a large, burly, muscle-bound elf. I expected a rock—what I got was a Rose. That was her name; she was take-your-breath-away beautiful. She was five foot, eight inches tall, with long, light brown hair reaching the middle of her back, and grey eyes that went right through you. She was a member of the royal family, an honest-to-goodness princess!

She showed up spectacularly. I was sparring with Ice Wind when I noted a shadow move across the sun. Looking up, I saw a legendary winged Pegasus dropping down to the ground. I rubbed my eyes and looked again, realizing that it was a pure white flying dinosaur. It was called a Quetzalcoatlus. It had a saddle and bridle on it. She leaped off its back and stood there eyeing me, measuring me.

Hers was definitely the last type I expected to train me in sword and shield work but when we started sparring, I realized she was the perfect trainer. She moved like lightning, able to outmanoeuvre any opponent she encountered, I was sure. By the end of the first session, there was no part of my body that did not ache, and I had a great deal of respect for Rose. Just like the flower, she was beautiful, but I had to watch out for the thorns.

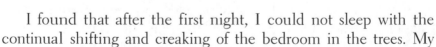

I found that after the first night, I could not sleep with the continual shifting and creaking of the bedroom in the trees. My companions knew that I did not care to sleep in the trees, so, taking care of their commander, they built a small cabin on the ground as soon as they were able.

Lying there, listening to the night sounds and slowly dropping off into sleep, I realized that I was not alone in the cabin. She slowly undressed in the room, and I could tell she had a stunning body. The moonlight filtering through the open window gently caressed her naked body. As I watched, I could see that the gentle, but slightly cool breeze made her nipples hard and erect. I could feel my manhood immediately responding to the nymph-like figure before my eyes.

I slowly approached her as she turned to look out the window into the dimly lit forest. I hesitated only briefly before starting to caress her from behind. I felt her shiver as I ran my hands down her back, following her spine from the base of her neck.

Then I softly nibbled on her earlobes and neck, feeling her body as it responded to my touch. She let out a soft moan of pleasure, and pushed her body backwards into mine.

I felt her trembling at my every touch and stroke of my strong hands as I searched for the right spot to make her completely mine. She let out a loud moan and almost lost her balance.

I gently lifted her up and placed her on the small bed in the cabin. I continued to touch her until she could stand no more. I knew what she wanted.

"Please," Rose said, trembling.

Her cries became more and more audible as I brought her to the heights of pleasure.

Afterward, we both lay exhausted, cuddled together in the dark room, listening to the sounds of the forest in the darkness. I drifted off to sleep, not waking until early the next morning. I wondered if it had been a dream, but knew deep down it was real. Besides, there was a note from Rose telling me to sleep in and then head up to the hall when I was ready.

There, I found a wizened elder seated in the sun, enjoying the afternoon warmth. The elder tried to stand the minute I entered the room.

"Relax, wise one. I am thankful for your hospitality, and I wait to hear the words of wisdom you would share with me, but only when you are ready," I said respectfully.

"You have brought change to the Elven people, and only history will tell whether it is for good or bad. But without progress, things grow stagnant, wither away and die. I am too old to make the trek to the top of this great tree without help. Will you help an old man gaze upon the great forest?" the elder elf asked.

I quickly replied, "It would be an honour to assist and spend time with you."

As we walked along the path leading up to the top of the trees, the elder spoke in general of Elven history and how the tree communities had been built in the forest. The elves had always been more comfortable and felt safer in the trees, away from any predators.

Stopping along the way for the elder to rest, we finally reached a platform at the top of the tree that overlooked the forest, which stretched as far as the eye could see to the north and south. In the distance, I could make out the great trees (as the elves called them) rise above the ocean of treetops.

"Some of the great trees have communities built around them. Others just have outposts to protect them from parasites and animals that would damage the trees," the elder said, explaining some of the Elven history and peoples.

He gave me a pendant on a simple piece of handmade leather. It was plain wood, with an intricate design carved on it which he said would be recognizable by any elf as a sign that I should be treated as a trusted leader. We spoke late into the afternoon But as the sun set below the tree line, he became quiet.

When it started to get dark and cool off, I politely asked if the elder was ready to go down but I found that he had quietly passed away, watching the sunset. Carefully wrapping him in my cloak, I remained there patiently until a guard showed up to light the lanterns on the platform. I told the guard of the elder's passing. The guard hurried away, bringing back a group who gently carried the elder down to the great hall. Following quietly to where the elder was laid to rest, I paid my respects silently. Turning to walk away, I saw Rose watching me from across the room.

"His name was Anax, the eldest of this community. He wanted to spend his last hours determining if you are worthy of our trust. I can see by the pendant you wear that he felt you are. He will be cremated, his ashes spread over the forest by a worthy warrior on one of our great flying beasts," Rose explained.

She further explained that normally elves would be buried, so the bodies could give up their nutrients back to the soil, helping the trees grow. Elders, who held special places in the hearts and minds of the elves, were cremated and the ashes spread out over the great forest.

"I would consider it a great honour if I were allowed to spread Anax's ashes over the forest. His wisdom touched my heart," I said quietly.

Rose said, "Since you have never ridden the flying beasts, I will instruct you starting tomorrow, until it is safe for you to fly on your own."

I slept fitfully; my mind was busy going over all that I had learned and all that had transpired in my life the last few months. Anax's cremation was held the next night, followed by a celebration of his life. As a courtesy to the dwarf warriors, the event was held on the ground.

The celebration carried on well into the night, and I saw that a drunken Yeti was a funny thing to behold. They were not used to consuming alcohol, so would probably suffer in the morning. I did not drink, as usual, as I wanted a clear head for the next morning, and flight lessons.

~ Sixteen ~

The Wings of Mercury

s Rose and I started the climb to the aviary where the flying beasts were kept, I heard a roar and saw a jet black dragon approaching from the east. As I stood there admiring the beauty of the dragon's coloring, noting as it got closer that it had a white mark on its forehead that looked like a star symbol, Gizmo came fluttering up to where Rose and I were standing, landing on my shoulder.

"Beautiful, isn't he? Mercury is to be the dragon mage's newest companion and transport. Elijah did not want you risking your life flying one of the lesser beasts—no offence meant, Princess Rose," Gizmo said.

"No offence taken, but why would one of our winged mounts not be suitable for the dragon mage?" Rose asked.

"This dragon is more intelligent, not needing direction at all times unlike your magnificent mounts. Mercury also has some magic abilities, and of course dragon fire. He has only to be given the simplest of directions, freeing the dragon mage to deal with other matters such as aerial combat or magic spells," Gizmo said. "Mercury is a very young dragon of only fifty seasons. Elijah hopes that he will learn much from the dragon mage. He is a direct descendant of Elijah, and it is hoped that he will be able to grow as wise as his great, great grandfather. This is intended as a great honour for in fact, Elijah was the dragon companion and mount for the last dragon mage, over ten thousand seasons ago."

Not wanting to scare the other mounts in the aviary, Mercury flew down to the ground around the dwarf warriors and engineers. He gave directions and soon enough, an area was cleared near my cabin. A large shelter was being erected in record time.

"It appears that the lessons have been postponed for the time being. Shall we stroll down to meet Mercury and see what all the details are, Rose?" I asked.

"I would dearly love to meet with Mercury, since I have never seen such a beautiful dragon in all my days. Also, it is a rare opportunity for me to speak to a dragon. The dwarves are very selfish when it comes to keeping their company," Rose said in awe.

"I will fly ahead to make the preparations for you to meet with Mercury, and for you to partake in the sharing of blood ceremony." Gizmo said. "You do not want to have to try to speak to Mercury while you are flying, as it is difficult to hear over the wind."

"Oh joy, another flagon of dragon blood to drink. I hope I don't develop an ulcer, because this dragon blood is very spicy," I replied sarcastically.

Mercury was just as striking up close. He appeared to be a little smaller than the dragon lords I had seen up to this point, but it was explained to me that dragons did not reach their full size until they were around two hundred years old.

"You have obviously been holding out on me in the information department, Elijah. How come I am just now learning that you were the last dragon mage's mount and companion?" I asked.

"Two reasons: you never asked, and I did not feel that the information would have helped you in any of your studies up to this point. Take care of the young one. He is very intelligent, but he is also very headstrong—he likes to do things his way, if he can get away with it," Elijah said with pride.

I walked up to Mercury and bowed. A lesser dwarf mage was standing there with a flagon of the evil-smelling mixture I knew contained dragon blood as well as other ingredients for the bonding magic. I was handed a knife, which I used to cut my left hand, allowing blood to flow into the flagon until I was told it was enough. I drank deeply of the brew, then handed the flagon to the mage, who poured the rest into Mercury's mouth.

"Greetings, dragon mage. I am Mercury, and I have been given the prestigious honour of being your companion, battle partner and mount. I look forward to many a glorious adventure in these dark days ahead that my great father Elijah has forecasted," Mercury said with excitement.

"It is an honour for me as well, to be able to fight alongside you, exploring this world that is new to me," I responded.

"As part of my duties to protect you, dragon mage, I will be staying in a shelter next to your dwelling. If you need assistance or help, you have but to think strongly of my name and I will be there immediately, regardless of when or where," Mercury said.

"Thank you. Since you and I will be working and fighting together so closely, you must call me Jim." I said to Mercury.

"With your permission, I will rest as the journey from the islands was a long one and I must recover before this evening's formal ceremonies. Tomorrow, Princess Rose, before we do some flight training, bring your mount down here so that I can meet it. It must get used to me not being a threat so that there are fewer issues if we are flying close together," Mercury stated.

"It will be so, as soon as you are ready in the morning," Rose replied.

I was tired after the bloodletting and made my excuses, heading to my quarters and crawling into bed to rest for a few hours. I told James to call on me at least two hours before the ceremonies were to start, so I could prepare. I was lightly dozing when I heard the door. Thinking it was James, I sat up in bed.

"Is it that time already?" I asked groggily.

"No. Sleep and I will watch over you Jim, 'til it is time." Rose said. With the secure feeling of Rose watching over me, I quickly entered into a deep and peaceful slumber, not waking until James came to tell me that my bath had been drawn. I climbed into the bath and noted that the cut on my hand had completely healed. I cleaned up and walked into the bedroom to change. On the bed was an elf garment, with a note from Rose indicating that it would be more appropriate for the ceremonies. I was to be recognized as an elf friend, at the same time as they celebrated Anax's life.

James had dutifully cleaned my Mithril shirt, which I put on first, as always. Then I donned the clothing. Light grey in colour, they felt soft and silky smooth, and were extremely comfortable. I put my gun and knife on, and then donned the grey cloak that came with the garments, fastened with a gold crescent moon clasp at my neck. I looked in the mirror, and thought I could pass for an elf at a quick glance.

As I exited the dwelling, the leaders of my companions from each race stepped into place behind me. They were all dressed in their finest garb for this sombre event, and were as alert as usual, to ensure the safety of the dragon mage, although in a very low key manner, so as not to offend our hosts.

The sun had set so it was a good thing that I had dragon vision, or else in the darkness, I would have stumbled into Mercury near the funeral pyre. The Princess Rose was standing nearby, wearing a garment the same color as mine, but more lady-like in design. She was also wearing flawless gem earrings, and a necklace that glowed like the embers of a fire.

The fire had to be started the old fashioned way, without magic, according to ceremony. I was asked to do the honours, so, pulling out my knife and some flint, I quickly lit a torch. I handed the torch to one of the holy men overseeing the ceremony, and the funeral pyre was set ablaze. As the pyre had been soaked in oil earlier in the day, it was quickly quite impressive.

Gladius made a speech about Anax's life, leading up to his last days, looking peacefully over the great forest, the perfect way for a man of peace to end his life. He did not end the speech, just transitioned to Anax's last duty of recognizing the dragon mage as an elf friend. He finished by saying that my opinion was welcome at any elf council, and my presence was also welcomed at any elf community in the world.

Then the party was on. I sat quietly on a bench, with Mercury lying near me. Mercury was telling me what his duties were and how he would assist me. Princess Rose strolled up to me, carrying a bottle and some glasses. She sat down beside me.

"Since you do not seem to be enjoying the festivities, I thought I would bring something to cheer you up. I hear that you have not been drinking of late, but this is a special wine, made by the elves, called Kritico. It will warm you, but your mind will remain clear and you will not lose focus," Rose said, with concern on her face.

After the first sip of the wine, I felt a warm glow spread throughout my body. My mind was clear as a bell, relaxing for the first time in a while. When the bottle was finished, I felt very tired and excused myself, heading to my quarters to sleep. Mercury followed silently behind me, settling into his shelter once I was safely ensconced in my cabin.

Waking up to the sun hitting the windows of the cabin, I rolled over to find Rose in bed beside me. I enjoyed just lying there, quietly watching her sleep. After a while, I went into the main room, where James had breakfast ready. I made up a platter and took it into the bedroom, waking Rose.

"Good morning, sleepyhead. Time to rise and shine. I never did ask you what you saw in me the first day we met. There seemed to be an immediate connection," I said.

Rose replied, "I was just drawn to you and the inner light that seems to emanate from you. I find myself safe and comforted when I am with you."

~ SEVENTEEN ~

Enemy at the Gate

After breakfast and a quick morning physical routine that Rose seemed to enjoy, I stepped out into the clearing to find Gizmo and Mercury talking, while an attendant was fitting Mercury with an unusual saddle. I walked over to examine the saddle, which was made up of some type of leather. It was the same color as Mercury's skin, and blended in nicely, almost invisibly.

It was a double saddle with a back rest and stirrups on the sides, so that the rider and his passenger were very stable while seated. It had a large leather belt that attached across the riders' laps, like a seatbelt. The riders put their feet in large stirrups, which were covered in the front to protect them from the wind. The most unusual feature was what looked like a perch for the little dragons, nestled in front of the lead rider, protected from the wind. There were no reins visible at all to control Mercury.

I asked Gizmo about the saddle, but she told me to talk to Mercury, as she had never seen a dragon saddle in her entire short life.

"Yes, that is a perch for a little dragon. Their grip is very powerful, and he or she will never fall off. As for reins, they are not needed. You simply direct me where to go and I will comply. If I do not, simply tap on my ear nodules and I will get the impression. Also, the eldest has already warned me about the dire consequences of not listening to you and stepping out of line," Mercury said.

"I have never seen such material as the saddle is made of. What is it?" I asked, examining it closely.

Mercury replied, "I do not know if I am supposed to discuss it. You will have to ask someone else that question."

Calling Elijah with my mind, I asked, "Elijah, do you know anything about this saddle that is being fitted onto Mercury? It seems to be made from some kind of leather that I do not recognize."

Elijah responded, "If you look closely at it, you might recognize the material. It is part of a ceremony that each dragon mount must go through to prove his worth. The saddle is made from the skin of a Tyrannosaurus Rex that must be killed by the dragon mount alone, to prove its worthiness. Each time a dragon mount is selected for a dragon mage, a new saddle must be custom made to fit."

Before I could ask any more questions on the subject, Princess Rose flew down on her aerial mount, and quickly alighted on the ground.

"Princess Rose, please step to one side in case your mount panics. It should be able to head back up to the aviary without anyone getting in the way and getting hurt," Mercury said.

Mercury stared at the Quetzalcoatlus and slowly walked toward it, allowing it time to settle with each step. Mercury was finally right beside the mount, and he allowed it to thoroughly examine him and breathe in his scent. After ten minutes, the Quetzalcoatlus grew bored and started looking for food.

"Princess, please leave your mount here and allow it to go back to the aviary. I would sincerely like it if you would join the dragon mage, Lady Gizmo and I for a ride," Mercury said.

"It is not often that anyone is offered a ride on a dragon. I would be extremely pleased to join you," Rose said.

As we were standing there chatting, Mercury suddenly stood up, sniffing at the air, and looked toward the newly-constructed walls and gate.

"There is danger coming. Be very careful, dragon mage," Mercury said, and before I could even ask Mercury what it meant, one of the dwarf warriors came running over to say that there was a stranger at the gate, wishing to talk with the dragon mage.

I walked over to the gate, Mercury, Gizmo, Isaac, and Princess Rose following closely behind.

"I believe it is the grand wizard Chavez. He is carrying a white flag on the end of his staff, but that does not prevent him from using it, if he wishes," Mercury said.

"I just want to talk to the dragon mage! I mean no harm to this settlement," Chavez yelled at the fence.

I could sense that the woods were crawling with orcs, although only half-dozen orc bodyguards were visible from the gate, and were standing well back from Chavez.

"Mercury, call for help from any dragons close by for backup, and be ready to attack if need be. Rose, please ask all the elves to watch the woods for movement of the orc horde that is out there. Get Blade and all the snow people out here for my bodyguard, in case of trouble," I said, directing the companions and dragons.

Rose quickly ran off to comply with my commands.

"Six dragons, five minutes," Mercury replied.

When the companions arrived, I stepped outside the gate with them, waiting for it to close firmly behind me.

Gizmo came with me, riding on my shoulder as I walked toward Chavez. The first thing that struck me about Chavez was his pale skin; almost albino. He measured around five-feet, six inches, and all skin and bones. He just stared at me as I walked toward him.

"I want to talk to you, not the little rat on your shoulder. Get rid of it," Chavez said.

"She will stay with me, but I will put my staff down to balance the terms of our encounter and she will remain silent during our conversation. You know that this conversation will get back to the dragons for clarification at least," I said to Chavez.

"Do you realize that you are being used by the dragons as a pawn in their great game of world domination in this dimension?" Chavez said, with venom in his voice.

"So did you come over from the same world that I did? When?" I asked.

"No, a different world—about three hundred years ago as they count. My world was a dying world of ash and nuclear waste. Once I came into my powers, I refused to obey the dragons and went my own way, trying to create a world order that would help the people everywhere," Chavez said.

"It does not sound too good, at this point. It sounds like a dictatorship, with you at the helm," I responded.

"The road to hell is paved with good intentions. Come join me, and we can make things better. Or I can send you back to your world, where you can go back to living a normal life. Of course, you realize that back home, magic only is available in a limited form. Unlike the nonsense the dragons are filling you with, the way back is open for only a limited amount of time. You do not have to stay here and be used. I can send you back to the ones you love and the world you know," Chavez said. "I have enough men here in the woods that I can whisk you away to safety; all you have to do is say the word."

Chavez seemed uncomfortable as he saw several large shadows pass between the sun and where he was standing.

"It appears I have your answer. If you change your mind, just contact me and I will take care of you," Chavez said, as a heavy fog drifted in rapidly. Chavez disappeared into it. I quickly withdrew behind the gate.

"Mercury, please thank the dragons and ask if they would hang around for another half an hour, before they go back to their homes. Ice Wind, take your men out. This is no different than a snowstorm back home. Just scout the outside perimeter and ensure that the enemy troops are leaving," I commanded.

"Someone get the Princess Rose, and ask her to join me in my quarters for a meeting in an hour. Gizmo, please have your husband Isaac join us, and meet at my quarters at that same time. Mercury, we will open the big window in the common room so that you can listen in on our conversation and add any information that you feel is important," I said.

I went to my quarters and splashed water on my face, reflecting seriously on what Chavez had said. I was also thinking of appropriate questions to ask the dragons. I felt lost. I looked at James and said, "James, round up some Kritico. I want to relax after this meeting is over, but I want to be able to still be good for something tomorrow. Also, I would like some food here in an hour— just stuff that I can munch on that is suitable for the dragons as well."

When I had everyone gathered in the common room, I looked directly at Isaac and Gizmo, saying, "I think it is time that you explain to me exactly what is going on. How much of what Chavez has told me was the truth, and how much was nonsense to try to get me to change allegiance?"

I went on to explain exactly what Chavez had said to me about the portal, and about just being a pawn for the dragons' world conquest. I had one of the dwarf warriors present to translate what Gizmo and Isaac were saying, so that Rose could be a witness to all that was said.

I did not want them telling me one thing and then changing the story for someone else. From my experience in law enforcement, the truth never changed, but lies changed all the time; even a little bit each time they were told.

Gizmo started off by explaining dragon history, as she had been taught in the dragon schools. She held nothing back, going into great detail about major conflagrations at some turning point in history. She went on for hours before getting weary, having to take several breaks. I could tell that she was telling the truth as she knew it. I quizzed her, but her historical details never changed from the original.

Thanking everyone for their help in making my decision easier, I excused everyone, with the exception of Isaac, who was asked to stay behind to clarify a couple of matters. When all of the others had left, I pulled Isaac aside to the table, sitting down to talk with him in earnest.

"What are you hiding, Isaac? Is there something that you do not wish me to know? I have been pushed in this direction, being led to believe that there was no way home. I was told that this was the best option for me to move on in my life," I said pointedly.

Isaac would not make eye contact with me, and kept looking elsewhere.

"I would like to know exactly what is happening! At this point, I do not know if it is really in my best interest to go home. My instincts tell me that I could do more good here, helping out my new friends and companions," I said to Isaac.

Isaac started to perk up at these comments, staring deeply into my eyes long and hard, and asked, "May I confer with the Eldest? One of us will get back to you within the hour."

~ EIGHTEEN ~

Air Time

aking some decisions after Isaac left, I summoned Mercury, having him saddled and ready to go. I talked to Rose, letting her know that I would be away for a couple of days. I had to get my mind organized and be ready for an important, life-changing decision. When Isaac came back with an answer to my question, I had something to say to him.

"Isaac, I am going to go to the Diamond stronghold to speak directly to the great dragon Elijah. I want you to accompany me, to provide companionship and input. I am going to fly on Mercury, so it will take no more than two days to reach him," I said. Isaac looked at me and nodded his head in agreement.

I went out to where Mercury was getting saddled up. Clothing, food, and camping gear were loaded on the saddle packs. We started to climb into the saddle and strap in, Rose ran up, carrying a small bag and smiling. Rose said, "I am coming with you. I was promised a dragon ride."

I sat there quietly for a moment, then nodded my head and helped Rose climb into the saddle behind me. Mercury sprang into the air, gaining altitude rapidly. Before leaving the large forest, I spread the ashes of Anax; watching as the gentle breeze caught it and carry it everywhere. After reading my mind, Mercury headed toward the Diamond stronghold.

"Elijah has spoken with me and will be ready to meet with you the moment you arrive at the stronghold," Isaac said.

I was exhilarated as the land flew by me below, feeling the breeze blowing in my face, and enjoying the cool air this high up. Conversation with Rose consisted of shouting back and forth; she was pointing out landmarks down below. The experience was fantastic. Mercury advised me that we would be landing at a small keep about halfway between the Diamond stronghold and the Elf community.

"Do they know we are coming?" I said.

Mercury replied, "No."

I sat quietly, looking at the horizon and enjoying the scenery. The sun had set and the first of the moons was rising. We landed several hundred feet from the keep and approached it on foot. I stepped into the torchlight and was immediately challenged by the guards.

"I am a traveller, just looking for accommodation for the night," I yelled at the gate. The watch commander came to the keep door and stepped out, the door locking behind him.

"Have the rest of your party step forward and be recognized before we can allow you into the keep," The watch commander said. When Mercury stepped forward into the light, the commander bowed deeply.

"If we had known, we would have prepared to receive you properly," the watch commander said. The gate was immediately opened, and as we all came into the light, the commander's eyes grew wider as he recognized an elf and a little dragon. It dawned on him who I must be. He sent someone to prepare a meal for all of us.

"Space is at a premium in a keep like this, but we will build a large fire for the great dragon to keep warm. A roof will be set up to keep the morning dew off the dragon. The others can share a dorm room on the ground floor, near where the dragon will sleep," The watch commander said.

The meal was simple but plentiful; no one walked away hungry. After a few mugs of mead, I headed to the dorm room and fell asleep. I awoke feeling that there was someone in the room with me. I lay quietly, listening to any noise around me. When the person was close enough to my bed, I lunged out, a wrist and throwing the intruder to the bed, causing all the torches in the room to light at once. There, looking a little startled, was Rose.

"I take this to mean that you do not want companionship tonight?" Rose asked sheepishly, a little smile playing across her face.

"One should not surprise a wizard in the middle of the night; the consequences could be dangerous," I said. With that, I extinguished all the torches, crawling back into the bed and Rose's arms. I eventually did fall asleep, waking in the early morning to an empty bed.

We saddled up Mercury after a quick, light breakfast and headed off into the sky once more. The rest of the journey was for the most part uneventful. I enjoyed watching the different landscapes and the herds of dinosaurs roaming the plains. We came upon a caravan that was being attacked by a tyrannosaurus. Mercury breather fire onto the dinosaur, and then we flew close so I could put the beast out of its misery, putting several bullets through its eyes and into its brain.

We landed for a short time, to see if we could assist with first aid. With the exception of two dead warriors, all other injuries were minor. The leader of the caravan thanked the party fervently, offering jewels and gold. Turning the reward down, we headed back on our journey right away.

~ Nineteen ~

The Dragon's Dark Secret

Because of the time we took to do battle with the tyrannosaurus, it was dark when we arrived. The courtyard was lit up like daytime with numerous torches, in anticipation of our arrival. Everything was taken care of the minute we landed. Rose was welcomed, and Isaac, Mercury and I were immediately escorted to the underground chamber, where Elijah was waiting. I was surprised that he was not alone. Three other older dragons were with him. These dragons were introduced to me as Adam, Joshua, and Zachariah (the unofficial dragon council).

"Lord Jim, we wish to share information that has been kept secret for centuries. This knowledge has not been shared with any of the inhabitants of this world since the days of old. We would have eventually told you but things came to the forefront with the visit from the wizard Chavez. We must make clear what is at stake and our point of view. That way, you can make an informed decision. Mercury was invited, as a dragon mount and his rider should have no secrets between them," Elijah said.

He started off by explaining that certain aspects of dragon history were not taught to the young, as they were secrets reserved for elders and leaders, once they reached an appropriate level of maturity. Apparently, all was not great in the history of the dragons; there had been a couple of wars in the distant past.

The First World War was amongst the dragons themselves, and in the Second World War dragons began bringing other species through to this plane of existence as troops that were brought to fight and slay other dragons. This approach did not last long, as most species were independent enough that they would only take orders for so long without asking why.

Then, five hundred years ago, there was a rift between the Dragons and the Malum. The Malum had been dragons at one time, but began exploring dark magic, dealing with death and evil. Their study caused them to become warped and disfigured over the hundreds of years that they had been practicing the dark arts. Elijah described how they looked one hundred years before. They looked more like a bat; they were almost blind and never came into the light, they were slightly smaller than the average-sized dragon.

Malum dealt with the outside world through intermediaries who were blinded when they took service with the Malum, so they could say nothing about how they looked. The assassins' guild was their idea, allowing them more contact with the outside world. On rare nights when there was no moon, which was once every four months, it is said that they liked to take flight and go hunting for fresh meat.

With the exception of the orcs, none of the other races liked the infrequent nights when there was no light at all. It was associated with death and the evil that came in the darkness. All the races made sure they were somewhere safe or at least well-lit.

"We do not know for certain this is true, but since a lot of disappearances happen on those nights, something is killing and taking livestock or people. We have set up a large field with livestock in a rural area, and a safe place for you to be well-guarded so you will be able to view the area for intruders. It is unknown whether one or more of the Malum will show up, but we want more evidence to show you that we are telling the truth. This is just part of the things that we intend to share with you, so you know we are holding nothing back," Elijah said sombrely.

Isaac was to go with me, since his sense of hearing and sight was still keener than my magically-enhanced senses. Rose insisted on bringing this important information back to the elves. After a lot of deliberation within the dragon council, they finally granted her permission. We arrived at the lookout in the late afternoon, and

Mercury left immediately so that his odour would not linger in the area for the Malum to scent.

There was a comfortable bench and some cots set up in the main part of the lookout. I lay down for a long afternoon nap, and was awakened just before dark by the companions for a cold meal so no light from a fire would give away our location. I settled down for a long night. Whether it was to be eventful or not, only time would tell.

Around the middle of the night, I was half asleep on the bench when Rose nudged me and whispered in my ear, "Something is coming."

I prepared myself and started searching the sky. I noted to the east there was something flying between the stars and our location in the lookout.

I watched as the dark shape descended, landing on one of the woolly rhinoceroses in the field. One of the younger companions gasped and the creature turned toward the lookout. The commander of the companions cursed softly and told his men to draw their crossbows. The creature gave a great leap into the air and flew directly toward us.

The companions let loose their bolts. I doubted if any hit, as the creature was moving very fast. I let loose a ball of fire from my staff into the path of the creature, and got a good look at my first Malum. Fortunately it was not my last. As the fireball hit the creature, it squealed in pain and flew away rapidly.

From what I saw, the dragons were very accurate in their descriptions of the Malum. The only thing they had not mentioned was that it was a pure albino, with no colouration, and the eyes were pink, but it did resemble a giant bat. The snout was much shorter than the dragons'. It was hard to imagine that centuries ago they were once dragons.

We lit some torches and unwrapped some magical light spheres. The commander thanked me for saving his men, and advised that he would talk to the young man who let out the exclamation. Without the fireball, the Malum would have made short work of the companions because it moved so fast.

Once the sun started to appear over the horizon, Mercury

showed up to give us a ride back to the stronghold. Isaac advised Elijah of what he had seen, and I went back to my rooms at the main keep. I was fast asleep in no time. When I woke up briefly, I found Sylvia nestled in the bed on my left and Rose on my right. I shrugged and fell back asleep for a few more hours.

When I got up, the bed was empty. I cleaned up and went into the common room to sit and think things through from the last few days. Rose and Sylvia were talking, and when I walked into the room they both got up and brought me food and drink. I told them that I had to go speak to Elijah again. Walking to the door to leave, Sylvia, then Rose, each gave me a passionate kiss goodbye.

Elijah had been briefed by Isaac prior to my arrival. He was grateful to me for scaring away the Malum, and at the same time allowing everyone to get a good look at the creature. The Malum had not changed in the last hundred years, as far as Elijah could determine.

"The next part of your lessons is the Orb of Pater. It is a powerful orb which can remove the fire and flight capabilities of any and all dragons. Pater created it to control the evil ones in case they should rise up in rebellion but instead they fled. The orb was stolen around the time of the last dragon mage's death, and it is not known where it ended up," Elijah said.

~ TWENTY ~

Quest for the Answers

"We believe the Malum are working with Chavez. They appear to be getting stronger. We wanted to have you trained more before you were to make an important decision, but since those we cannot trust have already extended an offer, it cannot wait. We need you to decide if you are going to stay and be the top cop, as your people would say, or go back to your world to be just another soldier, trying to make a difference." Elijah said.

"There may be time to locate and train another dragon mage, but it took us ten thousand years to locate someone with your qualifications. Without someone to intervene, eventually all the dragons will be dead. The other races will perish as well, or be enslaved. I know this is a difficult decision. Please take your time to decide—the portal to your world will be open for the next six months."

I bowed to Elijah and the council of dragons, slowly walking out of the underground, up to the surface of the stronghold. I wandered the walls and the public areas of the stronghold, so deep in thought I lost all track of time. When the first moon started to peek over the horizon, I realized that it was getting late, and I was late for dinner with the clan chieftain. I hurried to my room, finding my clothing laid out for me. I quickly dressed and headed to the great hall. Upon arriving, I apologized to the chieftain for not being there sooner.

"Lord Isaac has explained that the dragon Lords have tasked

you with a heavy burden, one that will take you some time to think over, to make the right decision. We understand that one does not suddenly rush into battle without a plan; that would be foolish. So, no excuses are needed," The Diamond clan chieftain said.

Thanking him, I went to sit down at the table. The only empty seat was, of course, between my two lovely ladies, Sylvia and Rose. I sat down and listened to the gossip and gentle banter between the dinner guests, losing myself for a couple of hours in the conversation around me. It was restful, as the conversation was directed solely on the day to day common things in the stronghold and nothing was discussed about orcs, Malum or Chavez.

I allowed myself to enjoy the sumptuous dinner and a couple of flagons of mead so I was feeling very relaxed when I headed off to my room and bed. The next morning I woke up alone, and when I went to the common room, only Isaac was there.

"I told everyone to leave you alone last night and this morning, as you were given an extremely important question to answer by the dragon lords. You needed time to yourself to consider everything," Isaac said.

Walking down to the central area of the stronghold, I called Mercury telepathically.

"I will be there momentarily. I was just in the chamber underground, speaking with the Great Dragon," Mercury answered.

"Mercury, how long would it take you to get back to the Elf community without passengers?" I asked.

Mercury replied, "Eight hours. I was going slowly because you were not used to flying."

"Tell Blade and my companions to bring the Ankylosaurus with the special platform here as soon as possible. Let him know that he only needs the basic supplies, as we will outfit it here. I will explain to you why I am doing this when you are back tomorrow, with his answer," I instructed.

Mercury nodded and took off at once, headed toward the sea. I asked Isaac, "Isaac, I wish to talk to Elijah, in person and private, to discuss further what the dragons have asked of me."

"Elijah has left word that you could interrupt him at any time to discuss this matter with him," Isaac replied.

Nodding, I headed toward the underground and Elijah's quarters. When I arrived, Elijah instructed the visiting dignitaries from other clans to wait outside for a few minutes. They started protesting until they saw the look on my face and realized who I was, and then they apologized and quickly stepped out of the room.

"Elijah, I need more time to make this life-altering decision. I plan on taking a trip with my companions to visit several communities. I want to take time to determine if I should give up my old life by staying here," I said, frowning, deep in thought.

"Thank you for not making the decision right away. You are a wise man to think this over. If it is all right with you, I will send Gizmo and Isaac with you so that if you have any questions, Isaac can answer them as he has been given all the knowledge of the elders. He has been told to hold no secrets from you. If there is anything that Isaac does not know, you can communicate with me anytime," Elijah said quietly.

I nodded and returned to the surface, telling the dignitaries along the way that the eldest was ready to receive them again. True to his word, Mercury was back early the following morning, and I explained to him what was happening.

~ TWENTY-ONE ~

Road Trip

ater in the morning, as I was walking the wall of the stronghold, I looked up to see a dozen of the elf flying mounts appear in the sky and approach the keep. A few of the mounts had extra passengers: Blade, James, Ice Wind, and all four of the snow people under my command. There were also four elves, sent by the community to be guards under Princess Rose's command. Blade and James looked ill, but the Yeti seemed to have taken the flight without any problems.

"Blade, when you feel better, get supplies together for up to a month for the companions, little dragons, Mercury, and the two ladies," I directed.

I designed a platform with 3 bedrooms, a common room and kitchen for Lady Sylvia, Princess Rose and myself. It was to have an area for the little dragons to sleep together, as well as a quiet nesting area; accessible to them only. I designed a large area on the roof for Mercury to rest comfortably in the daytime, and still be able to come and go by triggering a switch to open the roof and return whenever he wished. There was also a small room for James near the front of the platform, since he rarely left my side anyway, unless he was sent on an errand.

The Ankylosaurus that the companions were bringing with them would be outfitted for them to sleep and cook in. I inquired with the clan chieftain about locating and hiring a caravan master who could help in dealing with any patrols that may stop us. The best candidate the chieftain knew of was a dwarf called Creditum. He was well known throughout the land as a fair and honest trader.

Creditum was more than pleased when he received the request to join the dragon mage for a luncheon, to discuss possible business transactions. Elijah had informed me that this person was a great source of information for the dragons. His keen eye for detail and photographic memory allowed him to note tiny details, and impart them when needed. When Creditum came to the keep to join me for lunch, he looked like a typical trader; fat and jolly but from my enquiries I had learned that in close quarters when seconds counted, few could beat him at drawing his blade.

"Why, during this prime trading time of the year, are you sitting at home with your family—losing money?" I asked Creditum.

Creditum replied, "When Elijah speaks and tells you that you will be needed within the month, you wait and see what comes along. Elijah called on me one day early in my caravanning career to warn me that if I ran across a man with a certain name, to not trust him, as he was a spy for the orcs. On my next trip the man showed up and offered to sell me jewels. They had been stolen—I was being set up. If I had bought the jewels, I would have spent a lot of time in an orc jail cell."

"I want to travel incognito with a caravan to visit some of the larger towns and settlements, to learn more of their way of life." I said earnestly. This is part of my continuing training as the dragon mage, to expand my personal horizons. I can offer you one thousand gold coins, as well as a larger share of any profit made during the trip,"

"That sounds like a fair and equitable arrangement," Creditum said, with a broad smile on his face.

I sent him down to the dragons' treasure room in the underground. He was to pick through and find valuable items that were excellent trade goods, and were most likely to be purchased.

I found the ladies, and told them that we were going on a caravan trip, to different towns and strongholds. I handed them a bag of gold for shopping. Sylvia was very excited. When I arrived at the main keep, I told the ladies in waiting that Sylvia needed help shopping, and they rushed off to assist her.

With preparations started, I spent the rest of the day with Isaac, learning as much as I could about the history of all of the races.

"Little is known of the early years; documentation was not kept in as the races were brought over from their home worlds," Isaac said, shrugging.

"Also, I wanted to know, Isaac, if a watch of Chavez is being kept, to monitor his current whereabouts and what he is up to?" I asked Isaac quietly.

"Not at this time, but arrangements can be made. Have you some concern about him?" Isaac asked.

I replied, raising my voice slightly, "Yes, there is something bothering me about him. Find out, and also see if you have any information about when he showed up in this land and how he achieved his rise to power. I know he is not from here, and if he has access to more of his people, we could be in serious trouble."

Isaac rushed off to make arrangements, and the ladies came back with their purchases. They were very frugal, not buying anything too frivolous, sticking to comfortable travelling clothes and some small daggers for Sylvia for protection. She pulled out a small pendant that she had purchased as a gift for me; as she approached me to put it on, I felt my skin crawling with revulsion.

I quickly knocked it to one side and onto the floor. Sylvia was stricken! I explained to her that there was something dangerous about the pendant, and I would get Isaac to closely examine it with me.

"Would you be able to recognize the vendor if you saw him again?" I asked and Rose replied quickly, "In a heartbeat."

"James, come in here right away," I said. He rushed into the room, so quickly in fact that I wondered if he had been listening at the keyhole, which would not surprise me at all.

"Get Ice Wind and his men to go with Princess Rose and find this vendor, who appears to be selling dangerous magical jewellery. Then get the court wizard and tell him that I want him and his men down there right away, to examine the table closely for any more dangerous artifacts."

James rushed out of the room with the Princess, yelling for his men to attend him immediately.

After James had left, I took Sylvia in my arms, as she was crying uncontrollably. I said, consoling her, "You did not know, my dear. You were just thinking of buying me a trinket to show your affection. There is no harm done, because a mage can detect these things. Maybe someone thought I would be distracted, and not notice it. Go and lie down; I will be there in a minute to comfort you."

When she went into the bedroom, I called a guard in and talked to him in the common room.

"Grab a fire poker and use it to put the medallion onto the table. For no reason are you to touch it or let anyone else other than the court magicians touch it. It is very dangerous and you will guard it until you are relieved of that duty. Is that understood?" I said.

The guard nodded his head yes, his eyes wide in fear as he moved it onto the table. I then went into the other room and crawled into bed beside Sylvia, fully clothed. About twenty minutes later, the door opened and Ice Wind stood at the entranceway.

"Yes Ice Wind, what was the result?" I asked.

Ice Wind replied, "We just missed him, but he still is in the stronghold. The guard has been doubled and the keep guard has been tripled. The court mages have taken control of his table and wares, and the head mage himself is coming to take control of the pendant. We have his scent and are doing a room-to-room search, starting at the main keep."

"Carry on. Do not disturb me for a couple of hours unless it is urgent." I said gruffly to Ice Wind.

I lay with the Lady Sylvia until she fell into a deep sleep, then I laid a spell on her to carry her through the night. When I came out, I called one of her ladies in waiting to sit in the room to watch over her, as well as one guard outside the door. Isaac had returned to find everything in an uproar. He was shocked to find that another attempt had been made on the dragon mage.

I called for someone from the court mage's office to update me on the nature of the peddler's wares, as well as the pendant Sylvia had purchased. Shortly, the Court Mage himself arrived to explain what they had found.

"If you had put the pendant on, Dragon Mage, there is an

excellent chance that we would not be having this conversation. The pendant was enchanted with extremely powerful magic. In all my years in this position, I have only seen one other like it. To my knowledge, it had been spelled by the Malum. I will have to take this one down to the Eldest Dragon to be certain," the court mage said, with a look of concern on his face.

"Only if it can be done without any danger to Elijah. Otherwise, I forbid you to even bring it near him," I said angrily.

"We checked over everything else the vendor had been selling, and all other items were clean of any magic, including the vendor's personal belongings, which did not hold anything that would identify him," the court mage said.

"It is obviously another attempt by the assassins' guild. I would be really interested in knowing who was funding the contract. As a high-profile target, my assassination would not come cheap," I said.

Princess Rose showed up later in the evening, looking just as irritated as I felt. There had been no sign as yet of the would-be assassin.

"Rose, could you spend the rest of the night with Sylvia, keeping her company and protecting her at the same time?" I asked.

"I would be happy to. She is in the safest of hands with me," Rose replied.

I thought to myself that the two of them were getting along too well! This world was completely different in ways that I was continually learning. I slept on a couch in the common room. Warriors were coming and going all night, so I slept fitfully. Just after dawn, Ice Wind came to wake me and to tell me that they had found the assassin.

"We found his body. He appears to have taken his own life with some type of poison. There were, of course, no identifying marks or information found on his person. He was a dwarf. This has incensed the clan leaders—that one of their own people would stoop low enough to try to kill a member of a dragon household," Ice Wind stated, angry at missing the kill.

The court mage arrived at my rooms later in the morning to speak to me about the pendant. He said, "The artifact the assassin sold to the Lady Sylvia was definitely of Malum magic. The Eldest dragon smelled it, which was enough for him to tell that it was tainted by the dark magic that the Malum use."

Under the Eldest's direction, the pendant was placed in a special safe located in the underground, until a way could be found to destroy it and the other artifacts stored there. Once the body was confirmed the assassin, the guard was downsized and the stronghold was again opened for its daily routine.

"Isaac, is there any word on the companions, and how far away they are from the stronghold?" I asked.

Isaac replied, "They are making good time, and will be here in two days unless delayed for some reason on the road."

"Ice Wind, have the companions that stayed up all night rest. I will stay in the keep until late this afternoon. I will call you first before leaving the keep for any reason. The companions have been up for a long time and should take a much needed break, to be alert later," I said.

Ice Wind bowed in reply and quickly left the room. I entered the bedroom and observed the ladies sleeping side by side. Rose, guarding against intruders, woke up when I walked into the room, lying down again once she knew who it was. I crawled into bed between the ladies, to sleep for a few hours.

"The assassin has been found dead by his own hand; he took some poison, and his body was found near the wall of the stronghold," I informed Rose quietly. I then fell asleep immediately, not waking for four hours.

Once awake, I cleaned myself up and then walked into the common room, where I could smell something delicious. There were the ladies, with a sumptuous brunch for me to enjoy, but it was not free fare; I had to listen to their complaining about being kept in the keep for their own safety.

~ Twenty-Two ~

Chavez's Story

"I had to promise my companions, and Rose's bodyguards, that we would stay in the keep until late this afternoon, or else they would have had no sleep at all—and there's nothing worse than a cranky Yeti!" I said to the ladies.

The ladies just laughed at that and I was glad that the stress of yesterday seemed to have lifted from them already. Ice Wind showed up at around three in the afternoon and by then, they were more than ready for a stroll around the keep and the market. As we were on our way out for our stroll, I gifted both Sylvia and Rose with a golden broach in the shape of a dragon.

"This is a little trinket for each of you. When you are examining jewellery, or are around any item, it will vibrate a warning if there is magic attached to that item. It will pulsate if it is dark magic; it will vibrate steadily if it is white magic. That way, you will know to have me check it out before purchasing that item, in case it is dangerous," I said.

"Thank you so much for the lovely gift," Sylvia said, appearing fully recovered from the disappointment of the gift I had had to throw to the ground.

I walked out to inspect the construction of the new platform and accommodations for my travelling home. I was advised that it would be ready by tomorrow afternoon at the latest. I thanked the man and moved on, talking to Blade as he accompanied me. "Is everything ready to go in the way of supplies, etcetera?" I asked.

"Yes, everything is ready, and Creditum has selected his crew for the caravan and has chosen trading goods from the treasure room. He also said that he even found something that may be useful to you, which he will show you tomorrow," Blade said.

I sat up late into the night, discussing intelligence that had been gathered about Chavez since his first appearance over three hundred years ago. It was said that Chavez had shown up near the seashore in tattered rags, and has survived by stealing and killing on his way to Capital City.

The government at that time, which had been elected by rigged ballots, was run by twelve aristocrats who were more interested in lining their pockets than trying to run the country. They constantly bickered with each other, and assassination attempts were common.

Somehow, Chavez ingratiated himself with the staff members of a powerful aristocrat—one who led the governing counsel. He had worked his way up rapidly, being highly intelligent, and had quickly become the leader's mage. Once he had reached this position, he had bided his time for a few years, learning as much as he could about this country that he had stumbled across.

There had been so much inbreeding among the aristocrats that there were some really stupid men in line to inherit their fathers' positions of power. Chavez had convinced the leader that he would have more control if the buffoons inherited the positions as they did not know how to do the jobs. With their lack of intelligence, they could be manipulated easily. Unusual accidents had started to occur to some of the aristocrats; accidents that could be linked to their heirs.

The leader had had incriminating documents in his hand prior to the deaths of each aristocrat. And of course, each time the son was voted in with hardly a murmur; the people were so used to the system. Within no time, the leader had complete control of the counsel.

Chavez had manipulated the leader, who cared for nothing but women and drink. He had left Chavez to run things in his name. It reached a point where the People had become so upset with the taxes and brutality of the police force, they had begun demanding an election to replace the ruling counsel.

During the times of unrest, Chavez was able to learn quite a bit of magic from all sources. This included dragon magic, as well as dark magic from the Malum. In no time, he was very adept at multiple forms of magic.

The council had convened to plan how to appease the angry mob of people without losing their positions. This was the moment Chavez had been waiting for. The city hall, with all of the counsellors in it, had caught fire. No one had survived. Chavez stepped in and declared martial law because of this 'heinous act of terrorism,' over two hundred and fifty years ago. Martial law had never been repealed, and was still in effect, to this very day.

Chavez had continued receiving training in the dark arts. Sources believed that this instruction was coming directly from the Malum. This was speculation, but no one in this world, other than the Malum, had enough knowledge of that type of magic to teach it.

The toll that dark magic takes has a side effect on the body. At one time, Chavez could have passed for an elf at a glance. Chavez, three hundred years ago, had measured six feet tall, had a golden tan, light blonde hair, and blue eyes. Now he was no more than five-feet, six inches, as white as a ghost, with grey hair, and eyes that were clouded over like cataracts.

No one knows how old Chavez really was, or had been when he first arrived in this world. The information-gatherers speculated that he had been at least in his late thirties when he crossed into the dragon world. The dragons had invited him to meet with them when he first came to their attention after taking control of the government. He had shown up, but it only took one meeting for the elder dragons to smell the taint of evil on him. He was cast out and was told he was not welcome in any of the dragon strongholds.

The dragons had made a tactical error by not paying closer attention to this new rival. At some point during the years when he was solidifying his control of the government, he had been recruited by the Malum. Chavez shared the same goal that the Malum did—world domination. They had taught Chavez how to use dark magic. I wondered if either side had given any thought as to who was going to be in charge if they did manage, in fact, to take control of the world.

Chavez was not in the capital right now; his whereabouts were unknown. "All of the spies and contacts for the dragons are quietly looking for Chavez. When they find him, they will advise us right away," Isaac said.

The companions arrived the next day, looking very tired but proud that they were able to make it to the stronghold in record time. I told them to take the next couple of days off and had Sylvia and Rose supervise the loading of supplies and organization for the trip. The new platform shelter was ready, and Sylvia and Rose decorated it, preparing it for the trip.

I wanted to travel to Capital City first and pick up Mortimer, to see if we could extract any information from him related to his work with the assassins' guild. I needed to know where Chavez was, so that I would not have to face him (because I did not feel ready yet).

Information came in from a reliable source that Chavez had gone on his annual pilgrimage to the sacred mountains, south of the capital. He usually would be gone for a period of two weeks or more. No one seemed to know exactly what he did or where he went during these "pilgrimages". I speculated that he was meeting with the Malum for further training or consultation.

~ TWENTY-THREE ~

Holiday Time

Prior to our scheduled departure, Creditum asked me to join him for a meal. After the delicious repast, he pulled out a small box and handed it to me. He said, "This is a family heirloom, and has been with my father for many years. It was gifted by one who showed up and saved their family over two hundred seasons ago. My father believes it carries power; it radiates energy to the wearer. The previous owner, we were told, was a keeper of the law, like you."

Creditum handed me the box, and I opened it, finding a small oiled cloth in the box. When uncovered, it turned out to be a Texas Ranger Silver Star badge. Closely examining the badge and turning it over, I saw that the name, 'J. Martin' was scratched onto the back. I felt weak at the knees as I remembered my grandfather telling me a story, long ago, of my great, great grandfather being a Texas Ranger.

He had disappeared, and was never seen again. It was believed that someone had either killed him or he had died in an accident. His body was never found but his wife had never given up hope that he was still alive until the day she had passed away. The West was still pretty wild in those days so it was not unheard of for people to just 'up and disappear.'

"This means a lot to me. Thank you, and tell your father that indeed it comes from a keeper of the law in my world. In fact, it belonged to my great, great grandfather. He was well-respected by the people he met. I will cherish this gift for all my days, and keep it with me always," I said, my voice choking with emotion.

"My father will be very proud that this treasure was kept for one of the law keeper's kin to collect when it came time to pass it on," Creditum said.

"I would like to talk to your father, when time allows, because I never knew my ancestor. I would dearly love to hear any stories of him. He was one of the reasons I became a keeper of the law, when I was old enough," I said.

It would take a week to get to the largest city (the capital) along the roads with our caravan so as soon as the caravan was ready, we headed out. There was no indication of purpose. The dragons were kept out of sight until we camped for the night and no one was around to see us. Then, Mercury would come out as well, and hunt the area for any interlopers or prey.

To keep our façade, we stopped in every village along the way to the city where we traded with the goods that Creditum had packed in the caravan.

The only ones in the party who had to remain under cover were the dragons and the Yeti. The rest of the group were able to dress normally, but without any dragon markings; I dressed as an elf, with a cloak and appropriate clothing. My hair was combed to cover my ears, so I was able to stand back and watch the villagers.

We did not run into any patrols, as they travelled mostly along the main road while we stuck to secondary ones. The first orcs we saw were at the huge gates to the city. Creditum did all the talking to the captain of the guard at the gates, identifying himself and the others as part of his caravan, then showing them some of the quality items that he had for sale. The guard captain insisted on searching all of the platforms and storage areas. The rooms for Isaac and Gizmo were very well hidden (even for someone searching very closely). Mercury and the Yeti opted to stay in the woods surrounding the city until the caravan and I finished our business.

After passing through the gates to Capital City, we headed immediately to the usual lodging that Creditum stayed at when he was in the city. The inn keeper was an elderly gentleman of the People, who greeted him with open arms. Creditum spoke to him in private; the dragons were led secretly through the back stairs. Creditum advised us that the innkeeper could be completely trusted, as he was an agent for the dragons.

Princess Rose and the elves went out with me later in the afternoon; a group of elves would not be conspicuous in this city but if I had taken my mixed bag of companions, we would have stood out in any crowd. The innkeeper supplied us with a carriage and a trusted driver. The creatures towing the carriage looked like cousins of the triceratops, without the horns. The animals were about the size of large sheep, and the little carriage was only big enough to carry packages and the driver. We loaded a large chest onto the carriage, and headed out toward the seedy part of town.

I kept my hood up, so no one would notice the differences from the elves. It took an hour to reach Mortimer's shop. He was the only one working the shop, this late in the day. I initially let Rose do all the talking about setting up trading with merchants in the city. She also said that she had heard that strange curios could be found in his shop.

This late in the afternoon, the streets were very quiet, as most had gone home. Since the men working the night shift would not be arriving for a little bit, the likelihood of anyone coming to Mortimer's aid at this time of the day was slim. There were few on the streets to hear him yelling, and besides, he was not well liked. It was time for a confrontation.

I walked up to Mortimer, interrupting Rose's discussion with him. "I am the dragon mage, and I would like to know who wants me dead. I know, Mortimer, that you are a front for the assassins' guild, and have been for many years," I said, staring at him.

Mortimer just stood there with his mouth hanging wide open, and started to stammer about not knowing what I was talking about. The elves posted themselves at the only two exits from the shop, not saying a word—just staring at Mortimer.

"I have no idea what you are talking about! Now get out of my store before I call the guard and have you hauled away to jail," Mortimer said, with a sneer on his face.

"I can get you away from all these dealings with the assassins' guild if you help me. You can disappear and the guild would never find you," I said.

"I am interested in your offer, but you cannot hide someone with my distinct looks," Mortimer said skeptically.

"I expected that to be a stumbling block. Go look in the mirror now, merchant Mortimer," I said, pointing to a large mirror in the front of the store.

Mortimer looked in the mirror, and he saw not himself but someone of the proper age, who looked like a normal dwarf merchant, with the typical pot belly of an elderly man. "I will not give you any information, until I am safely away from the city," Mortimer warned me.

I nodded to the elves, who went out to the carriage and brought in a large trunk. Inside the trunk was a deceased elderly dwarf male (who had passed away from natural causes), whom they laid down behind the counter.

"Is there anything of sentimental value that we may pretend to steal before we burn the store down?" I asked quietly.

Mortimer immediately understood. He selected a few leather bound books and special items, then stepped inside the trunk, and was carried out to the carriage.

I pulled out a flint and some tinder, getting a fire started in the back room, and telling Rose to leave with the men. I then pulled out my magic ring of invisibility, making sure the fire spread properly, and exited the store, unseen. I had used flint and steel to start the fire, as I did not want any trace of magic to be anywhere around the fire. It had to look like a routine theft and murder, which would put the thieves' guild arguing with the assassins' guild.

As soon as we were back at the inn, I sat down with Gizmo and Isaac to make sure the changes made to Mortimer were permanent, using strong magic to add a powerful layer of protection. Creditum had completed his business, making a healthy profit as usual so we immediately packed up and headed out of town, fitting in with the rush hour of peasants leaving the city to return to their hovels.

The caravan came under less scrutiny leaving, due to the heavy traffic, than it did coming into Capital City. We continued on our way with the constant speed that any caravan would follow, so as not to raise any suspicion. We were about one day from the nearest dwarf stronghold, when we were stopped by an orc patrol.

"You will turn this caravan around right now and head back to Capital City to answer some questions!" ordered the orc captain.

"I cannot do this; I am expected to be in other strongholds! I will lose so much money! I have a wife and children to support! If you have any questions, I would be happy to answer them right here and now with complete honesty and detail," Creditum said in a pleading voice.

"If you do not turn this caravan around right now, your people are going to start dying," the orc captain snarled.

My mind was occupied, so I did not have time to waste with the orcs. I nodded at my escort, pulled my gun and started shooting orcs. In a manner of moments, the orc patrol was taken care of without injuries to any of my men. The members of the caravan quickly disposed of the bodies, off the road and out of sight.

I spent the following weeks sitting back quietly, listening to the people that Creditum spoke to, trying to absorb what was being said about the orcs, the dragons, and Chavez. I heard a lot about how everyone felt, and the positive feelings they had about the dragon mage, because now there was someone to stand up to the evil orcs, and restore order to the world.

Mortimer was very helpful. He didn't know who had paid to have me killed but he was able to give much insight into the running of the assassins' guild and who was in charge. Not surprisingly, the top man was the wizard Chavez, but he did not participate in the daily running of the guild. I thanked him for his assistance, and told him that we would set him up as a small business owner in one of the strongholds.

We found a campsite area for the evening in a glade surrounded by trees; it seemed like a nice, peaceful location to spend the night. The guards were posted, and everything had been cleaned up from the nightly meal. I was outside at the fire with Gizmo and Isaac; Mercury having taken flight to do patrols in the area.

I heard a woman's scream come from my platform. Everyone rushed to the platform, to find one of the caravan guards that Creditum had hired, wounded and unconscious in the common room. Rose was administering first aid to Lady Sylvia. She was seriously injured from several stab wounds! She would survive, but it appeared the child growing inside of her would not.

I instructed my companions to place the wounded guard someplace secure and tend to his injuries. As soon as he was conscious, they were to ask what had happened. I knelt down beside Sylvia's bed and cried for almost an hour, with Rose beside me, trying to comfort me. I sent Gizmo and Isaac with different groups to question the guards in detail, to see if they had noticed anything suspicious leading up to the assassination attempt.

I walked over to the guard, who was awake now and looking as pale as a ghost. All he could do was weakly mumble an apology for failing in his duty. He was able to tell me that an orc scout had broken into the dwelling, stabbed him and surprised the Lady Sylvia and tried to kill her.

I called Mercury in my mind and told him that he was looking for a single orc scout headed out from the caravan towards the nearest orc encampment or fortress. Mercury, with his keen night-time vision, located the orc in a short time. He disabled the orc and carried his unconscious body back to the caravan. Mercury then searched the entire area, finding two more orc scouts and telling us where to find them. They were captured and brought into the caravan for questioning as well.

The dwarf warriors took the first turn interrogating the scouts, followed by the Yeti, but all were unsuccessful. The orcs were very stubbornly refusing to share any information with the caravan party, especially about the attempted murder of Lady Sylvia.

I told them that they would be tortured to death, or released if they identified who had hired or directed them to try to kill the Lady Sylvia. When questioned at length, none of them knew who had tried to kill Lady Sylvia. It had to be someone from the nearby fortress to the north of them. Isaac scanned their minds, and said that their orders were to scout the area as usual. They were to kill whomever they came across, if opportunity presented itself.

Mercury was saddled and ready to go in minutes. I mounted and we flew toward the orc stronghold quickly.

"Mercury, please leave this area and do not interfere. Even though there is risk, I must do this alone," I said once we had landed.

He replied, "My oldest relative would kill me if I did not at least stick around and watch your back. So nothing you can say will send me away. We are bonded by blood, as you are with all the dragons. Your pain is our pain, and we must share the revenge, my brother of fire and claw!"

"The clans have been called." Elijah said in my mind. They gather to assist your revenge in this atrocity. One does not kill an infant of either dragon or dragon mage without consequences. I know that you wish to take revenge on your own, but your clan will help prepare things so that you remain safer. They will be here before dawn. There has not been such a gathering since the last dragon mage needed help."

"I will wait until dawn, and then I will attack—with or without them," I said.

Elijah replied, "I understand, and please do not think less of Mercury because he knew that we would want to know. This heinous act must be avenged. You are part of our family and we cannot let this sacrilege go without taking action against the perpetrator."

Mercury sat quietly with me throughout the night, killing any predators that dared come close to the dragon mage.

Just before dawn, a flight of thirty dragons landed near me, including two females who nuzzled me to show their concern. Isaac and Gizmo showed up as well, to offer support in my time of need.

I asked how Sylvia was doing and Isaac replied, "She is a very strong willed woman. I think that if not for her injuries, she would be by your side to exact revenge on this affront. She had to be restrained by the healer, as she wished to do just that."

I felt fire raging, overtaking me. I slowly walked closer to the orc outpost. Mercury later said that I became engulfed in the 'dragon rage,' which had only been seen rarely in the last century. When I was within ten feet of the entranceway, a sentry challenged me with a single arrow, striking my chest. It did not penetrate my mithril armour.

The horde of dragons flew to the attack, destroyed the walls of the outpost, and decimated the siege engines and heavy weapons that might threaten the mage or the dragons from a distance. The orcs were overwhelmed; they had never seen so many dragons in one place at the same time.

As I felt the anger taking control and growing stronger by the second, a wall of flame sprung up, encircling the outpost. In a matter of seconds, the entire outpost perimeter was engulfed in flames. My rage was fuelled by the fire. I had to really concentrate or else lose awareness of what was going on around me. Recollection of the entire event was a little hazy, and Mercury had to describe the incident to me later.

Mercury stayed in the area, watching the outpost, feeling through his connection with me the growing rage that was enveloping me. I lifted my staff and the gates were blown off their hinges, crushing a dozen guards behind them.

A volley of arrows sailed their way toward me, but within five feet of me, they were completely incinerated. Orc warriors ran toward me with their weapons drawn. They never made it close, incinerated by dragon fire.

Mercury could see the enclosures where the captives were kept but their doors had been blown off and people of all races were fleeing out the open gate. The orcs, however, did not survive their attempts to flee, bursting into flames as they neared the dragon mage.

The last building came crashing down, but a wall of flame remained around the encampment, containing the surviving orcs. Several attempts were made to get past the blockade or to attack the dragon mage, unsuccessfully and with usually messy results. All of the attackers burst into flame, screaming in their pain to their compatriots.

When there were only about two hundred orcs left, I felt the rage lessening.

"I want the officers who ordered the attempt on our lives brought forward. I will let the rest of you live to tell others that the dragons and the dragon mage will not be tampered with. The consequences will be severe, as you can see. This will not be tolerated by the dragons or by me," I shouted at the orcs.

Very quickly, three officers were dragged forward in front of the group, screaming their innocence as they tried to flee. I raised my staff and enclosed them in a circle of flame. Then, I engulfed them in one massive fireball that incinerated them instantly. At this point, I did not care whether they were innocent or not; I just needed to vent my anger.

"The rest of you may leave. Head north, away from where the captives fled, as I do not want them interfered with. I have ensured that there are enough supplies left from the fire in the stone storehouse. With the intact weapons lying around the outpost, you can safely make it to the next outpost, which is two days walk to the north," I said.

I disappeared into the darkness, walking back to a small hilltop overlooking the remains of the outpost. I lay down, falling fast asleep—my energy spent. Mercury landed next to me, extending his wing to keep me warm from the slightly early morning chill in the air. He called for Isaac and Gizmo to bring a litter to carry me back to the caravan. About ten of the dragons remained in the area to provide support and protection to the dragon mage's party.

The snow people and the little dragons showed up in a short time, and took me back to my room in the caravan and into bed.

The caravan healer delivered our dead baby girl, and started the healing process so Sylvia would survive. As is the dwarf custom, the infant was cremated the next day, and her ashes were placed in an urn that Creditum gifted to me.

"I still have contacts in and outside the guild." Mortimer said. I will find out who ordered this kill and whether you were the target and if the assassin took advantage of the Lady Sylvia being there."

I barely acknowledged Mortimer's promise, being in a deep and dark depression at that moment in time. Creditum suggested that we head back to the Diamond clan stronghold, and since no one challenged him, the arrangements were made. We travelled without incident several days but then we met a horde of orcs; three thousand strong waiting on the road. Mercury had noticed them the night before on his patrols so we were not surprised. A rider, asking to speak with the leader of the caravan, approached. They were looking for a large group of warriors who had destroyed the fortress to the north of their location. Creditum said that they had not seen any large force of men in their travels. The orc was invited to search the caravan if he wished. He declined but had us ride down the road through the orc encampment.

Creditum suggested that we speed up, as the orcs would not be long in figuring out that magic was involved in the destruction of the fortress. Since there were not many of their enemies using magic, all evidence would point to the dragon mage.

We reached the Diamond stronghold the next day. As soon as the sentries recognized the caravan, they opened the gates. The dwarves had kept the three orc scout captives safe and sound for the journey. At the stronghold, the captives were taken down to the dungeon for further questioning, to see if they had any other useful information.

Entering my quarters, I left instructions that I was not to be disturbed for any reason other than an attack on the stronghold, until I told the guards otherwise. I then spent the next two days only sleeping and eating. I was in a deep depression because of the loss of my unborn child.

After two days, I got out of bed and told my guard to run ahead and tell the companions that I was on my way to talk to Elijah. The guard started to say something about the need to make an appointment to see the Eldest, but saw the look on my face, and ran. Elijah was sitting patiently waiting for me, not saying a word; waiting for me to start the conversation when I was ready.

"As a lawman, I believe there is too much injustice in this world for me to leave things as they stand. I have suffered a loss at the hands of the evil ones. I will do my best to stop this from happening to others in this world. I cannot stand idly by and let this corrupt government enslave people when it wants to, without consequences," I said to Elijah

He replied, "Anything you wish will be yours if at all possible: manpower, money, weapons, supplies—you have but to ask."

"I will work alone at first, not under the dragon lord's emblems but it will not take long before the enemy realizes who is behind this," I said.

"Lord Isaac and Lady Gizmo will be your liaison with the

dragons. I can see in your mind some of the things that you need; I have a location in mind. I will pass the information on to Isaac, and arrangements will be made to fix up the quarters to your exact specifications," Elijah said.

I returned to my rooms with a new sense of purpose and energy. I instructed the guard on to ensure that all the handmaidens and other non-essential occupants on my floor be moved to other floors. This floor was to be used for me and my companions, until our relocation. I immediately sat with Lord Isaac, asking if I could obtain plans for the location Elijah and he were discussing. Isaac told me that the plans were to arrive the next day. There was a regiment of engineers headed to the location, to start the initial cleanup and repairs.

Sylvia came and joined me after a few days, completely healed thanks to the magic of the healers. Sylvia had been fortunate, as none of the stab wounds had hit any vital organs, just the baby. Sylvia was very stoic, looking at me and saying, "Now is not the time to mourn the loss of our daughter. Now is the time to avenge her death. You have started that already my love, if we kill a few hundred more, that will show them how much one of our clan is worth compared to their lives."

~ TWENTY-FOUR ~
Secret Rebellion

"Isaac, can you get a message right away to the engineers? They are not to clean up the outside of the keep. I want it to keep its rundown appearance from the outside, so no one realizes there are new occupants," I said.

Isaac replied, "That thought crossed our minds already. Since you hinted at stealth, they are not touching the outside at all. Just give me your list and we will do the best we can. We are not anticipating any problems, with the exception of dragon armour. I have never before in all my years seen such a thing, and will have to check to see if such exists, or whether we will have to make it from scratch. When did you want to head out to the new headquarters? We can be ready within twenty four hours," Isaac said.

I replied, "The sooner the better. Start arrangements right away."

Isaac flew out of the room, and I could hear dwarves yelling at each other about making packs and supplies up for travel right away.

"You have dark thoughts on your mind, Jim. It is hard to make sense of them, with the entire jumble in there," Gizmo said to me.

"Then I will try to slow down so you can get an inkling of what I have in mind for the near future, Gizmo," I said.

"You have a daunting task ahead of you. If you accomplish even a fraction of it, then you are a greater man than many before you," Gizmo stated.

I asked for the finest armourer in the stronghold. When he showed up, I sat down with him and started to explain what I wanted. "You will make the Lady Gizmo a mithril shirt that fits around her properly and will not fall off in flight. Then you will do the same for Lord Isaac. If anyone questions you, tell them that it is my request. You will also ensure that Lady Sylvia, Princess Rose and James all have mithril armour. The dragon companions will arrange payment when you need it," I said.

After taking measurements, the armourer bowed and left the room. Gizmo looked at me, with her head cocked to one side. I said, looking at Gizmo with concern on my face, "I am not taking any chances on those that are close to me; I have lost one too many already."

Gizmo nodded her head and flew off to attend to certain errands. I was tired, so I climbed into bed and was soon fast asleep, only waking for a moment when Rose climbed into bed beside me.

"Thank you for the present. No one has ever given me such a lavish gift before," Rose said as she cuddled close to me in the bed. She kissed me on the neck, and I was soon fast asleep again.

I learned the next morning that a set of dragon armour had been located in one of the old dragon storage places, and it was being brought here to see if it was useable, or if it could be copied for new armour for Mercury. When it was brought to the keep, it was presented to the eldest dragon for his approval. It was in such bad shape that it was only useful as a display piece.

Armourers were called to examine the armour as a template. We asked how long it would take to duplicate it, if we were in a rush. They said it could be done in one day, as they had materials on hand. They measured Mercury and said they would have it ready for morning, but last minute adjustments would be needed.

I felt guilty about being unable to take the necessary steps to save anyone under my protection from harm. When I paid my respects to the Diamond clan chief, I apologized about the loss of the infant's life while she was under my care. The chieftain not only accepted my apology, but explained that certain things were beyond the control of anyone; if she had not been the victim, it might have been the dragon mage instead.

I nodded and said to the chieftain, "I need fifty warriors to assist me in exacting revenge on the orcs in a way that they will not understand comes from the dragons. By taking out the slaver units covertly, it will take longer for them to realize where it is coming from.

"The warriors must not have any clan markings on them. It will help avoid repercussion from the orcs for at least a short period of time. There will also be elves, and warriors from the People. This will be a multi-race endeavour to deal a crippling blow to the orcs," I said.

The chieftain was eager to be able to help in whatever means he could. He immediately agreed, suggesting that the three companion commanders I had would be the best to make the selection from the troops. They would be able to make a suitable selection from all the volunteers. I thanked him and got up to leave, but the chieftain halted me.

"This small crystal is for you. It contains some of the infant's ashes. The rest will be kept in the crypts. You have at least a part to remember her by," The chieftain said, and I started to choke up with tears.

It took one extra day before we could head out to the new headquarters. Mercury's armour was properly fitted and in place. The mithril shirts were completed for all of my selected companions. We left with quite a bit of well-wishing on the part of the Diamond clan chieftain and the Eldest's dragon companions. Of course this was all done inside of the stronghold, as they did not want information leaked to Chavez that the dragons had given their blessing for this endeavour. Sylvia did not show up to wish me well, which I treated as a sign of her continued mourning, or anger at me for leaving her behind.

It took us five days to reach the run-down keep which was to be our headquarters. It looked dilapidated from the outside; however, once we got past the front gate, everything changed. It was amazing what the engineers had been able to accomplish in a few days.

While we were unpacking, a large chest was brought in, its contents making some unusual noises when it was dropped onto the floor. I quickly drew my gun and motioned my companions in the room to silence. I snapped the lid open to reveal the Lady Sylvia lying there.

"About time you opened this chest. It was getting rather stuffy in there," Sylvia said, smiling.

I just shook my head and said to Blade, "Blade, please help the Lady Sylvia out of the trunk, and get her settled in my area of the keep." I laughed, not being able feel mad at her. I admit, having her there made me feel better.

I headed to see how the rest of the unpacking was going, hoping not to find any more stowaways in the luggage, and directing things to be done the way I wanted.

The Keep was located on the edge of the great forest, and overlooked the ocean. We were in close proximity of a sacred great tree. Elves had set up a large outpost, to watch for unwanted guests. Built at a time when the dwarf population was sparse, to hold more dragons than dwarves the keep included an incubation chamber and nursery for young dragons, just in case they were needed.

There was a maze of tunnels underground. Two entrances opened on the cliff side, for dragons to be able to fly into the tunnels. Three other exits lead in each compass direction from the keep, well-camouflaged and allowing for access separate from the keep gate. When the engineers were finished, they also had enough room to house over one thousand people for a short period of time; longer with supplies.

The Lady Sylvia was in her element. She immediately took over control of the entire stronghold, including in the kitchen, ensuring things were organized to feed and keep the troops happy. She became the keep commander, with most of the warriors watching out for her and treating her like gold. Every time I saw her, she had a smile on her face.

I once overheard one of the kitchen staff make a disparaging remark about Lady Sylvia. Before I had a chance speak to the man, he disappeared. When next I saw him, he had several bruises and a broken nose; he never said anything about the Lady Sylvia again. I asked the sergeant on duty at the time about it, and was told that some of the warriors felt a little quiet discipline was in order. I told him that in the future it should be brought before me, but in this case, I would let it slide.

Everything I needed was ready. The elves, with practice, developed ways to fly low over a target and drop off warriors without any noise. Since they had been doing this type of warfare for centuries, I felt it best just to tell them what I needed done, letting them accomplish the task. I was getting used to being in charge; not bad for someone who was used to just taking orders.

I sent out scouts to watch the roads for orc caravans, wanting to cripple their slave trade to the point where they could get little done. They were not used to doing any of their own manual labour.

Since the caravans were running all the time, it did not take long for me to discern a pattern and formulate a plan on how to take out our first caravan target. I was sitting in the dark, watching the slave caravan set up camp in the valley below me. Scouts advised that the convoy had settled for the night; most guards were asleep, with the exception of those on perimeter patrol.

Companion wizards cast a sleep spell over the entire caravan. The scouts moved into the camp, prepared to dispatch anyone that might not be affected by the spell. The prisoners were removed and taken to a safe spot, and then the spell was cancelled. As they returned to consciousness, a disguised People warrior, planted among them, told them not to go to their home towns, but rather to travel to a group of towns in an area that was safe, and that would welcome them. These "towns" happened to be within areas of greater protection the orcs did not harvest any of their labour from.

Everything went smoothly; the orcs were allowed to wake naturally and were presented a mystery to solve and explain to their superiors. I had a meeting with the leaders at the fortress and explained to them that I wanted them to use their imagination to think of unusual ideas to free the humans from their captors.

Once the warriors were organized, I let them take complete control to deal with the slaver issue. I was then free to continue with my studies of magic and dragon lore. I spent long hours perusing old texts that I had been provided; enough to fill a small library. The dragons had even sent a librarian with the books, to ensure that they were cared for.

The representative of the elf and dwarf warriors kept me informed as to their progress in their raids on the slave caravans. Apparently, it took the orcs longer to figure out magic was being used than I had expected. The warriors, therefore, had time to come up with different plans of attack for the future. When the orcs started sending wizards with the caravans to cancel out any spells, the team was ready to adapt with a new plan of attack in place.

One day, I sat in the library, reading dusty texts. I understood most of the manuscripts but occasionally I had to get the librarian to translate some archaic words. Sylvia walked into the library, carrying a large platter with a light lunch and some fresh fruit. She said, "I brought you something to eat, since all you seem to do these days is study and sleep."

Nodding my head absentmindedly, I was deeply engrossed in a large tome about healing certain rare diseases, my attention was pulled away from the book by a pair of breasts leaning over the top of the large tome.

"I get the point. I will take the rest of the day off and spend some time with my Lady," I said, smiling.

Sylvia returned the smile, placing a bookmark in the tome and leading me over to an empty table, to share the simple luncheon that she had prepared. We chatted amicably for a while, and then went out to the battlements of the fortress to have a look at the beautiful scenery that surrounded the stronghold. The weather was nice, but with a gentle breeze coming off the ocean, the air was a little cooler than the normal stifling heat of the day.

I was standing with my arm around Sylvia's waist, looking out toward the ocean, listening to the sound of the surf hitting rocks not too far away when suddenly, I looked up into the surrounding forest.

"I have to run now, and go save someone's life. Not sure of all the details, but I am needed, I'll explain later" I said.

"Lord Jim, I await your victorious return. I will have an extra seat set at your table for company," Sylvia said, and she then stood on her tiptoes, gave me a gentle kiss, and pushed me on my way.

I ran down to my quarters, yelling at James, "JAMES, GATHER THE MEN! Get outfitted for a patrol!"

I still felt this overwhelming urge to be on my way to find the person who was going to need my help very soon. I stood by the gates, pacing back and forth, awaiting my team of men—the energy building up. Gizmo and Isaac flew down to where I was, and quietly sat with me. They were both dressed in the mithril armour I had had custom made for them, and were getting anxious, feeding off my energy, feeling the need to head out right away.

It felt like an hour, but my men were assembled and ready to go in five minutes. We quickly spread out in a defensive formation as soon as we stepped passed the gates. We made our way to the main road, which ran about one-half mile from the stronghold. I had my companions moving at a fast pace behind me, telling them we would slow down when we reached the area where we were needed.

~ TWENTY-FIVE ~

Godfrey

We travelled for about a half hour, moving away from the ocean along the trade road. When we reached a crossroads, there were large rocks at the edge of the road and I saw a cloaked figure sitting on one of the rocks. Surrounding him were a dozen orc corpses, and a couple of ogres as well. There were no marks on the bodies to indicate what killed them. I walked over to the cloaked figure.

"You don't look like you need any help from me. Why did you send the call?" I asked.

The man replied, "There are at least fifty more of their friends coming down the road in the next fifteen minutes. I am too tired to tackle that many bad guys."

There was something odd about the way that the stranger talked, but I would deal with that later.

Calling my companions over, I quickly explained what was coming down the road toward us. They immediately spread out, disappearing into the woods as if they had never been there in the first place. Standing in the middle of the crossroads, I waited to see what would come down the road. I knew my men had us well-covered and protected, and knew that no one would get past my group.

Signalling to Ice Wind, I asked him to have the Yetis visible on the road, since the orcs were instinctively afraid of the Yeti from experience, dealing with them in the North. It didn't take long before lead riders for the orc patrol showed up.

Right away, they saw the bodies, the stranger, the Yeti, and me at the crossroad. They did a quick about-turn, disappearing back the way they had come from.

It was not long before the orcs, along with a couple more ogres returned. The commander was immediately recognizable by being grossly overweight, and his uniform was covered in food stains.

"What the hell is going on here? Who killed my men, and who the hell are you?" the orc commander demanded.

"I am the dragon mage. I could tell you that I found them that way, but we would both know that would be a lie. They made the mistake of tangling with a mage and paid the price as a result."

Gizmo was on her usual perch on my shoulders, holding back her energy, just watching the scenario unfolding. She was looking into the minds of the orcs, and talked to me through their mind link:

"He is trying to decide if he could get enough space between himself and the action to survive the attack that is about to happen," Gizmo said.

I silently replied, "Gizmo, tell Isaac, your mate, to pass the word. Start killing the orcs at the other end of this contingent. Make sure that they haul the bodies into the bushes and out of sight, so if anyone is looking, they will appear to have run away."

When the yells started coming from the back of the group, the orc commander turned around and looked back to where the noise was coming from. I quickly pulled my pistol out, and the Yeti, following my lead, rapidly moved into a defensive position, with their weapons ready.

The commander turned to face me again, with a snarl on his face. Before he could utter a word, he was on the ground with a spear through his throat. The companions and I took care of the couple of ogres and the rest of the orc group before they had had a chance to reorganize themselves. The few survivors, who bolted, fleeing down the road, were caught before they got far and dispatched by the companions.

"Since time did not allow for introductions, I am the dragon mage Jim. I would be delighted if you could join me for dinner back at my residence," I introduced myself to this mysterious pilgrim, bowing slightly.

"I would be delighted to join you and to share a repast. By the way, my name is Godfrey. Since you were coming to see me a while back and never showed up, I decided to look you up and see what all the fuss was about," Godfrey said warmly.

We took the Ankylosaurus that the orcs had brought with their contingent, and loaded it with everything of value we could recover from the battle, riding it to the stronghold. I sat quietly as the platform swung with the movement of the animal below. Godfrey just sat there, looking at me. I was not sure why he was looking at me the way he was, but I knew, he would tell me when he was ready.

"You look a lot like your grandfather; you have his eyes," Godfrey said quietly.

"You knew my grandfather?"

"It is a long story, best shared over a drink and a full belly," Godfrey answered.

Although I was eager to hear what Godfrey had to say, I was learning patience, especially when dealing with wizards. It was best to wait for the time to be right. To rush the issue would anger Godfrey. He would provide less information if he was upset with me.

I had a couple of men run ahead to ensure that the troops did not become excited by the arrival of the Ankylosaurus. The last thing I wanted was to have guardsmen do something stupid in front of Godfrey, whom, for some unknown reason, I wanted desperately to impress.

Once we were inside the stronghold, safe from prying eyes, Godfrey was taken to a set of rooms to freshen up before the meal. I headed to my rooms and was greeted warmly by Rose and Sylvia. I shared the little tidbits of information that Godfrey had given me so far. They were both very excited, and went to the kitchens to ensure that he was treated to an excellent meal, to keep him in good spirits so he could share information that was important to the love of their lives.

The meal was laid out in the common room, near my personal

quarters. Sylvia, as the head of the garrison, knew that the guest was important to me, so she arranged for men to be in full dress uniform while serving the table. There were places set for four and for the two little dragons. Mercury had chosen not to attend as he was bored and wanted to make some night time patrols around the stronghold to ensure there were no more orcs.

I was impressed that the cook had provided such an excellent meal of seasonal fruit, fresh bread, and tender cuts of meat. Godfrey showed up for the meal wearing an outfit of simple homespun cloth. But for the air of power he carried and the mage's magical staff, he could have passed for a tall member of the People.

He was around five-feet, eight inches, with a slim build and had long, silver hair, braided with a strip of leather woven into it. He dug into the meal like he was starving, barely wasting a word other than to signal for a refill of his mug of beer. He only paused momentarily to exchange pleasantries with Sylvia and Rose, who had joined us for the dinner.

"He is no danger, and is exactly who he says he is. He has some amazing information to share with you, but it is nothing that cannot wait until you are alone," Gizmo said to my mind.

Godfrey had just finished a second helping of pie and was waiting for the servers to clear the table when he asked "Can we talk in private? I do not wish to share what I have to say with everyone."

I asked the servers to leave and once they were out of the room, instructed a guard to not allow anyone entry unless it was an emergency. I then looked at Godfrey and said, "I trust the dragons completely, and I would share whatever you have to tell me with my special ladies, so there is no reason they should not hear the information directly from you. If you are offended by this, then there is no point in carrying on a conversation, because they are my family."

"I understand completely. You have to have someone that you can trust, or else you spend too much time alone. Well, I have been here on this world for about one hundred and fifty years, coming over from what you would term the Wild West, to help out during a time of turmoil on this world. That is, after I found out that what was happening here needed my attention more than my home," Godfrey said, starting the long story of his life.

~ TWENTY-SIX ~

Godfrey's Story

He spoke of his years growing up as a farm boy, on his uncle's farm, after losing his parents to a Native American attack. This had happened while he was out checking cattle on a distant field. His uncle, a strict but lovable character, raised Godfrey to be a God-fearing young man who did the right things.

When old enough, he was drafted into the Southern army and was expected to report as soon as possible. Because of his beliefs against slavery, he ran to the North and enlisted with the army there instead. After the Civil war, he returned home, and found that resentment went deep against anyone from the North.

He left his uncle's ranch and joined the Texas Rangers at the age of twenty five. He quickly excelled in his new career so it was not long before Godfrey was well known. He was riding his horse one night, headed to a town to oversee a hanging. He had closed his eyes for a couple of minutes, and then had opened them to the sun shining in his eyes, and nothing looking familiar around him.

He had ridden his horse for several hours before he noticed a town in the distance. He had been about a half a mile from the town, when he surprised a tyrannosaurus eating a carcass of some type of herbivore. The tyrannosaurus had decided that Godfrey and his horse looked like dessert and had immediately set out after them. He had suffered some severe wounds from the tyrannosaurus' claws before he was able to roll away from his dead horse.

The gates of the town had opened and a large group of warriors

186

had distracted the tyrannosaurus. The rest had grabbed him and dragged him into the town, closing the gates quickly. His wounds had been beyond the skills of the town healer, so they had quickly transported him to the nearest dwarf stronghold. His greeting from the dragons had been a little unusual. They had asked him many questions, immediately offering to show him the way home once he was healed enough to travel.

He had told them that he had a wife and a couple of sons back home that he had to return to, so there was no question of staying once he had healed. It took longer for Godfrey to heal than it normally would have. The healer came to tell him that magic was all that had kept him from dying. The healer had advised that if he were to return to his home, the magic there was not as powerful and he would die from his injuries quickly.

Godfrey had not been sure what he should do, and had spent a couple of weeks pondering on his future. He had asked to see the dragon lord, where he was brought back to health. The lord had advised Godfrey that he was meant to be there, telling him that he would be taught to be a great healer, and one day he would pass on his experience and knowledge to another.

Godfrey went on to tell of the many conflicts that he was involved in, also doing great deeds of healing. He had met Chavez briefly, dismissing him as a second class magician of little or no talent. In later battles, Godfrey had realized that Chavez's power was increasing at an exponential rate, and he would soon be a threat.

Godfrey had learned of my arrival, and was excited to hear that this new arrival was travelling to meet him. When I did not show up, he kept track of me through his contacts with the dragons. After learning of my growing powers, and of my becoming the dragon mage, he had felt it was time to travel to see the dragon mage, to offer his assistance to me, in my continuing battle against evil.

"I also know your true name is Jonathan Isaac Martin. You see, it is my name too, as I am your great grandfather. That is my badge that you carry with you; a token of strength and honesty," Godfrey said.

I just sat there quietly, staring at my great grandfather, tears welling up in my eyes. Rose was wiping tears from her eyes, and Sylvia was crying for joy. I got up and went over to my great grandfather, gathering him in a bear hug embrace, and holding tightly.

"I am a little frail. If you do not loosen your grip, I will be your late great grandfather. It has been a long night and there will be time to talk tomorrow, but you must remember that our conversation here is private, as it could be used against you. I must be called Godfrey at all times. Good night grandson, I am so proud of what you have accomplished already in this world," Godfrey said.

I spent many long hours studying under my grandfather, delving into the healing and defensive aspects of magic. It was not long before the warriors at the stronghold referred to Godfrey as Gramps (since he appeared downright ancient, although he was very active and spry). I called him Gramps to his face once, and was immediately put through my paces, ending many days of practice stiff and sore.

He took me into the woods several nights, teaching me how to avoid detection from animals and people. He even offered a reward to the scouts, of fifty gold coins, for whoever caught him or me on our excursions. It cost me a few hundred coins before I started to learn my lessons. Scouts then were hard pressed to catch me, even when I was standing in close proximity to them.

I set out with him on an evening when both moons were full, giving enough light to almost be full daylight. I was growing closer to him every day, and as usual we were chatting amicably as we strolled down the road. Stopping suddenly, we could hear bare feet running down the roadway toward us.

We stepped to one side to spy on what was coming down the path. As we waited, we could hear other noises in the grass alongside the road. Something was out there hunting! Just then, a woman appeared around the curve in the road running, full-tilt toward us. Close on her heels were a couple of smaller raptors, which would catch her within the next ten feet.

Godfrey and I worked together like clockwork. He pulled the woman to one side, put her to sleep, and enveloped her in his cloaking spell. I waited for the raptors to stop in confusion, dropped my cloak and quickly dispatched the lizards with my gun.

~ TWENTY-SEVEN ~

Don't Wake the Dreamer

After making sure the raptors were deceased, I walked over to where Godfrey was administering to the woman's wounds. She was definitely not from around, she was not an elf and she was too tall for any of the other races I had met in my travels. Her skin color indicated that she would be of African descent in my world, but the fine features on her beautiful face led me to think of a more European heritage.

She was awake, staring at us. She said she was the wife of a chieftain, and had taken a long walk in the early evening near her summer home. A lion had attacked her bodyguards, forcing her to flee to the underbrush, where she would be safe temporarily. She had felt disoriented, and when she opened her eyes there was only the road and prairie around her.

Godfrey put her to sleep again. Looking up at me, he said, "She does not belong here and neither does the gateway that she has crossed. We need to summon some guards to secure the gateway and put her back where she belongs. We will have to get a Dragon master gate keeper to reseal this rift. The gateways into this world are there for a purpose, waiting for the right person to cross. This one feels like a tear that was formed by accident or design. If a new race finds it and comes across in any great number, it could cause all sorts of unpredictable problems. We are not ready to deal with that kind of change right now. The gateways are stable in specific spots where they can be monitored and incidents avoided."

I called Mercury and told him what was needed. He answered me that a contingent of men was on their way. I said, "Well, Godfrey, men are on their way now to guard the rift."

"I will place some false memories in her mind. When she awakens, she will think it was all a bad dream. She will not remember us, other than as hazy figures that saved her in her dream," he said, as we waited near the rift until elves and dwarves came to guard the opening into the other world.

We carried the woman through the rift, depositing her near another set of bushes, away from the gateway. We waited in the dark listening for the lion. I grabbed one of the bodyguards' spears. I didn't want to use my gun, as that would attract too much attention. We cloaked ourselves and waited until the woman's husband came looking for her. Once that happened, we stepped back through the rift.

"We will have to consult with the gatekeeper, to keep track of this world. I got the impression that they are a proud and strong people, and would make excellent allies if needed in the future," I said to Godfrey, as I sat down on a large rock to relax for a couple of minutes.

"I agree, but the impression I got is that they are not used to people with fairer skin than they have," Godfrey said in reply.

We called it a night and headed back to the stronghold, arriving without any further difficulties arising. I was sound asleep almost as soon as my head hit the pillow and slept until late morning feeling refreshed and full of energy.

Things went back to normal with Gramps (Godfrey) driving me hard to learn my lessons. I quickly felt more comfortable with all of the healing spells, and it would take one very skilled in magic to detect me when I was cloaked.

I awoke one morning to the sounds of a storm coming in from the ocean, battering against the walls of the stronghold. Everything was battened down and there was not much going on in or around the castle. Guards were rotating on shorter shifts, because of being soaked to the skin when they were out in the weather, so as not to catch their death of colds.

The storm lasted for a whole week. Everyone, including the

companions, was extremely bored and we were getting on each other's nerves. The healers reported injuries resulting from loss of tempers and fights. I had the companions training in the great hall, using the skills of Ice Wind and Blade to train the warriors in new ways to occupy their time.

I decided it was time to give the companions something else to do so I sent them out on patrol. They came back from their patrol soaked to the skin; the Yeti had the keep smelling like wet dog. After that, I kept the Yeti companions in the stronghold, delegated to leading patrols of the tunnels.

With the Yetis patrolling the tunnels, we were able to locate all the booby traps and disable them. There was an infestation of what appeared to be some sort of giant cockroach, which was dealt with in the Yetis' usual prompt and efficient manner. I decided to spend some more time exploring the tunnels even after the storm abated.

~ TWENTY-EIGHT ~

Of Seashells and Submarines

On the seventh day, the morning dawned clear and sunny. The sea air smelled fresh and invigorating as I took a stroll along the battlements with Rose and Sylvia. We noticed that the beach down below was littered with debris washed up from the shore. I called a small group of companions to take a walk along the beach with us and see what the storm had pushed up onto the shore.

The fish we found ranged in size from one foot, to some huge monsters that looked like something out of a nightmare. There were also shells of many sizes; walking along, I noted a large cylindrical shape at the far end of the shore.

I did not realize how large the shape was until we got close to it. The object was at least twenty to thirty feet in diameter and the cylinder was one hundred or more feet long. Part of the object was still immersed in the ocean. I sent one of the companions back to the stronghold to get some animals and men to pull the shape out of the water, to be examined more closely when time allowed.

This was definitely not from an animal or a sea creature that I knew of. This object appeared to be a fabricated machine of some unknown type, which I had never seen before. The first thought that crossed my mind was that it was a submarine. At this point I could not see what the driving power was or where the access was.

Then, I noticed a figure lying in the sand about two hundred feet from the 'submarine.' At first glance, I thought it was just another fish washed up onto the beach. Getting closer, I could see a resemblance to dolphins from my own world. The humanoid figure was approximately six-and-a-half feet long, with webbed fingers and toes, and was wearing a loin cloth. The being had an elongated snout, and a blow hole on the top of its head. The resemblance to a dolphin was uncanny—almost as if this were the next step in dolphin evolution.

I had the machine towed along the beach front until we could store it in the one cave entrance that was accessible to the water and I had a stretcher brought for the 'dolphin man,' and I received some strange looks from the companions when I ordered the blanket soaked down. I had to explain to them that, being a creature of the sea, it needed to be damp on the way to the castle.

The healers had no idea what to do with the 'dolphin man.' It was up to Godfrey and me to treat him. We alone had some idea of what the creature might be. There was a room in the stronghold with a large pool, which I arranged to be filled with salt water. A table was set up with various types of fresh fruit, breads, and fish for our guest to eat. We treated our guest, and once conscious, let him rest to heal on his own time.

I visited the creature every day, spending time talking to him, telling him my story but the creature only watched me, not replying to any of my comments. When it was obviously healthy enough to leave, the doors leading to the ocean were opened. I watched as my guest slowly walked down, disappearing under the waves. The entrance was then locked up so that the guest, if he wished to return, would have to knock. A guard was stationed at this entrance, with instructions to allow the visitor to return if he wished.

In the meantime, the engineers had been examining the machine they had found on the beach. They had found the entrance hatch, but could not figure how to open it. The machine, the engineers determined, measured four hundred feet long and thirty feet wide. Closely scrutinizing the hatch, I could see some sort of a shell design. However, without a key, or a proper opening spell, entry was not going to be without difficulty.

I consulted with the dragons as to what my next step was. Even if they could open the door to the 'submarine,' no one had the knowledge to understand what made it run and how to operate the controls. The dwarf engineers understood magic, but neither they nor I had any experience when it came to something technologically advanced like this machine.

After speaking at length with my cohorts, we decided to open the gate and allow the sea people the opportunity to take this unusual machine back into the ocean depths, where it belonged. This would be a token of good faith, hopefully opening a channel of communication in the near future.

They opened the sea gate where the machine was floating, sealing the rest of the stronghold behind strong gates. The sea people must have been watching, because the machine disappeared the first night that it was left unguarded. They left behind a small gift of a seashell-shaped amulet, which, when examined, would have been a match to the impression on the 'submarine' entry hatch.

I said to Isaac, "Well Isaac, one mystery left unexplained. Hopefully, the answer will come back to us in some form."

"Sometimes we are not meant to have all the answers. There are moments when it is best to not understand. If we are meant to have the knowledge, it will reveal itself to us when the time is right; otherwise, it is not for us to know," Isaac replied in a lecturing tone.

I just shook my head, heading back to my quarters to make plans for the near future. My men had everything under control. They had, through subterfuge or outright attack, destroyed twenty slaver caravans. I knew that it was only a matter of time before forces in the caravans would become too overwhelming to be taken out without danger to the men.

I had reached my limit, learning as much as I could. I decided to take a break for a week, to relax and absorb all of the training that I had been receiving. I maintained my physical training, but decided that I was going to be taking a break from the magical.

"Mortimer wishes to talk to you. He says that he has information about the assassination attempts on your life and the lives of those that are close to you," Ice Wind said.

"Tell him to come up to the common room and I will talk to him during breakfast. He is welcome to join us. I am not sure how much I should trust him with my personal safety so I want you here as well, ready to intervene if need be. Gizmo, Isaac, Rose, and Sylvia will be here as well, but I still want the strength of numbers in case things go wrong." I said in reply to Ice Wind.

"I will be here, and will step in at a moment's notice if there are signs of trouble." Ice Wind said.

The next morning, Mortimer, in his new guise, showed up for breakfast, I had briefed Rose and Sylvia about the information Mortimer was going to give to me. I also stated that I was unsure at this point of his intentions, but Isaac and Gizmo would warn of any falsehoods or planned evil from him. I said to Isaac, directing him, "Isaac, I want you to spend some time with Mortimer to read his mind and see what his intentions toward us are."

"I will peel him like a piece of fruit, and if he means evil, he will not live long enough to even enter the common room," Isaac replied.

When it came time for Mortimer to enter, I received a thought message from Isaac. "Mortimer bears us only good will. He is so grateful for his chance at a new life that he would give his to save yours. The previous person in his job came to an untimely end. There is no such thing as retiring when you are dealing with the assassins' guild."

"Sit down, Mortimer, or should I say Anthony? Enjoy breakfast with my family, which you are now a part of," I said invitingly to Anthony, indicating the table laden with food.

"My Liege, words escape me. I cannot say enough about what your comments mean to me. I have tracked down he who ordered your death," he declared.

"We have time; you will eat your fill first. Break bread with us, and become part of my family," I said, showing trust. As a rule, food was not usually shared with prisoners or enemies, as it might become necessary to have to kill them.

As per my instructions, there was an excellent breakfast, shared by all. Rose and Sylvia were extremely friendly and polite, treating Anthony like visiting royalty. At the end of the sumptuous meal, he looked expectantly at me.

"Anthony, I know that you have important information to share with me. Please—go ahead," I said.

"I am sure that it does not surprise you that Chavez has ordered your death, no matter the cost or effort that it takes. He initially set the price as one that would set up the assassin for life. Now, since you are getting harder to deal with, the price has risen to a king's ransom," Anthony said with concern.

"It is nice to be valued for a change!" I said laughingly.

~ TWENTY-NINE ~

Portals

The stronghold settled down to a boring routine. Everything out in the field was running smoothly and I felt comfortable with who was in charge. All my concerns were taken care of even before I could voice them. I kept waiting for something to happen.

I took the map the engineers had been working on, showing in detail most of the tunnels under the stronghold. I had the kitchen pack a lunch for me and I spent the better part of each day filling in the map and adding tunnels that were missing from the documentation.

For the first two days, I had company tagging along with me; the little dragons one day, my ladies the other. I got the feeling that they were just humouring me, so that I was not underfoot while they did all the things that needed to be done that did not require my approval.

By the second week, I was exploring the tunnel network alone; not even with my companion bodyguards, as there was nothing larger than a large rat in the tunnels, hardly a danger to the dragon mage. Without having company, I was able to cover more ground, lunching as I went.

I was probably below sea level, as the walls were damp and dripping. I thought it wise to turn around and head back to sunlight and my two beautiful sweethearts, when I felt my staff pulling me toward an archway that was bricked over and appeared ancient.

I closely examined the archway and the designs that were on the frame. They were a complex series of letters in either dragon or dwarven language, neither of which I could read. Following the lead of Draco, my staff, I loosened my grip and let it trace a complicated pattern that caused the archway to glow brightly. When the glow died down, the stones blocking it disappeared as if they had never been there.

The hallway that I could see leading off into the distance was bright and clean, with no dust or dirt visible. It eventually led to a room furnished with a desk and chair that looked very comfortable. I suddenly felt very tired, and sat in the chair to relax for a few minutes.

When I woke up, it was pitch black! The light in my staff had gone out when I fell asleep. Terror ran through me briefly, as I was momentarily disoriented, not realizing where I was until I had Draco glowing brightly and my eyes had adjusted.

I surveyed the room and noticed that five hallways stretched out away from the desk. I could see the short tunnel that I had just come down, leading back to the stronghold.

The symbols on each of the four other tunnels I recognized as dwarven, indicating each direction of the compass. Each corridor had a series of man-sized mirror as doors. Picking the tunnel marked 'North,' I stood before it to examine it closely. I touched a mirror portal with Draco. It had the consistency of water, rippling with the touch of the staff.

Walking back to the desk, I sat down and wrote a quick note in case someone came looking for me. There was a globe sitting in a stand on the desk. I reached out with my mind and energized the globe, so that it lit up the whole room. I walked over to the mirror that I had picked, and slowly stepped through the surface. It had a viscous feel to it, and felt like it was sticking slightly to my body as I stepped through it.

It was pitch black so I generated some light to see what I had stepped into. There was a duplicate room lined with mirrors like the one I had stepped through. As an experiment, I put my head through the mirror and saw the light and the desk. Everything was an exact copy of the room I had come from in the stronghold. This time, I left the globe dark, so there was a difference in the two rooms.

The only corridor from this room that had no mirror was blocked, so I walked up to the archway and let Draco guide me again with its magic, opening the doorway. The layout of the corridors appeared to be a duplicate of the stronghold one that I had just come from. I headed to the surface, finding another doorway magically blocked. The corridors were laid out in such a fashion that if you looked at them from above, they would be in the shape of a giant cross, with the magical doorway situated in the centre of the room.

Opening that magical doorway, I felt a very strong blast of cold air. This was not usual for a stronghold, as they were built close to or on top of volcanic regions for a natural source of heat. Walking through the area that would be the dragon residence, I saw that everything was dusty and dirty. Walking up to the surface, I could feel the cold. The door had been left ajar, allowing in frigid air, with snow gathering on the ground just outside the door.

Looking out to the inner area of the stronghold, I could see piles of snow and debris lying around. It was very apparent that this stronghold had been abandoned. Either it was not needed, or the cold had driven the occupants away.

Making my way back the way I came from, I headed back to the stronghold. I sealed the archway and made my way up to my rooms in the keep, where things, it turns out, were in an uproar.

The companions had started to search the corridors, looking for me. Deciding to keep the mirror information to myself, I told them that I had fallen asleep and had lost track of time.

In hindsight, I should have shared the information.. I did not, instead, keeping it to myself and spending a nice, quiet evening with Sylvia and Rose.

The next day, I was like a kid, excited to head down the tunnels again. Opening the archway, I chose to search the most southern doorway. The southernmost stronghold was in worse shape than the one to the north had been. It was warm, the walls collapsed in some areas, and the stronghold was surrounded by tropical forest and swamps.

As I walked around the outside of the keep, I was suddenly swept away by a flash flood, which engulfed me without any warning. I lost consciousness momentarily. When I came to, I saw a large tree floating by and grabbed hold of it, managing to hang on because I knew that if I let go I was dead. Dazed, it was very hard for me to focus on hanging on, never mind where I was or what was happening.

When I hit the shore, I was half-conscious, throwing up a large amount of water that I had swallowed. As soon as I was fully awake, I saw that I had lost Draco and my sidearm. Fortunately, I did not require either at the moment to survive. I gathered some broken branches and enough wood to last me for a while. I used magic to start the fire, although I still had flint and steel to start it. I was too tired to do it the hard way, wanting to get my clothes dry before it got dark.

As the darkness settled in and the stars became visible, I recognized that I was definitely in the southern hemisphere. There was only one half moon rising up in the sky at a different angle than I was normally used to. With my head pounding, it was hard to concentrate enough to call out with my mind for help from the dragons.

With my clothes dry, and a roaring blaze, I was able to keep the insects and the coolness of the night at bay. I slept fitfully, frequently disturbed by night-time noises coming out of the jungle, including the occasional scream of prey. The sun was well over the horizon when I dragged myself out of my nest, looking for something to eat.

Even with my head feeling like it was going to split wide open at any minute, I was able to gather enough energy to cloak myself in invisibility. I managed to find a dinosaur nest, and steal a few eggs. Gathering some berries, I headed back to my little camp to cook up my meal. Afterward, I started to gather my strength, starting the healing process as Godfrey had taught me.

Awakening to the roaring of one pissed off dinosaur, I cloaked myself again and moved away from the egg remnants and my campfire, which would probably draw the beast toward it. In my weakened state, with my head pounding, I was having trouble holding the spell that protected me from view.

I climbed a small hill, where I could view my latest camp site. It was only a matter of minutes before a raptor came into sight, sniffing at the remains left behind from my meal. I realized that I had picked the wrong nest to pilfer eggs from. The raptor smelled the air, calling out to its pack mates. The answering calls echoed all around my lookout.

The headache had temporarily dulled, but was now coming back with a vengeance and I was sweating profusely. I knew that it was just a matter of time before the raptors picked up my scent and tracked me down. Hopefully I would be able to defend myself without pistol or Draco, which I had used in all my battles since coming to this land.

Realizing that I was out in the open and that the raptors could come at me from all sides, I decided to return to the crumbling walls of the stronghold, hoping for at least a modicum of protection. As quickly and as quietly as possible, I began my trek to an area where one of the keeps was intact. This would give me protection from the raptors, forcing them to come at me one at a time.

Running back down the hill, I hit a patch of loose shale, which raised a lot of noise as I ran and slid down. I heard the roars of the raptors, and the scrabbling of claws as they got closer to me. Approaching the crumbling walls, I slipped on the muddy path, striking my head against a large rock. My last thought, before darkness overcame me, was that I would never see Sylvia and Rose again, becoming a meal for the raptors.

Coming back to consciousness, I found that all I could see initially was a set of scaled legs attached to something the size of a Great Dane dog, except wider and more muscle-bound. The tail was also long. It, as well as the body, were covered in scale-like armour. Moving very slowly, I sat up and noticed that there were five of the beasts surrounding me. They were holding two of the raptors at bay! The raptors were unwilling to attack as they were outnumbered by the smaller beasts.

The raptors, in the end, did not have the patience to wait for an opportunity to attack. They backed off into the bushes, and left the scene. I sat there, not daring to stand, awaiting the next move from my saviours. One approached me and gave me a thorough sniffing.

Then, sticking out a raspy tongue, it started to do what I could only guess was clean my wounds. After five minutes of this strange behaviour, I surmised the creatures had no intention of making a meal of me, at least not at that time anyway.

Although I was very wobbly on my feet, I managed to stand up and lean on the creatures, which moved in on either side to help me walk. Along the way, any time that I tried to change my path, they hissed at me and gently pushed me in the direction that they wanted me to take. They had a destination in mind, guiding me to a tunnel entrance guarded by one of their own.

Once inside the tunnel, the creatures gathered enough wood to last the night. One lit the fire the same way Gizmo had done when I first met her; a small jet of flame spit out of its mouth, setting the kindling ablaze. The other creatures brought dry grass in for bedding, creating a soft and warm nest for me to lie in. Quickly falling into a deep dreamless slumber, I did not stir until late the next day.

Awakening to a sharp pain in my ear, I quickly learned that the creatures had a litter of babies wandering the tunnel. Was I breakfast? That thought was immediately dispelled by one of the creatures, hissing at the babies and shooing them away from me. There was a stream of fresh water running along the tunnel. The creatures brought fresh meat for the babies, giving me a large portion as well.

Spending several days slowly healing, I did not venture from the tunnel (I was not sure they would let me go anyway). Upon waking on the fourth day, I found the pistol and staff I had lost in the floodwaters lying beside me. Looking around, I saw the one of the older females staring at me expectantly. When I spoke in a soft friendly voice, thanking her for my staff and pistol, her tail started wagging quickly and her tongue was hanging out of her mouth—just like a dog back home!

She came close to me, nuzzling me, and lay beside me on her back so that I could scratch the soft part of her belly. These creatures obviously had had someone in their lives in the past; they seemed too comfortable with my presence for anything else. I was just about ready to try and locate the mirrored doors to get back to civilization, but I was determined that I was going to bring these remarkable creatures with me.

I searched the cave, gathering strips of discarded skin and some larger pieces of wood which I fashioned a sled of sorts. At first light, I packed the puppies in the sled, under the watchful eye of the female who had bonded with me. Dragging the sled, the entire pack following me, the female close beside me, I headed toward the stronghold ruins.

~ THIRTY ~

New Companions

The raptors showed up again as we were all on open ground. My new friends set themselves up in a defensive circle around me and the sled. The moment three raptors showed their beady-eyed faces, my pistol sounded three times—dropping the raptors instantly. The creatures started to run toward the raptor carcasses, but I quietly told them to hold. They seemed to understand and held their ground until I told them it was okay.

They made a quick meal of the three raptors, bringing parts back to the two females that remained with me and the puppies. We encountered no more problems as we searched the stronghold, finally finding the mirror main room late in the morning. I oriented myself, choosing a doorway and stepping through it, coming through the other side into a hall filled with wizard companions and warriors.

"Hi Honey, I'm home!" I said jovially.

There was a moment of confusion as the creatures under my care came into the hallway and set themselves up to protect me and the puppies. The warriors reacted, drawing their weapons and moving forward to attack the creatures.

"Hold your positions and put away your weapons—these creatures are with me!" I yelled at the guard. As usual, when I raised my voice, my command was obeyed without hesitation on the part of the troops.

"Clear this corridor, and back away so that I have a clear path to the surface so that there are no problems. Someone run ahead and let the ladies and the dragons know that I am back. We have some unusual company!" I said.

"Only you could disappear for a few days, and bring back a species that was thought to be extinct 'til now. We had thought that Drakes had died off centuries ago! Who knew there were some left?" Isaac said in amazement.

Upon reaching the surface, Sylvia and Rose ran up to me, embracing me and covering me with kisses. I was surprised by the fact that the drakes did not interfere or even react to this sudden onslaught of affection.

"Those doorways lead to different strongholds all over the world. I am surprised that you did not know of them," I said.

"The portals are one of those secrets that were known by only a few, and became lost when the information holder passed on, without passing the knowledge to his or her successor," Isaac said.

"It is good that you are back safe and sound, Dragon Mage. As usual, we now have more mysteries to solve with your reappearance. The drakes, to my knowledge, are very empathic. That is why they let the ladies approach you, because they knew that there was no threat to your safety. The portals are another issue. They were believed to be just myths of dragon lore," Elijah said.

"I tried calling for help when I was in the south. Tell me, how it is that you could not hear me." I said.

I could hear Elijah give a mental shrug before he replied. "Isaac, Gizmo and Mercury act as amplifiers, otherwise, as I grow older, my range of communication is limited."

Gathering my ladies and my herd of drakes, I slowly wound my way up to the surface Where I found an empty pen and placed the drake puppies in there with the majority of the rest of the drakes. The oldest female followed me, even when I told her to stay. I smiled and shook my head 'no' but she continued to follow me.

"Lord Jim, you are hurt! Guards! Send for a healer immediately and have him come to the dragon mages' quarters to attend to him!" Sylvia yelled.

I lay down in my bed as Godfrey stepped into to the room took the healer's bag from him and shooed him away. The healer started to protest until the drake hissed at him. He took one look at the drake (whom I decided I was going to call Matilda), turned pale and walked out of the room without saying another word.

Exhausted and even though my head was still pounding, I fell into a deep, dreamless sleep. When I finally woke up, it was four days later. The sun was shining, and a breeze of fresh salty air was blowing into the room. I slowly sat up in bed, and Matilda looked up, wagging her tail like a happy pup. Godfrey walked into to the room and reached down, scratching Matilda behind her ears, before looking at me.

"I am glad to see you up and about, finally, after four days of lying there like a dead man. You barely moved an inch, and the ladies were worried that we were going to lose you. I assured them that you were made of tougher stuff and that it was only a matter of time before you would be up and about. My only real concern was your new pet at the foot of the bed. She has not eaten or moved since you lay down," Godfrey said.

"Well, I am going to call her Matilda, and I think we both need a healthy breakfast. So, Matilda, what do you think—is it time to eat?" I said to the drake.

Matilda wagged her tail and followed me out to the common room, where we both sat down and ate until we were stuffed. Sylvia and Rose came into the room as we were finishing.

"Ladies, I think it is time to stretch our legs and see if we can find which portal leads to Elijah. That way, we can get supplies safely, and pass information back and forth without fear of our messengers being intercepted," I said.

We went down into the tunnels again, and when we came to the central room for the portals, there were some guards and some of the companion wizards trying to make maps of where the portals led. I directed them to follow me. Gizmo was with me until I entered the central room.

"I will show you how to open the main entryway to the central rooms so that each can be explored. We will find the gateway to Elijah first. Arrangements must be made then to let the other dragons know to expect company through the tunnel system. Gizmo, please send on the message to Elijah and then stay here so that when I enter the correct portal I can confirm that by talking to Elijah through you as a relay," I said.

"The message has been passed to the great dragon. He will be searching for you with his mind, and will call you when you are in the stronghold tunnels," Isaac said.

I selected the east corridor, and it was only a matter of minutes before I could sense Elijah strongly calling me with his mind.

"Welcome, Dragon Mage. Wait a short time before you continue to the surface for Gizmo to join you. I will alert the companions and the guards to expect your coming out of the tunnel system to see me," Elijah said.

Gizmo joined me, with Rose and Sylvia, moments later. I made sure that the wizards were watching as I slowly recreated the pattern that unlocked the main entrance to the portal room. I waited patiently as each of the wizards in the group took turns opening and closing the entryway.

By the time the wizards had finished their lessons in controlling the entrance, a contingent of Elijah's companion wizards and stronghold guards assembled to enter the room and take control of security for the stronghold.

It was like I had never left; the guards we passed bowed out of respect for the party. No one barred our way and all doors were held open for us, leading to Elijah's quarters. Matilda saw Elijah and ran up as close as she could. She rolled onto her back, exposing her belly to be scratched.

"Obviously she trusts dragons implicitly. Other than me, she has not allowed anyone else to scratch her belly yet," I said, surprised.

"Historically, drakes were pets and bodyguards for dragons. They were also bred for protection of our young. During one of the dragon wars, the breed was believed to have been killed off. The dragons are again indebted to you. Drakes are instinctively bonded to dragons and to certain special people. Because you are inherently an honest and good man, they have bonded to you. Otherwise, they would have wanted nothing to do with you," Elijah said as he reached forward with a claw and scratched Matilda's stomach.

If we could keep the portals secret, I could appear to be someplace else and surprise slaver caravans. Chavez's spies would see me someplace else very public and too far away to pull off the attack and be back in public again. I was a realist, knowing that we would be only able to keep it secret for a short period of time before it leaked out, at least in rumour form.

I spent a few days enjoying the company of the Diamond clan. Sylvia was busy with her ladies, who were overjoyed at an opportunity to attend and spoil her. She kept a messenger close at hand to ensure that things which needed to be done were completed back at my stronghold. The pack of drakes was brought across and placed in an area near Elijah, where he could oversee their training, care, and breeding. Young orphaned dwarves, both male and female, were selected to work with the drakes and become handlers.

In total, the pack of drakes consisted of ten matched pairs of males and females, and two litters of puppies, totalling sixteen. That did not include Matilda, who was the Alpha and did not have a mate. I guessed that sometime in the past she had lost her mate, and there was no one suitable to replace him.

Elijah and I decided to keep the majority of the pack in the Diamond clan stronghold, and took breeding pairs to the other strongholds in the area. The drake's numbers would grow and the pups would be well cared for; all of them would be kept healthy.

Matilda and one of the breeding pairs followed me out of Elijah's quarters. I looked them over and they appeared to be one of the younger breeding pairs. I decided to call them Bonny and Clyde; a pair of young lovers that could cause lots of trouble if not watched.

I kept in constant touch with the stronghold through Sylvia, where my troops were still wreaking havoc with orc slavery caravans but I decided to give the Lady Sylvia the treat of being spoiled in the Diamond stronghold for a short while. Rose had gone back to her people, to help with the installation of fortifications along the forest floor by the dwarf engineers. Since everything was going smoothly, I decided I could relax before planning the next step to slowly bring down Chavez's empire.

Once the historians were let loose and set to studying the writing at the portal doors, they quickly determined that it was in an ancient dragon text. They were able to decipher it, with a little assistance from Elijah. The majority of the doorways led to strongholds, thus guaranteeing that no stronghold could be cut off from supplies as they could be brought in without the enemy even having a clue. Also, couriers could bring important messages in a matter of minutes instead of days.

The drakes raised a few eyebrows at first, but I took them on daily walks to get the populace used to their presence in the stronghold. Matilda made sure that Bonny and Clyde did not do anything out of line. She was quite often hissing at them or biting them gently to keep them out of the vendor stalls. Within a few weeks, the only people that were uncomfortable with the drakes were travelers or newcomers to the stronghold.

One sunny day on one of my walks with Sylvia, Gizmo, and Isaac (as well as the usual entourage of bodyguards and companions), Isaac and I were discussing new ways of using the portals to redistribute the freed slaves, as well as opportunities to be a thorn in Chavez's side, without being caught and starting an open war.

As we strolled through the market, we checked out a few shops. I, as usual, being the male, stood outside being bored. We heard someone shout from up the street, "Stop! Thief!"

The companions spread out as a young dwarf lad came running toward us, looking behind him and not where he was going. He ran straight into the side of Matilda, who knocked him down with her powerful tail and placed a foot on him to hold him down.

I was more interested in the interaction between Matilda and the boy than the heavyset, older dwarven merchant who came running up moments later. Matilda smelled the boy, wagged her tail and nuzzled him, obviously wanting him to scratch or pet her.

"She wants you to pet or scratch her head, boy. Why you were running away from that merchant and what is your name?" I asked.

"My name is Fred. The merchant was accusing me of stealing something that I did not steal," Fred said.

The merchant loudly interrupted: "He stole a valuable piece of jewellery from my shop. I demand that he be punished to the full extent of the law."

"The merchant lies. In his mind, I can see that he has it in his pocket. He plans to give it to his mistress as a gift of love," Isaac said to me, mind-to-mind.

~ THIRTY-ONE ~

Wrongful Accusation

eanwhile, Fred was busy petting Matilda, and she loved the attention greatly. Soon, Fred's hands were also petting Bonny and Clyde. They all pushed in toward the boy, fighting for his attention.

"Merchant, empty your pockets onto this cloak right now!" I demanded.

The merchant replied, "I shall do no such thing! Are you accusing me of dishonesty?"

"Yes, I am. Empty your pockets, unless you want to suffer the anger of the dragon mage!" I said gruffly.

The merchant turned pale, emptied his pockets slowly, hesitated for a moment, and finally pulled out the piece of jewellery that he claimed Fred had stolen. The merchant said, "I am sorry, Dragon Mage. I must have been mistaken."

"It is not I who deserves your apology but Fred, whom you have wronged by accusing him of being a thief. What is the value of the piece of jewellery that you have there?" I demanded.

"The necklace and gems are worth fifty gold coins, Lord Dragon Mage," the merchant said.

"Good. Then that is how much you will pay Fred to compensate him for the libel against his family name," I said loudly.

The merchant began to have a choking fit, and the guards laughed at him while pounding on his back until he breathed again.

Fred sat there on the ground, scratching the drakes, with his mouth wide open.

"I expect you to bring the gold to me personally, merchant, so that I can ensure the transaction is taken care of and that you do not forget again with your absent mind," I said, glaring at the merchant.

"Fred, I will escort you home to ensure there are no more problems with these merchants, who have misjudged you," I said to Fred.

Fred led us to the run-down section of the keep, where there was a small shanty town. It was a good thing we were in a warm climate; otherwise, the occupants would freeze to death in such scanty shelters. Fred entered one of the hovels, which looked a lot like all the rest.

"Mother, I am home, and I have brought company," Fred said as he entered the shanty.

"Have you got into trouble again, Fred?" asked his mother weakly. "Why have guards brought you home this time?"

"Fred, what is wrong with your mother, and why have you not called for a healer?" I asked.

Fred replied, "She has trouble breathing. I must care for her as much as I can; we cannot afford to pay for a healer."

After telling the guards to step outside and not disturb me, I bent over Fred's mother and asked if Lady Sylvia could touch her. I then placed my hands on Sylvia's arm, and reached out with my mind to find the illness. I found the infection that was filling her lungs and cleared them. As she coughed, emptying her lungs, I called for a litter and brought her with us, back to the keep.

"Fred, if you have anything that you want in here, grab it now. We will not be back to this shack again. You and your mother will be under my care from now on," I said. Sylvia gave me a big hug for the help I was giving someone else.

Fred nodded at me, not making a move to take anything. I walked alongside the litter, keeping an eye on Fred's mother, Susan. Under my direction, they carried her to the common room, and I summoned the stronghold healer. When he arrived at the room, he looked down at the woman as if to ask why she was there.

"Healer, I have started the process, but I am tired and cannot keep it up for the rest of the night. I want you to arrange for a healer to stay with her and give her strength to last the night," I instructed.

The healer nodded and left the room. I stayed until another entered and took over. I was very tired and went straight to bed. I slept soundly until I was shaken awake by Fred, who looked worried and pale.

"The healer has left to use the bathroom, and no one has come back. It has been over an hour, and mother is having trouble breathing again," Fred said, looking pale with concern.

Stumbling into the room, I started working on Susan again, feeling extremely weak. I said, "Isaac, wake up and go to the portal and summon Godfrey here to help this woman for I do not think I can keep this up for too long. Her health is in danger, and Godfrey will be willing. Tomorrow we can raise hell over the healer issue."

"I will fly to the portal and bring him back as soon as I can," Isaac said, and he was a blur as he flew out of the room.

Within fifteen minutes, Godfrey was there, bending over both Susan and me.

"Go to bed, Jim. I have this under control. The wonderful work you have done will not be wasted. She will be fine for the rest of the night," Godfrey said confidently.

"Fred, go to sleep. Your mother is in the care of the best healer in this world. He would be the one that I would want to take care of me if I was ill or injured."

The sun was well up in the sky when I woke up alone in bed. I arose, quickly dressed and went into the common room. Godfrey was dozing on the floor beside the litter. I woke him and steered him into my bed, closing the blinds so he could sleep for a few hours.

Looking around, I noticed that the drakes and Fred were absent from the room. When I questioned the guards, I was advised that they had gone outside. I checked on Susan, and could hear her breathing strong and clear. She was out of danger.

I found Fred standing outside of the door to the keep, arguing with the guards to let him in. There apparently had been a shift change, and the day guards did not know about the drakes or Fred. It could have gotten real ugly as the drakes were getting upset over not being able to get back to me. In a fight, I thought they would have been able to hold up quite nicely against the guards.

"Enough! This is Fred, and the drakes are with me. Make sure that they all have free access to the keep and to me! When the night shift captain comes on duty, have him come up to see me so that I can chew him out for not passing information along!" I said angrily.

"Fred, your mother is out of danger and will be fine. Come along with me. There is someone I would like to introduce you to. First off, since you seem to get along with the drakes so well, I would like to offer you a job taking care of them full time. I am also going to offer your mother a job when she is fully recovered," I said.

"Of course, Lord Dragon Mage. I would be honoured to take care of these creatures, although I don't know their names. Who is it that you wish to introduce me to, if I may ask, Lord," Fred replied.

"Of course, how rude of me; this one is Matilda, and these younger two are Bonny and Clyde. As to whom I want to introduce you to, it is the one and only eldest dragon, Lord Elijah," I said.

We headed to the tunnel entrance with the dragon companions saluting me and not even batting an eye at the drakes or at the boy (even though Fred was in rags). We headed down, and I called ahead to let Elijah know I was coming with company. We walked straight into Elijah's room, where he was having a meeting with some dignitaries.

"Greetings Dragon Mage and greetings Fred. Welcome! If you will excuse us for a few minutes, I must speak to the dragon mage and Fred for a few minutes alone," Elijah said to the dignitaries.

Fred stood there with his mouth wide open as they left the room and the door closed behind them. Elijah said to Fred, "Fred, I hear that you and your mother have accepted jobs with the great dragon mage. If you follow his orders and his guidance, he will treat you right and you will grow to be a great man. If he says your mother will be fine, you can take his word—he would not lie to you. Do you have any questions, youngling?"

"No, not at all, great one. This has been an exceptional honour, which I will cherish always," Fred said.

Elijah replied, "Do not thank me. The drakes chose you as their caretaker; they are good judges of character. Remember that, when you are dealing with people. If the drakes do not trust someone, that means you should not. Take good care of them, and they will take good care of you."

The next step was to take Fred to meet the tailor. I gave instructions for armour to be made for Fred, as well as an appropriate uniform. Fred and the drakes may end up in combat situations, so I wanted him protected with mithril, just like the rest of his "family" members.

I decided to check on Susan again while Fred was with the tailor, getting everything measured and fitted. When I entered the room, I found her sitting up in the litter, eating a light meal given to her by the Lady Sylvia.

"How are you feeling, Mistress Susan?" I asked, with concern in my voice.

"Good, My Lord. Thank you for saving my life and for taking us in. We will be out of your hair as soon as I am able to stand, and we will repay you as soon as we can," Susan said.

"I did not heal you for the money, or to have you walk out when you are healthy. I have given your son the responsibility to care for the strange creatures you saw with me. They like him, and so do I. Also, I would like you to take on the job of being in charge of my kitchen, to keep things running smoothly," I said in a commanding voice.

Susan said, "Thank you! If it is a chance to stay near my son, then you have my whole-hearted thanks. I will do the best I can for you and your men or ladies, as the case may be."

When Fred showed up in his new uniform, I let him spend quality time with his mother, explaining everything that had been happened to him. Although she was reluctant at first, Susan even let the drakes smell her, and she petted them.

A small room was prepared for Susan, so that she could sleep in a comfortable bed for once in her life. Fred was given a cot in the room next to her, so that he could sleep with the drakes. The merchant from the night before did not show up for the nightly meal, so after I finished yelling at the night captain, I instructed him to bring the merchant with the fifty gold coins to the keep; in chains if he refused to come.

The merchant showed up with the guards, who had obviously taken out their frustrations on him. He was upset, saying that he had friends in the Diamond clan household so he was not going to pay the money. After I let the drakes get close to him and rip up his clothing a little more, he was more than forthcoming with the fifty gold coins. I added insult to injury by giving it directly to Fred, who passed it to his mother.

The merchant was really upset, because I dismissed him without even looking at him directly. He complained about how he had been treated and said he was going to speak to the Diamond clan chief immediately, and he would make things right.

The next morning, the clan chief showed up, with the merchant in tow.

"If I see that merchant again, I will cut his hands off, barbeque him and feed him to the drakes. Get him out of here, because his constant whining is making me sick. Companions! Escort this piece of tyrannosaurus feces out of my sight. My Lord clan chief, go and speak to Elijah. He wishes to speak to you in regards to this issue," I said with hostility.

When the clan chief came back later, he apologized profusely for his friend the merchant's attitude. He also explained that he would speak to him about his bad behaviour.

Speaking to my companions later, I had them move Susan and Fred, with the drakes, back to my stronghold as soon as possible. I was worried about retaliation from the merchant. He might be too scared to deal with me, but he might be courageous enough to hire someone to try to kill Fred or his mother.

I called Elijah with my mind and explained that I was leaving quietly without fanfare and would speak to him as soon as I was rested. Elijah agreed that this was the best course of action, and said he looked forward to speaking to me later.

When we were down in the portal room, Matilda attacked a dwarf guard without provocation. I stepped in and pulled her away from the dwarf before she could kill him. Everyone was in an uproar until I yelled and got things settled down.

~ THIRTY-TWO ~

Betrayers?

"oes anyone recognize this dwarf? I have never seen him before in this stronghold. He is dressed as a Diamond clan guard, but I think there is something amiss," I yelled.

In his gear, I found a piece of paper showing a map of the tunnels and portals. I did not expect the secret to last long, but this was incredibly fast, even according to my expectations.

I instructed the guards to take the man to a healer and search him for any poisons, and then lock him up for interrogation. The men had heard of my ill humour in dealing with the merchant last night, and were quick to jump at my order. I instructed my companions to find Isaac at my stronghold and bring him back, to help with the interrogation of this man.

The clan chief was sitting outside of the cell waiting for my arrival, with a look of anger on his face. He said, with venom, "First you try to alienate me from a good friend of mine, who is an important merchant in this stronghold. Now you arrest one of my men and place him in a cell where he does not belong, after your pets attack him without provocation!"

Isaac arrived moments after my arrival at the cell door, and interrupted the clan chief's tirade. Isaac said, "What the lord dragon mage has said is true. This is not one of your men. This one comes from the Quartz clan. He is using your uniform to go unnoticed, while he searches and maps out the portal system to your stronghold to possibly get to the great dragon! This would bring great shame upon the Diamond clan, and take you from the top clan to the very bottom."

The clan chief turned pale and strode away, yelling to the guards. We could hear the alarm bells ringing as the clan chief demanded increased surveillance of the portal room and the great dragon's quarters.

"So, Lord Isaac, does this peon know anything else, or was he given as little information as possible, so as not to divulge anything if he was caught?" I asked, looking at the guard in the cell not saying a word.

"Unfortunately my friend, he knows very little. His orders came directly from the clan chief of the Quartz stronghold; they were not passed on to him by anyone else. No one else knew about the orders he was given. This was to prevent anyone from learning the truth. The Quartz clan has been without a dragon for many years. Otherwise, this subterfuge would have been discovered sooner," Isaac said.

"Return to the stronghold, please, Isaac, and gather a strike force together. We will enter the portal to the Quartz stronghold at first light and do some housecleaning when we get there. My only hope is that the rot does not extend to the roots and that we do not have to take out the entire army of the Quartz clan. If it is so, then we will destroy the clan and relocate all the uncorrupted members to other clans. If such is the case, Quartz clan will be no more," I said regretfully.

"I will get some dragons ready nearby, and as soon as you clear the portal rooms, call through Isaac and they will enter the stronghold. This will provide the distraction you need to enter from the underground," Elijah said.

Passing through the portal, I headed to my own rooms in what I had been calling the dragon mage stronghold. I told my guards that I needed to sleep for a few hours before heading out to battle. They advised they would keep the noise down while I slept. Sylvia was there to cuddle with me while I fell into a deep, dreamless slumber. Waking three hours later, I felt refreshed and ready to deal with this next disturbing challenge.

I made sure that all the troops had a hearty, nourishing breakfast before we made the final preparations for our excursion into unknown territory; this was going to be especially tough, as we were unsure how many were involved in this possible betrayal by the Quartz clan.

As the sun rose over the Quartz clan stronghold, Gizmo and I took Fred with the drakes in tow, through the portal to the stronghold. The minute we entered the portal room, only one guard started to run out of the room. Matilda grabbed him and pinned him to the ground. I identified myself, and ordered the rest of the guards to stand down.

"This one has a little more information, but not much. It would appear that the knowledge is known to only a few of the upper class and the clan chief himself. The information is a little confusing though; he thinks they are working for the dragons. Most of the troops are loyal to the dragons, and would die in their service," Isaac explained briefly.

Explaining what was happening to the rest of the portal guards as briefly as possible, I had them remain at the portal room to secure it and stop anyone that might run through here. That included the clan chief, if he tried to escape from the stronghold through the portal.

Isaac reported, "Three dragons have just landed in the main courtyard. They will ensure that the main gate is secure, so no one can exit that way."

To save confusion, I had the trustworthy guards of the Quartz clan go through the portal, taking the traitorous guard with them and securing the room on the other side. I instructed the men I left at the main room that no one was to exit without my personal authorization.

Reaching the main entrance to the tunnels, Lord Isaac and Lady Gizmo read the minds of the guards on duty and cleared them as faithful. I approached the three dragons that were in the courtyard, bowing as I approached them.

"Is all secure out here and to your liking? Do you need me to leave any troops here for your personal protection?" I asked the dragons.

"I am Betel. We have checked the loyalty of all of the troops surrounding us, and are completely safe in their care for the moment. I will be remaining here after this fiasco is over, to ensure there is a smooth power transfer if needed. My companions will be coming through the portals, so there should not be any further problems," Betel explained vocally.

"Thank you, Lord Dragon. I will keep you apprised of our progress through Lord Isaac or Lady Gizmo. I think the traitors are mostly in the central keep, with the rest of the troops unaware of what is going on," I said to Betel.

We quickly entered the keep, and discovered there only one or two high-ranking dwarves involved in the conspiracy against the dragons. That is, until we reached the upper floors, where the clan chief was sleeping. The guards watching his quarters were part of the conspiracy and would not let me (regardless of who I was) and my retinue enter the room where the clan chief slept.

As far as I was concerned, they were expendable, but I did not want too much noise, wanting to take the clan chief by surprise. Bonny and Clyde quickly saved me from any more planning by pouncing on and grabbing the two guards by the throat. They expired quickly and quietly. Looking back, I could see Fred smiling.

"Was that your idea, Fred?" I asked, looking at Fred.

He responded quickly, "Yes, Lord. With their speed, I thought they would be able to accomplish the task without any problems. I just concentrated on what I wanted them to do, and they followed through as if they read my mind."

"Good work, Fred. Keep it up with the drakes. We may need their speed and abilities in the future," I said.

My men quickly cleared the bodies of the guards and we quietly entered the clan chief's quarters. He was a light sleeper so he was already sitting up in bed and demanding to know what was going on. As the clan chief looked around, his voiced died in his throat as he realized that he was surrounded by individuals who did not have his best interests in mind. He grabbed for his dagger under his pillow, but I rushed him and knocked it out of his hand with my staff. The companions swarmed over the clan chief, trussing him up and gagging him.

Looking at his bed mates for the night, I spoke in a soft and low voice and said, "He may have betrayed the clan, the dragons, and himself. We are taking him to the eldest dragon Elijah, to determine how badly he has betrayed us all."

The girls just nodded at me, gathered up their things, and quietly left. I didn't think they would raise any alarm, but an escort would ensure it.

We carried the trussed-up clan chief and headed for the tunnel system, bringing him to face Elijah for questioning and judgment. As we left the keep, we encountered a group of fifty or more clan Quartz guards, blocking our path to the dragon quarters and tunnels. The captain ordered, "Stop where you are! Identify yourself and state your business."

"I am the dragon mage Jim, and I am here on dragon business. Your leader may have betrayed the dragons to the enemy. He is being taken for questioning. Interference will not be tolerated. Lord Isaac tells me you are a loyal servant. You must stand aside and let us pass," I said, warning the guards.

At that point, Betel landed between the groups, roaring and spouting flame, demanding to know what the guards were doing, blocking the dragon mage's path. We explained to the guards that I had Betel's blessing on this venture, and that Betel was moving into the stronghold to stay and bring honour to the clan.

The guard captain bowed to Betel, and directed his men to stand aside and allow me to continue on my way, with the clan chief in tow. We entered the tunnel system, and were back in Elijah's stronghold within ten minutes.

As we entered the tunnel system, there was a small contingent of dwarves exiting the portal to the Quartz stronghold.

"They are companions for Betel, to ensure his safety while he is organizing the stronghold." Isaac said. "Until we are sure about the rest of the Quartz clan, he has to have retainers he can trust."

We untied the Quartz clan chief and provided him with suitable clothes, as befitted his station. Then, he was escorted to the great dragon Elijah. Lord Isaac and Lady Gizmo were also in attendance, to assist Elijah with dispensing justice.

Elijah asked, "So, clan chief. Explain your actions and what you had planned for the future of your people. I am deeply interested in hearing your justification of betraying our trust."

"My people have been all but forgotten by the dragon lords!" The chief yelled at Elijah. "I thought a change was in the air when a dark elf came and said he was an agent of the dragons, with the promise of honour and reward if I would test the security of the strongholds. I stand by my decisions, and I do not regret any of my actions, right or wrong, or those of the people that I have tasked."

"Your plight and that of your people had not been brought to our attention. We will ensure that your clan is taken care of. A dragon lord will be staying at your clan stronghold to keep things running smoothly. The only question that remains is what to do with you?" Elijah said.

The clan chief prostrated himself on the marble floor of Elijah's chamber and said, "My name is Jeremiah, and I take full responsibility for the actions of my people. At this juncture, we have only planned. There has been no information exchanged with the elf who said he was an agent of the dragons. I realize now that I have been misled, and any information given to an enemy agent could be considered treason, for which the penalty is death. I only ask that you spare the Quartz clan and take my life in exchange."

"I hear your words Jeremiah. Go with Lord Gizmo and provide all the information you have in relation to this series of events. Any attempt to flee from those who watch you will result in the destruction of the Quartz clan. Is this understood?" Elijah commanded.

"Completely, Great Lord Elijah. I hope, with my words and actions, to show that my people have not gone beyond the point of redemption in your eyes," Jeremiah replied.

There were no chains or ropes to hold Jeremiah; he was not restrained in any way. He walked with his escort as if they were there to protect him, not as a prisoner. They brought him to the keep and put him in a set of rooms that were normally reserved for VIPs. Lord Isaac spent many long hours talking to Jeremiah, and confirmed that we had nipped the conspiracy before it began to flower.

Leaving the questioning to the experts, I took Fred and the

drakes back to my stronghold. As soon as we were in the main compound, Sylvia and Rose were there to embrace me. I also saw Susan, looking very healthy, grab her son Fred in a bear hug, with the drakes looking on, wagging their tails and looking just as happy as Fred.

"Susan is a blessing. Now that she is feeling better, she has taken over the kitchen. We have had to send the guards on more patrols, as they are getting fat from her delicious cooking. You will see at dinner; she has gone above and beyond as she heard you and Fred were going to be back for a couple of days," Lady Sylvia said.

"All has been quiet around the stronghold, Lord Jim." Blaze said. "The only thing of any interest is the occasional sighting of something large moving in the water off the shore. It appears to be large and metallic."

I replied, "Unless it causes a problem, or looks like it is going to land, there is not much we can do at this point, so I am not going to worry about it. I am going to spend some quality time with my ladies, relaxing and regenerating my energy so I am ready to deal with anything that comes."

I headed up to my rooms and sat down to relax in the common area. Sylvia took my boots off and bathed my feet, ignoring my protests. Rose went to continue her self-appointed task of being in charge of the security of the skirmish groups.

Sylvia rubbed my feet and I laid back, closing my eyes and feeling thankful for the ladies coming into my life. I was feeling very relaxed when she told me that my bath was ready.

"That was quick. You did not even leave my side, dear," I said quietly.

"While you were out and about, a few of the wives of the stronghold guards and companions volunteered to come help at the keep, as soon as they could do so safely, using the portals to travel. This reduced the risk of having to travel overland, and worry about attack from dinosaurs or orc patrols," Sylvia said cheerily. "That way, it frees me up to harass the guards and companions to ensure they are prepared for anything."

"That is great. Did you have to put a limit on the number of ladies?" I asked.

Sylvia replied, "Yes, we have only so much room, so we allowed only a limited number. It would cause too much conflict if we brought single ladies over, but now with the portal, single warriors can go home and we can rotate the troops."

I stripped down and crawled into the hot bath. Sylvia joined me and gave me a thorough cleaning (she did not miss any spots)! I had not had a chance to get this clean in a while, having to be happy with just washing up a little bit when time allowed.

I was clean and full of energy by the time dinner was ready. I wore my normal dragon uniform, and waved to the men, who roared a greeting when I entered the dining hall. I quickly waved them to sit down. As things settled, I sat down at the main table with my companions and ladies to enjoy the sumptuous banquet that Susan had prepared. I saw Fred carrying platters of food around to the different tables.

"Fred, you are a companion now, and your only duties are to care for the drakes and train with them. I do not want you to overexert yourself with these menial tasks. Come, sit down and eat with the rest of your fellow companions," I said to him, smiling.

Fred smiled, nodding his head and came and sat down at the table with the companions and me. I could see Susan in the kitchen, smiling with pride in her son. After the big meal, I left the warriors to enjoy themselves and headed back to my rooms.

"Sylvia, I agree with you. If I stayed here without some physical activity, I would be a fat old wizard in no time. But at least I know you will keep me active, at least a little bit," I said, eyeing Sylvia suggestively.

I spent the next two days spending as much time as possible with Sylvia and Rose, walking every day, checking on the troops protecting the stronghold. Godfrey announced that I was trained as much I could be in stealth and healing, but he would remain to assist in any way possible.

I was fully energized when I went back to inquire about the results of Lord Isaac's enquiries with Jeremiah. I asked Sylvia to join me, and she did not hesitate, jumping into my arms and giving me a very passionate kiss. "I take it that means yes?" I asked.

"Of course, my dear! Any time that I can spend with you is fantastic," Sylvia said.

It was a good thing that I asked Sylvia the day before I was to journey to the Diamond stronghold, because she took all day to organize and relegate someone to be in charge while she was away with me. I made sure that Matilda and Bonny and Clyde came with Fred.

Jeremiah had been treated well, with his wife being brought from home to attend and keep him company. Those closest to the dragon mage and the eldest dragon knew the truth; all others thought Jeremiah was there on a visit, as was common with the beautiful scenery and weather in this area. After a week of being at the Diamond clan stronghold, Jeremiah was brought to the eldest dragon again for sentencing.

"Eldest, Jeremiah is too ashamed to admit that he was tricked. He is willing to suffer death to keep what honour he has left. To Jeremiah to admit that he had the wool pulled over his eyes would be to admit that he is perhaps not fit to rule the clan," Isaac said, in Jeremiah's defence.

"Jeremiah, these few around you are the only ones that will know this, and I can guarantee that they will not divulge what is said here in confidence, on pain of death. Tell me the truth of the matter, that we can deal with it appropriately," Elijah said commandingly.

"Great Eldest Dragon, I prostate myself in front of you. The elf who came to me claimed to be a companion and had some instructions that I was to check the security of the strongholds, spying and seeing what information could be gained by watching and learning, so that any gaps in security could be sealed," Jeremiah stated, without any indication of shame.

"Interesting. I can tell that you have told us the truth. When was this person to come back to you to get the information, so as to remedy these gaps in security?" Elijah said questioningly.

"He did not say for sure, but he gave the impression that I would see him in a month at the most," Jeremiah replied.

Elijah turned his head, looking at Gizmo, and said, "Lady Gizmo, take an escort and go to Betel at the Quartz clan. Make sure there is a cover story with regard to the guards' deaths, and ensure that the families are compensated. They died at their posts, and full honour must be restored to the clan. The widows and surviving family members will be given pensions. There must be no word that they were killed by dragon warriors. Lord Jeremiah, you will gather your wife and return to your post with two chests of gold to distribute amongst your people.

Your clan is noted for their forging of weapons, and you will tell them that since you have pled their case, a large order for weapons and shields will be forthcoming shortly. False information will be provided for you to give to the enemy spy. The dragon mage will be speaking with you in your stronghold soon."

Jeremiah was overwhelmed that he was able to walk out of this meeting with his head still attached to his shoulders. He had to postpone his return to the Quartz stronghold. His wife was so overjoyed that she cried and held onto Jeremiah as if it was a dream. I felt that waiting one day would allow her to settle down and be composed when they returned home.

The historian and Lord Isaac were left with the task of making up a plausible story that would satisfy the spy but I knew that Chavez would not believe the information for very long. I sent a messenger through the doorways to let the Lady Gizmo know that they wanted to make it a big event, with a lot of fanfare, to dispel any suspicion that Jeremiah was in trouble.

We made sure that there was a large entourage and two large chests of gold, as the eldest had requested. When we were in the tunnels and entering the portal into the Quartz stronghold, I notified Jeremiah that the dragon lord Betel wanted to speak to him.

We entered the chambers where Betel and his companion protectors were. As a sign of trust, Betel asked his companions to leave the room so that he could speak to Jeremiah in private. Gizmo, Isaac, and I were asked to remain.

"Clan chief Jeremiah. Welcome back. You and I will have more opportunity to speak at a later time. I am remaining here in the Quartz clan stronghold to support your people. I am terribly sorry that they have not received the recognition that they deserved in the past. That will change as of now. We will make sure that we will write a new page in the history of the clan," Betel said.

"Lord Dragon, it will be an honour that the clan has not had in a few lifetimes to have you here. We will do our utmost to ensure that the respect you have entrusted us with is returned tenfold," Jeremiah said, almost coming to tears as he spoke.

Betel said, "I look forward to speaking with you in the future, my new friend."

Jeremiah's smile was ear to ear. He brought his wife and his entourage up to the doorway to the dragon chamber and tunnels where there was a great roar from the multitude of people who were there to greet him. I kept a low profile, and quietly headed to the rooms that had been prepared for my use. I left the speech-making to Jeremiah, planning on waiting until the banquet to make my own short speech.

The Lady Sylvia was waiting in my rooms, and cuddled into bed with me as I grabbed a short rest. I felt bad about taking the lives of the guards. Although I did not do the deed myself, ultimately it was my responsibility.

I slept fitfully. Sylvia, realizing that I was feeling stress, kept close to me and stroked my temples when I awoke. I finally drifted off again, and Sylvia watched over me, holding me close and comforting me. Awakening, I felt refreshed and revitalized. Sylvia was not there, but the tub was ready for me to get ready for the banquet.

She showed up all dressed and looking fantastic, like someone I would be proud to have on my arm for the banquet, and I told her so. I could see from her reaction that she appreciated my opinion. She assisted me with my preparation for the night's events, braiding my hair with a gold clasp in the shape of a dragon to hold it together.

I walked into the hall, quickly running the gauntlet of the receiving line and giving Jeremiah a big hug, as befitting an equal, which elicited a huge round of applause from the attendees. I kept my comments brief, advising that the Quartz clan was going to be needed to manufacture arms and armour for the companion protectors and other clans, in these troubled times.

Jeremiah was a very strong speaker, keeping the attention of the rest of the clan. No one looked bored; he held their rapt attention. When he finished, there was a solid two minutes of standing ovation from his guests and fellow clan members.

Pledging myself to sobriety, I had a few glasses of Kritico, which my companions had thoughtfully brought for me. This allowed me to keep a clear mind and observe the guests at the banquet.

I prepared to leave the next day. There was too much to do for me to relax for much time. I reviewed the false information that had been prepared for Jeremiah to review and pass on to the spy when he showed up. Jeremiah read the information over until he had it memorized. There was no mention of the portals. Chavez may not believe all the documents as gospel, but without the knowledge of the portals, he would think that strongholds could be blocked off from aid.

When I returned to my headquarters, I gave orders to Mercury to fly to the Quartz stronghold and spend time with Betel. I wanted him available in case I was needed when the spy returned to the Quartz stronghold.

~ THIRTY-THREE ~

Spy or Assassin?

A few days later, a companion came running into my chamber and advised that the spy was with the clan chief at the Quartz stronghold. I quickly dressed in dark clothing, and sent word with the companion to have Mercury ready and saddled up in case he was needed.

I brought Matilda only and left the other two drakes at the stronghold with Fred. Isaac and Gizmo, as well as Ice Wind and his snow people companions, came with me. I felt with their abilities, there was no way the spy would escape my attention. That is, unless he had some very powerful magic to cloak himself with. But I did not think that this was likely, as Chavez would not use such powerful resources just to gather information.

Jeremiah had received instructions beforehand to stall the spy as long as possible so when we arrived, the spy was still secluded with Jeremiah, where he was being wined and dined like a trusted friend. I had Mercury flying around the stronghold out of sight and awaiting any instructions from below as what to do next.

Lord Isaac was attuned to Jeremiah's mind, and advised that all was going well. The spy was giving no indication that he was at all suspicious of the information that Jeremiah had entrusted him with.

Anthony showed up while they were waiting for the spy to leave the Clan chief's quarters. I asked him "Anthony, what brings you here this late evening?"

"The great dragon requested that I attend to you, in case I may be able to recognize the spy from my past contacts. He may be a member of the assassins' guild, and as such I may have run across him before my untimely death," he said quietly to me.

"Thank you Anthony. Any assistance would be greatly appreciated," I said.

It was late—almost midnight—before the long-awaited contact finally staggered out of Jeremiah's quarters. This person appeared a novice since he did not feel threatened, seeing the state he was in. That lasted only until he was out of sight from the keep. Then he straightened up and walked normally toward the stronghold gate. I heard a sharp intake of breath from Anthony.

"Do you recognize him Anthony?" I asked, looking at him.

"Yes. His name is Tomar, and he is the most skilled killer in the guild. His targets, if they know that he has been given a contract for them, get their affairs in order and count the days 'til he comes. The longest anyone has been able to avoid his sights was one who hid in the mountains for six months before he was found and terminated," Anthony said in response to my question.

Anthony advised that Tomar was a dark elf, one who has given up all that the elves of the forest were associated with. Dark elves lived in the mountains; some practicing dark magic and offering fealty to the Malum. The only thing that distinguished them from the forest elves was the fact that they were very pale. It would take someone who knew the difference to know that they were dark elves.

I called Mercury and told him that the spy was headed out the stronghold gate and that he was an elf, not a dwarf. Mercury watched, circling high above the stronghold, and spotted Tomar the second he exited the gate. I waited until he was out of sight and made sure that all the lights were doused inside the gate before slipping out with my party.

Matilda instantly picked up his scent, and started to head in the direction that he had taken, but I held her back, as I did not want to jeopardize her life with the skills that this legendary assassin apparently had. I had Ice wind and his warriors spread out, and slowly followed the path that my target had taken. Mercury advised that the assassin was approaching a sheltered camp hidden in the woods to the north of the stronghold.

Mercury further advised that camp sheltered about fifty warriors and one Ankylosaurus hidden behind a stone outcropping, which hid their campfire from vision by the stronghold. Tomar slipped past the sentries and entered the building on the Ankylosaurus' back. I didn't know if he was resting, or passing the information on to the orcs.

The only way to tell was to wait. I had the ice warriors spread out around the camp and watch. I picked a safe spot and waited. Tomar was in the camp for several hours before leaving and heading to the west. I had a decision to make: follow him or follow the orcs.

I set a few of the ice warriors to watch over the camp, and directed Mercury to follow Tomar. I quickly decided on the best course of action to take, and advised my men that they must search out Tomar to find out what he knew, if anything.

I called Mercury down. Isaac Ice Wind and I, mounted up and flew ahead on the path Tomar was taking. I found a small hilltop, and set up a small fire with Mercury and the others out of sight. I sat roasting a small dinosaur that Ice Wind had quickly killed. It was not long before I sensed Tomar approaching cautiously up the hill.

"It is rather foolish to set a fire where it can be seen for miles, and then sit there blindly thinking one is safe," Tomar said loudly, so as not to surprise me—as if I did not know he was coming.

"Tomar, you are welcome to join me and share this meal. Or, as those of your calling are wont to do, you can try to stab me in the back. I am sure your master would pay handsomely for the price that is on my head," I stated, stoking the fire.

"You know my name, but I do not know yours. I do not normally kill strangers unless they are a direct threat to me or to a contract I have taken. I have no recent contracts outstanding at this time, so you are safe," Tomar said.

"I am the Dragon Mage Jim. I am sure that your lord and master Chavez would be disappointed if you missed the opportunity to slay me when you had the chance," I said, looking up at him.

"I am aware of the contract on your head, Dragon Mage, but since I have not been directly asked to slay you, I will not undertake this task and risk," Tomar stated in a matter of fact tone.

He sat down across from me and carved a piece of meat off the spit. He bit into it, with the juices running down the side of his chin.

I received a message from Lord Isaac in my mind.

"He has no other information with him, and has told you the truth as he knows it. He suspects that you are not alone, but does not know how many or where we are. He is as we were told, but he is very proud, not taking on a contract without being specifically tasked to the job by the head of the guild, who is Chavez, of course," Isaac said, mind-to-mind.

"May I ask what your plans are at this point in time?" I asked Tomar.

He said, "You may ask. I am headed west from this point until I receive further orders from my guild master. Since I have shared food with you, I will warn you if I receive the contract for your life, as a matter of respect."

He then rolled over, pulling his cloak around him, and went to sleep. I shrugged as Mercury landed next to me and enveloped me in his wings, warming me with his body. When I awoke, Tomar was cooking something else on the spit, which he shared with me. When he finished his meal, he wiped his hands, stood, nodded to me, and headed toward the west again. I let him go, and did not follow. Instead, I mounted Mercury and flew eastward, in the direction of the orc campsite.

The orcs had left, but it did not take long before we spotted them. They appeared to be heading for Capital City. Without allowing themselves to be seen, the ice warriors were following them.

I decided that it would make the information seem more important if we attacked the orcs but allowed our forces to be bested. It would make the falsehoods seem valid if it appeared that we were willing to attack the party to get it back. I looked at a map and saw that there were several dragon-held strongholds along the path they travelled. I sent Mercury ahead and arranged for a large party of dwarves to intercept the orc party.

The dwarves would show up in force, doing a sloppy search for the information, but not finding it. A second, smaller group would be dispatched closer to the orcs' destination and would allow themselves to be beaten off, after dealing the orcs substantial injuries. By the time the orc contingent reached Capital City, the information would seem extremely valuable.

Once that was arranged, I headed to the nearest stronghold to use the portal system to head home. Mercury would fly to the stronghold and join me soon as he could.

Bonnie and Clyde were there to greet me and Matilda with their tails wagging, looking like a couple of happy puppies. Of course, Sylvia was there, ready, calling for a hot meal and giving me a loving embrace to cheer me up no matter what the day had been like. It was good to have someone to come home to. Back where I came from, I had lived the life of a lonely bachelor.

Fred's mother, Susan, was there to greet me as well, with a heaping platter of fresh baked goods.

"Susan, this is awesome, but you need to cut back just a little bit; you are spoiling the troops. They are going to get fat and lazy," I said to her, munching on a sweet roll and eying other baked treats.

Susan laughed, saying, "I will cut back a little, Lord Dragon Mage, but they treat me so well, and I am grateful for the attention that they give me. Now with the gateways, I am able to get fresh products instead of stale, so I will try to feed them healthier meals."

"Don't forget to save a few treats for Fred and me," I said, smiling.

I contacted the historian at the Diamond clan stronghold in the hopes of learning more about the dark elves. No one had spoken to me before about them. I wondered if they were one of those things that were never spoken about like the dragon wars. The historian was not very helpful, stating that the only information he had was fairly recent, being less than fifty years old. There was nothing older in writing that he could find.

The dark elves were treated in general as second-class citizens, thieves, prostitutes, and murderers. Isaac told him that this was just a front, the dark elves in general keeping to themselves and rarely being involved with the other races.

Well, I thought, there was always the old fellow—Elijah, that is. Being the oldest dragon alive, he seemed to be the most reliable source of information. Who knows, maybe there was something embarrassing in the past that the dragons did not want recorded. I sought out Lord Isaac, who was my pipeline to all things dragon.

"Isaac, I think it is time for you to talk to Elijah again—this time about the dark elves. Since there appears to be little or no information in writing about them, we need to talk to him," I said, questioning Isaac.

"I will ask him and find out what I can, and get back to you as soon as possible," Isaac said, flying away to research my questions.

Two weeks later, I received an invitation to meet with Elijah in his chambers, with the Lady Gizmo and Lord Isaac only. This is never good news, I thought, especially when they did not want any others but dragons involved in the conversation.

Entering the chamber, I received another major surprise. There were at least ten large dragons and fifteen small dragons squeezed into the room. I had a sinking feeling in the pit of my stomach. This did not bode well at all. I bowed to Elijah as well as the other dragons in the room.

"The dark elves are our creation." Elijah said. "We used magic to do what you would call 'genetic engineering.' We wanted warriors who were fearless and able to fight in the deep, dark caverns of our enemies, the Malum. We found that the warriors we had wanted, once completed, were just as independent as any other species. We had created a new race of fighters who did not like taking orders from their dragon lords. We decided that we would no longer play creator, realizing too late that we were foolish to even try."

"Why do you need this gathering of dragons to give me this information, when it would have been just as simple to speak face to face?" I asked angrily.

"This is the Conclave, the ruling council of dragons, if you will. We rarely gather, as we are able to converse with each other by mind link. The reason we gathered here today is to honour you, and your continuing efforts for the dragons and the people of this world. Bringing back a species of animal that was thought extinct is just one example of the fantastic accomplishments you have achieved since coming here," Elijah stated.

"We trust you so much that all of our kin are being told that you are to be considered a dragon in all aspects." Gizmo stated to me quietly. "Your word is law, and even dragons will obey you. Even the conclave members will follow your lead. If they have any doubt, they will challenge you in private and not in front of others. Lord Isaac and I will be your channels to communicate with any and all of the conclave."

"Great Dragon Mage, have you made any plans to deal with the evil wizard Chavez?" Elijah asked.

"I am still trying to determine how best to approach it. All-out war is out of the question, as there would be too great a loss of life on both sides to risk it," I said to Elijah.

He replied, "We await your decision but know we will assist you in whatever way you need."

"Thank you. I will let you know my plans for dealing with Chavez, as soon as I have everything organized," I said.

I felt drained. It seemed to me that the dragons were no better than the men of my own world. They kept playing God, changing things for what they thought would be better and then realizing that they should have left well enough alone. Isaac and Gizmo started to talk to me, but I did not reply. They soon stopped talking, realizing that I wished to be alone with my thoughts.

I headed straight back to my stronghold and went to bed, ignoring everyone who wanted to offer me food or conversation. I instructed James that I did not wish to talk or be disturbed by anyone, unless the stronghold was under attack. Crawling into my bed, I had a hard time falling asleep, as my mind would not shut down. I wondered if there was anything else that the dragons had forgotten or withheld from me that would jeopardize or hinder my judgment in the future.

The foul mood that I was in could not be shaken. I strode the battlements of the stronghold, growling at the men. It was bad enough that the guards and my companions avoided direct contact with me, so as not to fall victim to my displeasure. It extended even to my adopted family. I instructed James gruffly that I did not wish any company in my bed chamber until I said otherwise.

Matilda curled up beside me as I lay in the bed. Not even bothering to change out of my clothes, I lay on the top of the covers, allowing her to keep me warm with her body. I awoke during the night to see that it was a rare full moons. Both moons were fully alight, giving the surrounding area enough illumination so that it was as bright as a stormy day.

Gazing out in the bright moonlight, I could make out creatures that normally would only be out in the daylight, moving around as they did in the day. I watched for a few hours until I felt tired again, undressing and crawling under the covers of my bed. I suddenly felt calmer and more at peace, realizing that regardless of what tampering with nature that the dragons have done, the world would continue on its natural course, with little or no impact.

Arising late in the morning, I cleaned myself up and called for a meeting of all the staff at the stronghold, including guards, kitchen staff, and companions.

"I am deeply sorry that I have been a little short-tempered with all of you in the last few days, but I have had a lot on my mind to sort out. I apologize for any slight you might have felt by my comments or actions. Things will be back to normal once again, as I have cleared my mind of the dark thoughts that were bothering me," I said to everyone in the stronghold.

"Speaking for most, Lord Dragon Mage, we realize that you have had a lot on your mind. We are glad to see you up and about, and definitely more like your cheerful self," Gizmo said.

Deciding that I needed to get away from everything, I planned a trip to the Quartz clan stronghold to reinforce the order for arms and armour for the clans, and to strengthen Jeremiah's standing as the clan chief.

I gave direction to my companions and the Lady Gizmo, taking Sylvia and my companions with me, including Fred, his mother, and the drakes. There was a little grumbling from the stronghold guards about the loss of their favourite cook, but they were more than happy when they found that she was returning back to them when the trip was over.

Sylvia had taken to wearing pants and armour so that she could be on the front line when it came to directing the guardian warriors. The companions were very well organized, and had three Ankylosaurus outfitted within a week. This also included my specially-equipped Ankylosaurus. I wanted to get away from everything and make this journey a little bit like a holiday. I sent a message to Argentum to see if he wanted to lead the caravan, with the idea of making a tempting target for bandits, to see if we could clean out any infestations before they became too troublesome.

Using the portals, I did not have to wait long before receiving word by courier that Argentum was thrilled to be of assistance to the dragon mage again. I prepared another Ankylosaurus with trade goods to show off and tempt any bandits. I then sent word to the other dragon lords, requesting that any unusual items that would draw attention be sent to Argentum for his caravan. Argentum was promised a percentage of the profits as incentive, although that was not necessary, as he was very excited about doing something to help eliminate bandits who had been preying on caravans for years.

Godfrey was to meet with Argentum at the stronghold, along with Lord Isaac, to oversee the organization and provisions for the caravan. I would have liked to be there when Godfrey introduced himself to Argentum.

~ THIRTY-FOUR ~

Bandit Hunting

rising early in the morning, I headed down to the main area where the companions were getting last-minute items loaded. Susan, by the smell of things, was going out of her way to give the guards something to miss her cooking skills by. I felt better than I had in a while. There were no serious worries on my mind, and I was looking forward to getting the companions out and honing their skills on a few bandits.

Mercury and the snow people were out, scanning the area to ensure the caravan would be unobserved when we left the stronghold. Mercury flew in, declaring all was clear, and settled into his hiding place for the day. The snow people were waiting for the caravan as it set out toward the great road. They would remain in the bushes paralleling the caravan, watching to ensure that there was no one out there watching the stronghold and waiting to ambush the caravan as it headed out.

The dwarfs blended in without a problem, but if I wanted to get some fresh air, I had to disguise myself as an elf. It wasn't common for elves to travel with caravans, but it did happen from time to time, depending on the cargo. The elves still sold valuable items such as certain crafts and rare saps used for making bows and specialty weapons or armour. The Lady Gizmo wrapped herself around my neck, and an Elvin cloak allowed me to blend right in.

We set up for the night in the very campsite we had first encountered the elves. As the camp was being set up with the usual speed and efficiency that I had witnessed in the past, a group of elves approached, walking from the great road toward the camp. I stood at the edge of the camp waiting patiently. A member of the group broke away and jumped into my arms. Rose gave me a great hug, and a long and passionate kiss.

"I am glad to see you too!" I said, returning the passionate kiss. Rose said to me, "You worry me too much, Dragon Mage. You disappear from sight for a few days, and then show up by magic with animals that I have only heard of in legend. I am glad that you are all right, and the more I get to know you, the more I realize you lead a charmed life, my love."

"I hope you don't mind if I tag along on your little excursion." Gladius said, interrupting Rose's kisses. "I could use the break from administration duties and would welcome the chance to exercise my sword arm."

"Of course. I am more than glad for the company and the comradeship," I said.

As the group of elves entered the camp, the Drakes came bounding out as if they were going to attack. At a sharp command from me, they slowed down, tails wagging. The elves allowed the drakes to smell them, not making any threatening moves until the drakes grew bored and slipped back into the darkening night around the camp. Matilda kept close to me but ignored Rose and the rest of the Elvin group, obviously accepting that they were not enemies.

"I hope you are hungry. Our head cook has come with the party, and she does an awesome job at meal preparation," I said proudly.

Rose smothered me with a huge hug, and a long, passion-filled kiss that filled me with a desire for more. She walked with me and greeted Sylvia with a hug and cheek kisses, overflowing with what appeared to be sisterly love. I could not grasp the whole situation between Rose and Sylvia. Back where I came from, there were very few wives who would accept other women in a man's life. The few exceptions were the ones on daytime talk shows or Mormon-based sects.

"We have decided to join your little trip, especially since I hear you will be hunting bandits during your travels," Rose said.

"Yes, I thought it would be good practice for my men and

dragons. They were getting out of practice as they have had little or no action lately. Your company would be more than welcome and I can see that Sylvia has already welcomed you to our mobile home," I said.

We sat down and enjoyed a tasty and satisfying meal. The fact that we were camping, so to speak, did little to lessen Susan's cooking skills. When it came to bedtime, Rose joined me.

"Not that I am trying to wreck this romantic mood you are in, but where is Sylvia this evening?" I asked Rose.

Rose replied, "She is sleeping elsewhere tonight; she gave up this time with you, since we have not seen each other for a while. Sylvia has had you all to herself, so this way you can remember why you and I love each other."

We had no confrontations on our way to the first of the strongholds along our planned route. Argentum made a point of flaunting all of his best goods when we were at the market. We stayed for a couple of days to allow word to get around of the wealth of this caravan.

I received a request, hand-delivered by a guard, to visit with the clan chief. When I went to the keep to speak to him, I found both of the little dragons present, along with Rose and Sylvia, who were dressed formally. Also there, along with Gladius and Argentum, were Godfrey and the leaders of each companion's race.

"I would like to have a couple of words in private with you, young man, to explain a few things," Godfrey said in a fatherly tone.

I replied, "Of course."

He led me to a small room, where James was waiting, along with my dress dragon mage outfit. Before Godfrey even started to talk to me, James started to strip me down and dress me in my best outfit.

"The ladies have decided that they wish to cement their relationship with you, and want to enter into a marriage of sorts. It is a standard of practice in this land, that a man can have more than one wife," Godfrey said, with a smile on his face.

He added, "As long as you can support them, you can have several mates. Rose and Sylvia both love you dearly and wish to be with you as long as they live. They have no problem sharing you between them; their love for each other is growing as sister wives. They could not wait for you to ask them, since you are unfamiliar with the way things are done. If you decide that you do not wish to do this, you have but to say the word."

"Of course, I love them both; I am just a little overwhelmed by the ambush wedding idea. But I am willing to accept both of them, and since they have no issue with each other, let's do this," I said.

When I walked back into the room where my soon-to-be-wives were waiting, I could see by the smiles on their faces that they were overjoyed at my decision. It was a brief ceremony, where we pledged our love and feelings for each other. We had a small meal, and shared a glass of wine together, then headed back to the caravan.

It was a long night. I spent a few hours with Rose first, then she left and Sylvia came to spend the rest of the night with me. Needless to say, I slept late the next day, not waking until both of my girls brought me lunch in bed.

Information arrived while we were in the stronghold that there was a large group of bandits along our route toward the west. I spoke to Argentum and made sure that we wouldn't leave the stronghold until late in the day. We made up excuses to make it look as though there was a real reason for not leaving until we did.

The elves and snow people, being the best at moving stealthily in the brush, separated early from the caravan, paralleling our path of travel.

We encountered no surprises, and set up camp for the evening in what appeared to be a poor defensive arrangement. I arranged a few dummies to look like stationary perimeter sentries. I didn't wish to place my men in a situation where they could be killed without having a chance to fight back.

I felt that this might be a long night without sleep, but we didn't have to wait too long. After the camp settled down for the night and the fires were dying down, the dummy guards were "taken out" by arrows.

A medium-sized group of twenty-plus bandits rushed into the

campsite and were running toward the platforms when they were met by the drakes and me, ready for a fight. The person in charge of the bandits was at the rear of the group, and yelled for his men to attack from there.

"I'm afraid you do not have anyone left alive to help you. They were taken care of by my men, before you rushed into my camp," I said to the bandit leader.

He snarled at me and started to back into the bush. When he turned around to run, he stopped dead in his tracks. There were Rose and four elf warriors standing in his way. He grabbed his sword and was ready to try to fight his way out but I stepped forward and rapped him hard on the head with my staff, knocking him unconscious.

"Somebody tie him up and put him in a secure area, under guard. Mercury, fly up and check the area to make sure there are no survivors going for help. If you find anyone, dispatch them right away. We can question this gentleman after we get some rest."

After getting a few hours rest and a hot meal, I was ready to talk to my unwanted guest. As tradition demanded, the enemy did not receive any food. I approached him with Gizmo and Isaac. The bandit glared at me, but didn't say a word.

"Isaac, Gizmo: Search his mind. I will ask him a few questions, which should get him thinking about where he comes from and if we have more work to clean up this infestation. The area will be a lot safer with this first bandit group eliminated," I said to Isaac, out of hearing of the bandit leader.

Then, I walked over to the bandit and sat down in a chair in front of him. I sat there looking over the dishevelled dwarf. He was filthy, smelling up the room with his unwashed body odour. He was of average height for his race; young enough that he did not have a beard yet. Dirty hair and clothes added to his smell. Obviously the sanitary conditions at his camp were less than ideal. I fired questions at him, keeping him distracted. He remained silent throughout the questioning.

The interrogation went on for an hour, and throughout the bandit was quiet, not speaking a word to anyone. What surprised me most was the fact that he did not plead for his life or offer to turn on his associates. He was either extremely loyal or afraid of the bandit chief. The guards escorted him to a holding cell, which had been set up in one of the Ankylosaurus platforms.

"Well, my friends, what were you able to glean from this one's mind?" I asked.

Isaac said to me, "Quite a bit, as a matter of fact. His mouth may have been silent, but his mind was racing with all sorts of information. We now know where his camp is, how many bandits have been left to guard it, and how many prisoners they have awaiting ransom or kept as servants. This one is named Liam. The only reason he is with this group is that his mother is a captive. He has killed no one, keeping well back of the group and waiting for them to finish. He has only helped with the task of escorting other captives or stolen goods back to their camp."

"Very well, keep him safe until we finish destroying their camp. I want to keep as small a contingent of warriors at this camp as possible, but first I want a detailed search of the surrounding area to make sure there are no threats. Isaac, I want you to send a request to the nearest stronghold for backup to take over any bandits that we capture, as well as to escort any of those kept against their will at the bandit camp," I directed.

"It is done as we speak. There will be a couple of dragon lords within calling distance by the time we reach the enemy camp," Isaac replied.

I spoke to Argentum after the search of the perimeter came back clear, leaving him with a minimal amount of warriors as protection. Isaac stayed behind with the caravan to ensure that he could call the dragons for backup if needed.

We slowly wound our way toward the bandit camp, finding and disarming about a dozen traps that were set along the path. We approached the camp, which had a stockade that blocked access to a series of caves at the end of the trail. I set my men up to monitor the stockade until it was time to initiate the attack. The sun slowly set; one of the moons rose, full and bright, casting soft, grey light over the forest as well as the bandit camp.

Once we were close enough, I could see that the compound was exactly as Liam had thought in his mind. We approached a point in the wooden palisade and I carefully used my dragon magic to burn a man-sized hole near the cliff face. My troops set themselves up between the caves cut into the cliff face and the rest of the bandit camp. The secure area where the captives were kept was obvious, with the door barred from the outside, and a guard sleeping outside. The guard was quickly dispatched and the cave searched for other bandits.

Once the cave was clear, I had my men spread out and check the other caves, which were being used as barracks. Any bandits were quickly overpowered, gagged, tied up and quietly stored in another cave near the captives' location. Gizmo read the minds of all those brought in, and several females were kept tied up, as they were family members of the bandit community. Others were untied and escorted quietly to the cell block area for protection.

The companions had all but five caves searched and secured, when the alarm was raised by an alert watchman. His warning cries were quickly cut off by an arrow to his throat, but the damage had been done. The bandit chieftain came running out of his cave, yelling at his men to man the palisades, and get to the walls and off their lazy rears! Too late, he realized the men in the compound were not his after all, as my forces grabbed him and quickly tied him up.

The rest of the bandits didn't give us much of a fight. They realized that their walls had been breached and the backup they were expecting was, in fact, my companion troops. This sucked all the belligerence out of them. They were used to situations where they outnumbered their targets by at least two to one. They were not up for a fair fight, especially when they recognized the shapes of a couple of dragon lords circling the camp, ready to join the fight.

The sun rose over the camp, showing a state of disarray after my men had ransacked it for anything of value, and made piles of everything.

Argentum brought one Ankylosaurus to the camp, and loaded up some of the more valuable items to make a profit and to pay his troops for their part in the caravan. This also allowed for my men to claim trinkets, as it was a tradition on this world to share the loot after the destruction of a group of bandits.

The dwarf troops from the nearest stronghold showed up in the early afternoon with three Ankylosaurus. They were there to pick up the rest of the treasure trove and to bring some comfort to the sick or ailing among the captives. They chained the bandits up for a day-long walk back to the stronghold. There they would be judged for their crimes, and appropriate punishment dealt out.

I watched as the bandits were being chained up. I noticed an older woman checking over the bandits, lifting their faces as if she were looking for someone. I approached her.

"Mother, can I be of assistance?" I asked.

She replied, "I am looking for my son, praying that he is alive. He joined the bandits only to keep me alive. He did not wish to become a killer, but he loved me so much and could not find an alternative."

"Well mother, if his name is Liam, he is fine and is waiting for you back at my camp," I said.

The woman exclaimed, "Yes! What are your plans for him? Are you going to execute him like all the rest of these black-hearted bastards?"

"No, as a matter of fact he has harmed no one; therefore, I plan on reuniting the two of you, and setting him free when we reach the next stronghold.

Liam's mother said, in tears, "Thank you, My Lord."

I sent the woman back with Argentum to my camp. After speaking to the leader of the dwarf expedition, I headed back with my companions to my camp. We spent a couple of days recovering before heading down the road into the area of the next bandit group. True to my word, I set Liam and his mother free, with enough money to set them up and live comfortably in a new community.

In total, we dealt with three large encampments of bandits over a period of a couple of months. My group became even more tightly-knit. Hardly a word was exchanged during battle, as each person knew his or her task, and little was needed in the way of orders. Fred kept close behind me, with the drakes watching my back. This allowed me to focus on what I was doing and not worry about was anything or anyone sneaking up behind me.

When we reached Elijah's stronghold, I sent the caravan back to my stronghold and told them to dispose of any orcs that crossed their paths.

I decided to take a few weeks off to rest along with my group of guardians and companions before I took on any other tasks. Sylvia and Rose settled in nicely to the suite of rooms that I had before I set up housekeeping in my stronghold on the coast. The Diamond clan welcomed us with open arms as if we were long-lost family members.

A feast was to be held in our honour, and the kitchen was abuzz with the chance to prepare their best for the dragon mage.

"Elijah, I will come to speak with you in the next couple of days, after I rest and gather my strength for the next phase of taking back control of this world," I said to him, mind-to-mind.

"You need not make any excuses, young one. When you are ready, come and speak with me. Otherwise, relax and sleep peacefully, knowing that you are protected within these walls, and you are as safe as I," Elijah responded.

The next days were like a dream, the fantastic banquet in our honour left me stuffed like a Christmas turkey. I spent the rest of the next few days sleeping soundly, and spending quality time with Sylvia and Rose.

Two days later, I awoke in the middle of the night in a cold sweat, yelling. All I could remember were dark tunnels, and shapes coming out of the darkness at me. It took me at least an hour before I was able to settle down and go back to a fitful sleep. It was time to go and talk to Elijah. I knew that he was waiting for me to come.

I did not arrange for the meeting, I just walked to Elijah's chambers, passing all the guards and companions. They just stood to one side as I strode through the main entrance, bowing or saluting, depending on their station.

Elijah looked up as I walked into the chamber, and dismissed everyone else from the room. Elijah said, "I knew you would come and speak to me eventually. I was there when you had the dreams. I don't think they were just dreams; I think they might have been visions of the task ahead of you."

"Not much in the way of detail in those dreams, and they were scaring the crap out of me!" I said.

Elijah said in a commanding tone, "Typical prophetic dream. They tend not to provide much in the way of details—they just give you a general push in the direction needed to do what you know you must."

"Gee, thanks," I said sarcastically.

"You have learned a lot during your time here, but there is still always more to learn," Elijah said to me.

Leaving Elijah's chamber, I started to mull over what he had said to me. I knew that I would have to deal with Chavez, and sooner rather than later.

I spent the next few days in deep meditation, finally sending for Godfrey to come and speak with me. It was only a matter of a few hours before he showed up. With the portal system catalogued efficiently, military traffic, unmolested by the enemy, was able to pass messages.

When my frustration level reached its peak, I started to wander the stronghold at all hours of the day and night. The drakes dutifully tagged along like little puppy dogs; no one interrupted my walks, because all it took was a growl from them and the staunchest warrior paled and stepped back. Also, anyone could see that I was deep in thought. One who had done so was usually not lucky enough to survive the encounter if they interrupted a wizard who was deep in thought. A startled wizard was extremely dangerous, as he might throw a spell your way before realizing you were an ally.

There had to be some way I could get past all the guards and locked doors between me and Chavez! Hopefully, I could do it with a minimal loss of life on either side. After all, there was always hope that the orcs could be civilized, after I took out their leader.

I went down to the dragon chambers to talk to Elijah late one night, knowing that I would not be interrupting any important meetings. The companions on duty tried to stop me, saying that Elijah was sleeping. I pushed passed them, with Matilda at my side glaring at them. Not a word was said to further impede me from the great dragon's chambers.

"I need to know if there is anything else that you are holding back from me. I must be fully prepared for my next encounter with Chavez, and if there is anything that is being kept secret from me, I must know. It could be used by Chavez to distract me enough that I may not be able to defend myself properly," I said to Elijah.

"There is one last thing that has been kept from you—it was felt that it was not relevant to the task at hand. We dragons are not originally from this plane of existence; we ourselves are from another world. We were servants of great mages, and when we escaped, we vowed never to be subjugated by other creatures. The original war that the dragons fought amongst themselves was between the mages and their servant dragons and the free dragons," Elijah said.

"That explains the first great war, but what about the second great dragon war, where you started bringing other races into this world to fight for you?" I asked.

Elijah responded, "That was during the time when the Malum and the other dragons broke away from each other. The Malum were keen on the manipulation of other species, to use them as servants and control them completely. We, on the other hand, wanted to work with the other species to be our hands, our agents while allowing them freedom in most of their decisions. They chose to help us in return for protection in a time of need, and our teaching of things beyond their ken."

"What about the Yeti and the Undine or dolphin people as we called them? Were they brought over?" I asked, searching for answers.

"There have been times in our history where larger gateways into this world have appeared for a period of time and races have crossed over. The Yeti are one such race. The gateway was open to their world for almost one hundred years before it started to close. They chose to remain here, as the hunting and area were ideal for their people. The Undines are an unknown quantity, as none of the races we brought here, or the dragons, can breathe underwater. For all we know, their gateway may still be open, or maybe they are indigenous to this world. We have had no dealings with them at all. There is one island chain where their vessels and people have been sighted occasionally. We have avoided interfering with them, to allow them to develop on their own without our influence," Elijah said.

"Well, at least I am glad to hear that you learned your lesson about messing with the development any of the races," I said.

Elijah said, contritely, "Nothing will be held back from you. If you have any questions, Isaac has been instructed to tell you everything, or to ask me if he does not know the answer."

~ THIRTY-FIVE ~

Emancipation

he next morning, I summoned Gizmo and Isaac and took them with me to check on how the drake pups were doing. As always, I took my personal greeting party of drakes with me.

Under the watchful eyes of their parents, the pups frolicked with Bonnie, and Clyde. They nipped at them and chased them around the pen as much as they were allowed to. They seemed to realize that Matilda was the alpha female, and left her alone to watch the proceedings.

While I stood there watching them play, I asked Isaac about the dark elves, and where they were. Isaac lowered his head in shame, and shared with me that other than a few, most were in a jail set aside in an old, abandoned mine. The prison was located near the mountains in the central southwest area of the world.

"Tell the conclave that this approach amounts to genocide. Deliberately detaining these people simply because of their race is unacceptable. I am issuing an order releasing all the dark elf prisoners and closing the prison forever, sending the dwarf guards back to their homes, thus freeing up warriors that could be used elsewhere."

"You are definitely testing the obedience of the conclave with such a strong order. I agree with you that this order has been a long time coming and needs to be fulfilled. Your request will be forwarded immediately and I will advise you of the reply." Isaac responded.

I knew that this was going to stretch the promise of the conclave to support me in anything I wanted. They had also agreed to obey my commands. Well, this certainly was going to open a real can of worms.

I was not surprised to hear from Isaac within an hour of my order.

Isaac said, "You knew that this might happen. The conclave is in an uproar. They are split about whether to support your request or think up an excuse to deny it. I think you know that the younger dragon lords and ladies voted in your favour."

"Ask Elijah to convene the conclave here, so that I may address them in person," I said to Isaac.

Elijah responded, "It has already been done, Dragon Mage. There has not been a more important vote in thousands of years. The result of the last one was to let the Undines develop by themselves."

I nodded and took the drakes back to my rooms, where I called Sylvia and Rose, as well as the companions. I explained the dark elves' predicament, as well as what I had requested. I then invited clan chieftains and elders from the Yeti, the Elves, and the People.

I also asked Anthony to see if a message could be sent to Tomar, the dark elf to discuss the plight of his people in captivity. Anthony knew where he could leave the message, but was not sure if Tomar would get the message in time. Furthermore, he may not attend, thinking it was a trap. I explained that the message would come with a guarantee of safe conduct. It would also contain my seal to forbid anyone from interfering with him.

When I spoke to the Diamond clan chief, he was more than glad to accommodate the meeting in his great hall. Then, I explained to him what the meeting was to be about in detail. He was a little hesitant to still host the meeting. The dark elves had been perceived as evil, even though no one, in his memory, had been harmed by one.

Within two days, the people invitees started to trickle in from everywhere. The most surprising of all was Tomar, who showed up at the gate late the second day after my invitation. They would not let him in the gate until I came down and yelled at the guards to open the gate. I introduced Tomar to Bonnie and Clyde, and advised him that they would watch his back while he was in the stronghold.

Tomar hesitantly said, "I have never seen this type of creature before. Are you sure I am safe with them?"

"You are completely protected. They will not let harm befall you while you are a guest. They are formidable warrior drakes, and can take out several guards or warriors in a go," I assured him.

By the end of the week, representatives of each race had arrived. During a large luncheon, Tomar stood up and told those in attendance about the dark elves, their culture and history. After he sat down, I explained what I had learned about the dark elves, and my request to the conclave to free those who had committed no crimes other than being of a misunderstood race. I left and asked Tomar to come with me, so as not to influence the council's deliberations.

Isaac had joined the meeting when I left, to listen to the consensus of those discussing the fate of the entire dark elf race. Within a couple of hours, he came to see Tomar and me in my quarters.

Isaac said, amazed, "I have never seen such a decision made in such a short time. If it were not for the fact that you have been treating all the races fairly, they normally would not even agree on what to have for dinner."

"What conclusion did they come to?" I asked.

"They unanimously agreed with your decision, throwing aside any old prejudices that any of them have held," Isaac said in amazement.

"Has the conclave gathered yet?" I asked.

"Yes, the final members have just arrived and are awaiting your presence," Isaac said. I gave him further instructions: "Tell the visitors in the hall to select no more than two from each race to come with me."

Isaac nodded his head, flying off in the direction of the great hall. He returned within a short time with two representatives of each race, as I had requested. I greeted everyone warmly, especially those that I already met and knew.

I told Elijah what I had planned, so that he knew, at least, what to expect.

Attending the meeting, in support of Wizard Godfrey and me, were: Yeti elder The Voice, elf representatives Gladius and Rose, the People elders Samuel and Joseph, dwarf leaders Adam and Jeremiah, and Tomar, the dark elf. Sylvia would not be excluded. She attended, in charge of my guardian companions. She was dressed the part in warrior armour and weapons.

I led them to the dragon chambers, pushing past the companions who attempted to stop the rest of my party from entering. I glared at them and they backed down. I broke into a coughing fit, trying not to laugh as Clyde walked over to one of the companions and lifted his leg, urinating on him.

As we entered, the dragons of the conclave raised an uproar, demanding to know why these other people were with the dragon mage. This was a closed meeting as far as they were concerned and only dragons and their immediate companions were allowed to attend.

"I invited these leaders to state their opinion of the dark elf situation. For the same reason, Tomar is here as the only representative of his people that I know of," I stated.

An elder dragon boomed out his voice: "Tomar is a well-known assassin. You have betrayed us, Dragon Mage. Guards! Seize Tomar and place him in custody 'til we can arrange an execution!"

The guards attempted to swarm Tomar, who had his sword out to stop his capture or die trying. The guards were stopped suddenly by the three drakes blocking their path, plus a wall of flame generated by me. I could feel the elder dragon trying to dampen down the flames so the guards could take Tomar.

Elijah roared. "Enough, this is my home! Guards—stand down. Tomar is here under truce, and his safety has been guaranteed by the dragon mage. Not that long ago, you pledged to stand behind him in his decisions and even obey his orders!"

The elder dragon who had ordered Tomar's capture said, "My apologies to Tomar and the dragon mage. I have exceeded my authority, and will abstain from voting in the conclave. I obviously have a deep-seated bias that I must deal with first, before making any rash decisions, like an impetuous youth."

Tomar said proudly, "Apology accepted."

"I also accept your apology. It is difficult to reach a decision when centuries of mistrust lie between the dark elves and the dragons, as well as those that work closely with them. We have pushed the dark elf race into a situation where they are forced to break laws in order to survive, as no one will deal fairly with them," I said.

So as not to further influence any vote on the part of the conclave, I excused myself, leaving the drakes and the Ice people companions to ensure Tomar's safety and good behaviour. The representatives of the races were in the room with the conclave of dragons until late in the day. The sun was setting as they came out of the dragon chambers.

"Isaac, Gizmo, how did it go, did you get any sense of how things are going to go?" I asked excitedly.

Isaac responded, "No. The youngest ones on the council are siding with you, of course, but some of the oldest have deep-seated fears and mistrust of the dark elves."

The conclave deliberated on the question that I had put to them. It took them five days to come to a decision. I was formally invited, in writing, the invitation presented by a companion in full dress regalia, to attend the conclave. I was a little wary of the way I was invited; I could only bring Gizmo and Isaac with me. No companions or others were allowed to attend.

When I entered the chamber, everything was silent. As the saying goes, you could hear a pin drop.

"Greetings Dragon Mage, I apologize for the delay. But the request that you put to us means a complete rethinking of our centuries-old beliefs," Elijah said.

I was given a parchment, with a seal on it, addressed to the keeper of the jail. I was told it contained instructions for him to stand down and return to the nearest stronghold for redeployment. It also instructed him to release all dark elves, allowing them to go when and where they wanted.

"Adoronac will arrange to be at the jail when you are there to validate the order, and to assist if there are any problems with the guards," Elijah said.

I slowly walked out of the conclave meeting to greet everyone. They were waiting with great anticipation for the dragon conclave's decision. I showed them the parchment and advised that I would be leaving as soon as possible, but that I wanted to have at least two Ankylosaurus, loaded with supplies and healers in case they were needed.

"Tomar, will you continue under this flag of truce, and come with me to explain to your people that this is not a trick of some sort?" I asked.

"I would be honoured to take part in the emancipation of my people. It will take a bit before they trust the elves and dwarves, and vice versa," Tomar said, bowing to me.

I spoke with the chieftain of the closest stronghold to the jail, explaining what I needed and advising him to keep track of all supplies. I promised him that he would be compensated for it later. As well, I requested the presence of two powerful healers from each stronghold.

The chieftain advised that the Ankylosaurus and supplies would be ready in two days' time. The chieftain set off at a run with his bodyguards and I sent a messenger to my stronghold, asking all companions and as many guards as could be spared to attend.

I called Isaac and Gizmo to one side to speak to them in private, mind to mind. "I want Tomar to come with us, but I am not ready to share the secret of the portals. He is still a member of assassins' guild, so ultimately he answers directly to Chavez. I am going to have Mercury transport both of us to the stronghold, meeting everyone else there." I said.

"Isaac and I agree that this would be the best solution. If you need to explain to Tomar, just tell him it is magic, which is technically true as the portals work by an unknown magic," Gizmo said quietly.

"Mercury, gear up and get back here as soon as you can. We have another interesting situation to deal with!" I called with my mind.

Mercury responded, "I am here in the stronghold. Great

Granddad felt that you might need my services on short notice. I can be ready to go in ten minutes; I have been resting and I am ready to go whenever you are."

"James, please find my travel kit, so that Tomar and I can take flight on Mercury and get to our destination as quickly as possible," I said to him.

James appeared crestfallen, until I pulled him aside and explained that I wanted him to take the portal system and have everything ready for when Tomar and I arrived.

James went running off to the keep, returning with Sylvia and Rose to say goodbye to me. After a quick kiss from my ladies, and once Mercury showed up, I had James pack the saddlebags. Tomar was eyeing Mercury hesitantly.

Tomar asked, "Is it safe? I do not see any reins to control this beast!"

Mercury said loudly, "I am probably smarter than you are, dark elf, and I am not a beast. I go where the dragon mage and I have decided to travel. Do not worry, I have not lost any riders yet… but there's always a first time!"

Tomar swallowed, but did not hesitate to climb into the saddle. He looked a little queasy initially, but Mercury, as per my orders, flew as steadily as possible. Tomar settled in to watch the landscape as we flew. We travelled for a day and a half, reaching the stronghold in record time.

When we landed, I could see Tomar's surprise at the companions and the rest of my company waiting for us. But he took it stoically, not saying a word. He did look at me and mumbled something about 'mages.'

As we were packing up the Ankylosaurus, I counted heads. We had a very large number of warriors from each clan represented in the group. I asked James, but he had no idea as to why our number of warriors had more than tripled from the initial plans. So before asking Elijah, I sought out Isaac and Gizmo to see if I could some information.

"Why have we amassed such a large contingent of men, just to relieve the jail commander and his guards?" I asked Isaac and Gizmo.

Isaac said in response, "My orders come directly from Elijah. First and foremost, the dragon mage must be protected at all times. Secondary is the shutting down of the jail, but information has been received that certain atrocities have been committed by those in the jail against the dark elf people of all ages. There are parties from all clans that are to witness and support the dragon mage if executions are required."

"Once we leave here, there will be a gathering of dragons within two minutes of flight to enforce any order that you feel is appropriate. The conclave of dragons has given you complete control of this situation, as you are independent of all races," Isaac said.

"Why wasn't I told of this before I left the Diamond stronghold, and before now?" I asked.

Elijah responded, "Young Dragon Mage, you have my word that this information has just come to light through one of the dragon lords in the area. They have been until now, looking the other way and ignoring any complaints that have reached their ears. Once the decision was made to support you, these dragon lords came to me to share what they had heard. I have given my word that they will not in any way be involved in the rectification of any problems that may surface.

"I did not want to disturb you during your flight with Tomar but I wanted you to have the information as soon as possible," Elijah added, with concern in his mind touch.

Great, I thought to myself. *If word gets out, they may dispose of any who would be willing to testify.* This would cause others to be too afraid of the guards to say anything against them. I called for Ice Wind as well as Rose and Gladius.

"Ice Wind, gather your snow people, head to the jail and secretly watch what is going on inside, reporting to me when I arrive," I said to him. Ice Wind nodded, running off, followed by the other snow people. They were out of the gate within moments.

I told Blade to gather all the dwarf warriors and head out right away, with a minimum of supplies for a forced march on the jail. They were to remain out of sight, capturing any patrols they came across, for questioning later.

"Gladius, are there any communities in this area where you could get Elven reinforcements?" I asked.

Gladius responded, "Yes, I could have up to one hundred warriors in the area of the jail by daybreak tomorrow."

"Good. I want you close by until the dwarf warriors arrive, and then pull back into the surrounding area for support. We may have to deal with some crimes committed by dwarves, and there are hard feelings enough between the races. It would be worse if you have to punish them or kill any dwarf. Just capture any patrols alive but injured if necessary for questioning," I told Gladius.

Tomar and I went to lie down on the Ankylosaurus platforms while they pulled out, under Godfrey's supervision. I sent Gizmo with Gladius, and Isaac with the dwarf contingent for long-range communications. Isaac was to coordinate some small dragons who would fly over and around the jail, watching what was transpiring and feeding information back to us.

Because Mercury was obviously exhausted from his long flight, I let him sleep as long as possible. When he awakened, Tomar and I strapped in and caught up with the dwarf warriors after two hours of flight. Mercury flew to where the other dragons were gathering. Awaiting me when we landed were five young dragon lords in their fighting prime, and ten younger dragons. In charge, to help the young ones keep their calm, was the Dragon Lord Betel.

I formulated a plan to fly in with Mercury and Dragon Lord Betel. The dwarves would pretend to be our companions. Ice Wind and his people would provide quite the distraction, as few had ever seen one of the snow people—let alone five of them.

We scheduled our arrival for late afternoon, when the guards working the day shift were starting to feel tired and not paying too much attention to details.

~ THIRTY-SIX ~

Gaol Break

Blade, with a small group, arrived at the gate first advising the guard captain that they needed entry immediately.

"A dragon lord has been attacked by a pack of predatory flying dinosaurs. He is being escorted by the dragon mage, and needs a clear patch behind the wall where he can be treated before we can proceed safely," Blade said.

The guard captain said, "This is a prison. He cannot land here."

"Are you refusing a dragon lord the right to land in the only safe place in the area 'til help can arrive?" Blade yelled at him.

"How long will he be staying?" asked the guard captain, who looked extremely pale, as though he needed to run to the outhouse, or just simply was going to pass out.

Blade said to the guard captain, "He can fly slowly, so we are waiting for other dragons to escort him safely to a stronghold to recuperate. We will be out of your hair in no time! Why, are you expecting a prison revolt or riot? I had heard that you have all the dark elves well under control."

"D—did you say more d—dragons? No, we—we are—fine. I just—have to get the—the commander," the guard captain stammered.

"You'd better be quick about it, here come the companions to the dragons. Lord Betel will be here in moments. You run along and get the commander, and I will supervise the gate, keeping it safe," Blade said with authority.

The guard captain looked at the contingent of companions that were coming at a fast trot. Blade told me later that when he saw the Yetis, the captain's eyes, as well as his mouth, went wide open. He stood there for a moment as if forgetting what he was going to do, then gave a start and was off in a run to get his boss.

The companions quickly cleared an area in the centre of the jail courtyard. The guard in the watch tower called out to everyone standing in the open area of the jail, "Dragons Ho!"

Betel came to a realistic-looking crash landing, bowling over a couple of the guards in the courtyard. I came to a quick landing beside Betel and Tomar and jumped off. I yelled to the companions, "Now!"

Tomar and the Yeti, as well as half the dwarf companions there, ran for the caves. Suddenly, the ten small dragons flew into the jail and also headed into the caves to seek out guards in order to get them to step down or disable them. The rest of the companions ran back to the gate and kept it open, while the huge contingent of dwarves and elves entered the keep.

As the troops entered the gate, the guards started to take up defensive positions to seal it.

Betel roared loudly, "Stand down right now! I do not want anyone hurt at this moment but if you resist the dragon Mage's troops, you will be struck down! I speak for the entire dragon conclave, and you risk our wrath!"

At that statement, the guards saw the six dragon lords settling on the walls of the jail.

A uniformed man ran up panting, "I am Commander Dagger, what is this all…about ..?"

He ran out of words as he took in all the warriors and dragons surrounding the open areas of the jail. He pulled his sword, rushing at me or Betel—I was not sure. A warrior stepped out of the group and tripped up the commander before pulling off her helmet to reveal it was Sylvia. She winked at me, unarming him and pinning him to the ground until some warriors tied him up.

"Put a guard on him; he is not to talk to anyone. But make sure of his safety until we can interrogate him. Find me the second in command, so that we can start this process as quickly as possible."

The guard captain who was at the gate turned out to be the most senior of the guards, so the command fell on him. He read the orders from the conclave, spit on the ground in front of me, and then gathered his men from the walls and barracks to form up in the main courtyard. He addressed the men, once he had them all assembled.

In a loud voice, he announced: "The great dragons and their conclave have come to the conclusion that we are to free these worms from their cages, so that they can go anywhere and do anything they want. The dragon mage has convinced them that they are not a threat to the clans!"

He read the order of the conclave as if it left a bitter taste in his mouth; everything that he had been taught or trained to believe was gone. He directed the men to remain in the jail until they had been debriefed by one of the little dragons.

I left the details of the debriefing of the guards to Blaze, who delegated little dragons and select trained interrogators to take care of the allegations of mistreatment of the prisoners. I walked into the mine tunnels to examine the living conditions that the dark elves had had to contend with.

The drakes and Fred followed me into the mines to ensure my safety, but I felt doubtful that any of the dark elves had enough strength to put up much of a fight.

The tunnels were damp and cold, with no doors anywhere in sight; the cool mountain air crept in everywhere. It was dark. There were very few torches and no cooking fires in the tunnels. The bedding consisted of straw, which was damp and full of mildew.

The caravan with healers and supplies arrived, and the supplies were distributed as quickly as possible. All of the healers went into the tunnels, spreading out as rapidly as possible.

The smell was atrocious; unwashed people and rotting hay, and the sickly-sweet smells that could only be gangrene. If the person or persons were found, fast action would be needed to save lives and limbs.

The caves reminded me of the unused tunnels and corridors in the land of the snow people. I quickly passed the word to the little dragons and healers to be careful for predators that might be hiding in the deep caves. You never knew what there might be deep down there, including some of the large cave spiders that I had dealt with before.

I shuddered as I continued to examine people who were exhibiting symptoms of malnutrition. I had yet to find the person with the infection that was giving off the gangrene smell. I knew, though, that I would have to move quickly to save whoever had the infection.

One of the companions came to me and pulled me aside to advise that they had found something that would interest me in the deepest part of the tunnels that led down into the undeveloped areas of the mine.

I was led past all of the residential areas of the mine. The mine opened up into a giant cavern that seemed to spread out for miles. Down in the pit of this huge space was a brick wall, which looked very small, dwarfed by the cathedral-like cavern that spread out around us.

The wall was covered in cobwebs, and protected by at least a dozen giant spiders that appeared to be the size of grizzly bears. Matilda and her two travel mates did not waste any time waiting for a command to attack. They went straight for the webs, setting them on fire and then going after the spiders with relish.

The drakes and spiders must have been instinctive enemies for centuries. The drakes knew just how to knock a spider down and make short work of it. When the drakes returned to my side I saw that, other than a few scratches, they were unscathed.

I caused Draco to light the area brightly. Writing was visible on the wall, with a door drawn in. Ancient writing surrounded the door, but it was only a matter of seconds tracing the lines with the magic staff when a portal opened up.

I directed the troops to clean out the rest of the caverns to ensure there were no spiders left. I then went back to the surface to follow up with the relief effort.

The entire process of questioning the dwarf guards was swift. A small dragon stayed in the room to search the mind of the dwarf for deceit. If the dwarf was lying during the interrogation, more questions were asked until the small dragon was satisfied, one way or another.

If any of the dwarves were dishonest, they would be placed in custody until such time as they could be transported, to be judged by Elijah at the Diamond stronghold.

All told, there were only six of the officer class and Dagger that were mistreating the dark elves. The rest of the guards did not care for the dark elf prisoners, but had taken no actions to mistreat them directly unless ordered by the officers to do so.

After exploring the entire tunnel system, only the one section was found with a wall of brick that held a doorway. The guards could find no other entrance to the mines.

A search team went through the portal. It came back to report that the tunnels opened up into a cul-de-sac in the Diamond stronghold that was almost completely hidden from view.

Both male and female dark elves were assessed for medical needs as rapidly as possible. The worst were taken through the tunnels right away to be treated. Those in less danger were loaded aboard the caravan and shipped out to the nearest stronghold for further treatment.

I selected a small team of companions, as well as Matilda and a few other drakes, to examine a small stronghold in a valley in the north that was well-protected by a pass. Coming along with us was Tomar, the dark elf, as well as Domar, the eldest of the tribe from the prison.

Our group was greeted by a large contingent of dwarf engineers, who were repairing walls and eradicating vermin to make this place more habitable.

"Is this another prison set-up for my people to waste away even more?" Tomar demanded.

"Don't be foolish young one! This is obviously a new home being cleaned up for our use. There are no guard posts; it will be up to us to defend ourselves, Domar the elder said.

"You are close to the truth. Kali will be here to guide you and help you settle into your lands," I said.

Domar asked, "Who or what is 'Kali'?"

"You will find out soon enough, eldest one. I will show you the storage rooms, where there are enough supplies to last you through the winter. You can grow your own crops in the spring," I said.

The head engineer advised me that the majority of the work was done and everything was in working order.

I escorted Domar and Tomar to its entrance to witness the last bit of my plan to seal the valley. Several dragons showed up, blasting the rock and causing a severe avalanche, which sealed the entrance.

Domar asked, "Does this mean that we are sealed into this valley, with no hope of escape? It would take us several years to dig through this rubble, to be able to get out of the valley."

I escorted Domar and Tomar to the portals in the tunnels, opening them up for their use and showing them the one portal which led to an access on the other side of the valley.

I explained where the other tunnels led and that they were free to use them for trading and meetings with other strongholds. I even traversed the one tunnel leading to the outside of the valley, to show that I was not lying to them.

"This way, your people are safe from harm or interference from the outside world. That is, unless you wish to travel to the world outside of this valley," I said to Tomar and Domar.

Once back in the stronghold, we were greeted by a young dragon, whose companions had gathered, awaiting us. Introductions were in order: "This is the dragon lord Kali, who will be your mentor in dealing with the dwarf and elf people. You must share in this potion with Kali, which will allow you to communicate directly with him."

Domar and Tomar looked at the flagon with caution in their eyes, so I grabbed the flagon and took a healthy draft from it. The other two joined me once they realized they would not be poisoned, or turned into something evil.

Kali said to us, "Now you can hear me, and I can hear you. And so shall it be 'til the end of your lives, or mine."

"This way, I can communicate with Kali as well as you can. Also, if you have need of me, Kali can call for my aid," I explained.

"I am simply here to guide you and to assist you with your re-acclimatization with life in the outside world when you are ready," Kali said with authority.

I arranged for the rest of the dark elves to be brought through the tunnels under a sleep spell, so that only the elders and certain warriors were aware of the system of tunnels. The others would be told when the time was right.

We traversed back to the Diamond clan stronghold, checking on the injured and elderly. Tomar approached me.

"Remember my word, Dragon Lord? I have received word from the head of the assassins' guild to kill you," Tomar said, looking at me.

"So. Do I have time to prepare or do you wish to fight right now?" I replied.

"I have sent a reply to the head of the assassins' guild that I am resigning and no longer wish to work for the guild. Under normal circumstances, I would be afraid of someone coming to get me, but since I am the best in the guild, no one would dare try to kill me. I hereby pledge my allegiance to the dragon master," Tomar said in a powerful voice.

He got down on one knee and offered up his sword to me, hilt first.

"I accept your offer of fealty, with the understanding that you give me as much notice if you wish to leave my service," I said.

Tomar nodded his head in agreement and promised, "I will stand at your side and guard your back, as long as I am able."

Elijah's mind cut into mine, saying, "At the rate you are going, you will soon have a member of each race as part of your companions."

It was a matter of about one week to finish repair of the old stronghold, to the point that it was secure and could be used to defend the occupants.

In the meantime, the dark elves received tender care by all the healers that were available in the Diamond stronghold. Once the stronghold was ready for occupancy, a strong sleep spell was placed on most of the dark elves, and they were moved quickly while they were slumbering. Only a select few of the elders and certain warriors were allowed to stroll through the portals awake.

The hardest part was locating dwarves that did not harbour any negative feelings about the dark elves. We needed a core group of dwarves who would assist the elves with getting settled. Fortunately, the small dragons did the selecting, and were able to find a select few that held no bias.

Everything was going smoothly and the dark elves were settled in their new home when Elijah said, "Kali has advised that the dark elves are extremely happy in their new homes, warm for the first time in years. They have begun building a statue of you in the centre of the stronghold. You are a hero in their eyes."

I was at a loss. I did not think of myself as a hero deserving a statue. Being thought of in such a way was a concept that I had never considered.

~ THIRTY-SEVEN ~

An Unexpected Event

I spent the next three weeks recuperating and focusing on learning different spells, both defensive and offensive. I spent quality time with Rose and Sylvia, and generally enjoyed myself.

We all returned to the secret stronghold, and took up house again. I was deep in thought and took to walking the battlements at odd hours of the day and night. This had two benefits. The guards and the drakes got to know each other and become more comfortable with each other. Also, they would ignore each other in a battle situation.

Late one night, I was walking the embattlements, checking on the guards. The next thing I knew, something grabbed me and carried me aloft into the night sky.

Once the shock wore off, I knew it was a choice between falling to the ground and possibly to my death or being part of a meal for this large flying dinosaur.

I decided that the fall could possibly kill me, but to be a meal for the dinosaur would definitely spell my end. I had dropped Draco in surprise when the creature had grabbed me off the embattlements and the beast had me in such a hold that I could not reach my pistol because of its claws.

My arms were still free so I was able to grab my knife out of my boot. I only hesitated briefly, knowing that the longer I waited, the less likely I would have a chance to do it. I slashed at the claws of the dinosaur. With a roar, the winged beast released me! That was the last thing I remembered for quite a while.

When I woke up, the sun was shining and I was lying in the middle of a field inside of something green and scaly. I tried to roll off what I landed on, but found I could not move my legs. The fall had broken my back!

The dinosaur that I landed on had died as a result of the impact, and by the smell, it had been dead for a few days. I could not see them, but I could hear something tearing at the skin of the dinosaur. It was just a matter of time before they got to me!

"Well, you S.O.B.'s, I promise to take a few of you with me!" I yelled at whatever was chewing on the dinosaur carcass.

That might have been possible if it were not for the pain, which took me in and out of consciousness. I started to get the feeling that I must have also hit my head when I landed.

I regained consciousness at one point just in time to see some sort of raptor reaching at me through the dinosaur carcass to try to take a chunk out of me. I shot it through the head and propped myself up, quietly waiting for the rest of the pack to show up.

I did not have a long wait. I heard the sound of arrows flying through the air and the occasional yelp of pain. Someone else was there! I could hear someone talking in what sounded like a Germanic tongue. This reminded me of what I had heard from the dark elves when they were rescued from imprisonment.

I tried to talk to them as they inspected me but they just talked amongst each other in that Germanic-sounding speech. They ignored my protests about pain and having a back injury, throwing me on a small cart. They took me several hours down the road to a small village filled with dark elves.

They dumped me in the corner of a musty-smelling shack. They stripped all of my equipment and put it somewhere out of sight.

After a week, I could tell gangrene had set into my injuries; the smell was intolerable. The only care that I got from my captors was the occasional bowl of gruel. They saw fit not to give me any medical treatment at all.

The following week, I decided to give them something to remember me by. I was able to gather enough energy to magically set the shack on fire. They were able to drag me out of the shack before the roof fell in.

"Aw, I was just starting to get warmed up, guys!" I said jokingly.

The elves did not respond verbally but one large fellow got a few kicks in. I was glad that I could at least touch a couple of nerves once in a while.

Elijah said in my mind, "If you can hear me, Lord Jim, try to respond with anything that might help us find you. All I can feel right now is your pain."

I responded to him, "Look for smoke."

I lapsed into unconsciousness as the large fellow kicked me in the head a few more times.

The next day the dark elves built a funeral pyre and lay me on top of it. The flames licked up, enveloping me. I felt warm, momentarily, before they started to burn me. It hurt, but the fire did not harm me otherwise.

I must have blacked out, because the next thing I remember was Rose and Tomar peering down on me with looks of concern on their faces. The whole village was swarming with dwarven warriors and at least six large dragons that I could see at the moment.

Tomar asked, "Do we need to take revenge and kill someone?"

"No. That large fellow standing sheepishly over there needs to be spoken to about how to treat prisoners. Take him into custody, will you, until I decide what to do to him," I said weakly.

Tomar responded, "It will be as you wish, Dragon Mage."

"I do not wish to alarm you Rose, but I think my back is broken. I cannot feel my legs, and I can't walk," I said quietly to Rose.

"Do not worry, my prince. All will be well. The greatest healers are available to help," Rose said.

"All that can be done will be done, Dragon Mage," Elijah said.

I was placed in a litter arrangement and flown back to the secret stronghold. The litter was then carried through the portal system to the Diamond stronghold and down to Elijah's chamber. Elijah was there to oversee a pair of aged healers work on me to make sure all the infection was cleaned up.

I could feel warmth emanating from Elijah, overcoming any pain and leaving me lying in a lethargic state, barely aware of what was happening around me.

Once they were finished, they placed me in the bed I had been used the last few times I had been stayed at the stronghold. The area was swarming with companions and more security than I had never seen before at the stronghold.

I was in bed for almost two weeks before the healers would even let me sit up. Another week passed and I was allowed to sit up for a while or be pushed around in a wooden wheelchair for a bit, before I was too tired and had to lie back down again.

Other than the healers checking on me, the only other people I was allowed to see were Sylvia and Rose. Sylvia made sure that no one disturbed my rest, and when I was sleeping, heaven help the poor person who made too much noise. Sylvia would find that person, and out of my hearing range, tear a strip off them for disturbing the dragon mage.

The dark elves were filled in as to what had happened. Domar and Lomar sat down and apparently had a long talk about the dark elf people's future. They decided to move to the valley. The entire village of two hundred people, including warriors, were moving within a week.

I sent for Tomar right away to speak with him about the move.

"Is there going to be any problem sending extra troops to ensure the civilians are safe from attack?" I asked.

"Initially there will be some suspicion but as time goes by, my people will realize that their safety is the priority," Tomar responded.

"Can the large dark elf who does not know how to treat prisoners be trusted now?" I asked quietly.

"His name is Neb, and once he understood the mistake he made, he pledged his life to you as I have. He initially called me a traitor but we were able to convince him once he spoke to the elder at the stronghold. Then we had a private chat about his respect for superiors," Tomar responded.

Tomar had a grin on his face when introducing me to Neb. I

could see the still-healing bruises on his face. Matilda came in and sniffed at him, and then gave him a good face washing, which to me was a good sign.

"I have spoken to Tomar, Neb, and I understand that you are trustworthy. Your family has been moved with the rest of the village, to the protected valley, where they will be as safe from attack as any of us. I have not made any decision regarding a possible penalty for the—shall we say—exuberant way you treat prisoners. But you have my word that if there is a penalty, it will levied on you only, and not your kin," I quietly said to Neb.

"Do you understand and pledge your service to me?" I asked.

"Yes, My Lord Dragon Mage. Whatever you need, I shall provide and more; I will lay down my life in your service. You have done much more to ensure the freedom of my people than any other in history," Neb said.

"What I need from you now is silence. You will push my wheeled chair, not uttering a word to me unless I ask you a question. I will let you know what your punishment will be, based on your actions. If that is acceptable, just nod and take your position," I commanded.

Neb nodded and took up position to push the wooden wheelchair. Matilda immediately came up beside him and I directed him to wheel me to Elijah's chambers. Our conversation was mind-to-mind, so Neb never heard.

Elijah asked, "Have you decided on a punishment yet?"

"Other than forbidding him speech until I can think of a suitable punishment?" I said.

"I will cast a spell to prevent him from talking, other than in case of emergency," Elijah said.

I kept Neb at my side to be my runner and handyman, fetching whatever I might need from anywhere in the stronghold. I sent Tomar and the dragon lord Kali to supervise the move to the stronghold. The dwarves may not listen to the dark elf, but they fell in line whenever a dragon was involved.

"Elijah, is there anything we can do to increase my mobility? I don't think I am much of a threat in a wheelchair," I asked one day.

Elijah responded, "We are searching all of the old ledgers to see if there is something we might do to increase or give you full mobility. Even if you are not physically battle-ready, we can still use your guidance."

The companions and I travelled via the portals to the dark elf stronghold. Neb and the companions came along with me, to ensure that no further injury occurred to the dragon mage. Knowing that I was coming soon, the elders had set aside accommodation suitable to my station, and to include the Lady Sylvia and Rose.

"Neb, I free you from your oath. You can stay with your clan, which has safely arrived. No one will judge you for your past action, as I have written up a pardon for you. I do not think your actions were done with knowledge of who I was," I said.

Neb lowered his head and walked away, looking for his clan.

"He is a troubled man, but he will talk to his family. I do not think we have seen the last of Neb. His father is an honourable man, and will ensure his son continues to bring honour to the family," Tomar explained.

I settled in and worked on ensuring that all the paperwork was done to get more supplies, to make sure there was enough for the winter months. I was half dozing in the wheelchair in front of a roaring fire when something touched my shoulder gently. It was Lady Sylvia, who advised me that Neb was back and wanted a private audience with me.

I had the room cleared of everyone with the exception of Matilda, who lay down on the floor beside me.

"Neb, come in and speak your mind. If you are here to kill me, there is a sword on the table and I am defenceless. Matilda will not interfere, and I have even written up a letter pardoning your crimes and preventing any from interfering with you. Take whatever action you feel you need to," I said quietly.

Neb stated contritely, "I have come to offer my service, whether it is to clean the drakes and clean behind them or to push your cart 'til I drop dead. My life is yours to control. Just say the word if you wish, and I will throw myself on my sword."

"Present yourself to Tomar, and study closely under him in the arts of assassination and fighting. When he says you are ready, you can come stand by my side and fight with me. With my understanding of your previous skills, it should not take that long," I said to him.

After he bowed deeply to me, Neb turned and left the room in search of Tomar. I heard a fluttering of wings as Isaac flew into the room, landing on the back of the wheel chair.

Isaac said to me, "You took a great chance there, he could have taken a sword to end your days swiftly."

"I may seem a little slow at times, my friend Lord Isaac but I knew you were in the room. I doubt that I could have even slowed Matilda down from going for his throat or prevented you from attacking him. He needs to control his anger, not be controlled by it." I said.

James came into the room to check in on me. Finding me all right, he started putting order in the room and offered to make me a light meal, which I turned down. He assisted me in preparing for bed and settled me in. Lady Sylvia and Rose joined me later in the evening.

~ Thirty-Eight ~

Surgery

bout a week later, the two small dragons, Gizmo and Isaac came to me to advise that they had discovered a solution to my problem. It was not easy and would entail another first for the dragon lords: I was to be taken to the great nesting site of the dragons.

The next morning, a large, closed-up litter arrived at the secret stronghold. I was taken down the tunnels and through the portal to the stronghold. I was not allowed company for this trip—just a couple of attendants, as well Gizmo and Isaac. Matilda, as well as another breeding pair of drakes, was onboard.

I received a strong draught to keep me asleep the entire trip, which took about a day and a half. My attendants were helpful and courteous, but I was to be blindfolded until I was inside the tunnels.

When the blindfold was removed, I could see huge tunnels, wide enough to allow two dragons to pass at a time. The whole tunnel setup and construction appeared ancient—hundreds of years old. I was brought up to a large, red, breeding female dragon.

My companion dwarf asked me, "Are you prepared for this procedure?"

"What procedure?" I answered. "I have received no explanations at all."

The dwarf said, "The Great Lady Neela was under the impression that you had been briefed completely on what was going to happen. One of the fledglings has had an accident, and it is only

273

a matter of time before he passes on to the next life. We are going to use some of his backbone to replace what was totally destroyed in yours from the fall."

The Great Lady Neela said, through my companion dwarf, "We have not performed this procedure in recent memory, and there is no guarantee that it will work. But we have high hopes, Dragon Mage that you will be able to walk again."

I gifted the breeding pair of drakes to Lady Neela, who was ecstatic. The drakes took to the dragon, playing like puppies around her and checking the nests, being very gentle with any eggs or hatchlings they found.

The Great Lady Neela, through my companion dwarf, said, "We have not had nest guardians here in a long time. We grieved greatly when they disappeared."

They took me to a luxurious room to rest and await the passing of the young fledgling dragon, 'Kai'. I immediately called the companions who were serving me, to tell them that I wished to be with Kai to help comfort him in his final moments.

The companions looked perplexed and answered that they would have to ask someone of authority for permission.

Upon his return, the companion dwarf said, "The Great Lady Neela thinks that it would be an excellent thing to be with Kai."

They took me to the young dragon, and I could see that he had been attacked by something and had taken a great fall. Blood was oozing from his body. A companion wizard cut my hand, added some of the dragon blood and made up the mixture allowing me to communicate with Kai. After drinking the mixture, I asked the companions to lay me down beside Kai.

As we lay beside each other, I allowed my mind to come in contact with Kai's, riding the waves of turmoil and pain and adding calm until his mind was flying high over the ocean and countryside, joy and contentment filling his young mind. I managed to keep the image of happiness until Kai grew weaker and slowly passed away.

I was taken back to my chamber, where attendants helped clean me, and then I was taken to a central chamber. Over one hundred dragons roosted around a table in the centre of the chamber. The companions lay me down face first, and I was administered a potion to numb my senses.

I could feel the warmth radiating in the room enveloping me as I felt a knife cut into my back, when I lost consciousness. The surgery took a while. I awoke lying in bed with all the torches in the room lit and the Lady Neela leaning over me, watching me intently.

She said to me, "How are you feeling, little Dragon Mage, and how much can you feel?"

"My head hurts like it has been hit by a hammer, but the tips of my toes are tingling. How is it that I can hear you in my mind without drinking the sharing potion, or having a translator dwarf?" I asked.

Neela responded, "You are part dragon now. You can talk to any dragon without any magic to make it possible. Your lifespan will probably be doubled, if not more, my little Kai, as the part of your spine spreads its magical energies throughout your body."

"Why are you calling me 'Kai,' Great One?" I asked

"Because part of you is Kai, who lives on in you. You made his passing so pleasant that he died with peace in his young mind rather than evil," Neela explained.

"I am pleased that I am even more part of the clan now," I responded to Neela.

I could sense now the love she was projecting toward me. Kai must have been one of her brood. She nodded her head as her companions placed me on a litter and carried me to the larger litter, which had been opened up so that I could see the entire island as the dragons spoke to me and each other.

I slept through part of the trip over the ocean, waking only once when the dragons called me by my new dragon name to point out some sort of sea monster lifting itself out of the waves.

Lady Gizmo and Lord Isaac kept to themselves, allowing me to adapt to these new feelings and the ability to listen to the dragons talking to each other.

When we landed at the secret stronghold, I thanked both of the dragons for their service. I could tell they were happy to receive my gratitude directly and not through a translator.

I rested for a week before attempting my first steps since I had broken my back. I realized that my new family and this new world were my new reality. There was no going back. Without the magic to maintain my body in my home world, I would be stuck in a wheelchair—if not worse.

Tentatively, I walked the battlements of the stronghold with Rose, Lady Sylvia, Matilda, Gizmo and Isaac. The wind was blowing, but I found that I could generate an area of warmth around us, not feeling any cold at all. We all stopped to admire both of the moons rising out of the ocean to light up the stronghold.

I had surmounted many dangers and met new friends and foes. I had taken many steps forward for the people I was trying to help in this world. I still had to ponder what to do about Chavez; he was the next major issue that I had to deal with, and soon.

~ CHARACTER INDEX ~

Adam   Leader of Diamond clan

Adoronac   Dragon Guardian of the North and provider of
                    counsel to the dwarves

Anax   elf — wise man elder — who in passing of old
                    age declared Jim an Elf friend

Argentum   Caravan leader (dwarf) travels south part of
                    world trading

Betel   young dragon lord taking charge of Quartz clan

Blaze   Dwarf — warrior — general — incorporated
                    into companions on clan edict

Blade   Dwarf — warrior — general — incorporated
                    into companions on clan edict

Bonny and   breeding pair of drakes that stayed with the
Clyde   dragon mage

Chavez   Grand Wizard — leader of the government and
                    one badass dude

Companion protectors from the People:

> **John** (Cpl) **Frank** (Cpl)
> Bill, Joe, Fred, Samson, Kevin, Karl, Larry, Lionel

Creditum   dwarf — caravan leader and trader, extremely
                    honest

Dagger   Commander of Dark Elf jail

Domar	eldest of Dark Elf clan
Dragon Council	three dragons: Adam, Joshua, and Zachariah
Drake	type of flightless dragon; about the size of a large mastiff back home.
Elijah	Eldest of dragons and member of the Dragon conclave, Elijah acts as the voice of the world's silent inhabitants. While attempting to do right, he may not always make the best decisions but is ready to make amends through his fealty to the Dragon Mage.
Envoy	Snow People – contact person between the sea people and his.
Fire-Tongue	Dwarf — warrior — general — incorporated into companions on clan edict
Flit	small dragon lord, known for speed and stealth.
Fred	Drake handler, falsely accused of being a thief taken under Dragon Mages protection.
Gizmo	Dragon companion and familiar to Jim, Gizmo, a female dragon of the smaller variety is wise, knowledgeable, courageous and very competent as Jim's companion and guide.
Gladius	elf — warrior and head of one of the elf communities that welcome Jim as elf friend
Godfrey	ancient wizard wise in the ways of all types of magic (other than dragon magic), also the dragon mage's great grandfather.
Ice Storm	Yeti (snow people) adviser to the Bronze clan in the north
Ice Wind	Yeti (snow people) Dragon Mage companion
Isaac	Gizmo's partner. Isaac is intelligent, capable and an excellent emissary for both Jim and the Dragon conclave, usually serving both quite well.

James	The Friday to Jim's Crusoe, James is the faithful, loving servant. Ready to defend, serve or kowtow to the Dragon Mage's every whim as it seems his destiny, James is always there.
Jeremiah	Leader of Bronze clan
Jim/Kai/ narrator/Dragon Mage	Former marine / police officer Jim is a quiet, introvert with a strong sense of right and wrong and a need to protect and serve. His courage, intelligence, resourcefulness and talent at magic and getting himself out of tough spots help him make believers and followers out of the inhabitants of the new world.
John	would be assassin (amateur) failed at attempting to kill dragon mage.
Joseph	Village Elder at one of the People villages
Joshua	twin brother to James of the People, sent to act as Jim's escort and servants, gave up his life defending Jim.
Kali	Young dragon, guide to Dark Elf clan
Kai	A young fledgling dragon that dies; also name given to Jim by dragon clan when the dragon's spine was used to cure him. Name given to Jim's first born son (mother was Rose)
Kaleigh	First born daughter of dragon mage Jim (mother was Lady Sylvia)
Lazarus	Dragon clan wizard trained to control portals to other worlds - dwarf
Lomar	elder Dark Elf from forest community
Luke	would be assassin (amateur) failed at attempting to kill dragon mage.
Malum	descendants of dark dragons —a bat-like creature that does not like light at all
Mark	would be assassin (amateur) failed at attempting to kill dragon mage.

Matilda	Leader of Drake pack, eldest female
Midnight	Pitch Black Dragon Seeker of things from other lands for Mother of Dragons
Mercury	Dragon steed and formidable ally, Mercury serves the Dragon Mage by conducting and protecting him while providing the voice of experience, all in an impetuous, irreverent, devil-may-care way.
Morlack	detachment commander for Orc encampment in the North
Mortimer/ Anthony	Merchant in Capital City (dwarf), front for assassins' guild, later ally for the dragon mage.
Neb	large Dark Elf, who was taken under Tomar's wing
Neela	eldest breeding female dragon, in charge of aviary
Orb of Pater	magical orb containing a crystal that steals power from the enemy and protects the bearer.
Pater	dragon — the father of all dragons dating back to the beginning of recorded dragon history
Rawlings and Smith	Detectives from Scotland Yard; sent to question Jim while he was in the hospital.
Rose	the strongest of the female characters, Rose is an Elven warrior that trains Jim in martial arts and later becomes his other wife
Samuel	Elder of the People (normal humans)
Snow people companions	Yeti — Snow Flake, Ice Runner, Snow Ball, Snow Storm
Susan	Fred's mother, nursed back to health and in charge of dragon mage's kitchen.
Susie	young dwarf lady — looking for love in all the wrong places
Sylvia	Dwarven widow and eventual wife, Sylvia is the "Ideal" partner in her silent, but commanding way, whether it be ordering the dwarven warrior or ensuring the household is run properly.

Tomar	Assassins' guild senior and most experienced killer
Torlak	Orc wizard
The Voice	Elder Yeti (snow people), leader and friend to Elijah

~ Items of Magic ~

Draco	Magical Staff — made of bone of ancient dragon, carrying strong dragon magic
Golden ring of Strength	Gift from The Voice of the snow people
Kritico	Elven wine — keeps your head clear, but warms your body and spirit
Mithril mail shirt	Gifted by dwarves of the Northern clans
Mithril Vambraces	(Arm braces) — Gift from Adoronac, to focus magical power
Orb of Pater	Magical orb containing a crystal that steals power from the enemy and protects the bearer.
Pendant	Intricately carved necklace, showing carrier as elf friend
Plain ring of Invisibility	Taken from wizard Torlak
Texas Ranger Silver Badge	Gifted by Creditum, the dwarf merchant: family heirloom, kept for over two hundred years. Seems to emanate energy to the wearer, giving him more endurance. Belonged to Jim's great, great grandfather, who disappeared over two hundred years ago.

~ ABOUT THE AUTHOR ~

Timothy was born in Chilliwack, BC in a military family. Even at a young age, he found his escape by reading science fiction and fantasy books, taking him to a place where he could dream of being a hero.

Upon completion of school, he started his career as a RCMP officer. After much success and 25 years of service, Timothy is now retired. He suffers from Post-Traumatic Stress Disorder and finds that writing gives him an outlet, helping him deal with this debilitating disorder.

Dragons and Dinosaurs is Timothy's first novel and with it, he wishes to share his passion for this genre of fiction with others.

He now resides in Grand-Forks, BC with his wife of 30 years and his service dog, Hunter. You can reach Timothy at timothysdragon@outlook.com

Printed in the United States
By Bookmasters